If the Slipper Fits

A Steamy Victorian Romance

Kimberly Keyes

Kimberly Keyes Romance

Contents

Before you start reading!

Hi! It's me, Kimberly Keyes, just saying thank you in advance for reading If the Slipper Fits, book 2 in my steamy Victorian "Hidden Hearts" series. You've probably already read book 1, The Trouble with Tigers, but if not, allow me to tell you it's available in Kindle, Kindle Unlimited, paperback and audible (1st edition only). There's also book 3, Beautiful Viscount, Beastly Bride.

Did you know that I have a newsletter? I send probably way too few emails (that's what the experts tell me!!) but I do like to keep my readers abreast of my sales, new releases, giveaways (whether one of mine, or a fellow author friend's giveaway), and I always share events where I'll be signing books and talking about the romance genre in general. You can visit my website at www.kimberlykeyes.net to sign-up!

That's all for now. Wishing you happy reading! I hope you enjoy Anna and Caden's love story as much as I loved writing it!

His eyelids grew heavy and his gaze dropped with languid grace to her mouth.

God, he was going to kiss her.

The heat in her veins turned scorching, melting her from the inside out. Her lips parted, and though she knew she should, she didn't, by word or deed, proffer the first protest. She wanted Caden's kiss, like she'd waited for it a lifetime.

Slowly, he lowered his head 'til his mouth hovered over hers. His warm breath fanned over her cheeks and goose flesh erupted over her entire body.

"I'm going to kiss you now. Is that all right?"

She swallowed. Nodded. And then, just in case he'd missed her nod, whispered, "Yes."

She'd barely uttered the word before his mouth covered hers, his lips exerting the merest pressure, as if savoring her, as if tasting her, one deliciously sweet sip at a time.

She'd imagined a thousand times how a kiss might feel. Her imagination had not come close to reality.

Chapter One

Femsworth Manor, York County, England 1879

Caden Thurgood came-to with a throbbing head, not entirely certain of his whereabouts.

Disinclined for the moment to open his eyes, he inhaled, long and deep, and allowed a few potentially pertinent facts to reach his consciousness: He lay on his back atop a lumpy surface. Dampness permeated his clothing where his body met the earth.

He grappled with his fingers and found dirt and grass. Muggy, lake-scented air surrounded him like a second skin. Add to that the incessant chirping of overly exuberant birds overhead and sunlight behind his eyelids, and, voila, he discerned he was somewhere out-of-doors.

But where, exactly?

There was nothing for it but to open his eyes. With reluctance, he did so. A gash of diffuse sunlight all but blinded him and he slammed his lids shut, but not before noting the haloed silhouette of a woman wearing an over-large bonnet hovering above him.

"Am I dead?" he heard himself croak, which decided the question. Dead folk didn't have voices, nor pounding heads.

"It would appear not."

The soothing, slightly amused tone of the woman's voice outweighed the risk of cracking open one eye, at least.

She was a pretty one, even frowning at him with such stern...disapproval? No, not that. It was more apt to say she studied him, as a physician might a patient.

As if in support of his theory, she wove cool, gloveless fingers gently through his hair, searching. Mm. Her light touch felt good.

Her tender ministrations coaxed him to sink into oblivion and close his one eye again. He fought the urge, opening both to study her in return.

She indeed wore a bonnet, a hideous one at that. It detracted not one iota from her beauty.

She had what appeared to be a bounty of rich, chestnut brown hair, currently restrained in a thick knot at her nape. Several wispy tendrils had escaped to frame a winsome, heart-shaped face. But it was her eyes that truly set her apart. Tilted, almond shaped, and amber in color, growing lighter closer to her pupils so they appeared to almost glow.

He knew her. Of course he did. But for some odd reason, he could not conjure her name.

He sent her a grin and attempted to sit up.

With seemingly no effort at all she held him down, one palm to his chest. The woman had more strength than the slightness of her frame implied.

"You mustn't do that. You've acquired a nasty bump on your head." She sniffed. "And seem to have imbibed a fair amount of spirits."

He'd been drinking? He smacked his lips. His mouth felt sticky and, yes, tasted slightly of whiskey.

In a rush of memory, his whereabouts came back to him. An expanse of morning sky, a quiet body of water, a perimeter of lush trees, and Harrison.

They'd set out this morning for the lake at Femsworth Hall where they attended a weekend house party.

They'd arrived last night, he at the bequest of his friend, Viscount Sterling Randall. Randall had requested Caden attend in his stead, to accompany his younger brother, Harrison, to, quote, keep him out of trouble, end quote.

This morning after breakfast, he and Harrison set out for a day of fishing on Femsworth lake. They'd also uncorked the fine whiskey Randall had proffered as thanks for Caden's escort. In retrospect, that had not been the best idea.

While the two of them hefted the skiff on their shoulders, the younger man reacted to a flying insect as if confronting his own mortality. He released his load to swat at the winged creature, somehow swinging the bow in the process, and thereby bashing Caden in his now understandably aching head.

Where *was* Harrison? He could ask his female companion. If only he could recall her name...

He drew a steadying breath. Got a nose-full of an elegant floral scent that he somehow knew emanated from her and not from any nearby flowerbeds.

"I beg your pardon, but I seem to have forgotten your name. Remind me?"

"Better yet, tell me of yours." She leaned closer, affording him a better view of her rosy complexion and heart shaped face. The floral scent grew stronger.

"Caden Thurgood, at your service, lovely." She *was* lovely, whomever she was.

"Well?" From several feet away came a sharp voice belonging to an older woman of some authority judging by her regal tone.

"He'll survive," lady amber eyes called in reply, smoothing those silky fingers over his forehead once again. "Now be a good prince and close your eyes," she murmured.

He huffed out a laugh. Had she just called him a prince? He wanted to ask but found himself more inclined to lie still while her blessedly cool fingers soothed the ache in his head.

***

"Thurgood, can you hear me?" Harrison demanded.

Caden's eyes opened and he sprang up onto his elbows. "Wha-where am I?"

He sprawled on a couch in a too-warm room with heavy drapes drawn so only meager light squeezed through. His head still ached, albeit more dully than before. How had he got here? How long had he been out?

Long enough to have the strangest dream.

He pinched the bridge of his nose and tried to capture the fading images. He was a boy again, gadding about on the grounds of Chissington Hall, the earl's estate. His playmate, an obstinate, bossy female with a head of dark blonde hair, insisted she take on the part of the stolen princess, with him in the role of Prince Charming—again. He laughed, then winced as pain lanced his skull.

"Glad you're feeling well enough to see the humor in the situation." Harrison drew the curtains open in one swift swipe, and daylight flooded what Caden now saw was a well-appointed parlor.

"We were at the lake," he stated. "How did I get here?"

"I drafted some of my aunt's footmen to convey you back to the manse."

Caden narrowed his eyes at the younger man. "After you brained me."

With a pained smile, Harrison rubbed his own head as if in commiseration. "Does it hurt overly? I really am terribly sorry. I didn't expect those damned bees to attack and—"

"—and you panicked, and swung the skiff like a weapon."

He had the grace to look contrite. "Sorry about all that, Thurgood. I trust the medicinal whiskey Sterling sent helped mask the pain?"

And made his mouth feel as if he'd swallowed cotton.

"How is the head now, by the by? You had me nervous for a moment, talking gibberish about Robinhood and Prince Charming in your sleep. You do recall we're at Femsworth Hall for my cousin's engagement party?"

"Of course I do." Caden sat up and swung his legs over the side of the couch. He fingered the knot on his scalp. Yes, definitely tender, but no caked blood. He'd survive.

"No real harm done, eh?" Harrison looked so puppy-dog hopeful that Caden opted to let the matter drop.

He did feel almost normal. He had one question, however.

"What happened to the lady?"

"What lady?"

"The one who tended me after you attempted to crack open my head."

Harrison eyed Caden with increased concern. "Mayhap I hit you harder than I thought. No one ventured out with us. Although..." He propped a hip against a side table, nearly toppling it in the process. He hopped up, righting the furniture.

Caden pinched the bridge of his nose. Earlier in the week, Randall mentioned something about his younger brother being whip-crack smart, yet a notorious hazard. Caden had laughed. Mayhap he'd laughed too soon.

"Although...?" he prompted.

"I attempted to help you up, only you lay there, limp as a wet noodle and I ran for help. When I returned you'd moved locations. I found you stretched out on your back on the grass as opposed to"—He cleared his throat—"face down in the mud."

Caden stopped himself just short of slapping a hand against his forehead.

"I'd assumed you'd rolled over on your own. Now I realize, some good samaritan must've passed by during my absence. In any case, I can't tell you how relieved I am at your improved state."

"So you keep saying," Caden muttered.

"Now can we attend the picnic? I'm famished."

He might need sustenance to survive the week. He unfolded himself from the couch. No black spots danced before his eyes. Encouraging. "Lead the way."

***

"I detest these over-blown things. If not for Beatrice being my favorite grand-niece, we'd not have made the journey south at'all." Lady Wentworth held up the lorgnette she wore on a gold chain around her neck and studied the expanse of lawn, dotted liberally with clusters of picnickers and servants.

Anna lowered the pimento-cheese finger sandwich she nibbled and regarded her employer. "Oh, yes. You like her so well, your first response was to decline the invitation. And it's

Bernadette." She popped the last corner of her sandwich into her mouth.

Lady Wentworth shot her a perplexed look. "I beg your pardon?"

"Your favorite grand-niece. Her name's Bernadette."

Lady Wentworth waved a dismissive hand. "I'm sure I said that."

Shaking her head, Anna wondered, not for the first time, what precipitated the dowager duchess's change of heart.

For herself, she'd quite forgotten the party invitation. After all, Lady Wentworth had issued her so-called regrets upon receipt. Then, with no warning, the lady announced her intention to attend the engagement party and it was all hustle and bustle and off they hastened, southward.

Anna hadn't recognized a soul at last evening's welcome reception, not that she'd anticipated doing so. But would anyone recognize her had been the question burning in her mind? More to the point, was anyone searching for her?

Nearly two years had passed since the harrowing incident, when she'd fled for her life after...what she'd done. Surely so much time having passed worked in her favor.

Then *he* walked in, and she proceeded to choke on her champagne, drawing several sets of curious eyes.

But really. Caden Thurgood, after all this time? Here?

And he could be no one else. She couldn't *not* recognize him. He'd grown from the young boy of her childhood acquaintance, but she'd know that face, those eyes, and that *presence* anywhere.

Despite her champagne-up-the-nose gaff, his gaze grazed past her without a moment's pause. She supposed his lack of notice owed more to her role as a lady's companion than anything else. The upper crust never remarked over members of the servant class. Still, she kept her eyes downcast and her neck bowed 'til her muscles ached from the strain.

Then this morning's disaster happened.

Beside her the dowager frowned at no one in particular. "Too many people milling about. I look forward to the week's end, when most of the guests depart."

"You don't say?" The statement made perfect sense coming from her recluse of an employer. What didn't was why she'd wanted to come to Femsworth Hall in the first place, her story concerning Bernadette being her so-called favorite notwithstanding.

Anna mulled the conundrum, swiping up another sandwich—chilled cucumber and butter this time.

Lady Wentworth's lips twitched. "You're an odd bird, Anna. A third my age and already more at home with these dry bones of mine and your notebooks than with people your own age."

Anna regarded her employer who regularly congratulated her on her good sense, touting the two of them birds of a feather. "Takes one to know one."

The older woman snorted. "Don't tell me you're not curious about that dashing young man you saved this morning—"

"I'd hardly call what I did that."

"As long as I live, I'll not forget the sight of you charging in to rescue Thurgood."

"You exaggerate, madam."

"Hardly. I've no doubt he'd like to thank you for your heroics. Any gentleman worth his salt would. It'll be a wonder if he spots you all the way out here, however."

"Am I to understand you'd prefer to relocate into the thick of things? As for the man in question, whomever he may be, I've no doubt he's quite forgotten my part in his little misadventure." Or so she hoped.

Her employer grimaced. "Surround ourselves with *them?*" She flicked her fingers contemptuously at the crowd. "Hardly. And his name is Thurgood. Caden Thurgood of Claybourne. Grandfather's an earl."

As she very well knew. She lapsed into a pensive silence while Lady Wentworth, humming, peered through her lorgnette.

Anna estimated the number of guests present at fifty. Fifty sets of eyes that had the potential to bring disaster down on her head. Or, more specifically, around her neck. They still hung murderers, didn't they?

Not that it had been murder. She'd merely defended herself. But would the court see it as such? Certainly Angelique would not testify on her behalf.

She fingered the brim of her bonnet, assuring herself it still sat low over her brow, while telling herself for the thousandth time her position as Lady Wentworth's companion made her invisible for all practical purposes.

Stumbling across Caden Thurgood this morning had simply been a stroke of bad luck—wrong place, wrong time. They'd not have crossed paths at all had Lady Wentworth not decided to join her on her morning walk, then insisted they aim for the lake.

When they happened upon a man facedown on the shore, Anna reacted without thinking, rushing to his aid. She credited her years of trailing after her father while he tended his patients for the inane impulse.

Closing her eyes, she relived the horrifying moment when she rolled the wall of a man onto his back and found Caden Thurgood, dead.

Not that he'd *been* dead. But for that split second, her heart seized and time itself seemed to stop 'til her father's voice sounded in her head reminding her to check the patient for signs of life. She nearly wept when she felt his hot breath tickling the fine hairs on her cheek.

It never occurred to her not to see to his injuries after that. Frankly, she'd quite forgotten the potential danger to herself—'til the moment he'd asked her name.

She'd feared he'd recognized her, at first. But then he'd asked her name, and she realized he hadn't recognized her, even up close. She'd gotten quite a bit taller, lost some baby fat, and, too, her hair color had gone from sun-kissed gold to dark brown.

She chewed the inside of her cheek. Might she chance a peek into the crowd to see how he fared?

Heart pounding in her ears, she searched the crowd.

Numerous party guests having finished their meals traversed the lawn, their lounge chairs and picnic baskets abandoned. A handful of liveried footmen scooped dishes and blankets into wicker baskets. Caden, however, was nowhere in sight.

"Any luck? I could lend you my lorgnette?"

Anna gave a start of surprise. She should have guessed her shrewd employer would know exactly what she was about, searching the crowd.

"Thank you, madame, but that's not necessary. I only wanted to see he survived his ordeal."

"That magnificent specimen of a man? Of course he has."

Anna cocked her head. "I beg your pardon?"

"I'm old, Anna, not blind. All the men of the Claybourne clan boast exceptional good looks, and Caden Thurgood is no exception, or didn't you notice? Tall and vital with that chiseled jaw. Thick tawny-gold hair a woman could sink her fingers into." Lady Wentworth shivered in dramatic zeal. "If I were only ten years younger."

Anna laughed. Lady Wentworth was sixty if she was a day, whereas Caden was closer to Anna's own age of four and twenty—perhaps one year her senior. "Only ten?"

Lady Wentworth smirked. "Very well. *Twenty.* I'd settle for either of the Thurgood brothers, but Claybourne's heir, Ezekiel Thurgood, recently married, crushing hearts across England."

"Did he really? I always thought him too busy adventure-seeking to take the time to choose a wife, let alone marry."

Her employer cast her a side-long look. "You're acquainted with the family, then?"

"Not at all. I'm sure I read something to the effect in the society column." She bit her lower lip then added, "I've never laid eyes on either man before today."

Lady Wentworth returned her attention to the crowd, once again employing the lorgnette. "There's the handsome rogue now, apparently none-the-worse for wear. I do wonder what laid him out to begin with." She sniffed. "We could have waited to find out."

Anna's heart pounded so hard she wondered it didn't crack her ribs. She spotted Caden in less time than it took to blink, no lorgnette necessary. He stood a head taller than every man present, and his thick head of tawny-blond hair gleamed in the afternoon sun.

Like a visiting dignitary--or a prince--he strolled amongst the other guests. "Charming everyone in his path with that pirate's smile, no doubt," she muttered.

"Beg pardon?"

She'd spoken aloud? She wracked her brain, finally coming up with, "I said it appears he could walk a mile."

"Seems true enough."

He was fine. She could put the entire incident—and him—out of her mind.

With only a modicum of reluctance, she adjusted her lounger, turning her back on the throng of people—and Caden Thurgood.

With a sigh, she pushed the rim of her bonnet back and reclined, eyes closed, savoring the warmth of the sun on her upturned face.

"I fancy another scone."

Anna sat up, yanking her bonnet down. "I'll fetch one for you." The possibility of encountering Caden had nothing to do with her leaping to do Lady Wentworth's bidding. Nothing whatsoever.

"Continue your sunbathing. I need to stretch my legs."

"I should at least accompany you, my lady. You might turn your ankle traversing the uneven lawn."

"Bah." Lady Wentworth, already on the move, waved her off.

Anna sank back onto her chair, relieved and disappointed all at once. But, no. This was definitely for the best.

She closed her eyes and allowed herself, for just a moment, to marvel over the coincidence. Of all the people in all of England, how had he ended up here, at the very same house party as she?

She had not laid eyes on him for too many years to count, enough that he rarely crossed her mind. But there had been a time when Caden, with his mischief-filled sky-blue eyes and breath-catching smile, occupied center stage in her thoughts, back when she was young and blessedly unaware of how complicated life could be.

How old had she been that last Summer? Going on fourteen? Which would put him at fifteen or sixteen. Not quite a man, but no longer a boy willing to act out her favorite pastime, *Prince Charming rescues his Princess.*

Except on that last day, when he'd offered. Obviously put-upon, he said he knew of no other way to shake her out of her dour mood.

She hadn't the will to tell him to stuff it as she ought. She'd been too aware she and her family would quit the country in a matter of days, and the lure of his attention focused entirely upon her proved too tempting to resist.

She'd lived on the memory of that last day for...far too long.

She hadn't laid eyes on him since. 'Til today.

In her mind's eye, Caden, the boy, faded, and she saw him as she had that morning, *after* she turned him over and felt his warm breath on her cheek. Lying there, half conscious, he'd smiled up at her and her wits threatened to scatter to the wind. Only through an effort of sheer will had she kept her head on straight.

She couldn't risk seeing him again. She certainly couldn't risk interacting with him. Still. Knowing he was here, so close and yet so far, was going to make for an infernally long weekend.

Chapter Two

"Harrison, introduce me to your friend."

Caden turned at the authoritative voice. He recognized it immediately as belonging to the woman who'd called to his mystery-nurse while he lay flat-out, lakeside.

Silver-gray hair and fine lines on her face marked her as of an age with the earl. She held herself like a queen as she eyed him up and down, clearly taking his measure. Interesting.

He flashed her his most engaging smile.

Her cheeks went pink, as most women's did.

Harrison hustled to her side, offering his arm. "Lady Wentworth, an unexpected pleasure. I distinctly recall my mother informing Sterling and myself you'd declined the invitation, as expected."

The lady arched her brows at him.

Harrison hesitated, seeming to recognize he'd committed a faux-pas, while also having no notion where he'd gone wrong.

He turned to Caden, a fresh sheen of perspiration dampening his forehead. "Thurgood, would you believe this great lady, the dowager duchess of Wentworth, is my grandmother's sister's sister-in-law?"

"You don't say?" Caden leaned down to Harrison, offering in a discreet tone, "You still haven't introduced us."

Harrison's face went ruddy. "Yes, of course. Thurgood, meet the Dowager Duchess of Wentworth, my great aunt by marriage. My lady, Mr Caden Thurgood, brother to Lord Ezekiel Thurgood, future Earl of Claybourne. "

Caden bowed over the lady's proffered, gloved hand. "A pleasure. Wentworth of Northumberland, my lady?"

She gave a regal nod, looking pleased.

Harrison spoke up. "Thurgood was good enough to accompany me to Lady Bernadette's engagement party in Sterling's stead. You remember my brother, the viscount? An emergency about which he would reveal nothing prohibited his attending. Of course, he hated to let Aunt Claudine and Bernie down. His loss, if you ask me. Had he known the infamous Lady Wentworth would put in an appearance, nothing could have kept him away." Harrison laid his free hand over his heart.

Lady Wentworth's lips twitched. "Keep it up, m' boy, and you may earn the spot as my new favorite...er...nephew or cousin or whatever." Waving a dainty lace kerchief, she said, "Now be a good lad and run along."

Harrison wasted no time obeying the lady's directive.

She pinned Caden with a stare.

She wished to speak with him privately? This grew more intriguing by the minute.

"Shall we stroll, Lady Wentworth?"

At her nod, Caden tucked her hand into his elbow and led her along the graveled perimeter of the green.

"Mr. Thurgood, how fares your head?"

He slid her a look. "Quite well, my lady, I suspect due to my having a rather hard cranium—a trait that runs rampant in my family. Pray tell, is it you to whom I owe my life? As I understand it, Harrison left me face down in the muck to either self-resuscitate or suffocate."

Lady Wentworth gave an unladylike snort. "No, dear boy, it was not I, but my companion, Mrs. Jones, who charged to your rescue. Indeed she dragged you from the shore onto the grass."

Mrs. Jones? The name didn't ring a bell.

"Dragged me, you say, my lady?" At well over six feet and a good fifteen stone last he'd checked, that would be no easy feat. "I'd very much like to thank your companion."

Lady Wentworth smile with evident satisfaction. "I thought you might."

She directed him to the far side of the lawn. As they drew near, he noted two lounge chairs, one turned to face away from the crowd. It had an occupant.

His eyes trained on the lounger as if the mysterious Mrs Jones would disappear should he look away. A ridiculous notion, and yet, neither he nor Lady Wentworth uttered a word as they made their approach.

A pair of well-polished black leather boots, crossed at the ankles, were the first he saw of the dowager duchess's companion. The fine boots were all the more noticeable peeking out from dull brown skirts.

Then his eyes lit on the whole of her.

She reclined, eyes closed as if in sleep. She wore a large, ugly bonnet, rim pushed back to expose a heart-shaped face. The corners of her full pink lips curved upward, just slightly, as if on the verge of a smile. She looked absurdly serene, like a cat, napping in a snug kitchen. He almost hated to disturb her.

Lady Wentworth, it seemed, had a similar disinclination, and, for a long moment, the two of them gazed upon Mrs. Jones.

Something must've given them away, however, because without opening her eyes, she spoke. "You found your scone, I expect?"

The older woman snorted. "I quite forgot the scone. But I did acquire a new friend."

Jones's lids flew open. In the next instant, she tugged her bonnet down so it covered her, forehead to lip, while springing to her feet faster than he could blink. The lounger sat between them like a moat.

Impressive agility. Odd, but impressive.

The Dowager patted Caden's forearm and went on as if Mrs. Jones hadn't leapt up like a hunted rabbit. "Quite by accident I crossed paths with Mr. Thurgood. Wouldn't you know he expressed a desire to meet his rescuer?"

Mrs. Jones made a noncommittal sound, something between a "Mmm," and a "Harumph," and angled a brief look at Caden from under the brim of her bonnet.

Lady Wentworth made the introductions. "Mr Thurgood, my companion, Mrs. Anna Jones. Mrs. Jones, your patient, Mr Caden Thurgood."

Mrs. Jones dipped an elegant curtsy, marking her as a woman of gentle breeding. No surprise there. As a companion to a duchess, she would have to meet certain standards. But she *had* seemed familiar to him. Perhaps they'd met in a social setting before she went into service—mayhap her family had fallen on hard times.

"Mr. Thurgood." Her voice was low and melodic, and, again, familiar in a vague sort of way.

He waited for her to raise her face, to meet his eyes. When she didn't, he chuckled under his breath, not so much amused as bemused. Last time he looked he hadn't grown another head, yet the woman could barely stomach the sight of him.

Perhaps he misread reticence for shyness? That made more sense.

"Mrs. Jones, may I say it's a pleasure to meet you. I half feared I'd imagined you—that is until Lady Wentworth confirmed your existence."

He could swear Mrs. Jones slanted an accusatory glare at her employer. Not that he could see past her massive gray bonnet despite the fact the top of her head reached his collar.

She may as well have thrown down the gauntlet.

Challenge accepted. He'd bloody well wait Jones out. He squared his stance and barely resisted crossing his arms over his chest.

Seconds ticked by until either curiosity or politeness got the better of her. She adjusted her bonnet to a less downward slant and peeked up at him.

Those eyes. Like liquid pools of glowing amber.

"Have we…" *met,* he'd intended to ask, but his voice croaked like a lad's who hadn't yet reached puberty, for pity's sake. He cleared his throat.

Mrs. Jones spoke as if he hadn't uttered a word. "I'm gratified to see you much restored—Mr. Thurgood, was it?—Thank you so much for your kind words. Completely unnecessary, I assure you." She curtsied again—in dismissal?—and addressed her next words to her employer. "Lady Wentworth, shall I go in search of that scone?"

"No, indeed, Anna." Lady Wentworth's tone had lost its gaiety.

Anna. He ran her full name over in his mind. *Mrs. Anna Jones.* Nothing pinged for him. But her voice, her eyes, her *spirit.* No doubt about it, he recognized her from somewhere.

"I see," Jones murmured.

It seemed she did see, because she drew what appeared to be a bracing breath, then lifted her face to send him a shy smile. No, not shy. Anxious?

"I must admit, Mr. Thurgood, you gave us quite a scare this morning."

His stomach dropped, and a bead of sweat formed on his brow then began a slow trickle down his temple. That voice. He *knew* her.

Her smile vanished in a flash and her wispy dark brows beetled. She moved toward him, hands outstretched, as if to take his arm. In a blink she retracted her reach, but her evident angst remained. "Perhaps you should sit a moment, Mr. Thurgood?"

He did feel odd. Off balance and a tad breathless, in fact. Lingering effects from his earlier, head injury? Whatever the cause, why not use it to his advantage? As Zeke, his paragon of a brother, had recently pointed out, living for himself was Caden's supposed modus operandi.

"I say. Don't faint on us m'boy. Sit," Lady Wentworth commanded.

Drawing a hand to his brow, he made a show of wincing. "I may have over done it. But, I couldn't possibly take a seat from a lady. A moment, if you please."

He didn't wait for Jones to argue—somehow he knew she would—but went in search of a third, unoccupied chaise.

Moments later, he settled his lounger opposite hers. He aimed his most devastating smile her way.

She slanted him a suspicious look. "How fares your head now, Mr. Thurgood?"

"Throbs," he lied, and just like that, her comportment softened. The woman had no future in poker.

"Anna, call one of the footmen for a lemonade."

"An excellent notion, my lady." Anna sounded nearly as authoritative as the dowager duchess. She eyed Caden, then threw a pointed look at his unoccupied chaise.

He dropped onto the lounger obediently.

Seemingly satisfied, she flagged a servant, procuring a lemonade and thanking him with a good deal more courtesy than she'd shown Caden thus far.

How perplexing. He could not recall a time a woman openly disdained his attentions. Perplexing and intriguing. Game on.

Chapter Three

Anna returned to Caden, leaning over him to press the ice-cold, crystal glass into his hands.

Eyes on her task, she still somehow felt his blue stare locked on her. Drawing a full breath seemed nigh on impossible.

"Thank you, again, Mrs. Jones. It seems I am once again in your debt."

His silken-toned voice flowed over her like a soft breeze, heightening her awareness and threatening to bring on a Caden-induced stupor. Out of nowhere, her mother's oft-repeated litany from long ago slammed into her consciousness.

Don't be fooled by his easy smile and charming ways, Gloriana. Never trust the blue-bloods.

She straightened, waving his words aside. "It's a simple matter of taking a glass from a tray. It's not as if I squeezed the lemons."

She almost regretted her waspish tone. Almost. Better he find her abrasive than guess the rich timber of his voice, the sky-blue of his eyes, the flash of his smile stole her ability to think. At this particular juncture, she very much needed to keep her head on straight.

She braced for his retort. The Caden of her youth would have sniped back—or stormed off. Apparently not Caden the man, however.

He grinned. "Didn't you?" he asked, the smile evident in his voice drawing her gaze to his handsome visage. His blue eyes twinkled up at her.

"Didn't I?" she repeated, losing the vein of the conversation.

"Squeeze the lemons."

A helpless, answering smile curved her lips. Damn the man and his innate charm.

"Lady Claudine and *Bernadette* are making the rounds with her intended and his family," the Dowager Duchess announced, stressing the bride's Christian name. "I may as well join them and get the introductions over-with."

Anna watched, bewildered, as Lady Wentworth marched into the lion's den for a second time in less than an hour.

"I agreed to sit only because I assumed you would follow suit," Caden murmured.

Face blooming with heat for no good reason, Anna lowered herself into the lawn chair opposite his. She took a moment to right her skirts, inwardly schooling herself to stop letting Caden's...*Caden-ness* addle her brain. She felt his eyes on her all the while, which helped not one iota.

Bracing herself, she lifted her chin intending to fight fire with fire. Let him squirm under the weight of her stare.

He appeared wholly unfazed by her appraisal. Meanwhile, the sight of him, sprawled in his lounger, somehow looking both decadent and elegant was doing funny things to her insides.

His focus shifted to the lawn behind her. "Funny. I heard your employer described as decidedly anti-social. Perhaps the upcoming nuptials tapped a hidden wellspring of sentimentality in her. It happened in my family. The mere *possibility* of a betrothal turned the earl into one of cupid's most avid assistants."

Her stomach sunk. Somehow she hadn't considered the possibility Caden might be betrothed. Or worse. "Have you recently married, then?" She could bite out her own tongue for asking such a personal question—except she did want an answer.

Caden shuddered in mock horror. "Me? No. I refer to my brother. The earl's finally achieved his fondest wish—the heir has settled down, in England of all places." A tight smile curved his lips. "I've never seen Zeke happier. Not that his wedded bliss did anything to improve his attitude."

Relieved beyond measure, and unsure how to respond to his latter statement, she commented on the former. "Lady Wentworth mentioned his recent nuptials."

He studied her, his stare direct to the point of rude.

Had a bug landed on her bonnet? Heat blooming over her body, she craned her neck, searching the thinning crowd for Lady Wentworth.

"Mrs. Jones, have we met?"

Her gaze shot to his face. "No. We've never had occasion to meet, Mr. Thurgood."

"You're certain?"

"Quite certain."

He dropped his chin in his hand, eyes narrowing. "Yet you seem so familiar."

"I have never set eyes on you before today. Never." She sucked her lower lip between her teeth and nibbled, hoping he believed her and would let the matter drop.

His taken aback expression told her she'd spoken with too much vehemence.

She forced a lighter tone. "One of those faces, I'm afraid."

"As to that, I couldn't disagree more." He crossed his arms over his chest and tapped a finger to his chin. "By your accent, I deduce you don't hail from Northumberland. Somewhere closer to London-town, perhaps, where I may have caught a glimpse of you at the park or an event?"

She blinked. Had he always been this tenacious? "Are you feeling better after your respite, Mr. Thurgood?"

He scowled, looking so much like the boy she once knew she would laugh were she not so alarmed.

"Why do you ask?" he drawled suspiciously.

She sent him what she hoped passed for a regretful smile. "I do have my employer to think of."

"In what regard?"

It was on the tip of her tongue to call out the presumptuous cur. Then she reminded herself they were not two old friends bantering. She was a servant. *A step removed.* Women in her station did not correct esteemed guests.

She lowered her eyes in what she hoped passed for a demure fashion. "She may require my arm, sir. She is rather advanced in years."

Caden laughed aloud. "In need of an arm? My dear Mrs. Jones, what would your employer say if she heard your summation of her, I wonder?"

"I said nothing derogatory." She'd never realized how very difficult it was to smile through gritted teeth.

"Merely that she's decrepit and incapable of moving around on her own volition." His eyes gleamed with devilry.

She meant to defend herself. Instead, her lips trembled with the effort it took not to smile.

"You have the most extraordinary eyes, Mrs. Anna Jones."

A thrall of heat suffused her entire body at the unexpected compliment. She ought to be offended by his unabashed forwardness, not knocked breathless. Certainly she had no idea how to respond.

A female's voice raised in triumph sounded from behind, and altogether too near, Anna's chair.

"Mr. Randall, I've found your missing friend loitering on the outskirts of the party."

Anna lowered the brim of her bonnet and tucked her chin as Caden slid his long legs over the side of the chair and stood. "Miss Egerton, Miss Applegate, Randall."

A ready made foursome, it seemed. With any luck, they would take Caden and leave without paying her any notice.

Caden's next words destroyed any hope of that. "I discovered the identity of my rescuer. Mrs. Jones?" He offered her his hand to help her up.

He meant to introduce her. Her, a lady's companion. Anna stifled a groan of frustration and placed her hand in his solid, warm grasp.

"Mrs. Jones, meet Mr. Harrison Randall. You may or may not know Mr. Randall is a distant relation of your employer's. The lovely ladies accompanying him are the Misses Applegate and Egerton."

Addressing the three newcomers, he said, "Mrs. Jones is Lady Wentworth's companion."

One of the young ladies flanking Mr. Randall sniffed, her message clear: She did not fraternize with the help.

Displaying none of his lady friend's reticence, Mr. Randall took her hand. "Very pleased to make your acquaintance, Mrs. Jones. I half feared you were a figment of Thurgood's imagination, conjured after I—after our slight mishap this morning. He asked after you immediately upon coming-to in Lady Fenton's parlor. He was quite vexed when I admitted I hadn't a clue as to your identity. Indeed, Lady Wentworth solved the mystery for us."

"And stole Mr. Thurgood clean away," one of the misses whined.

The other miss spoke up next. "Harrison promised to take us through the maze, and he avowed you'd make up our fourth, Mr. Thurgood."

Caden's glance shifted between Anna and his friends. "But why not five? Mrs. Jones, would you care to join us?"

"Do come, Mrs. Jones," Mr. Randall seconded.

The women scowled at each other in unspoken accord. They needn't worry their simpering little heads.

Anna silently chided herself for the uncharitable thought. Rather than fault them, she should seize the opportunity to rid herself of Caden Thurgood.

"I appreciate your kind offer, but my obligation lies here."

Frowning, Caden looked prepared to argue.

"Mr. Thurgood, we must go *now*, or we'll risk getting back to the manse too late for Lady Claudine's next event," one of the young ladies pressed.

"I'm ever so anxious to see the maze," the other added.

"Of course." Caden proffered one arm. Both ladies leapt forward, but one, quicker by half, won out. A moment later the foursome departed.

Helpless to resist, Anna's eyes followed their egress, as if drawn to Caden's shining tawny waves by an invisible hook. An odd ache filled her chest. Nostalgia, she supposed, owing to crossing paths with her long ago childhood friend who'd stolen her heart no matter how sternly her mother had warned her off of him.

Once was more than enough.

Abruptly, he glanced behind him, brows furrowed, a frown dragging down the corners of his broad mouth.

Perhaps he's disgruntled over being pulled away from me.

She scoffed inwardly. Why would he care if—

Her mind went blank as his gaze found hers. In the span of a heartbeat his entire demeanor changed, lips splitting in a brilliant, devastating smile.

Heat suffused her from head to toe as an answering smile she couldn't quell spread over her face.

Caden tipped an imaginary hat.

Anna's hand lifted as if of its own accord.

Briefly, he looked down toward the woman at his side who appeared to have his jacket sleeve in her fist. He patted her hand, before sliding his gaze once more to Anna. He sent her a quick wink and shifted his attentions forward.

He *winked*. Spine stiffening, Anna turned her back on him lest he look her way and catch her mooning over him again. It rankled, but Lady Wentworth had the right of it. Caden Thurgood of Claybourne was magnificent.

Lethal good looks aside, his mere presence stirred dangerous currents inside her, drawing her to him like a magnet to steel. She must resist the pull. Besides, turning into a goose around him as she always had, Caden might recognize her yet.

***

Anna drew the shutters closed, blocking out most of the late afternoon sun, and strode for the adjoining door of the guest suite. "Rest well, madam. Call out, should you need anything. I'll be just on the other side." She crossed the threshold, hand on the brass lever.

Lady Wentworth lifted her silver-haired head from her pillow and arched a brow at Anna. "Napping," she said in a flat tone.

Anna laughed softly. "Yes, napping."

The woman knew her too well. Anna never napped, yet she could hardly take her employer up on her suggestion she explore the grounds for the next hour or so. Too risky.

"At least you'll be rested for tonight's festivities."

"Yes. Now go to sleep." She closed the door softly and tried to tamp down the excitement coursing through her veins at the casually spoken words. *Tonight's Festivities.*

Earlier, the older woman had blithely announced Anna would accompany her to pre-dinner cocktails and, afterward, would partake of the evening's formal meal. "If I must suffer these fools, you must suffer alongside me," Lady Wentworth said by way of explanation—not that she needed one. She was Anna's employer.

Still, Anna ought to have argued. She knew what Lady Wentworth did not: Mingling with so many members of the upper crust had the potential to bring disaster crashing down on her.

Instead, a monstrous yearning rose up within her, dispelling all her fear—save for one. She could not bear to show up tonight wearing her tired servant's garb, and so she told the dowager duchess.

Lady Wentworth, it seemed, had taken care of that small detail.

Now, heart pounding with anticipation, she approached the wardrobe on stockinged feet making as little sound as humanly possible for no reason she could think of except she felt the need to do so.

The ornate wooden cabinet had previously housed only her servant's dresses fashioned of grey and brown wool. She pulled open the door on silent hinges and gazed at the half dozen shimmering gowns hanging inside. Bernadette's cast-offs according to Lady Wentworth.

She ran her fingers over the silk, chiffon, and tulle. Anticipation sang through her as rife a child's on Christmas morning.

She knew why. It was because of him. Bother. Why did the thought of him seeing her dressed in a gown fit for a princess have to thrill her so?

She closed the wardrobe and moved to the oriel window where she curled-up on the padded bench to gaze out at the pristine grounds below.

The late afternoon sun's rays bathed the gardens and rolling green hills in majestic gold, creating a vista so similar to one in her memories it hurt to look at it. Still, she didn't turn away.

Squinting her eyes, she imagined she saw the lush expanse of land comprising the border between her family's summer cottage and the fairy-tale castle-on-the-hill that was Chissington Hall.

On an afternoon like today her mother would be toiling in her gardens while her father hunted, or fished, or read his scientific journals. And Anna would be playing out-of-doors with Caden.

She saw him as he appeared the day they first met.

By pure accident, she had wandered upon him, his brother Zeke, and another of their friends on the riverbank, skipping stones across the river. A mere twelve years old, he already stood tall, lean and lanky. Whisking shiny gold hair out of his eyes, he introduced the three of them.

He aimed his gleaming, sailor's smile at her, and she was lost.

Anna covered the chaotic feelings within her with a veneer of hauteur she'd witnessed her mother employ on more than one occasion, informing them she was the daughter of Dr. George Masters, recently arrived from London, and that she intended to join them.

Zeke was not impressed. He wanted nothing to do with her. She was too young. Too small. Too *female*.

To her surprise, Caden had championed her cause—and afterward paid a hefty price.

Her heart squeezed a little remembering him standing there, hands fisted at his side, body quivering with indignation, as the two older boys mounted up and rode away sneering something about leaving *the girls* to play amongst themselves.

A wry smile twisted her lips. Poor Caden. She'd repaid his kindness by demanding he play what she wanted when she wanted at every turn.

She especially loved acting out Prince Charming rescues the stolen princess. He did *not* relish the role—save for the times he had to scale a tree, or storm a hill, or hack away a thicket to rescue her. The worst part, according to him, was the obligatory kiss. But truly, everyone knew a prince must bestow a kiss on his lady after saving her.

In the spirit of fairness, she had agreed to play his favorite game, as well. Robin hood. Everything about the dashing, heroic archer, appealed to him. She, on the other hand, disliked clambering awkwardly after him in skirts, pretending to be one of his merry men.

Despite the grubby nails and unkept hair that came with the role, appeasing him had one major benefit. When Caden got his way, he turned that blinding smile on her—just like today.

Without warning, her chin quivered and her eyes burned with unshed tears. He hadn't remembered her.

She recognized her lunacy, of course. She needed him not to know her. And, too, why would he? It had been eleven years since they'd seen one another. Her hair, golden from youth and days spent out-of-doors had since turned dark, just as her mother's had done. More to the point, unlike her, he didn't have the benefit of putting her real name with her face.

She scrubbed her eyes with her palms, firming her jaw and her resolve. For two years she'd been Mrs. Anna Jones, companion to Lady Wentworth of Northumberland, safely hidden from the authorities and Angelique alike. Everything depended on her maintaining her false identity. If Caden—if anyone—ever learned the truth of what she'd done, there would be hell to pay.

"What's down there that's drawn your menacing eye?" Lady Wentworth spoke from the now-open doorway linking the chambers.

Anna somehow managed to speak in a normal voice. "You know how your suitors scale the walls and disturb your rest when given half the chance. Speaking of which, you're up early."

"I tossed and turned, consumed with thoughts of those gowns Claudine had delivered."

Anna huffed out a laugh. "Why-ever for?"

Lady Wentworth gave her an appraising look. "I'm torn between the rose and the gold silk. Chop chop."

"Chop chop?"

Her employer gave her an exasperated look. "You must try them both on. My money's on the gold."

***

Caden inclined his head at something Harrison asked and forced his face into a politely disinterested mask, the polite part being the main difficulty. He brought the champagne flute to his lips and searched the crowded parlor for a plausible escape.

Any excuse to extricate himself from the foursome made up of himself, Harrison, the besotted greenhorn, and the Misses Egerton and Applegate.

Regardless of the sharp intellect Sterling Randall claimed his younger brother possessed, Harrison seemed oblivious to the ladies' attempts to out-maneuver one another to capture Caden's attention. He hoped to make-off before well and truly sabotaging Harrison's efforts to charm the unremarkable chits.

Caden had seen it time and again. For some inexplicable reason, women flocked to him. All ages, shapes, sizes, and walks of life. He'd long since given up trying to understand the why's and wherefores, choosing instead to accept what he'd heard too many times to count. He'd inherited his father's charm.

Where he'd gotten the devil's own luck—something his father never had—was anyone's guess.

Charm and luck. Was that the extent of what people saw when they looked at him?

He was, so he'd been told, more than passably attractive. However, for most women, looks did not make up for the lack of a title, of which he had none. Wealth could tip the scales, though for much of his life he couldn't boast that, either—though he had amassed a substantial base for himself between his quarterly allowance and, again, uncanny luck, both with choosing investments and at the tables.

He would no longer receive said allowance thanks to the recent argument between him and Zeke.

It galled him anew, recalling Zeke's sanctimonious presumption when Caden requested to avail himself of a large sum of money from the family accounts.

True, he'd recently admitted to his brother he occasionally gambled. Also true, he had refused to tell Zeke why he needed the money.

But damn it he'd wanted to surprise Zeke and Kitty as a sort of belated wedding present, and it wouldn't be much of a surprise if he told them what he was doing with the money.

Besides, he'd told Zeke he didn't gamble with funds he couldn't afford to lose—and he was not a liar.

So why had Zeke assumed he'd asked for money to cover a gambling debt? Because he expected the worst from Caden whose quote-end-quote lifestyle he did not approve of.

Zeke, the until recent-times world-traveler, adventurer, concerned with no one but himself, suddenly thought to measure one and all by his new and improved moral standards.

Caden would not stomach it. He told Zeke to stuff his brotherly admonitions, along with his quarterly allowance. Now he was as free as any man could be. Zeke no longer had any say in what he did or did not do with his life.

So why was he gripping the champagne flute in his hand so tightly it threatened to shatter? He relaxed his hold and forced his mind back on point—women, him, moths to a flame.

Usually, he rather enjoyed his good fortune of the female variety. Then there were situations like this, when a friend had his sights set on a particular female or two, *and neither happens*

*to be a tantalizing, amber-eyed mystery woman—and a widow
to boot.*

"I did so enjoy our exploration of the maze this afternoon,
Mr. Thurgood," Miss Applegate said, batting her lashes.

"As did I," Miss Egerton chimed, tapping her closed fan to his
forearm in an attempt to pull his gaze toward her. "How-ever
did you discover the path leading us to the exit so swiftly?"

"The truth is—" that he'd applied all his wit to the task,
hoping to resume his conversation with Mrs. Jones. Alas, she
and her employer had quit the scene by the time he'd navigated
out of the maze. "—It was as much Harrison's doing as my
own."

"Oh?" the ladies replied in unison, switching their attentions
to Harrison, who flushed a dull red even as an ear-to-ear grin
split his face.

"It was nothing," he denied, puffing out his chest a bit. "Did
I mention the maze located at Worley Manor?"

Caden seized the opportunity. He clipped a bow. "If you'll
excuse me? I promised Lord Fenton I'd discuss..." Drawing a
blank he coughed into his fist, flashed a grin, and took off for
the open terrace.

Half way across the parlor, he skidded to a halt.

He stared at the vision of Mrs. Jones in a curve hugging gown
of muted gold. Sans bonnet, she wore her lush hair pulled back,
not in any kind of intricate coiffure, but secured in an elegant
knot at her crown. A few artful tendrils hung loose to frame her
heart-shaped face.

Standing off to the side, apart from the crowd, she looked the picture of grace and, somehow, as if she she'd rather be anywhere else. He half expected her to wedge herself between the massive potted palm whose fronds she fingered, and the carved column it camouflaged.

Where was her tottering, old employer, he wondered, with a snort of laughter, recalling her earlier attempt to rid herself of him. *Him.*

Ah. Lady Wentworth stood talking with Lord Fenton a mere stone's throw away—also eschewing the bulk of the crowd, he noted. In any case, he saw an opening for him to approach Jones and meant to seize it.

Grinning, he drew the champagne flute to his mouth. Ah, yes. He'd drained the glass.

"She's a looker, I'll grant you."

Caden's gaze slid from Jones to the dark-haired man of a similar age with himself who'd sidled up beside him. He recognized the man. He would not call him precisely a friend. "Lord...Hardasher, isn't it?"

Hardasher's upper lip curled in a semblance of a smile, and he inclined his head. "Quite right, Mr. Thurgood. We met last year at the Huntford affair."

Huntford affair. Sounded familiar, though he couldn't conjure the specifics. Last year's--and the year's before for that matter--*affairs,* comprised of an endless round of parties, soirees, and balls, starting with the London Season, and carrying on through one Summer house party to the next.

This year promised to be more of the same until his brother returned from abroad, posted the banns announcing his engagement to a woman of whom no one had ever heard, and Caden raced home to Derby. Then the fun really began.

"Summer party?" he guessed.

"Quite right." Hardasher's eyes trained on Mrs. Jones.

Caden quirked a grin, though the man's intent scrutiny rubbed him wrong. He gestured with his empty flute toward Jones. "Lord Hardasher, do you, by chance, recognize her?"

His focus never wavered. "I can't say as I recognize her, though I did note something familiar about her the night of the reception, when I spotted her standing alongside the dowager duchess."

"She is the lady's companion."

"Is she, indeed?" The sly edge to Hardasher's tone drew Caden's hackles. Without a by-your-leave, he started toward Jones.

Annoyed, Caden followed. He would head-off any nonsense on Hardasher's part—the least he could do considering Jones had saved his life.

The dinner gong sounded.

Hardasher paused mid-stride. His head pivoted, then locked in place.

Caden followed the direction of Hardasher's gaze to the redoubtable Lady Wentworth, clearly en route to Jones.

Caden could almost read the poor sot's thoughts. He had no desire to tangle with the dowager duchess of Wentworth.

Sure enough, he hesitated one moment longer, tugged at the lapels of his waistcoat, then veered to join the mass exodus from the parlor.

Caden continued his now leisurely approach.

Before he reached them, Lord Hammond, recently named Earl of Whittenmore, appeared, proffering his arm toward the dowager in a courtly manner. As the lady of the most consequence in attendance, a high nobleman would need to escort her into the hall. Lord Hammond fit the bill nicely. Certainly Caden, the Claybourne spare, would never do.

He'd make an excellent escort for Jones, however.

"Lady Wentworth, Mrs. Jones, Lord Hammond, good evening."

Jones' face angled up toward his. Her amber eyes glowed as if they stole all the light from the stuttering candle flames illuminating the grand parlor. "Good evening, Mr. Thurgood."

Four words, welcoming enough, and yet, those eyes. He first thought he detected a glint of pleasure at his arrival. Then he read dread in their depths, or something akin to it.

He couldn't decide if he was vexed or amused. Certainly confounded. Women *liked* him.

Lady Wentworth shifted, dragging Hammond with her to bring the four of them into a semi-circle. Her eyes sparkled with mischief. She, at least, seemed happy to see him.

"Mr. Thurgood, delighted you appear to suffer no ill effects from this morning's mishap." Eyes still trained on Caden, she directed her next words to Hammond. "Mr. Randall whacked him with a skiff this morning, if you can imagine. Mrs. Jones and I discovered him and she rushed to his aid."

"Very impressive," Hammond commented, slanting an appreciative leer at Mrs. Jones.

Caden resisted the urge to step in front of her. Evidently no man alive was proof against the woman's charms.

She appeared oblivious, seemingly more concerned with smoothing nonexistent wrinkles from her skirts than noting any appreciative looks aimed in her direction.

"Mrs. Jones, may I escort you into the dining hall?" Caden proffered his elbow. "An extension of my thanks. Again."

Lady Wentworth nodded her regal head once in approval. She spared a moment to eye Jones down the length of her nose as if countermanding any argument before nudging Hammond to lead her away.

Caden swiftly understood why she'd sent the silent reproach. Unless he read the scene wrong, and he didn't see how he could, Jones meant to refuse his invitation.

Why, for God's sake? What had he ever done to her? Perhaps he'd been slightly, incrementally, forward. But she *was* a widow, and this was a Summer house party. Most women would be flattered. *If you do say so yourself,* an irritating inner voice--sounding very much like his brother's--scoffed.

His neck prickled with heat. Embarrassment, he realized. Lowering his arm, he cleared his throat. "Unless you'd rather—"

"Thank you, yes," she said in a breathless rush, almost as if forcing the words out, and placed her small, gloved hand into the crook of his elbow.

Relief akin to a shot of strong whiskey infused his entire body. He covered her hand with his and sent, he hoped, a blithe smile. "Shall we?" She gave a small nod and he started for the parlor door.

Society dictated high ranking guests enter the dining hall soon after the host and hostess, to then take their seats near the head of the table.

Caden, though a Claybourne, suffered no such constraints. He strolled along, Jones at his side, inclining his head toward other pairs to precede them.

Soon the number of milling guests dwindled to a mere handful. Caden had the sudden inclination to fill one of this afternoon's baskets with wine, bread, and cheese, and disappear in the garden maze till dawn.

Not that she'd agree to join him. What was it about the woman that awakened the mischief maker inside him?

He got another whiff of her intoxicating scent, woodsy and floral, elegant and stirring and felt his groin tighten. He didn't know whether to laugh or groan.

"Mr. Thurgood?"

He gazed down at her upturned face, locking eyes with her. "Mrs. Jones?"

"Is there some reason you wish to delay dinner?"

Yes. "Whatever do you mean?"

One corner of her mouth quirked upward and wry amusement danced in her eyes. "As my father used to say, if we moved any slower, we'd travel—"

"—In reverse," Caden finished for her, stopping dead in his tracks. An instant shock of deja-vu blanked his mind. He turned his gaze toward her, mouth open to explain.

Her face had lost all color. She ripped her hand free of his arm.

"Mrs. Jones, are you quite all right?"

She stumbled backwards, practically tripping over her skirts in her haste to put distance between them.

What the devil?

"I...no. I have the headache. Goodnight." Fisting her hands in her skirts, she turned and fled, her pace just shy of a run.

He stared after her, utterly bemused. There was no getting around the truth. The woman wanted nothing to do with him. It was the oddest thing. A woman whose interest he'd actually set out to engage shunning *him*.

Fine. He would not trail after her like some desperate puppy. He did not chase after any woman. Jaw clenched, he took one determined step toward the dining hall and stopped when he felt an object under his boot. He glanced down. Noted a mound of material that looked like...satin? Stooping low he scooped up what had to be one of Jones' evening slippers.

Rising, he tucked the lone slipper into his inner jacket pocket. Dinner could wait.

Chapter Four

An annoying stitch in her side forced Anna to slow her pace. She ought not be running like a thief through the dimly lit corridors in any case.

Thus far she'd passed no one in her quest to reach Lady Wentworth's suite. Good thing. Even now she would draw curious eyes. She glared down at the stockinged toes of her right foot peeking out from beneath her silk skirts with every other step. How on earth had she managed to lose one of her favorite slippers?

Her overzealous egress, that's how.

Stupid, stupid, stupid. First, she blurted out one of her father's sayings, next she gave in to female hysteria. What had she been thinking? She hadn't, that's what. Caden and that blasted, mind-melting smile had switched off her survival instincts, and the rote words from long ago had slipped off her tongue like water sluicing off a duck's back.

Once upon a time she had used every tool at her disposal to poke at Caden--including employing her father's litany of well-meaning advice.

Poor Caden. If he showed up one minute late, if he left more than a morsel on his plate, if he hurried, if he tarried, she had a trunk full of wise advice prepped and ready to hurl at him.

Her relentless teasing eventually led him to interrupt her and fill in the salient words himself.

Like tonight.

A tiny smile replaced her scowl. After all this time, they'd slipped into their old routine.

Her smile faded in an instant. She paused in the empty corridor and covered her face with her hands. She'd brought disaster down on herself.

Probably.

Her hands lowered to just beneath her eyes. She replayed the incident in her mind. She'd started the quip. He'd finished it, stopped dead in his tracks, and turned to stare at her, mouth agape.

Scratch that.

He remained as elegant looking as ever. Still. He had given her an odd look.

She fisted her hands at her sides and resumed her brisk stride.

Had he remembered her or hadn't he? No way to know now that she'd run off half-cocked.

Never make a stab in the dark. Examine facts, then make a calculated guess. Her father's words. She drew a deep breath and went over what happened once more.

He stopped in his tracks, turning to look at her. She reacted, pushing away from him. He had seemed concerned—all right, baffled. But he had not thrown a finger in the air with a resounding, "Ah ha!"

Assuming he had not remembered her, her panicked flight would lead him to one unavoidable conclusion: She was a candidate for bedlam. Likely he'd already made up his mind to avoid her. Which was good. The best possible outcome. She ought to congratulate herself.

She reached the door leading to Lady Wentworth's suite and leaned her head against the cool wood panel. Misery settled over her. She'd wanted one night with him. One night where she could enjoy his company like any other party guest might. If only she hadn't opened her big mouth.

Her stomach emitted a long, low growl. She snorted. Perfect. Certifiable and famished to boot.

She twisted the brass lever, yanked open the door, and kicked her lone slipper off with all her might. It landed somewhere in the dark chamber with an unsatisfying whisper.

"Now, what did that poor slipper ever do to you?"

She spun around, an undignified squeal bursting from her lungs.

Caden, the blackguard, stood not a stone's throw away, a crooked smile playing at his full mouth.

"Wh-what are you doing here?" Mortification and elation, dread and anticipation tangled within her.

He sauntered forward, waistcoat hooked over one thumb, his polished boots making nary a sound on the thick carpet.

The confidence he exuded both maddened and enthralled her. *Corinthian*, people called men like him, men of the upper crust, bestowed with an almost palpable vitality. Physically, perfect. Tall, powerfully built, immaculate. Except—his rich golden hair appeared mussed, as if he'd dragged a hand through it multiple times.

The thought cheered her.

"What sort of gentleman wouldn't ascertain a lady's wellbeing after she bolted from him like someone escaping the gallows?"

"The...gallows, sir?" An alarming choice of words, considering.

"An over-dramatization, perhaps." He shrugged and closed the distance between them, cocooning her in shadow as his height and the breadth of his shoulders blocked much of the meager light from the lamps lining the corridor.

She shivered, though not from cold. The heat of his body encircled her, and carried with it an intriguing scent of spice and essence of pure male.

She tilted her head back to regard him. Though her breathing had gone choppy at his arrival—from fright, she told herself, she managed an even-toned reply. "I apologize for any inconvenience I may have caused. As you can see, I'm perfectly fine."

His eyes narrowed and he tunneled a bare hand through his hair, rearranging the golden waves anew so that more of his thick mane stood on end.

His obvious discomfiture threatened to coax a smile out of her. She pressed her lips together.

"I see. And now I'm the brute who's hunted you down and dragged an apology from you." He huffed in evident frustration.

Now she did giggle, though she quickly covered her outburst with a cough into her fist.

His eyes went to slits. "Are you...did you just *laugh*?"

She shook her head, afraid she'd let loose with more giggles if she tried to speak.

"You *did*."

A peel of laughter escaped her despite her best efforts. "I'm terribly sorry. It's just, you appear quite vexed."

"I am not vexed."

"You clearly are." She bit her inner cheek to stymie another giggle. He brought lightness to her spirit without even trying. He always had.

He crossed his arms over his chest. "Assuming you're correct, a point I am not conceding, by the by, why on earth would that amuse you?"

Her lips quivered. "I don't know?"

His expression remained stern for half a heartbeat before an ear to ear grin split his face followed by a hardy laugh.

Shoulders shaking with silent mirth, she couldn't resist asking, "Why are *you* laughing?"

He reigned in his humor and gave her a crooked smile. "Damned if I know. The same reason I was vexed, perhaps?" His expression sobered. "Because of *you*."

"Me?"

He threw his hands in the air and paced away from her. "You. First you save me from certain suffocation in the muck—"

"—An over-dramatization."

He barreled on as if she hadn't spoken. "—then you make it crystal clear you want absolutely nothing to do with me. *Me.*

"Even so, I made a concerted, dare I say *gallant* effort to offer my thanks by escorting you into dinner, while, I'll add, warding off that blackguard, Lord Hardasher, and for no apparent reason you flee the scene with nary a care for your reputation or mine."

Anna blinked and tried to digest his multi-faceted diatribe.

He steepled his fingers at his lips. "Everyone is sure to conclude I'm somehow to blame for your disappearance. Perhaps it would have been better for me to proceed, post haste, into the dining hall, but how could I in good conscience?"

"You couldn't go in to dinner because you were worried for my welfare and my reputation?"

"Mmm...yes."

"But, by following me, you most likely caused more tongues to wag than if you had not?"

His pacing brought him toe to toe with her once more. His voice came out a masculine purr. "Is it any wonder I'm vexed?" His gaze roamed her face as if searching for answers, finally making an unsettling stop on her lips.

She fought the urge to moisten them with her tongue. Heat suffused her, limb to limb, concentrating low in her belly. "Allow me to reassure you, sir. I'm no one for anyone to remark upon."

"So you say." He cocked his head, and in a quicksilver change of topic, asked, "My dear Mrs. Jones, how fares your head?"

"My head?"

"Did you not claim to have the headache?"

She'd completely forgotten the hasty fabrication. Her hand flew to her brow. "A bit better. Thank you."

He clasped his hands behind his back and leaned closer. "I think you made it up."

Her skin prickled with awareness—of him, of the limited space between them, of his wickedly spicy aftershave teasing her nostrils.

"Your opinion, of course, is entirely your affair."

A slow smile spread over his too-handsome face. "Not a denial."

He lowered his head further, as if he meant to whisper in her ear. Instead, he inhaled, slow and deep through his nose.

The whisper of sound curled through her, making her insides quiver.

"Darling, are you absolutely certain we've never met? Because, there's something so familiar about you..." He inhaled again, and the long draw sent tendrils of fire all the way to her toes.

She had to say something, anything, to distract herself from the wickedly delicious sensations flooding her. "Are you, by any chance, *sniffing* me?"

"I..." he broke off for a beat, straightening away from her. "...am. I beg your pardon, but your perfume tantalizes me. You pass by and it's there, calling to me, just out of reach, utterly intoxicating. I make out cedar-wood, and another flower..."

"Tuberose," she whispered.

"And?" he whispered in return, his gaze dropping to her mouth.

"Amber," she replied, her voice barely audible.

"Ah. Good old amber."

They might as well be the only two people left in the world. Gooseflesh broke out over her entire body, and her legs turned to so much pudding she collapsed against the wall for support. For the life of her, she couldn't conjure one intelligent thought, much less form a word.

His eyes lifted, locking with hers.

The warmth in his blue gaze captured her completely. She could not look away, nor did she wish to.

"Tell me you don't know me."

As if he'd mesmerized her, an almost overwhelming desire to spill her every secret welled-up inside her. Of *course* he tempted her. He always had done. With one look, one softly spoken word, he melted her like butter on a hot skillet.

The yearning to confide in him burned through her.

No. She slammed her lids shut and gave herself a mental shake. Would she never learn? Last time she relied on someone she thought she could trust, she'd barely escaped with her life, and *she* hadn't even belonged to the nobility. Hadn't her mother warned her about trusting one of their rank, and Caden specifically?

Inner walls semi-restored, she opened her eyes and forced a polite smile. "I promise you, sir, we do not know each other." And so they didn't. Not anymore.

The warmth in his eyes dimmed, replaced by a subtle, but distinct message: *Challenge accepted.*

Oh dear. Not that. The Caden she remembered never backed down from a contest of wills.

She must convince him. "Unless you've frequented Durham." She nibbled her lower lip, adding, "I come from a small, *very* small village in Durham County."

***

She was lying, and right to his face. She'd been about to divulge where they'd met—and he knew to his bones they had, indeed, met. Then, something caused her to dig in her heels and lie. There had been a tell. What was it?

He closed his eyes and replayed the last few moments.

Her lower lip. She drew that plump, rosy flesh between her straight white teeth and he *knew* she lied.

But how did he know that tell in particular? Blast it all, why couldn't he recall the chit?

"What are you doing?"

He arched one brow, but kept his eyelids shut. "Thinking."

She made a nondescript sound of annoyance and must've shifted because there was that scent again, invading his senses and dulling his brain.

He cracked open one eye. "Distracting me with your lovely perfume again. Clever. I'll never smell it and not think of you."

She laughed softly and lowered her gaze. "You certainly will not."

"You sound very sure of that."

She gave a graceful one-shoulder shrug. "It's my own recipe. It's never exactly the same twice."

Like a key turning in a lock, her words loosed a fragmented rush of fuzzy memories. She'd had an obsession with someone's oils and herbs. Her mother's? Her father's?

Her mother's.

And her father...He'd been a doctor, hadn't he?

Of course. He saw her as she'd been. Shorter by a mile. Dark blonde hair, curlier then, and going lighter by the end of summer. Same heart shaped face, smiling, bossing, teasing. The "*as my father always says*" sayings, that, yes, now he understood had caused that momentary brain fog outside the dining hall. And finally, the lip-chew for the tell.

Exaltation soared through him. He'd known her a lifetime ago, in Derby, by God. Damn he wished Zeke was here to confirm his suspicion.

But assuming it was she--one *Miss Gloriana Masters.* Yes, *that* was her name—why not admit the truth?

"You look very strange." She drew out the words, eyeing him with wary suspicion.

He crossed his arms over his chest and the lump in his coat reminded him of her pocketed slipper. He ought to give it back.

"As it happens, I spent a fair amount of time in Durham." A blatant lie, but mark him, he'd trip her up. So much more fun than confronting her outright. "What's the name of this tiny village from which you hale?"

Anna's eyes widened in alarm, and Caden nearly snorted. He couldn't wait to hear what she'd come up with next. A small town in Durham, indeed.

"I did not mean to say I was born there. I merely worked there for a prolonged time."

"Did you?"

"Er, hadn't you better return to the dining hall? For my reputation's sake?" she squeaked.

He grinned and rocked back on his heels.

"Quite right. I should put in an appearance, if only to apologize for my tardiness. Perhaps I'll see you tomorrow and we can resume this little chat—assuming your headache resolves."

She lifted a hand to her temple. "When one of these comes on, they tend to last for days."

He nodded, his face a mask of grave understanding. "I see. How-ever does Lady Wentworth manage with you out of commission so often?"

Her hand fell to her side and irritation flashed in her amber eyes. "I never said it happened often."

He shrugged. "Right. Only that it debilitates you for days on end."

Her lips firmed and she glanced pointedly behind her into the dark antechamber. "If there is nothing else, sir?"

He tapped his coat over his ribcage, assuring himself the slipper tucked in his inner pocket remained, snugly in place. "No, indeed. I bid you good evening, Mrs. Jones."

He turned on his heel and sauntered away.

Chapter Five

Anna didn't wait to see if Caden glanced over his shoulder. She dove into the night-dark antechamber and slung the door closed behind her with more force than was, strictly speaking, necessary.

Fumbling in the pitch blackness, she struck a match, cupped the flame—with shaking fingers, blast it—and lit the sconces framing the draped window.

Bathed in the soft glow illuminating the chamber, she stripped off the beautiful gold silk gown she'd borrowed for the evening. Rehanging the dress, she smoothed her hands over the fine material. She'd felt a bit like a princess wearing it. Even Lady Wentworth had exclaimed over her appearance.

Dear God, Lady Wentworth. She'd been so preoccupied with Caden, she'd failed to consider the fine fettle she'd gotten herself into.

What would Lady Wentworth say regarding Anna's blatant disregard of her explicit directive? More to the point, what would she *do?*

Irrespective of the undergarments she still wore, Anna paced the small space, her mind racing anew. The dowager duchess had her quirks, some might argue flaws. Particular, demanding, eccentric, reclusive. But she was also fair-minded. Anna had never known her to sack one of her employees for a minor infraction.

The question was, would she consider Anna ignoring an express order *minor?* Anna thought not. She paused in the middle of the room to cover her eyes with one hand and tried to imagine Lady Wentworth's reaction.

She would be disappointed. Maybe hurt? That thought alone settled in her stomach like a brick. She might have—all right did have— a tough exterior, but she always treated Anna like a member of her inner circle.

She slumped into an armchair and stared morosely at her stockinged feet. In the two years of her employ, never once had Anna been the recipient of the lady's wrath, and this was how she repaid her kindness.

How intimidated she'd felt interviewing for the post of companion to the dowager, owing primarily to her made-up references, or rather the fact they'd not, apparently, passed muster. Witness the minor noblewoman who had hired her prior to Lady Wentworth only to summarily rescind her offer of employment a day later.

The placement agency gave no explanation for the client's retraction, and Anna hadn't asked. She hardly wanted to draw attention to the most likely reason. Her potential employer must have attempted to verify her falsified letters of recommendation.

Oddly, the agency had not sent her packing. Instead, they informed her she would soon interview for the post of companion to the highest-ranking member of society she'd ever lain eyes upon.

The pinched-faced agents had taken great pains to warn her of the noted recluse's exacting standards. They did not have to spell out the obvious: Anna stood little chance of securing the post.

Yet to their mutual surprise, Lady Wentworth hired her on sight. When they boarded the Wentworth travel coach bound for Northumberland the very same day, Anna silently surmised the lady had filled the post in haste and thus had no time to check her references. She could only thank her lucky stars.

For two years since, Lady Wentworth's exclusionary world had provided a haven of safety for Anna. The unexpected boon was the bond which had sprung up between them almost instantly. Lady Wentworth felt like home to her, and she liked to think her presence added something worthwhile to her employer's life.

Tonight, thanks to losing her head over Caden, thanks to indulging her silly, fanciful holdover dreams from childhood

where she was the princess and Caden her prince, she'd jeop-
ardized all of that.

She could practically see her mother shaking her head in that
I-told-you-so way Anna so disliked.

She couldn't undo what had been done. She'd do the next
best thing. She would apologize to Lady Wentworth the first
chance she got, pray for a second chance, and hope she still held
her position come morning.

***

The groan of a door hinge sent Anna half out of the wingback
chair where she dozed. Heart racing, she gripped the armrests
and glanced around the dimly lit chamber anticipating the sight
of dust-covered velvet drapes, a sagging gold-tasseled canopy
over a lumpy four post bed--and the scowling face of Angelique,
her father's widow.

The stuttering candlelight instead revealed rose and cream
papered walls, a large wardrobe and folded cot, and Lady Wentworth coming through the chamber door. Relief swept through
her.

Then she remembered the mess she'd created.

Knuckling her eyes, she sat upright and braced for her come-
uppance.

"Good evening, Lady Wentworth."

"Anna." The older woman moved toward her, peeling off her
kidskin gloves.

"I suppose you're wondering what happened tonight?" Anna queried in a small voice.

Lady Wentworth settled herself on an adjacent chair. "I might have done, if not for the enlightening conversation I had with a certain handsome gentleman with the devil's own charm. I believe you know the one?"

She believed she did. Unfortunately, she had no idea what he might have said. "I...see."

"He told all and sundry how he stumbled while leading you to the dining hall. Claimed he suffered a bout of dizziness due to his recent head injury." She cocked her head slightly, a considering look on her face. "Shame he laid you out in the process."

"Me?" she yelped. "Laid out?"

Lady Wentworth's lips twitched. "Naturally the ordeal left you distraught, with no appetite to speak of, and you hobbled back here to recuperate."

"I see," she said again. This was how he protected her reputation? By painting her as a clumsy invalid? Anna's belly gave a low growl as if in solidarity with her indignation.

"Tell me, was any part of the handsome fiend's tale true?"

Caden had provided a plausible excuse for her disappearance. But lying to Lady Wentworth felt wrong. "Perhaps he stalled due to a bit of dizziness, but he did not stumble, nor did I wind up prostrate on the floor, for heaven's sake."

Lady Wentworth gazed on her with a knowing expression. "An opportunity to flee presented itself and you took it before thinking it through?"

Anna twisted her hands in her lap.

"I could ask why. I could press you for answers, but I suspect your response would be your usual vagary. You do value your privacy. Reminds me a bit of myself."

Anna blinked. She'd never dreamt Lady Wentworth noticed her skirting any but the most innocuous questions relating to her past.

"I have developed a theory of sorts." Lady Wentworth paused, as if deliberating her words. "Something tragic happened in your past, likely involving your late husband, perhaps even your parents. Now you're playing it safe. Maybe too safe. Maybe even allowing life to pass you by."

Anna couldn't speak. Lady Wentworth had deduced a fair amount. More, rather than speaking to her in anger, she seemed to understand, even sympathize with her.

A fond smile curved the older woman's lips. "Do you know why I wanted you to attend tonight's festivities?"

Anna shook her head and, curse it all, stared at the silver-haired dynamo through a misty haze.

"Because you remind me of someone I once knew whom I..." Her words abruptly halted. Her eyes lowered to her pale hands, clenched in her lap.

Alarm flashed through Anna. She hated to see the indefatigable lady distressed, much less on account of her. "My lady?"

The older woman shook her head once then leveled her gaze on Anna. "It's a house party, Anna, in the country. Not all of society's rules apply--especially not as concern widows. Your husband may be dead, but you're not, something a particularly dashing man of your recent acquaintance has clearly noticed."

An image of Caden as she'd seen him hours ago, smiling, hair gleaming, aiming those lethal blue eyes in her direction, flashed in her mind. She replayed the sound of his voice curling into her ear. *"Your perfume...tantalizes me..."*

With brutal effort she suppressed the sudden, fierce yearning swamping her senses.

"I have some understanding of what goes on at parties such as these, Lady Wentworth, and I thank you for your..." She broke off, searching for the word. "...concern. Rest assured I am quite content with my life as it is."

Not precisely the truth, but not a total lie. While she enjoyed Lady Wentworth's companionship, she sometimes longed for something more—a husband, a grand passion, even a career of sorts. Thanks to what she'd done—beginning with misplacing her trust—she could have none of those things. Not without risking her very life.

The older woman frowned in evident bemusement. "I see. I'm glad to hear it. Still. I can't help feeling you're missing out."

Pressing her hands into the arms of the chair, she hefted herself to her feet. "Now if you don't mind, I refuse to spend one moment longer in this blasted contraption. I swear, men designed corsets as part of a devious plot to torture the fairer sex into submission." Her words faded as she disappeared into the adjoining bedchamber.

Anna stared at the empty doorway. Her employer had let her off easy tonight. Her leniency was more than she deserved.

But what she'd suggested—that Anna might enjoy Caden's company, without censure, at least for a little while—hurt beyond measure. Because Anna couldn't risk the one thing she suddenly wished for more than anything else in the world.

***

Anna arose with the sun, despite suffering a sleepless night. She relished her daily walks, breathing in the brisk early-morning air. From the start of her employ, Lady Wentworth permitted the practice. Anna showed her gratitude by not allowing it to interfere with any plans the lady might have for the day. To that end she held to the maxim, the sooner she left, the better.

Pulling the simple tan linen walking dress over her head, a slip of shiny gold at floor level caught her eye. Ah, yes. She tied the cord at her bodice and frowned at the poor, lone slipper lying against the baseboard where it had landed last night.

She scooped up the slipper, admiring its hand-stitched embroidery briefly before tucking it away in the wardrobe beneath her folded nightshift. She doubted very much she'd see the missing half of the pair ever again. But she'd take a look nonetheless.

She pulled on her gleaming, black leather lace-up boots. Tying off the first bow, she smiled briefly. Only last week she purchased both the boots and evening slippers from the cobbler's shop she'd discovered on one of her off-days. The owner adored

Anna. And why wouldn't he? She spent a pretty penny in his establishment.

True, the quality of her low-heeled boots marked them as too dear for a woman on a companion's salary. Anna had deemed the risk low considering the unlikelihood anyone would notice the help's shoes peeking out from beneath plain gray and brown and tan skirts. *People see what they expect to see*, her father always said.

Indulging her penchant for beautiful, well-made shoes was one small luxury she allowed herself. Not that her funds would last forever. Still, spending the money she'd acquired from pawning her mother's ruby pendant—the very pendant Angelique claimed to have sold to pay her father's debts—felt like a small victory in a sea of losses.

She had forfeited her freedom and all tangible ties to her late parents, but Angelique had *not* ended up with her mother's prized ruby.

Shoulders back and chin up, she let herself into the corridor.

***

Caden shifted on his feet and thought longingly of the lone cup of strong black coffee he'd imbibed before taking up his watch. He stared past palm fronds down the empty corridor from his post—a recessed alcove off the main concourse leading to the dining hall.

He pulled the watch from his pocket and frowned. He'd waited here three quarters of an hour. No sign of Anna yet. He'd been so sure. Perhaps he'd misjudged.

After Lady Wentworth's casual mention of her companion's penchant for early morning walks last night, he'd lain awake trying to work-out how he could use the knowledge to his advantage. The brilliant scheme finally came to him as the sun's fiery rays lit the horizon.

Invigorated, he'd arisen, washed, shaved, and ventured downstairs in search of strong coffee and a good stake-out position.

Ah, well. Another cup wouldn't go amiss. He sidled out from behind the potted palm, and froze as Anna came into view. Satisfaction pulsed through him. His hunch had proved correct.

Sliding back into place, he crossed his arms over his chest and allowed himself a smug grin. Gloriana Masters, or Mrs. Anna Jones depending, had returned to the last known location of her lost slipper.

Another tell, Mrs. Jones.

If she wanted him, hell, *anyone*, to believe her story about haling from a remote farming village, she'd need to make several adjustments to her persona, and not solely concerning the incompatibility of her footwear to her station.

Right enough, her usual dresses, like the one she wore now, marked her as a servant. But her clothing failed to disguise her gentle breeding. The grace with which she moved, her regal posture and incline of her head told a story all its own. Put the woman in silks such as she'd donned last night, and voila, she resembled nothing so much as a member of the nobility with the bluest blood running through her veins.

Eyes on the floor, she moved steadily toward his alcove. The hated, ever-present bonnet for once hung loosely from her fingers.

It was a rare moment, indeed. No bonnet, no ducked head, no palm fronds obscured his view of her. She was breathtaking to behold. He straightened away from the wall and rubbed a hand over a chest that felt suddenly tight. Damn sleepless night catching up with him, no doubt.

She reached a cross section in the corridor. Brows knitted in concentration, she clasped her arms behind her, zigged one way, then zagged the other.

A twinge of regret pricked his conscience. She'd never find the recalcitrant slipper, especially as some perverse instinct bade him leave it in his bedchamber. Still, her focus impressed him. She apparently didn't notice the Fenton's oh-so-proper butler eyeing her with concern.

"Madam, may I assist you in locating...er...the breakfast room perhaps?"

She jerked upright and bit her lower lip.

Caden stifled a snort.

"No, indeed. Just taking a turn 'round the manse, stretching the legs." She patted her skirts in emphasis.

"Very good, mum." Frowning, the spit-shined butler turned on his heel and strode past Caden's alcove.

Time to make his move. He smoothed a hand over his hair and stepped into the corridor.

Anna did not look up. She'd resumed her search.

As he closed the distance, his blood simmered with a heady sense of anticipation, something he hadn't experienced since—well, he couldn't remember the last time.

"Mrs. Jones."

Anna let go a tiny, strangled shriek. Her eyes, wide with surprise, locked on him then narrowed. "Mr. Thurgood? Why are *you* here?"

He snorted. "Why am I here? I believe I was invited. Or rather, Randall was invited and I—"

"I meant, why are you here, in this corridor, at this hour?"

"Stretching my legs," he said, in a parody of her words a moment ago.

She slanted him a skeptical look.

"As to the the time of day, I always rise early, Mrs. Jones."

"You don't say?"

He shrugged, then said honestly, "I enjoy the relative quiet mornings offer, and the time it affords for contemplation. And you, Mrs. Jones?"

She arched a brow and a corner of her lips crooked upward. "Contemplation? Of what, pray tell?"

Caden opened his arms wide. "Solutions to the world's problems? At least in my small corner of it, Mrs. Jones."

Her semblance of a smile vanished. "Why do you keep saying that?"

"Exactly what, Mrs. Jones?"

A most becoming pink tinged her cheeks. "Mrs. Jones," she said between gritted teeth.

He grinned. He was having more fun than he'd had in ages. "It is your name, is it not? Nevertheless, I shall refrain from addressing you as such."

She gave an exasperated sigh. "It seemed unnecessarily excessive."

Craning her head, she glanced over his shoulder, giving him the impression she meant to skirt him.

He stepped closer. "And how fares your head this morning, ma'am? I presume ma'am is acceptable?"

The pink tinge on her cheeks which had begun to fade blossomed with a vengeance. "Much improved, sir. Thank you for asking. How is your..." She flittered her gloved fingers over the crown of her head.

"Oh, yes." He rubbed his cranial lump a-la-Harrison. Still tender. "I hardly remember it's there."

The smile that curved her lips turned genuine.

"May I ask what has captured your interest so intently?" He waited, his expression all innocence, or so he hoped, despite the fact his gaze kept dropping to her mouth. But he didn't want to miss the tell-tale nibble that was sure to come.

Only it never came. Instead she moistened her lips with the tip of her tongue. Those rosy, perfectly-shaped-for-kissing lips.

With effort he dragged his gaze to her eyes, then decided the view wasn't half bad there, either.

"Last night when we...that is, you didn't happen to..." She huffed out a breath. "Never mind. It's not important. If you'll excuse me, Mr. Thurgood? Pleasant day to you." Picking up her skirts, she turned and set off at a brisk pace.

She meant to leave him in her dust.

In two strides Caden fell into step beside her. "No breakfast for you?"

The look of consternation she slid him nearly teased a bark of amusement from him. Or annoyance. She'd given him the cut direct. Again. It was the damnedest thing.

"I prefer to take my morning stroll before breakfasting."

As he'd guessed. "Your morning stroll, you say? How's that for a lucky coincidence. As it happens, I am also heading out for a walk. Might I accompany you?"

Her clear reticence made him want to retract his request. He realized he disliked feeling like a beggar, an unwanted one at that. Teasing her was one thing. But he'd be damned if he'd resort to forcing his attentions on a woman. "I beg your pardon. I won't infringe—"

"No, no," she cut in, linking her hands behind her back. Her shoulders rose and fell in a deep sigh. "Your company is most welcome, sir."

An unfamiliar, heady warmth suffused him. "Lead the way."

Chapter Six

Anna breathed in the fresh scent of foliage and damp earth. She turned her face skyward. This was her favorite time of day, when the morning sun tangled with layers of clouds. Today's, thick and smoke-colored, painted the sky fuchsia, orange, lilac and purple.

Her cheeks seemed to drink up moisture from the very air. She felt like a child breathless with the first hint of spring. Only it was Caden exhilarating her senses. So much for her good intentions where he was concerned.

Less than an hour ago she'd stepped from the guest chamber, staunchly committed *not* to see him again, regardless of her employer's thoughtful, if odd, encouragement to the contrary. Yet here she was, strolling beside him in companionable silence along the meandering, tree-canopied trail.

There was nowhere else she'd rather be, and no one else she'd rather be with.

It felt like coming home, except for the part where her heart raced every time he smiled. That felt like something else entirely.

"The polish on your boots rivals my own, Mrs. Jones. I shall have to mention as much to my valet."

He'd noticed her boots? Leave it Caden to belie her assumption no one noticed the help—much less their footwear.

"Thank you," she muttered and shortened her stride to cover the tips of her boots with her skirts.

Caden grinned down at her. Even his eyes smiled as if he noted her discomfiture and reveled in it. "Last night you mentioned you come from Durham."

"Did I say I haled from Durham? How silly. It must've been the headache talking. That was the location of my last post." She silently congratulated herself on the story she'd invented during her sleepless night. She'd somehow known, given the chance, Caden would renew his interrogations. "Lancashire is home. High in the Pennines. Boulsworth Hill, specifically."

As far as she knew, nobody but cheese makers lived there. Of equal importance, the terrain made traveling to the region difficult. She couldn't imagine the polished, social chameleon that was Caden Thurgood venturing to the sparsely populated upper moors of the Pennines for holiday. She ducked her head, hiding a smug grin.

"I see." Somehow with two little words he communicated both amusement and disbelief.

He'd always been too bright for his own good.

"Where did you grow up, Mr. Thurgood? London proper?"

In her experience, men loved talking about themselves. She'd employed the tactic to distract men from the pain of having a bone reset, a wound stitched, or worse still, from their worries over an ill loved-one. Her father's trick. She'd never seen it fail.

"Partly, yes. Growing up, my family split time between London and Derby. The earl, always, and my father, oft times, resided in London when the House of Lords was in session.

"Summers and holidays were spent in Derby, but of course, my brother, Zeke and I both attended Eton, and then Cambridge, so...London. The latter part of college I leased an apartment. The habit stuck, and I keep one there to this day. But Derbyshire's home. At least"—He blew-out a stream of air—"It was."

She opened her mouth to ask what he meant, but before she could utter the first syllable, he redirected the conversation.

"Do you know the area? Derbyshire, I mean."

So much for her never-fail theory.

"Derbyshire?" she aped. Images of rolling green hills, a lush riverside, dense clumps of fragrant forest, and a formidable castle on a hill rushed into her mind like a high speed train.

In a flash, the visions narrowed in scope, and she saw a cozy limestone cottage at dusk. Inside, she and her parents sat around the table, talking, laughing, eating stew flavored with the pungent herbs from her mother's garden.

As if she were here, her mother's stern warning came to her. *Keep-up your guard around that Claybourne boy. With nobility the title always comes first, even before family.*

"Yes. Do you know it?"

She cleared her throat and shook off her memories. "No. Is it nice? Oh dear."

Seemingly from nowhere, three fat drops of rain splatted on her, leaving damp splotches on her skirts. Sudden sharp gusts of wind grabbed at the hair pinned at her nape, pulling tendrils loose to whip her cheeks.

Glancing up, she saw the magnificent hues of the early morning had given way to a bottomless gray. She'd been too caught up with the man at her side to notice.

"We probably ought to head back," she said without enthusiasm, instead of thanking her lucky stars for the perfect excuse to shake off the blood hound that was Caden Thurgood.

"Bah. Just a bit of wind." Cupping her elbow, he urged her onward.

Her good sense and inner resolve melted at his touch. "You can tell the weather?" she asked in lieu of making any real protest.

"I can. However, in the event a heavy branch shakes loose, you should probably stay close." He tucked her gloved hand snuggly into the crook of his arm.

Even through his clothing and her glove she felt his well-muscled arm flex beneath her fingers. Warmth radiated off of him, warding off the damp chill of the morning and making her want to purr like a kitten. She hadn't noticed the cold seeping into her bones until his body heat dispelled it.

The wind shifted, and a lovely hint of his spiced cologne teased her nostrils. Lady Wentworth's words from last night came to her, and, for the briefest moment, she had the indecent urge to curl into him.

A singularly bad idea. Still, she did not retract her hand.

"Where were we? Oh, yes. Derby. Pity you haven't experienced the splendor, especially during summer months."

He stretched his free hand out before them as if painting a scene. "Picture rolling hills, dense forests that turn the air almost green when you stand within their thickets mid-day, and a winding river running through all of it."

"It sounds lovely."

"I spent much of my youth there. It's a wonderful place for rearing children. I came close to settling there on a more permanent basis myself, recently."

To raise children? Fool that she was, she hadn't considered he might have an intended. Her heart rose up to choke her.

"I see." *Don't say it. Do not say it.* "There's to be a Mrs. Thurgood soon, I take it?"

"Thought I'd mentioned," he replied, flippant as you please.

She glanced over her shoulder. She should have insisted they return to the manse when she had the chance.

"...about Zeke's recent marriage. He and the future Countess of Claybourne have taken up residence in Chissington Hall, the earl's seat.

"As far as raising children, I referenced my own childhood, but, I will say, based upon their"—He scratched the side of his nose—"That is, I suspect there'll be a little Ezekiel or Christine before long. As for me, I am blissfully unattached. In case that was what you wanted to know."

"Oh, I didn't...I wasn't asking if..."

"Of course not. Silly me." His smug grin belied his words.

She couldn't seem to work up any annoyance. He wasn't on the verge of marrying. She could breathe again.

"I am confused about one thing, Mr. Thurgood. It sounds as if you prefer Derbyshire. But you reside in London?"

He shrugged. "London's not precisely home. I do let an apartment there, but it doesn't get much use after the Season. In fact," he paused, his expression turning resigned as if admitting to something he'd rather not, which made no sense to her whatsoever. "Let's just say for the last several years I've traveled extensively."

"Oh? On business?"

"Business? No."

She waited expectantly. When he didn't elaborate, she pressed. "Any reason in particular?"

"So many parties, so little time," he said breezily. But his eyes didn't reflect the devil-may-care attitude his words portrayed.

"I see. How very..." she broke off, not certain how to finish her sentence. She didn't know how she felt about Caden wandering the countryside, aimless, going from one party to the next. "Entertaining."

Something like anger flashed in his eyes, then vanished as swiftly as it had come. "Are you sure you never met my brother?

You sound exactly like him," he muttered. "At any rate, I'd given some thought to settling in Derby recently and have since changed my mind, and that's that."

There was something here. Something eating at him which he clearly didn't wish to discuss. She ought to let the matter drop. "May I ask why you opted against doing so?"

"Aren't you the inquisitive one?"

"I hate to call you the pot..." She let her words dwindle, hoping he'd take the bait.

He huffed out a laugh. "Fair enough, Jones."

His expression turned considering. "How to make a long, boring story succinct? There's a limestone quarry on the estate, the uses of which I looked into during Zeke and Kitty's absence. I had a notion to head up some projects utilizing limestone to benefit the earl's tenants and local villages, beyond buildings and roads. Circumstances caused me to change my mind. Suffice it to say, after this party, I'm considering an extended holiday abroad. Mayhap I'll simply ride the Summer party circuit again. Who knows?"

"More parties, eh?" She sniffed. "I can tell you if I had a choice to live in a castle on a hill, I'd choose the castle every time."

He drew to a sudden halt then fixed her with a stare, an odd gleam in his eyes. "I didn't say anything about Chissington Hall being a castle."

Her mind went blank for a moment that stretched like an eternity. Then she formulated a realistic reply—she hoped.

"No, but you did mention Derbyshire housed the earldom's seat. I merely assumed."

One corner of his mouth quirked upward. He patted her hand still tucked into his elbow. "Of course you did, Mrs. Jones."

They walked on. The crunch of fallen leaves, and scent of pleasantly sweet, decaying foliage, surrounded them. She closed her eyes and allowed herself, just for a moment, to pretend--that Caden hadn't become a practical stranger. That she wasn't on the run. That she hadn't been forced to do the unthinkable and now suffered the consequences.

A burst of wind ripped through the tunnel of trees producing a wolf-like howl and chilling Anna everywhere Caden's body heat did not reach. She opened her mouth to insist they start back, only to be forestalled by Caden's next words.

"Boulsworth Hill, you say. Is that where you met your husband?"

A shiver coursed through her, though whether from the dropping temperature, or the macabre image of her so-called husband as she'd last seen him, she couldn't say. "I-I would prefer we not discuss my late husband."

He made a tut-tut sound. Drawing to a halt, he gripped her shoulders with gentle pressure and shifted her to face him. "My dear Mrs. Jones. I didn't balk at your questions."

"You don't understand. You can't. Your world is parties and soirees and deciding between your London address, a country estate or a trip abroad. Mine is...not. Won't you allow me this moment, walking beside you as if neither of us had a care in the world?"

Genuine concern darkened his sky-blue eyes. "You're right. I don't understand. But I want to."

Her insides thrummed with a an unfamiliar heat. The entirely too-pleasant warmth threatened to steal her good sense, because more than anything, she wanted to tell Caden everything, right here, right now, starting with her mother's illness and finishing with this moment.

She shook her head to clear it. As if in direct opposition, wind and leaves swirled around them, picking up speed in time with the chaos inside her.

Then, abruptly, the wind ceased. Silence and stillness engulfed them. Her tongue darted out to dampen her dry lips.

Caden's gaze fastened on her mouth, tracking the movement. "Help me understand," he repeated.

"Why?" she whispered, his answer suddenly of vital importance.

He inched his big body closer, bringing them toe-to-toe, and forcing her to tilt her head back to look him in the face rather than stare at his bright white shirt and broad chest. "Because you seem in need of a confident. And because..." Caden swallowed hard and lifted his hands to cup her cheeks.

At some point, he'd removed his gloves, and the feel of his palms on her skin felt unbearably intimate—and utterly divine.

The blue of his eyes reflected the clouds overhead and swirled like a churning sea, stealing her breath. She couldn't speak. Could only shake her head.

His eyelids grew heavy and his gaze dropped with languid grace to her mouth.

God, he was going to kiss her.

The heat in her veins turned scorching, melting her from the inside out. Her lips parted, and though she knew she should, she didn't, by word or deed, proffer the first protest. She wanted Caden's kiss, like she'd waited for it a lifetime.

Slowly, he lowered his head 'til his mouth hovered over hers. His warm breath fanned over her cheeks and goose flesh erupted over her entire body.

"I'm going to kiss you now. Is that all right?"

She swallowed. Nodded. And then, just in case he'd missed her nod, whispered, "Yes."

She'd barely uttered the word before his mouth covered hers, his lips exerting the merest pressure, as if savoring her, as if tasting her, one deliciously sweet sip at a time.

She'd imagined a thousand times how a kiss might feel. Her imagination had not come close to reality. An ache of need she'd never known stole through her, turning her bones liquid.

He nipped at her lower lip, and she gasped at the unexpected thrill. The scent of him filled her nostrils. Soap, subtle, woodsy cologne, warm male skin, *Caden*. She wanted to nestle into him and breathe him in, but that would mean breaking off the kiss, and that she absolutely could not do.

"Anna." One of his hands smoothed up her nape to cradle the crown of her head, tilting her face upward. With a groan, he deepened the kiss.

Her hands found his hard shoulders of their own accord, snaked around his neck to cling to him as she rose onto her tiptoes, silently demanding more.

He responded to her invitation, sliding the tip of his tongue along the seam of her lips 'til her mouth opened slightly, and his hot tongue dipped inside to feather over hers.

Her own soft mew sounded. Swift embarrassment had her pulling back.

Emitting a low growl, Caden held her fast, one arm banding around her waist. His mouth turned demanding, voracious.

Nothing had ever felt so right as the delicious friction of his lips on hers, of the hard planes of his body against hers.

Her fingers threaded into the silky golden hair brushing his collar making her wish with all her might she had removed her gloves as he had.

He shivered under her touch. "Anna, my God, Anna," he whispered against her mouth, before sealing his hot, damp lips over hers once more.

A low pounding sounded in her ears. Her heart beat, growing louder with each passing second. Slowly, the truth permeated her kiss-drugged mind. Not her heart. Horse hoofs thumped in the not-too-far distance.

Reality flashed through her. What in blazes was she doing? She jerked away from him with the force of an ax-split log.

"Wh-what…Anna?" Caden's chest heaved as he sucked in air. He stared at her, looking so charmingly befuddled she would have laughed under different circumstances.

After a moment of awkward silence, he gave a shaky laugh. "I wasn't planning to take you on the forest floor, if that's what you were thinking."

She gaped at him. "I beg your pardon, Ca-Mr. Thurgood? There are people nearby."

"And? This *is* a house party. I doubt any passers-by would have stopped to chat."

She blinked. "Why do people keep saying that?"

He scowled. "People? Who else said that to you?"

"I think the more pertinent question, sir, is what sort of woman do you take me for?"

His expression turned wary and he tunneled his fingers through his hair. "I never would have started the business except…you are a widow, are you not?"

The way his eyes narrowed on her face, he actually meant the question.

"Of course," she replied, with a bit too much vehemence.

He nodded once. "As such, no one expects you to play the virginal debutante. Not at a house party at any rate. Still." His expression turned contrite. "You have no reason to believe me, Mrs. Anna Jones, but you make me forget myself."

The huskily spoken words reached inside her, spurring her to confess he had the very same affect on her. But that much was obvious. She'd put up no resistance whatsoever, indeed, had in fact, welcomed his heated kisses.

"I rather thought you wanted me to kiss you. Was I wrong?" he asked, echoing her thoughts.

She could not deny the truth. She shook her head.

One corner of his mouth crooked upward, giving her a glimpse of straight white teeth. "I'd begun to think I'd picked up a foul odor or grown another nose or something the way you avoid me."

She had attempted to do just that, albeit without much success.

He barked out a laugh. "Mrs. Jones, may I make a suggestion?" Not waiting for her an answer, he grasped her hand and tucked it in the crook of his arm. "Never take up gambling."

"My father may have told me that once or twice."

"A wise man," he muttered, leading her back to the gravel path from which they'd strayed before speaking again. "Anna—Mrs. Jones—Perhaps I should apologize, tell you I regret what happened. But I can't. Not without lying. I haven't many hard-fast rules, but I do have one against telling falsehoods."

"No apology necessary. There were two of us involved in—" she cleared her throat "—what happened." Her voice sounded decidedly husky to her own ears.

Evidently, he noticed. He drew to a halt, shifted to face her. "Careful. I may start thinking you want me to kiss you again." Twin blue flames lit his eyes.

She did want him to kiss her again. But she'd forgotten her tenuous circumstance twice now since arriving to this blasted party—both times thanks to Caden. Regardless of whether or not she, a lady's companion and widow, could be forgiven a house party dalliance, she did not need to lose her head over the man.

She must remain vigilant, which, apparently, she couldn't do while in his presence. It was like he was a magnetic rod and she tiny shavings of steel. She might have herself all neatly lined up, but the moment he drew near she spun about, forgetting all but him and the way he made her feel.

She'd wanted his kiss, and enjoyed it immensely. But it mustn't happen again.

She sent him what she hoped passed for a politely regretful smile—as if she found the prospect of another kiss akin to watching water boil. "It's past time I returned. Lady Wentworth will be awake and may require assistance."

"Of course. I didn't think. Must be that bump on my head again."

Though the muted sun had climbed higher in the sky, the day had not warmed. If anything, the temperature had dropped. Past the edge of the tree line, hovering above Fensworth Manor, clouds congealed, creating a dome of gray as thick as smoke. Air, heavy with moisture, clung to her like a second skin.

She might wish him to think he held little interest for her, but in truth she relished the heat eking from his body to hers where their arms linked, where his hand covered hers.

Devil take it.

"Speaking of your injury." She shifted to face him and stripped off one glove. Her face burned with the blush she knew stained her cheeks, but she didn't care. She had to touch his hair, just this once, to see for herself if it felt as silky smooth as it promised to be when she'd sifted it wearing gloves.

She reached up, eyebrows arched in a silent demand for him to lower his head. When he complied, she riffled gently through his shiny hair—luxurious silk beyond measure—and gingerly fingered the small lump.

Caden held himself stock still, scarcely seeming to breath. A muscle ticked fiercely in his jaw.

"Does it hurt much?" she whispered.

"Not in the way you think," he answered in a rough voice.

She hesitated, uncertain what he meant by his odd reply. Finally she withdrew her hand. "You're very lucky. Head wounds can be deadly." A gust of icy wind stole up her skirts sending a shiver down her spine.

"My head's too thick for one thump of a skiff to crack it." Caden moved to stand in front of her. He pulled the empty glove she held from her grasp and attempted to slide it onto her bare hand.

It was a task easier done by the wearer.

He laughed when she tugged her hand and glove away from him.

"My first foray as a lady's maid ends in dismal failure. I enjoyed the brief endeavor, however."

She tried to scowl at him but found herself fighting a smile as she donned the glove, then flexed her fingers in the tight-fitting leather.

"Your hands are elegant and smooth skinned, feminine yet strong." He met her gaze. "Apparently I like everything about you, Mrs. Jones."

She gave him a chiding smile, unsure if he meant the profuse flattery, yet unable to still the flutter in her belly his words caused.

"I suppose I must get you back, or the dowager duchess will have my head." He tucked her hand into his elbow and urged her closer to his side than society deemed proper for an unmarried couple. Incorrigible rake.

Still, Anna allowed the impropriety. What was one more indulgence in the grand scheme of things?

All too soon they neared the back of the Manor.

Caden slowed as if he, like she, hated to see their time together end. "I'll see you later today, amongst the other party guests, no doubt."

"I will be wherever Lady Wentworth wishes to spend her time." She gave Caden a frank look. "Most likely that rules out any of the planned festivities."

"I see. But tonight. You'll be present at dinner." He said the last as if stating a well-known fact.

Anna gave a non-committal shrug. Let him think what he would. If she had any say, she would not see him at dinner, or again, period. She had tempted fate enough, lingering overlong with him this morning, allowing him to kiss her.

Not that she could bring herself to regret the impulse. She would never forget their kiss as long as she lived.

They reached the portico, climbing the last step as the grey skies overhead opened, releasing a heavy rain.

Chapter Seven

C aden exited the gentleman's wing en route for the grand hall and this afternoon's activity, whatever it may be.

His plan had worked this morning. He'd intercepted Anna before she'd headed out for her walk and spent a glorious few hours with her. He'd kissed her as he'd wanted to from the moment he'd laid eyes on her stretched out on that lawn chair.

So why was he in such a foul mood?

Scratch that. *Horrendous* mood.

The fault lie entirely with the chit, Anna, or Gloriana, or Mrs. Jones, or whomever she claimed to be at the moment. She wanted nothing to do with him. He'd read her disinclination on her face as clearly as if she had spoken the words aloud.

And this was *after* he'd kissed her.

As to why her rejection mattered so much, he couldn't say.

Except that it made no sense—especially after that divine kiss. He hadn't been the only one affected by it, of that he was sure.

She'd practically melted in his arms. He could still feel her lithe body, pliant against his, could recall that elegant scent, uniquely hers, enveloping him, teasing his senses in a way he'd never experienced. *Christ.* He tunneled a hand through his hair. Remembering the heaven of holding her in his arms was driving him mad.

Clearly, he'd been too long without the charms of a woman—between Zeke's wedding and the tasks he'd taken on in Derby, not to mention this last minute party, there hadn't been time. Yes, that was the problem. Whether or not he laid eyes on *Mrs. Jones* again made no difference to him.

He had wanted to see her expression when he revealed he knew her true identity—assuming he was right about who he thought she was. He was ninety-nine percent certain.

He merged with a handful of guests ascending the wide marble steps marking the entrance of the grand hall. Wading into the crush of people, he pasted a jovial smile on his face. This was a party, after all, and he was Caden Thurgood of Claybourne, the consummate party guest.

The room was blasted hot, and smelled of warm bodies—more than fifty at a glance—and liberally applied perfume. The muggy air sneaking in from outdoors had created a ripe, stifling atmosphere.

He tugged at his cravat and decided the knock he'd taken on the head yesterday sufficed to excuse him from today's fun-filled activity.

He turned to leave in time to witness a liveried servant closing the double doors and sealing his fate. Nothing for it but to soldier on.

Movement out of the corner of his eye drew his attention. Harrison, his young friend, stood in the thick of things, madly waving in a come hither gesture. The Misses Applegate and Egerton once again flanked him. The prospect of fending off their advances held as much appeal as it had yesterday.

Pretending not to see them, he slipped into the crowd and started in the opposite direction. His steps faltered before his brain made the connection as to why.

Anna.

For a timeless moment he drank in the sight of her, slight and elegant in a fine yellow day dress, the furthest thing from servant's attire. She wore another unfortunate bonnet with an over-large brim. Although he could not see her eyes for the bonnet, he caught the wry smile she aimed at her employer.

Lady Wentworth spoke in an animated fashion. Her narrowed gaze shifted about the room landing on this person, then that. Her accompanying scowl told him she did not hold the assembled guests in high esteem.

He wondered why on earth the woman had agreed to attend the celebration, family notwithstanding. Not that he had any complaints. Make that *many* complaints.

He shook himself out of his stupor, squared his shoulders and strode toward Anna and Lady Wentworth like a man fully confident of his reception. In truth his insides quaked like a schoolboy's about to take his first pony ride.

The dowager spied Caden first. Her faded eyes twinkled in silent greeting, as if the two of them shared a secret. A moment later, she shifted and, to Caden's eyes, purposefully blocked his approach from Anna's view.

He was really starting to like the grande dame.

A firm hand clasped his shoulder from behind. "I say, Thurgood, did you not see me over there?"

Harrison. Caden had only himself to blame, standing there gawking at Jones.

Resigned, he turned. Harrison's entourage hadn't accompanied him, it seemed. He smiled. "Over where? I've only just arrived."

"The ladies and I have a glass of champagne for you. Why're you bound hell-for-leather toward the fringes of the party?" He craned his neck to look past Caden, then grinned. "Oh. I see what you're about."

Heat crept up his neck belying his casual, "I don't follow."

Harrison's *come now* look said he didn't buy Caden's act. "Unless you're hoping to further your acquaintance with the dowager duchess, I assume you're after her lovely companion, Mrs. Jones."

"*After* is hardly a word I'd use. I simply wished to express my gratitude."

"Right. Because she didn't catch your thanks the first several go-rounds."

Caden scowled but didn't voice a rebuttal.

"Jones is a looker, I'll grant you that. But braving Lady Wentworth"—He scratched the side of his nose in apparent befuddlement—"It would take more than a pretty face to induce me."

"Is that not your grandmother's sister's sister-in-law you besmirch?"

Harrison looked pleased. "You were listening. Quite right, my great Auntie's husband's sister, she is. So, you know my intel on her is beyond accurate."

Caden glanced over his shoulder. Lady Wentworth's stare, punctuated by an imperially arched brow, strongly discouraged further delay.

He turned back to Harrison, mouth open to issue a hasty farewell.

Harrison plunged on undeterred. "What my Auntie told my grandmother about Lady Wentworth, who told my father—"

"The Marquis? The paragon himself, gossips about the dowager?"

"It's not gossip when it's family history. Do you want to hear the tale or not?"

Not right now, he bloody didn't.

Evidently, he didn't have a choice. Harrison lowered his voice to a conspiratorial murmur. "As my father tells it, Lady Wentworth—then Lady Greyson prior to her marriage to the duke—once had all of society eating out of the palm of her hand. Dad says she got invited to all the best parties and held court everywhere she went. How do you think she snagged Lord

Wentworth? He could have had his pick. The bluest of blood ran through his veins. Ladies far and wide vied for his hand, they say."

"Indeed. Listen, Harrison—"

Caught up in his account, Harrison continued unabated. "In the early years of her marriage she didn't hole up in Northumberland as she does now. Indeed, for years she and her daughter accompanied the duke to London, staying the duration of the season. Post season, they did the summer circuit, hopping from house party to house party."

A glance over Harrison's shoulder revealed the imminent arrival of the misses Applegate and Egerton, the two cutting a swath through the crowd like eels through water.

Harrison's voice lowered to a whisper. "Until one summer—"

"Sorry, old chap, your family history will have to wait."

Harrison looked aggrieved. "But I'm just reaching the climactic point."

"Later."

He approached his quarry, glancing about to assure himself Harrison's group hadn't trailed after him. They hadn't, but damn it all if Lord Hardasher wasn't skulking about, mere feet away. He eyed Anna with a single-minded intensity that stirred Caden's hackles. He knew a lascivious glint in a man's eyes when he saw it.

And what of your intent?

What of it, he silently retorted. He had a history with Anna. At least he thought he did.

Lady Wentworth shifted, giving Anna a clear view of him.

She graced him with a polite smile, but he caught a flash of wariness in her eyes. Not exactly the warm welcome he hoped for.

"Good afternoon, ladies. What a pleasant surprise. For some reason, Lady Wentworth, I was under the misapprehension you meant to eschew today's event." He slid Anna a brief, speaking look.

The dowager gave an unladylike snort. "On the contrary, Mr. Thurgood. Evidently, your *source* underestimates my sense of familial duty."

Anna gave the woman an arch look which she cheerfully ignored.

"Your duty is my good fortune," Caden said.

"Good fortune all around, m'boy. Nothing like a handsome man to help pass the time, especially at affairs like these." Her gaze flicked over the crowd, her expression pinched as if she smelled something foul.

She shifted her focus to Anna. Mischief glinted in her eyes. "Don't you agree, Mrs. Jones?"

Anna's face flushed crimson. "Is it warm in here?"

"Nothing a glass of lemonade won't cure," Lady Wentworth said. She inclined her head at a nearby footman carrying a silver tray laden with crystal glasses of lemonade and he started in their direction.

"I didn't catch your assent, Mrs. Jones," Caden murmured, emboldened by the dowager duchess.

"I'm sure I have no idea what you mean."

He laughed softly and had the pleasure of seeing her lips twitch as she fought an answering smile. Her rosy, eminently kissable lips.

Seconds later she cleared her throat and he realized he'd been staring.

He dragged his gaze from her mouth and sent her his most devastating smile, guaranteed to make a woman swoon if his friends were to be believed.

She all but rolled her amber eyes and very deliberately shifted her focus to the milling crowd.

He laughed outright. He was having more fun then he'd had in an age. Mrs. Anna Jones brought the playful side out of him.

Or rather, Mrs. Gloriana Jones. He had no further doubt this was she. Standing with her head held high as if surveying her domain, rather than the hide-her-face-under-a-bonnet business she'd been up to, her demeanor finally matched up with her face, marking her as none other than a grown up version of the girl he remembered.

Did Lady Wentworth know? His gaze slid to the older woman. Impossible to say, but he'd wager no. Still. She did seem fond of *Anna*.

She gazed on her now, a slight, indulgent smile on her face. Yes, definitely fond. Whoever said the dowager duchess had a dour temperament had it at least half wrong.

"Ah. Here's Lord and Lady Fenton now," Anna offered, oblivious to their scrutiny.

"Whether to put us out of our misery, or bring on more suffering, we'll soon find out," Lady Wentworth muttered.

In the room's center, their smiling host and hostess patted the air, shushing the crowd.

Caden shifted, inching closer to Anna, purportedly to get a better view of the Fentons.

He caught a faint whiff of her perfume and lowered his head, inhaling deeply. The elegant melange of cedar, rich botanicals and the essence of the woman herself had his mouth watering like he was a starving man and she a prime bit of mutton. In truth, he wanted to eat her alive.

Meanwhile, he suspected he could leave without her even noticing. He'd never found himself in such a lamentable position. Confounding.

"Ladies and gentlemen, we had intended a tournament of croquet for your entertainment this afternoon, but as you can see, Mother Nature decided otherwise. But never fear, we shall have great fun indoors playing a game devised by Lord Fenton and I. We call it *House Party Hunt*." Lady Fenton glanced around the room, eyes alight with anticipation. "You'll play in teams of two. One male, one female."

Caden stifled a groan. No doubt a random pairing would commence. An entire afternoon stuck with someone about whom he couldn't care less, when he could spend the day trying to unravel Anna's mysteries. Oh, all right, and make another attempt to kiss her senseless.

He couldn't get that kiss out of his head. She'd tasted so sweet. And the way their bodies fit fully clothed, he could only imagine the perfection of...

"... and the first couple to return with a full card wins."

Damnation. He'd missed the rules. "What did she say? Objects on a card?"

Anna sniffed. "Your partner will fill you in, no doubt."

Was that petulance he heard in her tone? Not completely disinterested in him, after all. The thought cheered him.

She inclined her chin toward a side door and aimed a loud whisper at her employer. "Perhaps I should head out now, before—"

"A moment if you please, Anna." Steel laced the older woman's words.

Anna's smile of acquiescence seemed forced. "Of course."

Caden stretched his neck 'til it popped. He'd read her wrong. Again. She couldn't rid herself of him fast enough. Fine by him.

A feminine voice rose from the crowd of bystanders. "How are the pairs to be chosen?"

Lady Fenton held up two woven baskets, filled with scraps of white parchment.

Here it came. The dreaded name-drawn-from-a-hat pairing.

Lady Fenton's answer rang out. "The names of each person present have been written on a—"

Lady Wentworth's booming voice cut her off. "Nonsense, Lady Claudine. Such a process is far too time-consuming."

"Er…It is?" Lady Fenton asked, her exuberance dimmed.

"Of course. Instead, every lady shall turn to her right—" Lady Wentworth's skirts swished as she angled her body toward Caden "—and touch the arm of the first man she sees." She tapped his forearm. "That man will be her partner."

After a moment of silence, the sounds of scuffling boots and slippers, feminine giggles and raucous male laughter filled the room as people shuffled hither and yon, seeking to accidentally-on-purpose sequester his or herself with a preferred partner.

Caden considered the elderly woman whose gloved fingertips rested lightly on his sleeve. He could fare worse, and damned if he didn't like the old—how had Harrison phrased it?—she-dragon. He might learn a useful thing or two about her companion, to boot.

From the corner of his eye, he spotted Hardasher, heading straight for Anna. He gritted his teeth as everything in him railed against the notion of Anna paired with the man.

"And you, Mrs. Jones, shall stand in my stead." Lady Wentworth, sounding decidedly pleased with herself, took Anna's gloved hand and slapped it on Caden's arm where hers had rested a moment before .

"But—" Anna began.

Hardasher stalled in his tracks, his response echoing hers. "But—"

Caden clapped his free hand over Anna's so fast, he surprised even himself. "Sorry old chap. The lady has spoken." He bared his teeth at Hardasher.

Hardasher's lips compressed into a thin line. "See here," he began, but a glance in Lady Wentworth's direction, evidently, caused him to rethink his objection. He broke off, sent Anna and Lady Wentworth an ingratiating smile, then said, "At least grant me the favor of an introduction, Thurgood."

"Yes, indeed, Mr. Thurgood, do introduce us to your game partner," came a woman's plaintiff voice.

Miss Applegate, Miss Egerton and Harrison had opted to join them.

"Hullo," Harrison said with a finger waggle. "The girls insisted we make our way over." The apologetic look he gave Caden said he knew they weren't exactly welcome.

Caden returned an affable grin, not the least bothered by their arrival for some odd reason.

"Harrison," Lady Wentworth said with a nod of acknowledgment. The others, along with the requests for introductions, she ignored. "I need a word with the Lady Claudine before I retire to my chambers. Anna, I leave you in Mr. Thurgood's capable hands." Nose aloft, she swept away.

Anna stared after her, a look of longing in her eyes. Damn but the woman vexed him.

"Well, Mr. Thurgood?" one of the misses prodded.

Caden frowned, unsure of what she expected from him.

Harrison cleared-up the matter. "But the two of you met the infamous Mrs. Jones yesterday, if you'll recall. The woman of the hour? She who rescued Thurgood at the lake?"

Lady Applegate narrowed her eyes, studying Anna as if considering her for purchase at auction. "Oh, yes, Lady Wentworth's companion." She spoke the last word as if it left a sour taste in her mouth.

Irritation pricked him. What unspeakable rudeness. For a split second he considered calling the woman out. Gentlemanly restraint won out, however. Lambasting her would accomplish nothing other than to assuage his own temper. He doubted Jones would thank him, in any case. He opted to take a page from Lady Wentworth's book. He ignored her.

"Lord Hardasher, may I introduce my game partner, Mrs. Anna Jones?"

Only then did he notice the regal, head thrown back Anna was gone. The downcast, face-hidden Anna took her place.

"A pleasure to make your acquaintance, Mrs. Jones." Hardasher grasped her hand and bent over it.

"Lord Hardasher," Anna murmured, tucking her chin even further and dipping an elegant curtsey.

Hardasher stooped as he attempted to peer beneath the rim of her bonnet.

Caden sympathized with the man. He hated the thing himself. Why on earth did she wield her bonnet like a shield? Did the upper-crust so intimidate her? The Gloriana from his childhood didn't cow to anyone. What happened to change her so?

"Mrs. Jones, I never asked what inspired you to offer assistance to Mr. Thurgood?" Harrison asked.

Anna's head jerked in his direction, as if taken aback by the question.

Caden too wondered at his friend's odd turn-of-phrase..

"Anyone would have done the same," she murmured.

Harrison smiled genially. "Anyone who felt they could do some good would, yes. For my part, I went in search of help. Yet you swooped in like an angel of mercy."

"I don't know about that. My father was a do—" She broke off.

Harrison arched his brows, gazing on her with polite interest. "You were saying?"

Her shoulders slumped. "A doctor of medicine," she all but whispered. "I...assisted him in his practice from time to time."

Ah. She hadn't meant to reveal the small detail, probably hoping to keep Caden from discovering her identity. *Too late, darling.*

"And your mother?" Harrison prodded.

"My...mother?" she squeaked.

Caden eyed Harrison, his suspicions roused. Did every man present wish to throw his hat into the ring as a potential suitor to the chit?

"Mrs. Jones' lineage is all very interesting, I'm sure, Mr. Randall." Lady Egerton sounded anything but intrigued. She drew a breath as if she meant to go on, but Caden had his own interests to protect.

"Indeed. Ladies, Harrison, Lord Hardasher? If you'll excuse us? There's a game afoot." Not waiting for a reply, Caden scooped Anna's palm in his and pulled her toward the couples lined-up, awaiting game cards. Once in the queue, he tucked her hand snuggly into the crook of his elbow.

Her fingers squeezed his forearm lightly.

Caden glanced down as she turned her face upward.

She gazed at him, a small, seemingly genuine smile curving her rosy lips and softening her amber eyes.

What's say we play Prince Charming rescues the stolen princess, Glory. That should stop your sulking. The memory slammed into him.

He'd suggested her favorite pastime, he claimed, because she seemed glum at the prospect of her imminent departure from Derby. He did not share his own, secret motive for doing so.

In the handful of times she'd asked that summer, he'd refused. She probably assumed he simply preferred more rough and tumble games—skipping stones, climbing trees, Robinhood and his band of merry men. After all, in previous summers that had been his stated reason for not wishing to play Prince Charming rescues the princess.

That summer, however, at fifteen going on sixteen, he'd wrestled with something else entirely. Something he couldn't explain if he wanted to, even to himself—though he had *not* wanted to.

Days before she was to depart, *he* had asked her to play act the princess—albeit with a belligerent air, as if he did her a favor. No surprise, she accepted with girlish delight.

That had been her last summer in Derby. He hadn't known when her family's coach departed for London it would be the last time he ever saw her. Even so, her leaving hurt like hell.

***

She could breathe again, thanks to Caden dragging her away from too many eyes and too many questions, focused entirely on her.

Lord Hardasher with the spine-chilling stare caused the hair at her nape to stand on end. She'd spotted him hovering at the edge of the party near she and Lady Wentworth. She tried telling herself he, like the two of them, disliked crowds.

Only when he attempted to partner with her for the game, her suspicion that he had a particular interest in her resurfaced.

Then Mr. Randall arrived and started with *his* questions. They'd seemed innocuous enough at first. But he kept digging. The deeper he dug, the more she grew convinced he, too, had an agenda.

She nibbled the inside of her cheek. *Don't go borrowing trouble, Glory,* her father would say.

Right. Was it more likely Mr. Randall and Lord Hardasher both plotted against her, or that their interest in her reflected nothing more than polite curiosity? The latter, of course.

The problem here was Caden. Caden, and his ability to scramble her thinking without even trying. The *problem* should have taken care of itself, with Anna steering clear of the six foot two glorious male specimen, and would have—if not for Lady Wentworth's machinations.

She, at least, Anna trusted to have no ulterior motives. She simply wanted Anna to have a little fun.

What, she wondered, did Caden want?

They moved forward in the queue.

He lowered his head to murmur low in her ear. "You're thinking very hard about something."

She suppressed a shiver of pleasure as the deep timbre of his voice sent a tickling sensation curling through her. "Nothing in particular," she lied.

"Hmm." A dubious glint shone in his blue eyes, as if he knew she held something back.

She didn't recall Caden, the boy, having a particularly inquisitive nature. But Caden the man could give lessons to a dog sniffing out a bone.

"Mrs. Jones?"

"Yes?"

"I pray you, at least, listened when Lady Fenton announced the rules."

She gave a one-shoulder shrug. "How hard could it be?"

His complexion went ruddy. He ran a finger under his cravat, as if to loosen it, and muttered, "You have no idea."

Before she could ask what on earth he meant, they reached the head of the line. Caden accepted the letter-sized card, and the Fentons shewed them off with well-wishes for a good showing.

"And we're off." Card in hand, he led her down wide marble steps into the long gallery. They passed several couples, heads bent over their game cards. When they reached a semi-secluded alcove, Caden drew her to a halt.

"Now then." He held out the card, but fixed his eyes on her. "The rules?"

Helpless to resist the magnetic draw of his gaze, her eyes locked with his. The sleepy intensity of his stare set off a flurry of butterflies in her belly.

The sensation was oddly familiar. It reminded her of how he'd made her feel as a girl. That searing blue gaze of his had left her dizzy and full of breathless anticipation. At the time, she hadn't fully understood that he was who stirred those delicious feelings in her. She had known she secretly enjoyed having attention fixed solely on her.

"I take it we need to ask someone?" he asked with a wry grin.

Irritation—at herself or him, she couldn't say—had her snatching the card from him. She studied it while piecing together what she'd heard of Lady Fenton's instructions. "You see the rows and columns of squares?"

He leaned in. The heat from his body and his wickedly delectable scent, a mix of spicy cologne and something fresh—his soap or shampoo—filled her nostrils. Her heartbeat fluttered against her ribs like a hummingbird's wings in flight.

"We're to locate these items," she said, hoping he missed the breathless quality of her voice.

"All of them?"

He sounded so appalled, she chuckled. "We only need to complete one consecutive row or column. Then we return with our finds. The first couple back wins."

He reached out to angle the card toward him, his gloved fingers partially covering hers. The contact felt somehow intimate and claiming, as if he had every right to touch her.

"Lady's broach. Gothic novel. Feather. Miniature portrait. Silver comb. Lady's gold slipper."

"Gold slipper? Where do you see that?"

"Oh, isn't *gold slipper* there? My eyes must be playing tricks."

She scanned the items, frowning. "I don't see anything you could confuse with slipper."

"Shall we?" His free hand grazed the small of her back, urging her toward the recesses of the manse—away from the general flow of guests who swarmed the well-stocked library, music room and sitting areas nearest the grand parlor.

"Speaking of slippers, yours are a lovely shade of blue with what looks like very skilled hand-stitched embroidery. This after the expensive walking boots you sported this morning. I begin to see a pattern."

She blinked. First her boots, now her slippers? Even Lady Wentworth had never commented on Anna's footwear. "I'm sure I have no idea what you mean."

"Ah. I do apologize." He ducked his head as if chagrined, and guided her down a narrow corridor splitting off from the main.

She glanced behind her, aware she no longer heard other guests. A sense of contentment suffused her. She could almost convince herself she and Caden were two friends who happened to find themselves at the same party, not a care in the world save playing a game.

She grinned to herself. "You apologize, sir? For what, pray tell?"

A regretful smile curved his lips. "You admittedly didn't pack a slew of party dresses. I assume Lady Wentworth not only garnered gowns, but also slippers and boots for you, as well. Rather uncouth of me to broach the subject, however."

Her spine stiffened. So much for forgetting her current circumstances. Clearly Caden had not. Worse still, he saw her as a servant reduced to wearing another's shoes.

He sighed. "What have I said wrong now?"

"I have no idea what you mean."

He drew to her to a halt. "Out with it, Jones."

She lifted her chin. "I am not wearing borrowed slippers, nor did I borrow those boots."

He flashed her a crooked, pirate's grin. "Just so."

She frowned, feeling vaguely tricked.

He regained her hand and resumed leading her in a leisurely stroll. "Odd though."

Wary now, she slanted him a glance. "What's that?"

"For one with such high standards in footwear, your choice of bonnets leaves a great deal to be desired."

Her mouth fell open and she stopped abruptly. "I beg your pardon?"

He released her hand, and glanced back from whence they'd come as if to ascertain no one followed. With a grunt of satisfaction, he made fast work untying the bow at her chin.

"What are you doing?" she demanded, though she made no move to stop him.

He plucked the bonnet from her head and jammed it in his coat pocket.

"Well," she huffed. "Now you've likely crumpled it beyond repair." Not that she wasn't secretly glad to be momentarily rid of it.

He looked not the least repentant. "It was already there, darling. Besides. That *thing* was blocking my view."

She threw up her hands and glanced around the corridor. "Your view? Of what pray-tell?"

"Of your beautiful, amber eyes."

Beautiful? *Amber*? She snorted, batting back the flush of pleasure at his words. "Please. My eyes are nothing if not boring old brown."

He crooked a hand under her chin and guided her face upward 'til their gazes locked. "There's nothing boring about your eyes, Jones. They seem to capture all the light in any room and glow like expensive brandy held before the fire."

Her eyes glowed? She didn't know whether to smile or scowl at his brazen flattery—except her mouth kept trying to pull into a grin, so that wasn't exactly true.

"Shall we go on?" he asked as if he hadn't just given her the nicest compliment she could remember receiving, ever.

"I take it you have a destination in mind?" she asked, mostly to fill the silence.

He grasped her hand, once more folding it into his elbow. "I haven't any notion of the layout of this sprawling manse, but I do have some experience finding my way around meandering architecture. The earl's estate in Derby. You remember."

"I...recall you mentioning it this morning."

He flicked the briefest glance her way. "I propose we begin our search at the furthest reaches of the manor then work our way back. Any objection?"

"None." Not because it meant she'd spend more time alone with Caden, she told herself. She merely appreciated relaxing her vigil against the unwanted notice of other guests.

"Excellent. We're of a like mind—for once."

"How better to outpace the competition than choose a less traveled path?"

He barked out a laugh. He tucked the card under one arm, freeing his hand to cover hers. His fingertips skimmed her gloved knuckles in a light caress she felt all the way to her toes.

"I'm all for weeding out the competition. I have a question, by the by."

"Oh?" Inwardly, she groaned. They were approaching two open doorways. A dim glow of light shone from within the rooms. Anna scanned the first rooms's interior searching for possible game items, or anything that might distract him from resuming his interrogations.

"Mrs. Jones, are you," he cleared his throat, "as glad as I am to find us partnered this afternoon?"

"That's rather forward, sir." The answer was an emphatic *yes,* but she did not want it to be so, and, in any case, she could hardly say so without seeming forward herself.

He shifted to face her, heaving an exasperated sigh. "You are correct. I apologize. My only excuse is finding myself in the unusual circumstance of"—He huffed out a bemused laugh—"begging for scraps."

She blinked. "I don't follow."

He rubbed a gloved hand over his jaw. "I suppose I'm looking for some sign I'm not alone in this..." He broke off, grunting in evident frustration. "...fascination? For my part, at least, finding you has quite elevated this entire affair."

The sincerity in his words sent a dangerous burst of warmth through her, leaving her breathless and utterly speechless.

He enthralled her. The sight of him, the timber of his voice. A mere five minutes in his presence led her to make brainless decisions, like agreeing to walk with him this morning, and then allowing him to kiss her.

Oh, all right, and kissing him back.

He also made her feel safe and protected, like Prince Charming incarnate, come to rescue her. But *was* she actually safe with him? Or had her past with Caden, the boy, blinded her to the potential perils of Caden the man? In truth, she didn't know him at all. Not anymore.

"Why?" The one-word question spilled out, without her having made a conscious decision to ask.

"Why?"

In for a penny, in for a pound, her father always said. "What about my company do you enjoy?"

His eyes locked with hers. "Isn't it obvious?"

She shook her head, unable to speak.

"Damn," he uttered softly. "You're not lying. How is it you're widowed and still so innocent?"

"I don't follow," she said for the second time in as many minutes.

"Forget it, Jones."

"Oh, no you don't. You can't say what you did and not explain yourself, sir. What does my supposed innocence have to do with anything? For that matter, you said, *you're not lying*, as if you knew for certain. Are you claiming to read minds now?"

He gave her a considering look. "You have a tell."

She laughed. "That's preposterous."

He shrugged.

She pulled her hand free and crossed her arms over her chest."What is this tell, then?"

His lips twitched. "As if I'd reveal my one advantage."

"You're bluffing."

In the warm glow of the wall lamps lining the corridor his thick hair gleamed and his eyes sparkled like blue gems. "On the contrary, Jones. One thing you should know about me is that I notice things."

He moved closer, and instinct had her retreating backwards 'til her back collided with the wall and they stood toe to toe. The chill of cold plaster permeated her gown, a sharp contrast to the heat pulsing through her.

She drew a bracing breath and the scent of him, a subtle mix of spice and warm male skin teased her already enlivened senses. "You're claiming you noticed things about me?"

He nodded once.

Curiosity burned through her. "Such as?"

"I know you have a penchant for fine shoes, and an abominable collection of over-large bonnets which you garner like a shield. I know you prefer to keep to yourself, which probably explains how you won the affections of your employer, the noted recluse, with whom you share anti-social tendencies. I know you indulge in regular morning walks." He leaned closer and his voice lowered. "And you always smell like flowers and elegance and mystery."

She licked her lips. "Mystery?"

His eyes tracked the movement, like a cat stalking a mouse. "Definitely."

A terrible craving for the damnably charming rake to kiss her threatened to topple all her good intentions. She wanted to close her eyes, twine her fingers around his neck, and feel his mouth pressed to hers. How did he do that?

He traced one finger along a tendril of her hair, and her insides quivered. "You're a mystery I can't help wanting to unravel." His voice lowered to a rough whisper. "You could always share. Your secrets are safe with me."

His words, his nearness, his bloody irresistible magnetism wiped out any coherent thought in her head save *kiss me*.

Heat swirled in his blue eyes. "Your face tells me how badly you want me to kiss you. Yet if you could leave this very minute and never lay eyes on me again, I've no doubt but that you would. You arouse and confound me." He leaned forward, bracing one forearm on the wall beside her head. "Anna, say something."

Emotions tangled inside her, robbing her of reason. "I..." She peeled her gaze from his too-handsome face and peered over his shoulder though the open doorway directly across the corridor. "I think..."

"Yes?" His face lowered incrementally toward hers.

"...I see a feather."

He closed his eyes briefly before shifting aside. "Of course you do. Kindly lead the way."

Chapter Eight

Anna sprang off the wall and crossed the hall, desperate to put space between herself and Caden. Keeping her wits about her seemed entirely reliant on keeping him at arm's length.

The smell of sweet dried flowers and herbs greeted her as she entered the chamber. Low burning wall lamps framing a closed, shuttered window provided enough light to illuminate the space.

Silver and pale-rose striped paper covered the walls. To the right a woman's escritoire sat ready with parchment and writing implements neatly laid out on its surface. To the left a small settee, armchair and side table comprised a modest sitting area. Behind her, a narrow bookshelf filled with slim, leather-bound books covered most of the wall. All in all, a very feminine decor. She concluded she'd wandered into a ladies office.

She strode to a tall, oriental floor vase containing an arrangement of dried eucalyptus, cat tails, and ostrich feathers. Careful not to disturb the rest, she withdrew one feather.

"We can check this box." Smiling in triumph, she turned on her heel in time to witness Caden drawing the chamber's heavy paneled door closed—or nearly so. He pressed one eye to the crack of space between the door and the door jam.

"What are you—"

"Shh." Peering into the hallway, he held one long finger behind him to staunch further protest. "One of the couples followed us," he whispered. "I presume you don't want them pilfering your cache of feathers."

She hastened toward him. Rising up on her tiptoes, she struggled in vain to see over his broad shoulder. "Would you..." She squirmed her way in front of him and put her eye to the crack. Then she saw *him*. She gasped and jerked backward into Caden's hard chest.

Lord Hardasher *was* following her.

Saying nothing, Caden held her fast, circling one arm around her waist as the other reached past her to close the door with a soft click. Then he grasped her shoulders and turned her to face him.

His teeth flashed white as he grinned. "Your level of competitiveness astounds me, Mrs. Jones. Not to worry. They'll soon pass by."

But they wouldn't. Of course they wouldn't. Not with Lord Hardasher hunting her. Did he work for the Yard?

She grabbed his hand to drag him from the door toward the sitting area on the furthest side of the room. "Caden, who is Lord Hardasher?" she whispered. "How do you know him?"

He frowned down at her. "Hardasher? Not well. He holds a minor title. A baronetage, I think? I met him some time ago—at my club, or perhaps a house party. I can't recall precisely where. Why?" Suspicion laced the one-word question.

Unable to keep still, she twisted her hands in front of her. "That's all? You did introduce us."

Caden's eyes narrowed. "Has he approached you? Propositioned you in some way?"

"N-no. N-not precisely." Damn her quavering voice.

Concern softened his face. He grasped her shoulders in a warm, gentle grip. Abruptly his expression changed to one of alarm. "What the devil? Anna, you're shaking. What's this about?"

She searched her mind for a plausible answer and willed her tremors to desist. Nothing came to her and, if anything, her trembling increased.

"Anna?" he prodded, his voice quiet steel. "Tell me, or by God, I will leave this room and drag the answer out of Hardasher himself."

She gripped his waistcoat lapels intending to hold him in place by any means necessary. "*No.* Lord Hardasher has done nothing untoward. I-I'm competitive, as you said."

"A competitive streak doesn't explain your trembling, Anna."

"I've caught a chill." In truth, sweat trickled down her back, but she soldiered on, her words coming faster and faster. "If anyone has given me pause, it's you, tossing my given name around willy nilly. I don't recall giving you leave. I ne—"

Only Caden's sharp, "Anna," cut off her rapid-fire speech. Or babbling, depending on one's perspective.

He drew her to the settee. Dark pink velvet, she noted, dazed, as he pressed her onto the bench.

Just as well. Her legs wouldn't hold her upright much longer. She stared at the door, dread hollowing out her insides. Any minute now, Lord Hardasher would burst in. And then what would she do?

Caden stood before her, hands splayed at his hips. "I'd like to point out, you were the first to use my Christian name, by the by."

She dragged her gaze from the door to Caden.

He studied her, jaw clenched. He bore the comportment of one who'd made-up his mind about something and expected resistance.

God, now what? She couldn't think straight as it was.

"I have an alternate question, *Anna*. Rather than ask why *I* used your given name, *Anna*, why are you?"

The over-stressing of her name, accompanied by the certainty she read in his eyes, penetrated in an instant. Her blood turned to ice. He knew. He'd known all along. She'd had it all wrong. Caden, not Hardasher, hunted her.

Or perhaps they hunted in tandem.

It explained everything. His undeterred interest in her. His questions.

She'd walked right into a trap, lured by irresistible bait—Caden Thurgood.

She decided to play dumb and buy herself a little time to think. "What other name would I use?"

He gave her an almost pitying look. "Miss Gloriana Masters, perhaps? Or Mrs. Gloriana Jones, your married name—assuming you are, in fact, widowed. But you're not who you're pretending to be."

She blinked rapidly, batting back a wave not of panic, but pain. Caden meant to betray her? She could hardly fathom the notion. Never mind she'd been lying to him. But that'd been for his own good, to keep him from becoming embroiled in her mess.

What was his plan, she wondered, bitterness swamping her? To drag a confession out of her and deliver her to the magistrate? She would not go without a fight. She glanced around the room. The door was her only means of escape, unless she wanted to dive through panes of glass, but there went any hope of subtlety.

"For pity's sake, quit acting like a cornered rabbit. You'd think I meant to cart you off to be drawn and quartered. It's not a crime to pretend to be someone else, darling."

The tiny bench creaked in protest as he lowered his big frame to sit beside her, then took her hands in his. "Anna—Glory, tell me what is going on. If you're in some kind of trouble, let me help you. I'm more resourceful than I look. As it happens, I've a bit of experience in aiding damsels in distress."

And just like that, the bricks she'd begun erecting around her heart crumbled, probably because she wanted so desperately to believe he didn't—couldn't—mean her any harm.

She searched his face for any sign of duplicity. He looked so dog-eyed hopeful she almost smiled.

From nowhere, her mother's words played in her head so clearly they may have been uttered only yesterday—*Watch yourself with that Claybourne boy. He might not be in line for the title, but he's nobility. With them the title always comes first. Even before family.*

She sobered, pushing her fanciful hopes aside. Caden's lineage notwithstanding, she dared not place her safety in anyone's hands but her own. Hadn't her own step-mother led her into the trap that landed her here?

"You can help by telling me who sent you, Mr. Thurgood."

"Sent me? Nobody, unless you want to count Viscount Randall when he asked me to accompany Harrison in his stead. Something about a family emergency involving their sister."

She glared at him. What else could she do?

Caden traced his fingers along her jaw.

Heat curled through her insides like smoke.

"You needn't look so peeved that I worked out who you are. In fairness, I didn't put it together at first. I only knew I recognized you. Then, last night I asked you where you came from and you bit your lip, and—there goes my ace." He chuckled, but his joviality seemed forced and did nothing to hide the concern in his blue eyes.

Longing welled-up inside her, birthing a sliver of hope she could not seem to squelch. *Could* she trust him? How could she possibly know for certain?

He peeled off his gloves, eyes on his task, a crooked grin creasing his cheek. "For your information, when you speak something, shall we say, less than truthful..." He broke off, set his gloves aside, then raised his gaze to meet hers.

"Yes?" She prodded, breathless.

"... You bite your lower lip." He brushed the pad of his thumb over her lip as if to illustrate.

Like a spark igniting a flame, warmth spiraled through her.

"On the way into dinner last night you mentioned one of your father's sayings, and my memories stirred. *My father says thus and such* you used to say—usually as a means of getting your way, I now recall.

"I still didn't put it all together, however. Not 'til the moment you told me you came from Durham and nibbled your lip." He crossed his arms over his chest and leaned back against the wall behind them.

He was so handsome, it almost hurt looking at him.

"My memories came back in a rush. A foggy rush, mind you." He waited, expectant.

She had no words. He remembered her. She should be frightened, and she was. But for some reason, an overwhelming joy blotted out most of it.

He spread his arms. "Come now. Derbyshire? Summertime? Robin-hood and his merry men?"

She was helpless to stop the wobbly smile curving her lips.

Triumph lit his blue-eyes at her silent admission, and the last of her resistance crumpled. "Prince Charming and the stolen princess, you mean?"

He hooted with laughter. "The very same. Now, kindly tell me what in hell is going on."

Chapter Nine

Caden didn't consider himself a particularly gifted man. However, he had been born with one notable skill his father would have paid dearly to possess. He could read people—probably explained his luck at the tables. Mayhap his luck with women, as well.

Now, leaning back against the wall in the chamber where Anna had led him, balanced on a precarious pink settee, he employed his gift, holding his tongue while reading Anna's inner struggle over whether to trust him with her secrets—or not—all over her beautiful, expressive face.

Impatience tore at him. He was so bloody close. But he sensed if he pressed her even a fingernail's clipping harder, she would turn tail and run.

He would wait. She would talk.

Muffled voices sounded from the hall and Anna's already pale face turned ashen. Eyes wide as a doe's, she stared at the closed chamber door as if the devil himself loomed on the other side.

Blood boiled in his veins. One thing was certain. He would make Hardasher pay for whatever he'd done to inspire such terror in Anna.

But first, he had Glory or *Anna* or whatever she chose to call herself to deal with.

The settee groaned under his weight as he shifted his weight. He crooked one finger beneath her chin and drew her attention back to him. "Calm yourself. I locked the door."

Renewed suspicion darkened her amber eyes as they locked with his. She swallowed audibly. "You're not...working with him?"

"Working with him? Working with him, how? What do you take me for?"

She searched his eyes a long moment then surprised him by launching herself into his chest. "Oh, Caden," she choked.

His arms banded around her. He hadn't a clue what she meant by *working with* Hardasher, and, right now, didn't much care. He closed his eyes, savoring her softness, inhaling the elusive, elegant scent ever-clinging to her skin and hair. The urge to tilt her head back and feast on her sweet mouth screamed through him.

He'd read terror in her eyes, though, and still had no clue as to why. Why was key.

Clenching his jaw, he steeled himself against his weakness for the woman and allowed his arms to fall to his sides. "Tell me about Hardasher, darling."

She slanted him a considering glance. "He looks at me. Every time I round a corner, there he is, leering."

"But has he approached you? Has he attempted to…"

Her chestnut brows beetled in evident confusion. "To what?"

She couldn't possibly need him to spell it out.

"To. What?" she repeated, articulating each word.

He threw his hands wide. "To seduce you, Glory. Has he tried to seduce you?"

She drew back as if shocked by the notion. "Why would he do that? We've hardly spoken two words."

He didn't know whether to laugh or check her brow for a temperature. "Must I remind you this is a house party?"

Annoyance flashed in her eyes. "Your point?"

"My point is, you're a beautiful, unattached, widow. Most likely, Lord Hardasher is simply after…" *a bit of sport.* He couldn't bring himself to say the words. Something about the crass way they sounded, even in his head.

And about the way they hit a little too close to home, Thurgood?

Dawning understanding lit her eyes. "You're saying, he wants…" She cleared her throat, and her expression turned…hopeful?

No, that couldn't be right.

"Do you really think he wants to have his way with me?"

She *did* sound hopeful.

"Is that something you want?"

She looked aghast.

His jaw relaxed and a smile threatened to spread over his face. Funny. Until that moment, he hadn't realized he'd been gritting his teeth. "If you aren't concerned he has a romantic interest in you, what about Hardasher frightens you?"

She nibbled the inside of her cheek, never taking her eyes off him. "I feared he may have recognized me."

The hidden identity thing, back in play. He crossed his arms over his chest and leaned one shoulder into the wall behind them, hoping the settee wouldn't collapse beneath them. "I think it's time—past time—you tell me what is going on."

Her expression turned mulish.

He summoned an encouraging smile. "Let's start with the name you're using. Mrs. Anna Jones. You're a widow? That part is true?"

Her mouth firmed, but she did not bite her lip. "Yes."

Not lying, then. An inexplicable stab of pure jealousy pierced his gut at the thought of her wedded to—and bedded by—another man. How utterly ridiculous.

Her hands fisted on either side of her skirts and her eyes turned pleading. "Can't you leave it, Caden? You know the name I went by as a girl, and you know who I am now. A widow in the employ of Lady Wentworth. As to the rest...believe me when I tell you, you don't want to embroil yourself in my affairs."

"Anna." He took her hands with his own, one at a time, unfurling her gloved fingers.

Her hands felt delicate and feminine engulfed in his. Her diminutive size slipped his notice much of the time because she carried herself like royalty, just as she had as a girl, convinced she could snap her fingers and the world would rearrange itself to her liking. Now, however, she called to mind a fragile bird with a damaged wing. He had the inane desire to scoop her into his arms, carry her out of here and...what?

Hell and damnation. Until now he hadn't thought beyond getting her to admit her identity and stealing more kisses. Perhaps more than kisses.

Sudden, fierce resolve filled him. He *would* help her. He hadn't lied about having experience aiding damsels in distress. His brother's wife's recent situation had involved danger, intrigue, kidnapping, even attempted murder, and he had played no small role in untangling her from her snares. Anna's difficulties couldn't possibly surpass Lady Kitty's.

"I can handle messy, but I need the truth. And that starts with why you're so concerned with keeping your identity secret."

She pulled her hands from his and wrapped her arms around herself, her face a study in misery. "Please don't ask me, Caden."

For the love of everything holy. The need to move, to prowl, filled him, and he unfolded his body from the settee.

"Anna—Mrs. Jones—whatever you'd like me to call you. It's clear you're in trouble. It's clear you need help—and I'm offering to lend a hand. But how can I if I don't know what I'm up against?"

Her spine stiffened and her chin lifted a fraction. "I don't *want* your help. I never asked for your help. In any case, you could not hope to extricate me from my"—She pressed her lips together, briefly—"situation."

And there it was. She doubted his capacity to assist her. Cold seeped into him, as if the room's temperature had dropped by twenty degrees. It would serve her right if he turned his back on her and left the chamber right now. He bloody well should.

Instead a bull-headed resolve to match hers reared up inside him. He *could* help her. He would prove it—to both of them.

"Start with why you're lying about who you are."

She groaned and slanted him a vexed glance. "You're not going to let this go, are you?"

"Not a chance."

"Very well." She heaved a sigh. "If you must know, I lied on my employment application. After the death of my..." She broke off, pinching the bridge of her nose.

Gad, was she fighting tears? He hoped not, with every fiber of his being.

"Your husband?" he prodded.

She half nodded, half shook her head as if she wanted to move past a painful memory. No tears dampened her cheeks, thank God.

"...I discovered myself to be not only alone, but destitute."

"Discovered, you say? You had no fore-knowledge of your depleted fortunes?"

"None."

"I see."

A sardonic smile curved her lips. "A man in *your* position—"

"—My position?"

She waved one graceful hand. "Being of the nobility."

He rolled his eyes and carefully resumed his seat beside her. "Surely you recall I'm a mere mister. My brother and grandfather hold the titles. I'm a regular bloke."

He sidelong glance proclaimed her unconvinced. "I'll rephrase. A man of your *background* may or may not realize how few options exist for a female of no means on her own. There's marriage, there's scant employment, and there's the street."

He arched a mocking brow. "I'm cognizant." He propped his elbow on his knee. "One thing I am unable to fathom, however, is how you landed in such dismal circumstances. Surely your father left you an inheritance?"

Masters had been a man of some means, he recalled. When had he died? There was so much about her he didn't know. He thirsted for every scrap of information.

She pressed her full lips together. "Father did leave me well off—hence Mr. Jones' proposal."

"You're saying Jones married you for your inheritance, squandered it, then died? What sort of man did you marry?"

She fixed him with a hard stare, somehow giving the impression of looking down the length of her nose at him.

Touchy on the subject of her husband, then. "I apologize. Pray, continue."

She licked her lips. "I knew I must find a position quickly, or starve—or worse."

He nodded once, taking her meaning all too well.

"My particular skills—knowledge in horticulture and the preparation of medicinal tinctures—didn't lend themselves to procuring a post. In short, ready work could only be found as a lady's companion or governess—if one had references. I did not."

Unable to sit still, he rose from the settee again, jammed his hands in his pockets, and stalked over the rich carpets in silence rather than cast further aspersion on her late husband. To have left her penniless, without the decency of warning her of her impending doom? What kind of scoundrel did that? And how had he done so without her knowledge? Had he gambled away their resources? He knew that sort all too well. He'd been sired by one.

"What of your family? You said your father passed, but what of your mother? Surely you have relatives."

"My mother died a long time ago—within two years of the last summer we spent in Derby. She, herself, was an orphan, with no family to speak of. My father passed more recently. Like me, he was an only child and his parents died before I was born. If I do have any family"— she opened her arms wide—"their existence and whereabouts are a mystery to me."

He leaned against the wall beside the settee, propping one booted foot behind him. Her unwillingness to speak against her husband told him she'd loved the miscreant, regardless of his ineptitude in seeing to her welfare. Meanwhile, Caden wanted nothing so much as to reach into the grave and punch said husband in the mouth.

"Why did you and your father never return to Derby after that last summer?"

She lowered her head. "Mother developed a lung illness on the journey to London that last summer. When it came time for our annual exodus to the country, her illness had worsened. Father hoped if we didn't push her, if we let her rest, her condition might improve. It didn't."

"I'm so sorry."

She nodded. "After she died, father never broached the subject of Derby again. I did eventually ask him about going back. His answer didn't surprise me. He couldn't bare the reminder of happier times." She paused and plucked at her skirts. "He...met someone in the latter part of his life."

"He remarried?"

She nodded.

"And what of his new wife? Unless...did you lose them both at once?"

Abruptly she covered her face with both hands. He'd hit a nerve.

"Could we talk about something else?" Dropping her hands, she gazed at him with pleading eyes. "Tell me more about your life. You mentioned an interest in the quarry? Something to do with overseeing its production for your brother and the earl?"

Pushing for answers and dredging up her past had clearly caused her distress—and to no avail. He was no less in the dark concerning why she felt compelled to keep her identity secret than when he first posed the question. Applying a modicum of tact going forward wouldn't kill him, and might garner better results.

"I contemplated overseeing it. Past tense." He sighed. "Somebody ought to and, if my brother's wife has anything to say about it, doubtless will. Limestone has many uses which, properly implemented, would bolster the estate's property values as well as raise the standard of living in the surrounding communities."

"Many uses, you say? Besides providing the foundation for building blocks and cobblestones?"

"A plethora."

"Such as?"

Her look of genuine interest sparked his own passion for the subject.

"There's repairing and building roads and, yes, buildings. Additionally, the lime derived, spread over depleted soil, has been shown to improve crop yields. Too, the right amount of limestone minerals added to a town's water supply can make it more healthful for drinking. And, not to get too detailed, but used as a flux in metallurgical processes—refining, alloying, extracting metals," he put in at her querulous expression, "it lowers the melting point, helps to purify metals, etc."

"How extraordinary."

"Exactly." Unfortunately talking about the project reignited his ire toward his brother. Damn Zeke and his sanctimonious, supercilious, self-righteous attitude which had caused Caden's own over-the-top, knee-jerk reaction.

He should be heading-up repurposing the mill in the coming months. Instead, following the Fenton's party he was off to who-knew-where for who-knew-how-long to subsist on God-knows-what.

Weeks ago, on the cusp of their argument, cutting ties with his family had seemed like a grand idea. And it was. He hated Zeke's holier-than-thou condescension. It didn't help there was some truth to his brother's accusations, nor did the fact his brother held himself to the meticulous standards he touted. Zeke didn't have an irresponsible bone in his body.

He shook off the dour thoughts and refocused on the beautiful, mysterious woman beside him. "You may recall the quarry isn't far from the cottage your family let."

"Yes. On the river."

He heard the smile in her voice and felt his own mouth curve upward.

"Such enthusiasm from a man who, by his own admission, spent the last year flitting from house party to house party."

It was as if she'd spotted his weakness and purposefully jabbed him there. "Your point?" he asked, working hard to keep his tone light.

"I'm wondering what sparked your interest?"

"Ah." The sting from her too-keen observation faded at thoughts of his new sister-in-law. He smiled, unable to not. "I believe I've mentioned Lady Kitty, Zeke's wife?"

She nodded.

"Yes, well, the lady is," he gazed toward the plastered ceiling as he considered how best to describe her. "...quite something. Among other things, she's a self-appointed champion for all of humanity. When she learned Zeke had been de-facto providing limestone for the royal navy's arsenal, she commenced one of her legendary lectures on the moral degeneracy in allowing said practice to continue."

He stopped and narrowed his eyes on her. "You know, I think the two of you would get along. She's another strong-willed, opinionated female."

Both her brows shot up.

He'd meant the comparison as a compliment. Mostly.

"Her claims piqued my interest, and I did some checking. It didn't take long to decide the lady made a fair point. "

"Why? What did you find?"

He studied her a long moment and considered what he'd learned about how limestone had been militarized, particularly by the navy. *Greekfire* used by the British navy, was an incendiary blend of chemicals, the primary being limestone, that even water wouldn't douse. Quicklime, a powder substance tossed on a standing army, caused blindness and burned the skin.

He shook his head. "I think it's best I refrain from detailing the horrors of militarizing limestone. Suffice it to say what I learned spurred me to research limestone's alternative uses. I planned to present my findings on the benefits of repurposing the quarry, as well as my offer to head up the the project as a kind of"—he shrugged—"wedding present for my brother and Lady Kitty."

Deep approval glowed in her eyes. "I think that's wonderful, Caden. May I ask what changed your mind?"

He'd happened upon Zeke and the earl's heated discussion—about him and his apparent, derelict ways. "Turned out, he had someone more qualified in mind."

She made a scoffing sound. "Then why hadn't he already installed this person? In any case, it's perfectly clear the role should go to you. Nobody could be better suited."

He stared at her, reluctantly fascinated.

She surprised him, then, reaching one gloved hand to cover his. "You were born to defend innocents and right wrongs. It comes as naturally to you as breathing." Her tilted amber eyes seemed to capture every bit of the meager wall lamps' golden light.

"You must be confusing me with someone else."

She shook her head. "From the moment we met, you impressed me with your gallantry. You never hesitated to do what you thought right, even when you paid a price." A tiny smile pulled at the corners of her mouth. "That's why you made the perfect Prince Charming."

"Oh, is that why? And here I thought it was because you liked my kisses." And, my God, but he wanted to kiss her just now.

She withdrew her hand and burst with laughter. "Of all the pompous—"

"—You aren't going to deny you demanded I kiss you after each and every rescue?"

Abruptly, she sobered. Her gaze lowered to his mouth. "I don't recall. I'm sure it had nothing to do with...It was just the way the storyline went. The prince rescued his princess and, of *course*, bestowed a kiss."

His body, already simmering with suppressed need, tightened with arousal. "I see. You're sure?"

She lifted her chin. Two matching splotches of pink stained her cheeks. "Quite sure."

"I propose an experiment."

"What sort?" she whispered, but she raised her fingertips to her lips as if cognizant of what he intended.

Blood pounded in his ears. He was playing with fire, but couldn't seem to make himself stop. He locked eyes with her and wrapped one arm around her waist, drawing her close. He cupped her nape, fixing her head at precisely the right angle for his kiss. Her skin was cool and silky smooth beneath his fingers.

"Well, then, Princess. Shall we take this up post-rescue?"

Her magnificent eyes widened. "Post-rescue?"

"I've freed you from the villain and transported you to safety." He waited several torturous seconds for her agreement—or rebuttal—tense and ravenous.

"Thank you, my prince," she breathed, and closed her eyes.

Heart slamming against his ribs, he did not hesitate. He closed the distance between them, brushed his mouth over hers, and swallowed a groan of pure ecstasy.

Her lips were soft and warm and pliant beneath his. Using the merest pressure, he tasted, savoring hints of sugar and mint and awakening feminine passion. He ached to deepen the kiss and plunder her sweet mouth, but he held back, needing a sign the same heady desire thrummed through her.

When her hands landed, feather light, on his shoulders and crept up to twine around his neck, he nearly gave in to the deafening clamors of his body to take more. Instead, he teased her senses alive with tender kisses that strained the limits of his control.

Finally, *finally* she leaned closer, her hands simultaneously tugging at his neck.

He did not budge.

She pulled harder, drawing her torso more snugly into his.

Still he resisted her efforts—until he heard her low, barely discernible whimper of need that turned the blood in his veins to liquid fire.

His mouth sealed over hers, his tongue sliding over the seam between her lips, seeking entrance.

She opened for him on a gasp and he plunged into her intoxicating warmth. With each greedy slide of his tongue, the flames of desire licking at his insides burned brighter, hotter.

She responded with a sweet ardor, kissing him back with abandon, weaving her fingers into his hair.

His hands roamed over her, committing to memory every curve of her body, reveling at the tremors coursing through her at his touch. She was soft and lithe like perfectly ripe fruit, ready to be plucked from the branch.

A conflagration of need and agony filled him to the brink of his limits, urging him to take her, *now*. To lay her back, peel off her gown and grant his hands and mouth and cock the freedom to pleasure her while sating his own desperate cravings only she could fulfill. He could make her want him, could make her want to give herself to him. He knew it like he knew his own name.

And yet, in the dim recesses of his brain, alarm bells clanged. This was Glory. She deserved far better than a quick tumble in a back room of a stranger's manse. And, what would come after? If she was to be believed, she would leave him in a matter of days without a backward glance.

Shaking with the force of his desire, something akin to terror filled him. Had he ever wanted a woman so badly? Had he ever known this overwhelming, all-consuming passion?

He ripped his mouth from hers and pressed his damp forehead into her neck, dragging in ragged breaths, steadying himself through sheer force of will. He'd teased her about liking his kisses, but, in the end, found she possessed a near sorceress's power over him.

When he felt almost steady, he raised his head, noting her own dazed expression. Gods she was beautiful, with that heart shaped face, that luminous skin, those tilted, exotic eyes.

"Caden?" Her fingers toyed with the hair at his nape. She licked damp lips, parting them as if in invitation.

He rose from the settee, crashing into an adjacent armchair in his haste to get away from her and the spell she'd cast over him. He had to get a grip on himself. Master this feeling, this bottomless yearning.

Then it hit him. *This* was *familiar*. Reminiscent of that last summer with her, in Derby.

For three long months, he'd avoided playing Prince-Charming-rescues-his-princess, mainly because he feared the effects of the obligatory kiss on his senses when simply being in her vicinity tied him in knots.

She wasn't like the other girls he knew. She was feisty and funny and didn't melt at his smiles the way every other female, young and old, seemed to do.

The last day they spent together she had seemed so forlorn. If he was honest, he felt rather morose himself, knowing she would leave in a matter of days. To cheer her, or so he claimed, he offered to play her favorite game, rescuing her and carrying her to the riverbank.

Then he'd kissed her.

That kiss had turned his insides into a tangled mass of wanting and agony, pleasure and torture, and he'd bolted like a scared rabbit.

Less than a week later she was gone. His youthful heart had ached for months afterward. He missed how she made him feel—alive and challenged and completely off-kilter, like standing atop a precarious cliff, staring down at crashing waves.

Exactly like now.

How had he entertained the notion of a dalliance with *her*? Then again, one second in her company, and how could he not?

"Caden?" A combination of vulnerability and concern shown in her eyes.

She likely expected an explanation for why he'd jettisoned away from her as if she'd suddenly caught fire. Too bad he couldn't offer her a reason that made any damned sense.

Sorry, love. Kissing you feels too damned good, makes me want too damned much, makes me ache in places I'd just as soon forget existed, and oh, by the way, you seem to have had this power over me since forever.

No. He could not explain his reaction to himself, much less her.

He waited to speak until he had his practiced mask of banal civility in place. "Anna," he finally said in response. Not bad. He sounded normal, even to his own ears.

Her brows knitted with confusion as she smoothed her skirts. "I've never...that is, that was..."

"Quite a kiss, and more than proved my point, wouldn't you say?"

She stilled. "Your point?"

He grinned like a cocksure ass and somehow resisted the compulsion to jam his hands through his hair. He needed to get them out of this room—for both their sakes. He needed to think, and he couldn't do that with her in arm's reach.

He'd imagined a lighthearted fling between like-minded adults, and old friends to boot. The problem was, this—her and him—felt like *more*. Everything in him ached to reach for her. To kiss her and touch her and whisper promises he'd never made to a woman in his life, promises he'd never wanted to make, promises he had no clue if he could keep if he did make them.

If they stayed in this room, they'd wind up making love, which should be fine. It was a house party. And yet, he knew, to the core of his being, if he made love to her, and she left, she'd be his undoing.

It made no sense. He felt like a perfect idiot.

"Your point?" she repeated, sounding irritated now.

He paced toward the door, and safety, then, helpless to resist, moved back in her direction. "You do like my kisses."

Nothing like a dose of arrogance to force a wedge between them. It couldn't be helped. Creating distance was his only possible recourse for the moment.

"I like *your* kisses?"

He chuckled at her offended tone and tugged at his too-tight cravat. "Oh, I like yours, too. Never doubt it." Too damned much.

"Oh." She sniffed and made an obvious effort to appear unfazed by his comment, but he saw the tell-tale trembling of her lips as she fought a pleased smile.

That damned hint-of-a-smile threatened to overturn all his good intentions.

"Do you suppose we ought to finish our discussion?" he asked.

Her good humor vanished. "But we have."

"No, we haven't. Not by a long shot. I still have questions. Is Jones your actual married name, by the by?"

She unfolded herself from the settee, shimmied past him leaving a trail of her heavenly scent in her wake. She made for a small, gilt-framed wall mirror he hadn't noticed, hanging to the right of the door. Women always seemed to know where those things were, even in rooms they'd never entered.

The fact she had not answered him did not escape his notice.

Gazing at her reflection, she made an inarticulate sound of horror, and her nimble fingers went to work, smoothing and re-pinning her hair.

He moved to stand behind her and met her eyes in the looking glass. His insides tightened with a maddening desire to drag her into his chest and nuzzle the tender skin at her nape.

Instead he shoved his hands into his trouser pockets. "Good as new, Glory," he said, voice gruff.

She lowered her eyes. "Caden, may I ask that you refrain from referring to me by that name? I wouldn't want you to slip. Indeed, sticking with Mrs. Jones would be best. And I shall call you Mr. Thurgood."

She may as well have slapped him. "I won't give your secrets away by word or deed, Glo--An—*Mrs. Jones*," he corrected himself with mock severity. "But why bother maintaining the charade? Come clean with Lady Wentworth, and your need for secrecy disappears altogether. She seems genuinely fond of you. You don't seriously believe she would dismiss you if she learned the truth?"

It was on the tip of his tongue to promise he'd take care of her in the unlikely event the dowager duchess did turn her back on her, but his words died when Anna twisted around to face him, eyes pleading to the point of desperation. "Please, Ca—Mr. Thurgood. Promise me you won't say anything to her. Not to anyone."

Sheer panic shone in her eyes. What was he missing? "I've already promised, haven't I? You must believe I'd never do anything to harm you."

She searched his eyes a long moment, before nodding once. He didn't know whether he felt relieved or insulted.

"Now, then," she began.

He crossed his arms over his chest and waited to hear what she would say next.

"Shall we make an effort to fill some more of the squares on our game card? Where did I leave that feather?" She set off in search of it.

He blinked. She wanted to go on as if nothing out of the ordinary had happened between them.

"A moment, if you please. Hadn't we ought to finish discussing Hardasher, at least?" He fisted his hands at his sides to keep from reaching for her, whether to hold her, or give her a little shake, he couldn't say. He wasn't stalling for five more minutes of of her time. Hah.

She plucked the recalcitrant feather from the ground where it had landed near the settee, and turned to face him, skirts swishing at her feet. "I am no longer concerned. You quite convinced me his interest in me lies more in the way of a, er..."

"Lascivious nature? I'm happy to handle *his interest* for you." Imagining planting his fist in Hardasher's face had a satisfying edge to it.

Her eyes went wide. "Mr. Thurgood, promise me you won't approach him about me."

Mr. Thurgood. "Another promise? You're demanding quite a lot of those, aren't you?"

She pressed her lips together.

"I suppose you also want my promise not to badger you about your future plans. You know you can't continue indefinitely as a lady's companion, An—Mrs. Jones."

She slipped around him like water 'round a river rock, making for the door. "Why-ever not?"

"Because you were meant for something more. Anna," he began gently, "if it's money you need—"

"*No.*" She grasped the door lever and looked over her shoulder at him with stern eyes. "Get this through your thick skull, Caden Thurgood. I require neither your money nor your assistance. I shall live my life as I see fit. Regardless of how pleasant seeing you has been, nothing of my circumstance has changed, nor do I wish for it to."

"Pleasant," he aped in a neutral tone, nodding. Ironically, he'd said similar words to women over the years. He'd had no notion how much the rejection, however nicely phrased, stung.

He ought to be thanking his lucky stars that he'd reined himself in, resisting his body's demands to make Anna his. She could not be any more clear. She intended to walk away at the party's end, never to see him again, just as he'd suspected.

He glanced around the room. Spotted his discarded gloves and the abandoned game card. He stalked over, snatched up both and proceeded to re-don the kidskin gloves with meticulous attention. Anything to avoid looking at her.

From the corner of his eye he saw her press her back to the door.

"Caden, it has meant the world to me to see you again."

He snorted. Now she meant to let him down easy? Too rich.

"Your kindness—"

"—Enough. You don't want my help and you want to be left alone. I don't foresee a problem, Mrs. Jones. Shall we rejoin the others? I have an idea where we might find a few additional items along the way, if you'd like to make a good showing."

He closed the distance between them and reached around her to open the heavy door. "After you?"

She laid a hand on his forearm. He bit back a curse as his entire body clenched with need.

"Please, believe me. You don't want to get tangled up in my life, Caden. It would only cause you trouble."

He forced a smile. "Duly noted. Shall we?"

She searched his face a long moment. Finally, she stepped into the empty corridor.

A sinking feeling settled in his gut, like he'd gambled all he had on a weak hand and lost. But he hadn't. That was the point. He had kept his head. So she meant to leave—again. So be it.

Chapter Ten

True to his word, Caden located two more items on the game card as they made their way back to the grand parlor. Not that it led to any spirit of frivolity.

Anna made a pretense of enjoying the escapade—at first. Caden did not. By the time they reached the front half of the manse, the very air between them crackled with tension.

She wanted nothing so much as to kick him in the shins. She had hoped to revel in the memory of this last interaction between them for years to come.

Caden with his sullen attitude had ruined everything.

So she'd pricked his male pride by refusing his gallant offer of help. He'd done the same to her—with that kiss.

For her the kiss had been magical, bone-melting, heart-stopping.

He'd sprung away from her as if suddenly realizing she carried the plague. One minute he couldn't draw her close enough, the next he shot across the room like lightning.

Had she done it wrong? She must've done.

She glared at his hard, gorgeous profile. She'd hurt him by not allowing him to sweep in and save the day, had she? Well, he'd hurt her by his rejection of her very femininity.

And she mustn't forget that snide comment about how very much she seemed to have enjoyed his kiss.

"I take it the game is won," Caden offered dryly.

Busy steaming, she'd neglected to notice the entrance to the grand parlor, now in eye shot. It appeared most of the other guests had reconvened. Excited chatter and revelry spilled out of the large chamber to echo down the corridor.

"Oh, mustn't forget this." He stopped and pulled something from his pocket.

Her crumpled bonnet.

He slipped it onto her head, adjusting it with surprisingly gentle fingers. He tied the straps into a bow under her chin, and, to her mind, lingered over the task.

The veneer of anger she'd erected crumbled in an instant.

"Thank you," she whispered, ridiculously on the brink of tears. *Her*. She could not recall the last time she'd cried prior to this weekend. When her father had died? Yet, since arriving to this infernal house party, she'd misted up twice, first, with Lady Wentworth, and now with Caden. Hadn't she learned long ago tears accomplished nothing?

He grunted his reply, and tucked her hand into the crook of his elbow to lead her into the parlor.

She ducked her chin, anticipating moving through a mob of people.

Caden paused at the threshold, glancing around the room. Without a word, he heaved a sigh, ushered her past the bulk of the crowd, then stepped in front of her.

He was shielding her from direct view with his body. Even piqued with her, he had her interests in the forefront of his mind. How like him.

A hard lump formed in her throat, and she tried with all her might to swallow it back. No use. Her face contorted. Wonderful. On the rare occasion she did succumb to tears, she resembled nothing so much as a baked apple.

Thanks to Caden, no one saw.

Lady Fenton's cheerful voice rose above the din. "Ladies and gentleman, your attention, please." She paused as the room grew quiet. "Our champions," she announced.

Applause rippled through the room, amplifying Anna's misery. In a moment she would say goodbye to Caden, in all likelihood for forever. Oh, they may see each other in passing a few more times over the next several days, but, by unspoken agreement, the light-hearted flirtation which had sprung up so naturally between them had vanished.

Anger at her situation, the unfairness of it all, bubbled up inside her 'til she wanted to scream. Despite his sour attitude, despite his evident disappointment in her lovemaking skills, she didn't want to say goodbye. Not yet. *Not again*.

She could set things right between them. Offer to tell him her dreaded secret. Allow him to realize on his own how impossible helping her would be.

Who was she kidding? He was Caden, *her* Caden. He would never admit defeat. She could not live with burying him under the mountain of trouble that followed in her wake.

She had to let him go.

She stared at his square shouldered, broad back through a blurry haze. Finding him after all this time, being held in his arms, being kissed by him, had been like stumbling head first into heaven. In saying goodbye, she may as well be cutting out her very heart. But better hers than his.

"You've gone quiet on me again." Hands on hips, he twisted his torso to glance back at her.

She couldn't bring herself to meet his gaze. Could barely choke out a reply. "Just wondering where Lady Wentworth got off to."

"Probably resting in her guest chamber. Best if you run off and join her like the obedient little companion you are."

A wry huff of laughter squeezed through the stubborn lump in her throat. He'd intended his biting remark to sting. Even so, the heroic vein at his core shone through. He'd spoken in a voice loud enough for her ears only.

She attempted a smile and cursed the stubborn quiver in her chin. With any luck, the bonnet he so detested hid her lapse in control. "Thank you for today."

He snorted and shifted 'round to face the other guests, stance wide, arms folded over his chest. "Not quite sure which part of today you enjoyed enough to thank me for. If you reference what I think you do, I can assure you, the pleasure was entirely mine."

She meant to take offense at his caddish remark. Instead, his last statement lightened the darkness engulfing her heart. *The pleasure was entirely mine.*

If that were true, why had he gone from hot to cold in the blink of an eye? She must have done something wrong. Abruptly it was all too much.

She turned and bolted for the side door uncaring of who might witness her graceless egress.

***

Caden felt the air stir at his back. He glanced over his shoulder in time to see Anna bolting for the small, servant's door at the rear of the overheated grand parlor. He glowered after her. She hadn't even bothered with a fare-thee-well.

But then, could he blame her? His attitude had grown increasingly snarky.

He may as well leave, himself. He hoped like hell no one tried to stop him. He was not in the mood to fraternize.

Pushing past several guests, an image of Anna's flight from the room replayed in his mind. Skirts fisted in her hands, her bonnet-covered head more downcast than usual, as if—No. He would not feel guilty. She had lied to him, repeatedly, only coming clean when cornered. Even now, she guarded her secrets. It was all well and good to allow him to kiss her. But trust him to help her out of whatever conundrum she faced? That, apparently, was out of the question.

Damnation, but she confounded him, like no woman he'd ever known. Tied him up in bloody knots. One minute he wanted to bed her, the next throttle her, the next run from her, then the cycle started all over again.

He breathed a sigh of relief as he exited the close confines of the parlor and started for the bachelor's wing.

What a bust this weekend was turning out to be. He'd departed Chissington Hall intent on having the time of his life amusing himself with women, wine, and winnings, knowing Zeke *really* wouldn't like the latter.

Although, in fairness to his brother, a friendly card game would hardly draw his ire. It was the hells he disapproved of.

Damnation, why was he defending his brother, even in the privacy of his own thoughts? The point was, he'd chosen the wrong woman with whom to form a temporary liaison.

He could sort this. Pausing mid-stride, he gave his waistcoat a sharp tug and turned to scan the thinning crowd. He *would* enjoy his idle, irresponsible, purposeless life. Blast, Zeke, and the earl, and Mrs. Anna Jones.

He caught sight of Harrison and raised a hand in greeting. The younger man shot Caden an affable smile and hurried toward him.

"Thurgood, hardly seen you since we arrived. I say, old chap, why do you look as if someone stole your last farthing? Don't tell me that head injury still plagues you?"

Blasted woman.

"Good day to you, Harrison. The knock I took? I hardly recall it now." He resisted the urge to pat the tender crown of his head.

"Glad to hear it." Harrison glanced over his shoulder in a conspiratorial manner. "Did you enjoy the afternoon with your new lady friend?"

Caden shrugged. "Well enough."

"She has a way about her that strikes me as…" He rubbed his chin. "Familiar in a way. Did she happen to mention if she and Lady Wentworth are distant relations? You know how often the well-to-do take in those family members whose fortunes have declined."

"A common practice, I'll grant you. But in this case, the answer is no. The dowager went through an agency to procure Jones' services." Caden arched a brow. "Frankly, I'm surprised you have the time to ponder yet another woman. One would think you have your hands full with the two who haven't left your side for the duration of this affair."

Harrison's eyes gleamed with undisguised amusement. "No need to get your feathers ruffled. I've no intention of poaching—not that I'd stand a chance against the famed Caden Thurgood if I did. I'm simply curious. Collector of useless information, here. One of my many charms."

"What utter nonsense. I've no claim on the woman. None whatsoever. I barely know her."

He clenched his jaw, regretting his outburst. He sounded defensive even to his own ears.

"Of course not." Harrison pressed his lips together as if suppressing a smile. "Any interest in a friendly game of lanter-loo? My brother claims you're quite the sharpie."

"Randall said that?" Was Sterling another one cataloging Caden's so-called misdeeds?

Harrison took a hasty step back. "Maybe I'm remembering wrong. Look, Thurgood, if you'd rather not join us, it's no skin off my teeth. We'll make do."

He had no interest in joining the game. Why enjoy a bit of sport when he could spend the hour sulking and obsessing over a certain vexing female?

He *could* help her, by Jove. He could wipe out her destitute state in one fell swoop. Or he could've had he not recently financed the quarry project. In any case, he was not without resources. Why refuse his offer of help?

"If you've enough takers, I'd rather..." He broke off. "Who's playing?"

Harrison ticked names off with his fingers. "Myself, Sir Geoffrey, Lord Hardasher—"

"Love to," Caden said, slapping his back. "Where and when?"

Harrison flashed a surprised grin. "Gentlemen's parlor, and now."

***

Caden peeled up his cards, pretending to study his hand while eyeing Hardasher on his immediate left.

The man brooded better than a hen guarding eggs which refused to hatch. Granted, the poor sot had loo'd the last several rounds, while Caden had managed to snag at least a third of the pot five times running. Any man's pride would be pricked, especially in light of Caden quashing his scheme to get Anna alone earlier. Not the man's day.

His mouth curved upward at the thought. He could be for-given for taking enjoyment out of Hardasher's failures as con-cerned Anna, couldn't he? He hadn't had the best day himself. Misery and all that.

"Thurgood's grinning like the cat who stole the canary," Harrison announced wearily. "I'll take it as a sign. Pass."

Caden winked at his young friend and tossed some coin onto the table to raise the stakes. "Trump."

A collective groan sounded as, one by one, the other players slid their cards toward the table's center.

"Never say you win again?" Hardasher grumbled, gathering the deck as the game's next dealer. He shuffled the cards, a marked scowl on his face. "With luck like yours it's a wonder you didn't take the grand prize this afternoon as well." After a beat he added, "Or did you?"

The man's thinly veiled slur on Anna's virtue rankled. Never mind Caden *had* made advances.

"The prize of a beautiful woman on my arm? So I did."

Hardasher arched a brow. "You've become fast friends since the first night when you asked if I recognized her."

"Are we playing or would the two of you rather yammer like a couple of kitchen maids?" asked Sir Geoffrey, seated to Caden's right.

He ignored the outburst.

Anna had secured his promise to not approach Hardasher to question him about her. But he hadn't brought her up. Hardasher had. Would she consider that splitting hairs? Probably.

He reclined in his chair, slinging one arm over the back, and responded to Hardasher. "You didn't, as I recall. Recognize her that is."

Hardasher pursed his thin lips as he dealt. "Indeed. I'm convinced I never laid eyes on Miss...Jones is it? before this weekend."

"Mrs. Jones," he corrected absently. Tension he hadn't realized he held eked out of his shoulders. The man did not know her. "Last hand for me, I'm afraid."

"That gives us one last chance to recoup our losses, lads. Ante up," Harrison enjoined the others.

One by one they tossed coins onto the table.

Hardasher contributed last. "As I recall, she did look familiar, however."

Something about the man's canny tone, as if he knew something Caden did not, sent a chill skittering up his spine. Impossible, he assured himself. Of all the party's attendees, Caden alone knew the woman's true identity.

"Right. Then you realized you'd seen her earlier in the day, in the company of Lady Wentworth," Caden said.

Several players demanded replacement cards. Hardasher doled them out, accordingly.

Caden gave the signal to keep the hand he was dealt, not that he had a clue what he held.

Hardasher took his time discarding, peeling off replacements, fanning out his hand. Then he grinned.

Caden resisted the urge to repeat his last statement. Did Hardasher know Anna or not? Of course he didn't. He couldn't. Still. He *had* followed the two of them into the recesses of the manse.

Good God, Anna's paranoia was catching.

Hardasher tapped a blunt finger under his nose. "The thing is, over the last several months, a sizable ad has run repeatedly in the *Times*, seeking information on the whereabouts of a lady bearing a striking resemblance to Mrs. Jones."

An ad? Who placed ads for missing persons? A runner might. He shifted in his seat and felt a bead of sweat trickle down the center of his back.

Other than admitting to falling on hard times, Anna's answers had been deliberately vague. Might she have committed a serious crime, such as larceny, in order to survive?

He rolled the idea of a thieving Anna over in his mind. He simply could not fathom it. He needed to rein in his imagination, by jove.

"What was the woman wanted for? Let me guess. Murder?" With a chuckle, he eyed his hand for the first time. God awful.

Harrison chuckled alongside Caden. "Right. Lady Wentworth's hired a murderess."

A small smile played at the corner of Hardasher's mouth. Eyes on his cards, he gave an unhurried reply. "No murder involved. Evidently the lady in question was abducted during the wee hours of her wedding night." He paused, his glance sliding toward Caden. "...to Baron Bolton. He's offered a substantial reward for her safe return."

"How in hell does one steal a bride on her wedding night?" Harrison scoffed. "You'd think the groom would pay better attention."

Several men snickered. Not Hardasher, however, whose eyes remained fixed on Caden.

"Bolton?" Caden spat. "That drunken lech? He's old enough to be her father."

Across the table from him, Harrison folded his hand. "Calm yourself, Thurgood. It's not as if your angel-faced rescuer married Bolton. The sketch merely resembled her."

"Photograph," Hardasher put in.

"Photograph, sketch." Caden waived a dismissive hand. "Harrison's correct, Hardasher. Whoever you saw emblazoned on that advertisement couldn't possibly have been Mrs. Jones."

Hardasher cocked his head. "Out of curiosity, how are you so certain?"

Baron bloody Bolton, that's how. He *knew* Bolton. The baron had once numbered amongst his late father's posse of immoral, over-imbibing, gaming-hell cohorts. The lout wasn't fit to carry Anna's gold slipper now safely ensconced in Caden's chamber, much less marry her.

Caden propped his elbow on the table. "Simple. Bolton needs an heiress to fund his estate thanks to years of neglect under his watch. Lovely though Jones is..." He shrugged and left the rest unsaid. Anna was no heiress.

"It's true Bolton's estate has seen better days." Hardasher broke off, revealing his cards with a smirk. "Trump, I believe."

A grumbling consensus ensued.

"Congratulations, Hardasher. Looks like Lady Luck finally smiled on you." Caden shoved back from the table.

Hardasher scooped-up his share of the winnings. "I detect an air of censure concerning Bolton, Thurgood. I submit *many* amongst the nobility must wed in order to restore the family coffers. Not all can be born a Claybourne, with access to the Claybourne connections and fortune, and thus the ability to withstand a few years bad luck. Men do what they must to survive."

Harrison looked aghast. "I say, Hardasher."

Caden sent Harrison a quelling look. No need for the afternoon to degrade into a cock fight, when he himself couldn't care less what Hardasher thought of him, never mind he had it all wrong.

True enough, the Claybourne estate boasted substantial wealth. But not because buckets of money had passed down through generations, as Hardasher insinuated. Nor had Zeke married into money.

Instead, through ingenuity, hard work, and wise investing, his brother amassed the fortune necessary to restore the estate after their own ne'er do well father drained it nearly dry.

Caden had benefited, of course. Quarterly stipends, club memberships, the use of familial estates. Better still, under Zeke's tutelage, he learned the art of investing well to grow a tidy nest egg of his own—the very nest egg he'd pilfered recently in his efforts to re-purpose the quarry. Not that Zeke had thanked him for it.

"The point is, Lord Hardasher, Mrs. Jones lacks the means to save the hapless Bolton, victim of tradition though he may be. And now, gentlemen, I bid you good day. Thank you for an"—He patted the bulging pockets of his waistcoat containing the coin he'd won—"enriching afternoon."

He made his way to the exit with a spring in his step, a whistle on his lips, and a plan forming in his mind. True, he had made up his mind to cut Anna a wide berth for the remainder of the party. However, the news he had to share with her thanks to Hardasher's illuminations changed things. She would appreciate knowing she had nothing to fear from the man. He had simply confused her with the hapless woman who'd had the misfortune to marry Bolton.

He snorted. In all likelihood, the poor chit had not been abducted at all, but had wised up after the ceremony and fled for her life.

***

Caden scrutinized his appearance in the dressing mirror beside the wardrobe. Clean shaven, tawny waves oiled and tamed. Crisp white shirt, simple cravat. Black superfine, lint-free and expertly pressed from his jacket to his trousers.

He snorted even as he inspected the sheen on his boots. He'd never worried overmuch with his grooming. He'd never really needed to. Women found him appealing. They liked his looks. They lapped-up his charm. Why should Anna be immune?

Still. He felt more than a little foolish, actively *trying* to make a favorable impression. But, damn it, he would have her eyes on him and him alone.

He pulled his pocket watch from his waist coat and checked the time. Early.

A pounding on his door sounded alongside someone—Harrison?—bellowing his name.

He strode for the chamber door, jerked it open, and found Harrison, fist elevated, mouth open—and he was shirtless.

"Something's missing from your attire. Give me a moment. I'll think of it."

"Oh, bloody ha ha. I'm half dressed because I'm having a wardrobe malfunction."

"An interesting choice of words."

"Literally, Thurgood. My armoire is jammed shut. Damned door won't open. I gave a good yank and broke the handle clean off. I tried to pry the thing open 'til my fingernails practically tore off." He held out his hands for inspection.

Caden huffed out a laugh. "Only you, Harrison. Give me a moment." He slipped off his dinner jacket and hung it over the valet. "Between the two of us, I'm sure we can figure a way to free your clothing."

For once, Harrison's uniquely bumbling ways would work in his favor. He wouldn't arrive downstairs so early he'd appear over eager. Women didn't like that. Or so he assumed. Prior to Anna, he'd never had cause to test the theory.

Harrison trotted ahead. "I appreciate this, Thurgood. Shouldn't take more than a moment with both of us working at it."

Chapter Eleven

"Good God, have more guests arrived?" Wearing an expression that said she smelled something foul, Lady Wentworth swept through the open double doors into the grand parlor.

Anna followed close on her heels. One foot into the large chamber, and she shared her employer's dismay. The din of excited voices and the warm, still air of an over-crowded room with windows closed against the elements seemed to engulf her. If only Lady Wentworth had not insisted she join her this evening.

"Anna, stay close."

She shimmied nearer to her employer, eyes fixed on the back of her silver coiffure. How better to avoid a chance collision of gazes with a certain handsome rogue?

She had quite made up her mind to avoid any further run-ins with him tonight. Not that she supposed Caden would go out of his way to speak with her. Not if his curt attitude, somehow made all the worse by the kiss that had melted her bones—*and not his*—were anything to go by.

Lady Wentworth's steady swath through the crowd slowed to a sudden crawl in the center of the melee. Guests seemed to press in on them from every direction.

Anna chanced a furtive glance around. The candle-lit parlor teamed with party guests and flushed liveried footmen bearing flute-laden silver trays. The thick carpets, velvet drapes, and tapestry covered walls turned clinking glasses, conversation and laughter into an indecipherable roar.

Without meaning to, she strained her ears for Caden's deep timbered voice, then, unable to resist, craned her neck, scanning for the taller-than-average, devilishly handsome man.

"Champagne awaits, Anna. This way." Lady Wentworth shouldered more than one guest out of her way, only to draw to a halt as the milling people ahead of them congealed into a seemingly impenetrable wall.

"For pity's sake," she hissed.

Anna silently commiserated. She could not move in any direction without either knocking elbows with someone, trampling a lady's skirts, or having hers caught under someone's boot or slipper.

"I beg your pardon. Tight quarters here. Mrs. Jones, isn't it? Lord Hardasher, at your service. We met earlier."

In spite of the warmth resulting from the crush of bodies, goosebumps sprouted over her suddenly clammy limbs. A deafening rush of blood pounded in her ears, blocking out all other sound. Everyone, save the dark-haired lord standing entirely too close to her, faded into the background.

Anna forced her lips into a semblance of a smile. "Good evening, Lord Hardasher." Though her rational mind knew she was perfectly safe, her breath turned choppy and her knees wobbled.

She must get hold of herself. Hadn't Caden already given her the most likely explanation for the man's interest in her? He was a rake. She was a widow and a servant at a house party, and thus, fair game.

He leaned down, eyes narrowing on her face—and all her self-assurances flew out the window. She could scarcely draw breath. With a sick certainty, she knew he recognized her.

"What lovely eyes you have, Mrs. Jones. Such an unusual shade."

Anna lowered her gaze as if that could protect her from his scrutiny. "You're too kind, my lord."

"Anna, I see a way out. Come." Lady Wentworth grasped her forearm, and with surprising strength, dragged her forward.

"My lord." Anna sent Lord Hardasher an apologetic smile as relief washed through her.

The man smirked in acknowledgment, dark eyes glittering with promise.

He *knew* her. He had to. Hadn't he?

The further she moved from Lord Hardasher, however, the more she chided herself for her bout of hysteria. Certainly Caden found the idea of Hardasher as some sort of investigative spy as preposterous.

Caden. A sudden, intense longing for him welled-up inside her, as if his mere presence by her side meant safety and security and...home.

What was wrong with her? He wasn't any of those things.

Although, he had offered to help her. If he knew the truth, though, that she'd killed a member of the nobility...*Watch yourself with boys like him, Glory. He's of the nobility. With them the title always comes first, even before family.*

Why why why would her mother's words not cease plaguing her? She'd never seen any proof her obsessive claim held water.

On the other hand, she'd never had any cause to test it.

Dear Heaven. She couldn't recall ever having such a divided mind. She supposed it all came down to...wanting. She wanted to believe in Caden. In his integrity as a man. In his steadfast friendship.

At last, they emerged from the bubble of people and, as if by magic, the air around them seemed cooler by at least ten degrees.

Lady Wentworth sighed in a dramatic fashion. "Thought we'd get eaten alive in there."

Eyeing the cluster of guests from which they'd escaped, she leaned close to Anna. "I don't care for the look of that fellow, Hardasher. Something feral about him. Stay away from him, my dear, eh?"

Anna's laugh sounded tinny to her own ears. "I couldn't agree more."

"Good girl. Let's away to the terrace."

She crossed the threshold behind Lady Wentworth to stand under the open skies. A welcome breeze carrying the scent of flowers from the garden beyond the terrace cooled her flushed cheeks.

Not quite dusk, the sun had dipped below the thicket of oaks, elms and birch to the west, lining the tree tops with a silver light. The domed sky, aglow with the last remnants of sunlight, and hanging paper lanterns transformed the gravel-covered terrace into a setting worthy of a fairytale. All she needed now was her prince.

An image of Caden surged to the forefront of her mind. Her traitorous heart leapt, anticipation swarming through her.

Lady Wentworth perused the intimate groupings gathered along the length of stone balustrade. After a moment she tsked. "He's not out here either, I'm afraid. I've seen neither hide nor hair of him. Have you?"

Anna blinked. She contemplated for the briefest moment feigning ignorance as to which *him* the lady referred. But there was no use trying to outwit the old fox.

"I have not—not that I've been looking."

Lady Wentworth gave her a dubious look. "I'll wager he's not yet arrived. Otherwise that pesky baronet wouldn't have gotten within arm's length, much less cornered you. Come. Harrison's holding court at the rail. Perhaps he can shed some light on Thurgood's whereabouts."

Anna stifled a groan. Did Lady Wentworth mean to outright ask after Caden? Worse yet, what if Caden appeared at his friend's side the moment she did? Half reluctant, half enthralled, and with no actual choice in the matter, she followed.

Harrison addressed several enraptured onlookers, gesticulating wildly as he did so, clearly acting out a scene.

"...Unbeknownst to me, he had wedged a shoehorn under the jammed cabinet door. Meanwhile, I caught hold of my cravat which had somehow caught in the hinges, causing the whole mess. I gave a good yank." Harrison mimed a full body heave-ho. "And whammo!" He gave a loud clap of his hands. "The cabinet door gave way, flying open. Thurgood's shoehorn went airborne, and the next thing I know he's on his backside with a gusher shooting from his forehead, and making a god-awful mess I might add."

He waited for the horrified gasps, chatter, and laughter of his audience to quiet before continuing. "He's a lucky bloke, that Thurgood. Caught him right here." He tapped his brow. "A mere half inch lower and he might have lost an eye. At first I thought he had, what with all the blood. The poor girl who came to clean the mess nearly fainted at the sight."

"One can only imagine what Thurgood had to say," one man commented. More laughter ensued.

Lady Wentworth chose that moment to make her presence known. "Yes, indeed, Harrison m'boy. What did the so-named *lucky* lad say? Is he still on premises? If he has any sense he's got himself as far away from here as possible."

Harrison went from lounging against the balustrade to standing ramrod straight. "Lady Wentworth, Mrs. Jones, I didn't see you there. Good evening to you both."

"Never mind that. What of Thurgood?" Lady Wentworth demanded.

He cleared his throat. "As to that, last I saw him, he was abed getting his wound tended. I doubt he's of a mind to travel, my lady."

The dowager duchess eyed him almost pityingly. "I rather meant if he had half a brain he'd remove himself from your presence lest your next foible permanently maim him."

Harrison's friends fell out laughing.

When the raucous laughter died down, Harrison offered, with only a hint of underlying sulk, to fetch them both champagne.

"I should love one," Lady Wentworth replied. "However Mrs. Jones must attend a small errand for me."

Anna met the older woman's eyes. The kindness she read there left no room for doubt. Lady Wentworth somehow knew she had to go to him.

Seconds later, she pushed through the crowded parlor, uncaring of whether Lord Hardasher spotted her or whose dress she trod upon or whether anyone might remark over her haste. None of that mattered now.

***

Lying atop his bad, shirtless and fuming, Caden held the wrapped ice to his brow. How in hell had it happened that aiding Harrison had ended with him bleeding and *not* enjoying pre-dinner cocktails, while the younger man, fully clothed thanks to Caden, had probably just finished his second aperitif?

Harrison was a bloody hazard, that's how. Next time Randall tried to pawn his younger brother off on Caden, he'd tell him to stuff it.

He wanted to get up from this bed. Wanted to don a fresh shirt, head downstairs, and find Anna. Not that he wanted her to see him looking like someone's punching bag.

Last he glimpsed himself in the mirror, the left side of his forehead had a swollen gash and a blossoming blueish green tinge. More to the point, every time he sat upright and removed the pressure from his latest head wound a-la-Harrison, the bleeding recommenced.

Harrison had suggested sending for a doctor to staunch the blood flow. Said he'd seen a wound of this sort before—caused it no doubt—and in his opinion Caden needed stitches.

Caden roared at him to remove himself from his chamber, and Harrison complied in swift order. Had he ever been more frustrated in his life?

What of Anna? Where was she at this moment? Probably sipping champagne, grateful for the chance to enjoy a respite from his constant attentions.

He closed his eyes, re-positioned the dripping ice pack, and forced himself to lie still. In another few minutes, the bleeding would stop. Then he could decide if he wanted to bother joining the party.

Maybe this was for the best. Maybe Harrison had actually done him a favor. The whole notion of speaking to Anna about Hardasher now seemed foolish and desperate. As for his plan to wow her with his devastating good looks? Pathetic, not to mention impossible now.

A rapid tapping sounded at his antechamber door. A chamber maid with a fresh towel and more ice, perhaps? Surprising. When he'd bellowed at Harrison earlier, he'd frightened-away the maid and footman who'd come to help as well.

He opened his mouth to tell whomever it was to go away, then closed it when he heard the interior door open and shut. He knew better than to abuse the help simply because he'd had the misfortune to travel with Randall's accident-prone brother.

Soft footfalls padded over the thick carpet. Skirts swished. A hint of something elegant and delectable teased his nostrils. His stomach tightened into a hot fist before his mind fully registered who had entered the room.

Anna, here? Why, precisely? Pride or curiosity or anger, he couldn't say which, bade him not move a muscle.

Her footfalls ceased halfway to the bed. A long minute passed. Caden's heart thudded so hard against his ribs, he wondered she didn't notice and outright accuse him of lying in wait.

After several more interminable seconds, she resumed moving, her stride brisk and determined.

He knew the moment she reached his bedside because her signature scent—tuberose, cedar, and everything feminine, danced in and out of the air he breathed. He inhaled, long and deep. He *had* to. No woman had ever smelled so tantalizingly good. His entire body screamed for him to reach for her, drag her into him, and kiss her senseless. His lower region stirred to life as if he had.

At least his blood flow had found an alternate direction.

She cleared her throat, then spoke in a soft voice. "Caden? I don't wish to startle you. It's Anna."

He nearly cracked a grin. As if she needed to give him her name.

She cupped his cheek on the non-injured side of his face with cool, silken fingers. "Cade, it's Glory."

His insides twisted at the sweet surrender. She'd used not only his Christian name, but her own.

He eased his lids open—keeping them closed at this point bordered on the ridiculous—and lost himself in the amber depths of her almond shaped eyes.

The tenderness he read there hit him like a punch to the gut. A painful ache radiated up his chest, lodging in his throat where it burned like hot coal. Why did it hurt, looking at her?

On second thought. He slammed his eyelids shut.

What in hell was happening to him? He could hardly think above the cacophony of emotions she aroused in him. Yearning and lust, resentment and confusion. Maybe he *should* have let Harrison send for the doctor.

"I'm not dying. It's just another annoying head injury, courtesy of that bumbler I once called friend. You needn't have troubled yourself to come by. I'll be right as rain any time now."

She drew back, pulling her blissfully cool touch with her.

He couldn't blame her. He sounded like a petulant child, once again illustrating Zeke's assessment of his character.

Her lack of a reply had him slitting his good eye open to study her.

The softness in her expression had vanished, leaving a shuttered look in its stead. And something else. Embarrassment? It was almost as if she couldn't look at him.

He probably looked like a monster—except the ice pack covered his bruise. He was bare chested. Could that be the issue?

"Mr. Randall detailed how you got knocked flat by his armoire. He explained you bled quite a lot. That's often the case with head wounds."

Though her face was angled in his direction, her focus seemed fixed on the headboard above his head.

How in hell was she still so modest around the opposite sex? Never mind. Her business, not his.

"Is that right?" he asked, drolly.

Another dainty throat clearing sounded. "I'd like to examine your injury myself, if I may?"

"I don't require a nurse."

More, he did not need her pity. He had his pride. He turned his head away from her in clear dismissal.

The mattress dipped slightly. Had she actually edged a hip onto his bedside? Damn her eyes.

He fisted his hands to keep from reaching for her.

"Caden, please." Her imploring tone tore at his defenses.

He turned to face her, his insides clenching at the sight of her pleading expression. "Very well. Have your way with me." His mouth curved in a deliberately sardonic smile.

She pressed her lips together but didn't voice a rebuttal. She reached for the ice pack and gently peeled it back. She studied him, both brows arching.

"That horrible, is it? Has the bleeding stopped, at least? I haven't dared take the pressure off to sit upright since the initial gusher that destroyed my cravat and shirtsleeves."

He watched her gaze track down to his Adam's apple, then drift lower. Staring, she licked her lips.

Just like that, he went ramrod hard.

Inwardly cursing, he propped-up one knee and rested an elbow on it to hide his inconvenient arousal as best he could, then cleared *his* throat.

Her eyes shifted upward, a satisfying flush staining her cheeks.

"What do you think?" His husky voice revealed too much of what he felt, at least to his ears.

Her lovely, tilted eyes went wide and her rosy lips formed a perfect O before she squeaked, "What do I think?"

By God, she could not fake this level of innocence. Mr. Jones must've been a dead bore in the bedroom. An oddly cheering thought, that.

"About my wound. Shall I heal, or am I to be branded for life?"

"Oh. Right." She hinged forward to study his brow anew, all business save the twin splotches of red on her cheeks.

His gaze locked on her lips. Hunger hollowed out his insides, urged him to do something stupid like rise up, mere inches, to claim her mouth with his. No matter that a few short hours ago kissing her had rocked him to his core. No matter that he knew she deserved better than being treated like a party favor by the likes of him. No matter. He wanted to kiss her more than he wanted to breathe.

"A slight edema has formed, but the bleeding's stopped. Any larger of a slice and you'd have required stitches. You may bare a scar. A bit of salve would help." She traced the area above his brow with her fingertip.

He felt the caress all the way to his groin. He swallowed hard, words failing him.

She met his eyes, sending him a resigned grin. "No doubt a scar will only serve to make your perfect face even more dash-ing."

"Perfect, eh?" He arched his injured brow, instantly regret-ting it as stabbing pain had him raising a hand to the site, which he regretted more. "*Ouch.*"

"Poor Caden." She brushed his hand aside and reapplied the ice with practiced care. "Better?"

He gave an inarticulate grunt as, inside him, a war raged. His last shred of good sense ordered him to send her away before he did something stupid. He reminded himself she would rather live her life as a servant than consider an offer of help from him. Reminded himself she'd had no trouble informing him she could take him or leave him, *would* leave him without a backwards glance at her first opportunity, even knowing their paths might never cross again.

Never again. The mere thought gutted him like he was fifteen all over again.

All the more reason to send her away.

His gaze fixed on her lips as he worked up the nerve to do what he must. "Anna?"

"Yes?" Her breathless answer threw fuel onto the fire burning within him.

I need to kiss you, his insides wailed. He swallowed the truth. He would stick to his guns. Do what he knew was right—for both of them. Though he couldn't pry his focus off her mouth, he forced out the words. "You'd better go. You'll miss dinner."

She somehow managed to stiffen in offense while still leaning forward to hold the ice in place. "I see. What about you?"

He gave a one-shoulder shrug.

"I could fetch you a plate, and the salve I mentioned."

He opened his mouth to reject her offer then choked on his reply as the tip of her pink tongue darted out to lick her goddess-inspired lips.

"Very well—if you join me." He was an idiot. He could live with that.

***

"Might I have a moment of your time, Lady Wentworth?"

Lady Evelyn Wentworth turned to study young Harrison, her distant relative by marriage.

A dark haired, gangly man of medium height. Affable by anyone's standards. But...there was something in his eyes. A sharpness lurked there, visible if one happened to pay close enough attention.

Dis-ease coursed through her. "We have some time yet before the dinner gong sounds. You may escort me on a brief tour of the Fenton gallery."

"An excellent notion. I know a short cut." Harrison proffered his arm, and she hesitated long enough to offer up a prayer he wouldn't manage to do her bodily harm before their conversation reached its end.

Neither spoke as they wove between clusters of guests. Eventually, they passed through two massive carved wooden doors into a long, narrow gallery. Harrison paused to close the doors behind them before once again taking her arm.

"How fare's your father, the marquis?" Lady Wentworth asked.

"He's well and sends his regards." Harrison paused in front of a large, gilt-framed oil painting depicting one of Lord Fenton's predecessors.

The man in the portrait did not resemble Fenton in the slightest. He was, in fact, far more handsome.

Harrison nodded toward the painting. "It's amazing, is it not, how people can be related by blood, and yet have few physical similarities."

A fresh frisson of alarm skittered up her spine. Ridiculous. She had nothing to worry about from this young man. How could she? How could he know anything? Although something had precipitated his request for this little tète-a-tète.

"I disagree," she said, deliberately contrary. "Take this…"

She drew the lorgnette dangling on a chain round her neck to her eyes to read the name plate under the frame. "Lord Gerald Fenton. One can assume he's a direct relation to the current Baron of Femsworth. Note the all too familiar overly large forehead."

Harrison regarded the portrait. "Mmm. I see what you mean. Look hard enough, and you're bound to find some sort of tell."

She sniffed, gave a none-too-subtle elbow tug, and he resumed leading her down the line of portraits.

"I'm afraid I didn't express myself well. Aside from whether or not relatives tend to look alike, they sometimes share similar characteristics. One wonders if they pass down through the bloodline. Say, a manner of carrying one's head, or pursing one's lips. A narrowing of the eyes, perhaps, or a gate."

"Yes, yes. What of it?" she snapped. Her heartbeat raced in her chest, and a bead of perspiration dampened her upper lip.

"I find it intriguing."

Schooling her breathing seemed nigh impossible. She jammed to a halt in front of the next portrait and stared at it unseeing as she concentrated on inhaling and exhaling, slowly, through her nose.

"Imagine, if you will, a grandmother and granddaughter separated for all of the child's formative years, yet still sharing distinctive mannerisms."

Cold suffused her. How had he come to know her darkest, most closely guarded secret?

He went on. "Why, the two, or at least one of the two, might not even recognize the other as a relative, even in the face of those glaring idiosyncrasies. And let's say one of the two, the grandmother?—for illustrative purposes, we may as well stay with grandmother, granddaughter paradigm."

"By all means."

He sent her a benign smile. "Let us say the grandmother possessed knowledge of the true nature of the relationship, and knew precisely how it came to pass the two had never made each other's acquaintance, all hypothetically, of course—"

"Of course."

"—one could see how a conversation about the why's and wherefores of their separation might be difficult to broach."

"What do you want?" she hissed.

He crossed one arm over his chest and drew his opposite hand to his chin in a contemplative posture. "Want? This is merely a hypothetical scenario."

She opened her mouth to speak, mortified to feel her chin trembling.

He continued unabated. "Let us suppose this granddaughter happened to have got herself married to one of the worst dregs of society, albeit a member of the nobility. Mightn't she set out to right her mistake, by, say, vanishing into thin air? How fortuitous if a long-lost grandmother chose to aid her in this endeavor."

"Indeed."

"Given enough resources, the young woman could hope to maintain her freedom. Unless..."

"Unless?"

"Unless she happened to attend a house party where she also happened to be recognized by someone who desired the reward for uncovering her whereabouts."

Her fears for herself, for being discovered, evaporated in a blink. Still, terror gripped her. Legs trembling like they'd turned to water, she placed one hand against the wall for support.

After all she'd done to assure Anna's safety, to have it all go wrong now. All the money and status in the world didn't contravene a husband's bloody *rights*.

"What would a grandmother do in such an instance, in your opinion?"

"Why, secret her away. Immediately. Hypothetically."

Chapter Twelve

With the jar of salve clutched in one fist, Anna rapped twice on Caden's antechamber door then let herself in.

Heart racing from her mad flight to find a footman to request a dinner tray, on to her chamber to retrieve the salve, then back here, she pressed an ear to the adjoining door and heard only her own choppy breaths.

She opened the door, her gaze shooting to where Caden lay atop the bed, chest rising and falling in a steady manner indicative of sleep. He had not donned a shirt as she had feared—expected—he would. She drank in the sight.

Dusk had turned to full-on night and the candelabras framing the walnut four-post bed barely touched the shadows engulfing the room.

But those flickering candles bathed his supple looking skin in a soft gold that bade her fingers to touch and explore. Oh, he was beautifully formed. Broad shouldered with a muscular chest that narrowed to a trim waist and a hard, flat stomach.

Heat infused every inch of her body, coiling through her to a searing concentration low in her belly. It was an odd, strangely delicious sensation.

She inched closer, not so much as blinking.

His thick, tawny hair, lay mussed against a white pillow. The thick fringes of his lashes cast shadows over his broad cheek bones, and even in repose, his mouth curved in seductive invitation. Despite the bruise marring his brow, Caden epitomized male perfection.

"Are you going to stand there all night, or are you going to apply your magic elixir?" He regarded her through slitted eyes.

"I thought you'd fallen asleep. I didn't want to disturb you." She spoke in a breathless, too-rapid manner.

He snorted softly. "I'm quite awake."

"Then why are you lying shirtless?" The fact one had nothing to do with the other, added to the tell-tale breathlessness of her voice, told her she might have missed the hoped-for affronted effect.

A lazy grin curved his lips. "Bother you, does it?"

"Did I not say so?" Oh, would that he believed her scandalized.

"Pardon me, darling. I thought it obvious I needed help getting into my robe—what with the bleeding and dizziness."

"Dizziness? You never mentioned feeling light-headed."

"Only when I sit upright. I s'pose for decorum's sake, I should've risked a minor faint. Terribly sorry."

She might've believed his apology sincere if not for the devilish gleam in his eyes he didn't bother to mask.

"I'll just slip into my robe." He reached for a bed post and started to drag himself up.

"No." She rushed forward to press her hand into the center of his chest.

His skin felt exactly as she knew it would. Hot. Supple.

She yanked her hand back as if burned. "S-Sorry."

"Whatever for, Anna?" Caden asked in a velvet soft voice.

To her horror she giggled. She hadn't suffered a fit of nervous giggles since...Bother. She couldn't remember the last time.

She sniffed and willed her expression to sober. "I'm...er...sorry I didn't offer to help you don your robe. Tell me where to find it, and I will."

He arched his unmarred brow and directed her to the valet beside his wardrobe. "Beneath my dinner jacket."

She crossed the darkened room to where the garment hung. Grasping the heavy silk, she caught a faint whiff of Caden's spicy aftershave. Only the knowledge he watched her kept her from pulling the silk to her nose. She strode back to the bed, holding it at arm's length.

She stalled a foot from the bed. How to help him without touching all that glorious skin?

Caden gave her a long, considering look. "I can manage, Anna." He may as well have added, *if you're afraid.*

She could do this. She must. The man needed her help. Any exertion might start his wound bleeding again. And besides. That *skin.*

Without warning he hoisted himself to a sitting position.

She stared, mesmerized by his rippling abdomen. Then he swayed like a drunken sailor.

"Not so fast." She rushed forward, bolstering him upright with an arm 'round his broad shoulders. She lay a palm across his forehead, careful to avoid his aggrieved brow, then tested the temperature against her own. Not much difference there.

He smiled, and batted his lashes at her, twice. "I'll be right as rain, now you're here."

It would serve the charming rogue right if she let him topple. "Shall we get this on you, then?"

She considered the heavy silk grasped in her fist. He leaned into her rather heavily. If she released him to wrap the thing around his shoulders, would he crumple onto the pillows, or worse, fall over the side of the bed to land in a heap on the floor?

Her gaze drifted to his now up-close, naked torso. Her heart thudded against her ribs causing the sound of her own blood to rush in her ears. With an effort of will, she focused on her task.

Mentally bracing herself, she slung the robe one-handed across the front of him, hoping to catch it with her other hand currently occupied with holding him upright. She missed.

There was nothing for it. She angled her torso across his, robe in hand, essentially wrapping her arms around him, and found her face inches from his, and her breasts pressed against his warm chest.

Her nipples tightened. A small squeak of dismay sounded in her throat at the same time Caden hissed in a breath.

She froze, afraid to move. "Did I hurt you? I'm so sorry." And she was. But perhaps, hurting him had kept him from noticing the condition of her nipples.

"No," he ground out.

"But you…"

"Just leave the damned thing."

"Fine." She unwound herself from him, then gaped as he sat erect with seemingly no trouble at all.

"I'm a terrible patient," he muttered, not looking at her. "You didn't hurt me. It's just…"

"Yes?"

He lifted his gaze to hers. Primal heat burned in the liquid blue of his eyes.

"You're an enigma to me, Anna. One minute, off-putting to the point of rudeness, insisting you need no-one and nothing save being left alone, the next, you act as if there's no place you'd rather be than here, by my side."

Hands trembling, she reached for the jar of salve she'd dropped on the bed in her haste to catch him, gripping it like a lifeline. "I don't need your help."

He grunted in annoyance.

"Caden, I'm trying to keep you out of a situation far more complicated than you comprehend."

"So you keep telling me," he growled.

"As for me wanting to be here and nowhere else, you're right there, also." She laughed softly, less embarrassed than she ought to be. If anything, her admission left her feeling more free than she had in a long time

She opened the pot of salve, and held it to her nose. Lavender, frankincense, honey, thyme. She'd pieced together one of her mother's recipes with another she'd found in a herbal she'd discovered in Lady Wentworth's library, of all places. Such mixtures not only aided in healing bruises and scrapes, they had an added benefit as an aromatic tonic for nerves. Apparently she needed more help than it could provide.

She set the jar on the side table with a click. "Are you going to say anything?"

"Yes."

She slanted him a glance, waiting.

His mouth curved in an apologetic smile. "I do need help getting into this thing." He held the robe out to her like a peace offering.

A helpless, answering smile tugged at the corners of her mouth. Shaking her head, she took the garment and draped the rich silk over his broad shoulders easily, now that she didn't need to hold him upright. A cozy sense of intimacy unlike any she'd ever known seemed to envelop them.

She pulled the lapels open wide. "Right arm first. Slowly."

The simple act of lifting his arm had his chest muscles flexing and his abdominals firming. A delicious tickle started in her belly. Her hands tightened reflexively on the lapels.

"Now the left," she whispered.

He obeyed, and her gaze dropped to the narrowing trail of tawny hair that disappeared under the waistband of his snug-fitting black trousers.

"Did I miss an errant spray of blood?"

Her gaze shot to his face. "Er...No. That is, I thought perhaps I saw some...thing?" she finished weakly. Damn the too-observant man.

"Mm."

How he laced the one-syllabic answer with such evident amusement was beyond her. Lifting her chin, she pretended not to notice.

Making no further comment, he tugged the lapels of his robe from her clenched fingers. In seemingly no particular hurry, he closed the robe, cinched the tie, and settled back onto his pillows, folding his arms behind his neck. The repose left his throat and collar bones bared to her.

Face burning, she grasped the open jar and dipped her finger into the luxurious ointment. "May I apply your salve now?"

"By all means, Doctor Jones."

She swallowed and shifted to face him, schooling her features into a mask of detached professionalism. She hoped.

She'd seen any number of things while accompanying her father on any number of house calls over the years, men's throats, partial midriffs and more. Yet glimpsing the slight depression at the base of Caden's throat where his heartbeat pulsed made her want to do brazen things like lean forward to demand he kiss her like he had this morning.

She wouldn't, of course. Pride, not decorum saw to that.

She could not forget him breaking off their kiss as if his life depended on it. One minute she was entering heaven's gate, the next, he was across the room boasting about how much she enjoyed his kisses.

No, she would not demand he kiss her. If he refused, she would die of mortification.

With care, she dabbed the gooey tincture over his laceration, working her way outward 'til she'd spread the mixture across the entire inflamed area.

"Better?" she asked.

"I'd say it feels too damned good."

The husky growl of his voice had her gaze snapping to his.

Caden's eyes, twin swirls of wild blue, blazed.

She couldn't be absolutely sure, but she thought he wanted to kiss her. She licked her lips and brought her face incrementally closer—just in case.

He swallowed hard and lifted one hand to trace the curve of her cheek. "This is not a good idea, Glory."

Her insides melted at his touch, the fever in his eyes, her name on his lips. As if drawn by an invisible cord, she leaned closer still. "Are you saying you don't want to kiss me?" she asked, her voice barely a whisper.

Caden huffed out a laugh that seemed equal parts exasperation and frustration. "No."

His hand on her cheek slid to cup her nape, anchoring her in place with a palm that was hot and slightly damp. "I do. So. Badly..."

The glass jar she held slipped from her fingers to land on the carpet with a thud.

"...but it's not a good—"

She closed her eyes and pressed her lips to his.

***

He'd recognized her intent one second before she silenced him with her kiss. Thanks to their previous experimentations, the ensuing explosion of need coursing through him came as no surprise.

But Anna's outpouring of sweet, reckless passion left him reeling. She wound her arms 'round his neck and clung to him as if she could not bear any distance between them.

God, how he wanted her. Wanted to devour her whole in one swallow. But he had to stop this now—before he couldn't stop at all.

With an agonized groan, he turned his head, breaking off the kiss. "Anna, you don't know what you're—"

"Shh." She cupped either side of his face and guided it back in her direction. Then she angled her soft lips over his and he was well and truly lost.

She lay against him, her body half draped over the side of the bed. Much too far away.

He scooped her up, dragged her across him, and, rolling, tumbled atop her onto the center of the bed.

He propped himself onto his elbows, arms bracketing her, eyes drinking in the sight of her—skin luminescent in the candlelight, lips softly parted. "Gods, you're beautiful."

Shaking with the effort it took to rein in his need, he kissed her with a tenderness that cost him. He wanted to ravage, to plunder, to feast, but her lips, so soft, so sweet, begged to be nibbled, tasted, teased.

His tongue cruised over the seam of her lips 'til she opened for him on a delicate gasp that acted like a feather duster down his spine.

A low moan sounded in his throat as he lost himself in her warmth. His hand snaked up to cradle the warm nape of her neck, fingers tangling in the once neatly twisted knot of hair.

"This won't do at all," he murmured.

"Mmm?" came her dazed reply.

Without another word, he set about removing her hair pins. Soon he had the majesty of her dark, chestnut hair fanned over the bedcovers. Looking at her almost hurt.

"You're beyond anything, Anna. You intoxicate me, rob me of sense 'til I feel I'd rather cease breathing than stop kissing you."

Her cheeks flushed a deep rose and an uncharacteristically shy smile tugged at her perfect lips. "Then don't. *Please.*"

Satisfaction roared through him, and his cock, already straining against his trousers, went painfully hard.

He had to calm his violent need for her or risk humiliating himself—and he had a decision to make. Unfortunately, he feared nothing had changed since he'd faced the same decision earlier today.

He lowered his head to nibble at her delicate ear lobe and nuzzle the tender underside of her jaw, a war raging inside him. He wanted her, and she seemed to want him equally. He could make love to her here and now, but then what? Watch her walk out of his life, an impoverished, helpless servant? Impossible.

Trembling with the force of his desire, he pressed his forehead to her collar bone and resisted the urge to howl.

Her fingers toyed with the hair at his nape. A shiver rolled though him.

"Caden?" His name on her lips tore at his insides.

"I...can't."

"Oh. Of course." Her hands fell away from him.

Everything in him mourned the loss of her touch.

Gathering his strength, he lifted his head to stare into amber eyes filled with so much hurt and confusion it took everything in him not to gather her close and kiss her again.

He clenched his jaw against the wave of temptation, and showed his hand. "I can't make love to you and leave you to your current circumstances. Hear me out," he said, rapid-fire, when he saw stubborn resolve fill her eyes.

He must convince her to accept his help. That alone would free him to make love to her 'til neither of them could walk out of this room.

And after that?

After was where the terror came in. *One step at a time, Thurgood.*

"I spoke to Hardasher."

Her eyes went wide and she jolted to a sitting position despite his best efforts to stay her.

"But I asked...*You promised*." She stared at him as if he were the very devil. As if he'd betrayed her.

He wanted to shake her. He would never hurt her, damn it.

He sat up and swung his legs over the edge of the bed, beyond frustrated. With Anna, with himself, and with the clamoring needs of his heavily aroused body.

"Hear me out, please?" He stared at her over his shoulder, unblinking.

When she gave a single nod, he rose, tightened the sash of his robe, and paced.

"To clarify, I did not ask Hardasher about you. *He* broached your name."

The color drained from her face. Jesus, she was that worried about losing a post? He could take care of her if it came to that.

The thought brought him up short. He truly was getting ahead of himself.

"What did he say?"

Caden sent her what he hoped passed for a reassuring smile and moved back to the bed, propping his hip on the edge of the mattress. He reached for her hand, which she gave him with evident reluctance.

Brushing his thumb over her knuckles he said, "He didn't recognize you, darling. You caught his eye because you look similar to some poor wench who had the misfortune to marry one of the most detestable members of the British nobility to walk this earth."

"Dear Heaven."

"Precisely. Evidently, on this vile creature's wedding night, he lost his bride to an abduction or some such thing. According to Hardasher, an ad ran for some time asking for any information—what the devil?"

She'd jerked her hand free of his and flung herself off the bed to land on her feet. She looked not the least relieved. More like a cornered, wild animal.

Doubt whispered through him. He rose, and with measured steps, circled the mattress to stand before her.

"Anna, do you have something to tell me?"

She lifted a trembling hand to her mouth. "He's not dead. Thank God."

Chapter Thirteen

The fairytale setting of Caden's candlelit bedchamber faded. Her mind raced. She felt as if she stood at the entrance to a very large, very dark tunnel. Her ears echoed with the sound of her breathing and her own pounding heart.

Baron Bolton, the man whom she had been forced to marry, then summarily killed, was not dead. She would neither go to prison, nor face execution. The proverbial noose had been lifted from 'round her neck.

But freedom from retribution took second place to the realization she had not taken another's life.

It was like a boulder had been lifted from her shoulders.

"Anna, for the love of everything holy, explain yourself." Caden's large hands gripped her shoulders.

She looked up at him. He studied her as if she was an escapee from bedlam. How long had he been questioning her?

"Tell me you're not bloody married to *him*. This is beyond anything."

"I..." She spread her arms wide. "...am."

He released her as one might a glowing poker. Before her eyes, his expression morphed from one of tenderness and longing to betrayal.

So much for his profession to understand the limited avenues open to a woman on the brink of destitution. Privy to a mere a shred of her history, a history she'd tried to shield him from, and already he'd judged and sentenced her.

"How could you marry *him*? Here I thought...I thought...but you only left because you thought him dead?"

"An oversimplification, but—"

He jerked a thumb over his shoulder toward the four-post bed. "—And what was that all about? I actually struggled with bedding you and subsequently leaving you to fend for yourself, a penniless servant, when all the while, you would happily depart my bed to go back to *him*?"

He scrubbed a hand over his mouth and glared at her. A muscle rapid-fire ticked in his jaw. "And now? I suppose *now* you'll relinquish your servitude to rejoin *him*?"

His last words hit her like a pail of icy water. *Rejoin him...*

No. She wouldn't. She couldn't. Only, her so-called husband—and Angelique, no doubt—had evidently posted an advertisement with her picture, promising a reward for assistance in locating her.

"Well?"

"Please, Caden. I have to think."

Assuming Hardasher had, indeed, recognized her, he may have already sent word. Baron Bolton and her dear, sweet step-mother might, even now, be on their way to Femsworth Manor.

She had to leave. Now.

Caden paced the room, muttering under his breath. "Of all the scenarios I could have conjured, this one would never have entered my mind. I understood you loved your husband, even if he did sound like a cad. But Baron bloody Bolton?"

Having reached the far side of the room, he pivoted and stalked back toward her. "I dismissed the possibility of you and Bolton out of hand, I'll have you know."

He stopped a few feet from her, nostrils flaring, hands fisted. "I misjudged you completely. I don't have a clue who you are, do I? *Christ.* If Zeke and Claybourne could see me now, and the fool I've made of myself over you, they'd laugh 'til their eyes bled."

He may as well have slapped her. He thought *himself* a fool? The prize went to her. She'd known better than to trust him, but in the end, her heart overruled her head. A moment ago she'd have given him anything. Everything.

How terrible to realize her mother had been right all those years ago.

She steeled herself against the tidal wave of pain she had not seen coming. "I must go."

"Excuse me? *Go*, you say? Have you looked at yourself in the mirror?"

She blinked, seeing him through a haze. No. She would not cry over this man. "I haven't, no. So sorry my appearance doesn't meet with your approval, sir."

He pinched the bridge of his nose. "I *meant*, if anyone catches sight of you they'll assume…" He huffed out a mirthless laugh. "Never mind. The point is, you can't leave before we talk this through. Help me understand…any of this, Anna, please."

His anguished plea pulled at her heart strings. With ruthless will, she recalled to mind his words. *I misjudged you completely…If Zeke and Claybourne could see me now, and the fool I've made of myself over you, they'd laugh 'til their eyes bled.*

She blanked her expression. "Understand? But you already seem to know the prescient facts. Why lower yourself with any further association, Mr. Thurgood?"

She shoved past him, striding for the basin and the shaving mirror hanging above it.

She stared at her image in horror. Hair loose and hopelessly tangled, cheeks flushed. She looked as if she'd just taken a mad ride on a wild horse.

With swift fingers, she twisted her hair into a semblance of a knot and glanced down at her rumpled, borrowed gown.

She bit back a groan. Caden had the right of it. If she encountered anyone in the meandering corridors leading to Lady Wentworth's chambers, they would have no doubt how she'd spent the last hour.

It couldn't be helped.

She squared her shoulders and, not sparing another glance for Caden, made for the antechamber door. Every step she took felt like losing a piece of herself—even knowing the truth. He saw her as beneath him, just as her mother always warned.

His words echoed in her head. *I misjudged you completely...if Zeke and Claybourne could see me now.* Her heart burned like she'd swallowed live coal.

"Wait." Caden, who'd stood silent and motionless, now caught her in two ground-eating strides. His warm palm closed around her elbow in a gentle, firm grip.

"Please, Glory," he said in an achingly tender tone that tore at her insides. "Don't leave like this. Not before we clear the air. I was caught off guard. Can't you understand? One moment you're in my arms, the next you're married to the devil incarnate. I thought..."

She turned to face him, eyelids stinging. Not that she was crying, for the love of the saints.

Looking into his beautiful eyes, her shield of anger vanished, leaving her bared and raw. "I know what you thought, Caden. You thought to entertain yourself with the help, and rekindle an old friendship while you were at it. Maybe toss some coin my way to help you feel better about my bad end."

His face paled. "No. It wasn't like that. I swear on everything I hold dear."

She cupped his cheeks with shaking hands. Thoughts raced through her mind, things she wished she could say to him. In the end, there was no time and even less point.

"Goodbye, Caden." With that, she turned and fled.

"Anna, *wait.*"

She spared one last look as she charged down the corridor—and nearly collided with Mr. Randall. Only his outstretched arms averted disaster.

Grasping her shoulders, he studied her with grave concern. "I beg your pardon, is it...*Mrs. Jones*? It is you. Are you quite all right?"

Mortified, she twisted free and raced on.

Caden's voice sounded behind her, entirely too close for comfort. "Harrison, what the devil are you doing? Get out of my way, man. What are you—*let me go.*"

"Listen, man, there's something I need to tell you that can't wait."

Swallowing a sob, she raced on.

Chapter Fourteen

Pressing at a stitch in her side, Anna jogged through the dimly lit, blessedly unoccupied corridors leading to Lady Wentworth's chambers.

The enormity of what lay ahead penetrated her very bones. She reminded herself she'd managed to flee with little more than the clothes on her back—and her mother's ruby—once before.

On the plus side, she wasn't leaving a dead body in her wake. Not that Bolton had actually *been* dead.

Bolton, alive. She reviled the man for what he tried to do. Even so, she had never come to terms with having killed him, even in self-defense.

How unfortunate she had no time to enjoy the freedom from her ever-present guilt, nor any time to contemplate Caden, and what he must think of her.

What *he* thought? Bah. What about the awful things he'd said? *Can you really blame him?* an irritating inner voice demanded.

No. Definitely no time for mulling over what transpired with Caden. Her life hinged on a razor's edge. If Angelique and Bolton got their hands on her, she'd exchange one death sentence for another.

Get the deed done, Bolton. I don't care what you do with her afterwards. Toss her in the Thames for all I care. Do it and we're home free. Angelique's words before she stormed out left little doubt of the pair's intentions regarding Anna.

She entered the night dark antechamber, turned up one of the low-burning oil lamps, and glanced around the shadowed room. What to bring? Her servant's clothes, of course. What of her tinctures and oils?

The Antechamber door creaked and swung open wide. Lady Wentworth crossed the threshold.

Anna blurted the first thing that came to her mind. "I...I have to go." Her eyes stung. The thought of leaving this irascible woman who, against all odds, had become synonymous with home, threatened to break her like nothing else tonight had.

"I know."

"You do? But—"

"There's no time to talk. I packed your things and had them sent down."

"You packed for me? Sent down where? I don't understand."

The older woman held up one gloved hand, palm out. "We haven't the time for a lengthy discussion. You must leave, and quickly. To that end, I've made certain...arrangements." She cocked her head as if contemplating her next words. "You may find them slightly uncomfortable, but do bear in mind you'll suffer this discomfort for only a brief time, and the small sacrifice far outweighs the alternative."

"Which is?"

"Leaving here with Lord Bolton."

Her insides froze. "He's here?"

"No. But I believe his arrival is imminent."

Anna's head spun. Lady Wentworth *knew* about her marriage to Lord Bolton?

Had Caden told her? No. He wouldn't have had time. She searched the dowager's face.

"Anna, do you trust me?"

She'd known her employer only two years. She'd been betrayed by others whom she'd known much longer. Still. She inhaled deeply, praying she wouldn't regret her decision. "Yes."

Lady Wentworth's demeanor conveyed a palpable sense of relief. "Follow me."

***

Caden slunk back into the well-cushioned bench in the travel coach Harrison had lent him and stared morosely out into a night as black as death.

Horse hoofs clattering over cobblestones drowned out the gusts of wind tearing through the surrounding trees as the driver atop the box held the handsome pair of grays at a steady clip. Lord knew how on a night like this. Not a star penetrated the thick clouds blanketing the sky overhead.

Between the inky darkness outside and the glowing lantern illuminating the coach interior, Caden could make out nothing through the small windows.

He glowered at the luxurious velvet cushions and swaying curtains that made up the entirety of his gilded cage. With a flick of his fingers he extinguished the lamp and plunged himself into a profound blackness which matched his mood.

He rubbed at his temple, near his uninjured brow. His head throbbed with a dull ache, whether from his first injury, or his second, or from plain, bloody frustration, who could say?

He rapped on the trap above his head.

The driver slowed his team to a roll and slid open the trap. "Aye, sir?"

"If this storm breaks, we'll need to stop for the night. Keep an eye open for an inn."

"Aye, sir. If'n the weather turns." The trap slid shut.

He dug in the pocket of his great coat and withdrew the flagon of whiskey Harrison had shoved into his hand upon seeing him off. He couldn't remember the last time he'd eaten, and partaking of the spirits would likely knock him sideways. If only they'd mute the deafening accusations echoing in his head.

He thumbed the cork off and raised the silver pint in a silent toast to nobody before taking a long slog. He welcomed the liquor's burn as it slid down to his empty stomach.

He was off to Chissington Hall, summoned by Zeke, as if his dramatic declaration of less than a month ago had never occurred. For once, Caden couldn't fault his brother. This was about the earl. Still, he couldn't help but wonder what sort of reception he'd receive.

To say their last interaction had been caustic would be putting it mildly.

The afternoon had started out so promising. He'd gone in search of the earl and Zeke with a spring in his step, eager to finally share his findings about the many uses of limestone, along with his offer to personally oversee repurposing the mill.

He'd anticipated Zeke's reaction with a quiet sense of pride. First would come surprise that Caden had taken on the project of his own recognizance. Perhaps he'd express chagrin about not granting Caden access to the familial funds, leaving Caden no choice but to borrow against his own investments.

Next, Zeke and the earl would listen with interest to the myriad heretofore untapped benefits of limestone to the estate which Caden would outline in detail.

Finally, and most importantly, would be the satisfaction and pleasure in Zeke's eyes when he realized how Caden's plans for the quarry would ultimately please his future countess.

Too bad he never got the chance to deliver his news.

Standing just outside the open door of the earl's den, he listened to the two men he respected most in the world discuss him and his many character flaws as if he were no more than a child rather than a man fully grown.

"*What* about *Caden? Where are you going with this, Zeke?*"

"*Kitty and I've been wrestling with the serious question of what to do about him. You know very well he's spent the last several years galavanting 'round England, gambling, sometimes in hells by his own admission—*"

"*—Zeke, we've established the boy does not have a gambling problem.*"

The boy.

"*He's not like your father, Zeke.*"

Damn right, he wasn't.

"*No? Then why did he come to me asking for a large sum of money? Money which, I might add, he refused to explain his need of.*"

"*I'm sure he had a valid reason.*"

"*Like the last time?*"

"*You refer to what happened at Oxford? Zeke, that was a long time ago and he learned his lesson. What did he say, precisely?*"

"*He requested family funds to finance a so-called business venture, then refused to name the venture. I told him we'd discuss it once I returned.*"

"*That does not sound like a gambling debt to me. Perhaps the lad simply wanted to do something on his own, without the oversight of his big brother.*"

"If so, he got his wish."

"Zeke, why so harsh?"

"Mayhap I haven't been tough enough. I agree, he's not lost to his vices like our father. But what kind of life is it to jump from party to party, feasting on women and wine and all manner of sport without a care in the world—except for appeasing his own carnal appetites?

"And this request for money? What's happened to all he's amassed? A pretty penny, I can assure you—all gone in a blink? I tell you, it sounds too similar to the last time he needed a large influx of cash."

"You really suspect a gaming debt, then, despite all his assurances to the contrary?"

"My best guess? Yes. And if I'm right, he's fast on the road to ruin, just like our father. And the blame lands squarely at my feet."

Caden didn't know what he found more offensive—the fact his brother hadn't believed him about the money, the idea he found him a ne'er do well, or that he dared take ownership for Caden's actions as if he weren't a man, able to answer for himself.

And the earl's biggest show of support was to deny Caden gambled in the hells in a manner akin to their father? Indeed he did visit the hells occasionally, he wanted to shout. He just didn't lose.

Having heard enough for a lifetime, he marched up to his bedchamber to pack.

His brother saw him as nothing more than an overgrown child intent solely on self-gratification? One who couldn't manage his own life without his big brother's guidance? Caden was happy to prove him right and to hell with the money he'd spent on the quarry. Zeke could choke on it when he finally figured out what he had really been up to.

Randall's request for Caden to accompany Harrison to their cousin's wedding party in his stead arrived that very afternoon. It could not have come at a better time. He leapt at the opportunity. But not before informing the earl and Zeke he needed neither their money nor their influence nor their time, since he was such a disgrace in their eyes.

Then he left, feeling damned good about his decision to write them off.

Only now that the earl had taken ill, his actions struck him as nothing short of a child's tantrum, perfectly illustrating Zeke's point.

And why stop there? Witness this situation with Anna. He'd barreled in, so certain he could solve all her worldly problems without the least idea what her problems entailed—namely a husband whom she wanted back from the grave. No wonder she'd rejected his help.

Scowling, he slunk deeper into the cushions. In fairness to himself, all she needed to do was give him her real name.

Gloriana Masters *Bolton.*

Damn it. Much as it galled him, he couldn't pin the blame solely on her. She'd told him repeatedly to leave her alone. Stubborn, arrogant ass that he was, he hadn't listened. Not until it was far too late—for him at any rate.

How had she got so far under his skin in the span of a few days?

She hadn't. The girl he knew had. The girl she once was. The one that got away, who he never forgot, whose mischievous smile ruined him for all others.

Except...why did looking at *her* turn his blood to fire? Why did the thought of kissing her consume him, and the actual press of his mouth to hers destroy him? He'd never experienced anything like it in his life.

The woman owned him from the moment he opened his eyes and saw her hovering above him, lakeside. Thank God she didn't know, as she could clearly care less.

Except...when the latest Harrison-debacle happened, she'd come running. Why? She nearly had him convinced she gave a damn.

Then she'd kissed him. God, if he hadn't pulled away to make one last ditch effort to win her trust, what might have happened?

They would have made love, that's what.

God help him, everything in him wished he could go back and restrain his instinct to do the right thing. What did that say about him? Nothing good. Exactly like the caustic words he'd hurled at her learning of her marital status said nothing good.

Not that he could repair the damage he'd done. She was *married.* To Baron-bloody-Bolton.

Damn her eyes for misleading him. She'd stated unequivocally she was widowed.

But then, she'd thought Bolton was dead, and, oh yes, he mustn't forget her heartfelt *Thank God* when she learned he wasn't. Two small words that cut deep.

She loved the man. He couldn't wrap his mind around it.

He took another dram of whisky.

He needed to get the infernal woman out of his head, and focus on getting home to his grandfather—which would prove a much easier feat if his mind would stop playing tricks. He could still smell her tantalizing scent. Cedar and tuberose and an elegant intangible something he couldn't name.

He slammed a halt on his cogitations about Anna and turned his thoughts to the earl's unknown malady. After all, that was why he careened down this isolated road into a brewing storm in the middle of the night.

According to Harrison, the messenger Zeke sent hadn't conveyed any specifics about the earl's decline in health. The runner relayed only that the earl's condition was serious, and that Caden should return home immediately.

He drank more whiskey. At least Harrison's coach was comfortable, and his horses fresh. He should reach Derbyshire by daybreak—unless the weather worsened. By the sound of this wind, that was a distinct possibility.

***

A sound akin to a woman's sharp cry dragged Caden from a fitful slumber.

He sat bolt upright and peeled open gritty eyes. He could see nothing in the jostling, dark carriage. He rubbed at his neck, stiff from the awkward posture he'd assumed after nodding off. What had awoken him?

Outside, the wind howled in violent fury. That answered that.

He pushed the curtain aside to peer, bleary-eyed, through the rain-spattered pane. The moon had managed to sneak from behind the clouds, enough so he could make out sheeting rain and downed branches.

A monumental gust of wind slammed into the carriage, causing it to lurch up onto one side. In less than a blink, the wheels slammed back down. Caden heard an alarming crack, but the coach barreled on. *Enough.*

He thumped the trap door above his head. It opened a sliver, and rain sluiced inside.

"Aye, sir?"

"We haven't passed an inn?"

"The lord and lady ordered me t' make haste and t' stop for naught."

"What utter nonsense. Stop at the very next inn you see. We'll wait out the storm and recommence our journey come morning."

"Aye, sir," he said, his relief evident.

A quarter of an hour later, Caden felt the carriage slow and turn off of the main road.

Several flashes of lightning revealed a two-story inn, and what looked to be a working stable and barn. The windows of the establishment glowed, offering a cheerful welcome and respite from the inclement weather.

He could well imagine sitting before a hardy fire eating a hot meal, washed down with a frothy ale. His stomach growled in anticipation.

The driver halted his team beneath a hanging sign announcing the establishment *The Jolly Pumpkin.*

After directing the groomsman to the stables, Caden vaulted to the graveled courtyard, eschewing the carriage stoop for expediency sake. He would gather whatever luggage he needed for himself, should there be a vacancy. If not, he'd bunk down with the horses. Whatever the case, they were through traveling for the night.

A round faced, rosy cheeked proprietress greeted him just inside the door. She wore a beaming smile missing only one or two teeth, and barely blinked at the lump over his right eye. In swift order, he procured a room, pocketed his key, and headed back out.

He stood on the porch a moment, filling his lungs with the cool, damp night air, then hiked up the collar of his great coat and crossed the courtyard toward the stables.

He took his time, allowing the icy rain to revive his senses and dispel some of the effects of the whiskey. The liquor might have dulled the pain from his latest injury and slowed his obsessive thoughts about a particular woman, but neither result lifted his mood in the slightest. He gave a self-derisive snort. Apparently he preferred to suffer with a clear head.

Inside the stable, a lone lamp burned. He quickly discovered the stowed coach.

The groom was nowhere in sight. From the loft area, muted voices and a slit of light beneath a closed door, likely the stable master's private room, told him Harrison's driver had found a billet for the night.

Now to see to his own needs.

He opened the coach door, hoisted himself up and leaned inside—then froze for a full second while his brain caught up with what his eyes were seeing. The luggage compartment stood open, and Anna, wearing the same gown from earlier, hovered over the bench, one leg in, one leg out of said compartment.

He dove the rest of the way into the carriage, yanking the door closed behind him. Darkness enfolded them. Cursing under his breath, he pulled a box of sulfur tipped matches out from beneath the bench and relit one oil lamp.

As though turned to stone, Anna stood frozen, skirts fisted in her hands. She stared at him, skin ghostly pale, eyes wide as saucers.

"I *can* see you. You might as well complete your exodus from the luggage well. And while you're at it, would you mind telling me what the devil you're doing here?"

***

Anna teetered, one leg in the hold, one knee pressed onto the bench cushion.

"Oh, um, hello." She started to hoist up her skirts to pull her other leg over the trunks and through the opening, then paused, her cheeks flushing with heat. "Would you mind averting your gaze?"

After first rolling his eyes in an unnecessarily dramatic fashion, he complied, gesticulating with his hand for her to get on with the thing.

She did, sparing a moment to close the cupboard behind her, before perching atop the bench opposite Caden. She cleared her throat.

He turned to face her, fixing her with a stony stare.

She licked her lips. "I didn't know it was your coach I got into."

He arched a brow. "No, indeed? Whose did you think it was? This is your usual means of transportation?"

She tamped down her irritation, deciding she owed him a degree of patience.

"I didn't ask whose vehicle it was. Lady...er...rather, the advice given me suggested climbing aboard your conveyance was the most expeditious, perhaps only, option available to me."

He tapped his lips with one finger, brows furrowed.

She blinked rapidly. "I had no reason to think I might be riding with you. Not until I heard you speak to the driver, at any rate. You certainly shared no plans to leave tonight when last we spoke."

"When last we spoke," he said, his tone deceptively neutral. "No, don't s'pose I did."

She lowered her eyes and plucked at her skirts. "Is it because of what happened between us you left?'

His derisive snort drew her gaze back to him. She thought she detected a ruddy stain on his cheeks, although in the yellow lamplight she couldn't be certain.

"As it happens, a family emergency called me away. I'm heading for Derby. I hadn't intended to stop tonight, but the weather had other plans. And here I am answering *your* questions, while you feed me your usual vagaries. What is going on, Anna? The truth for once."

She did owe him the truth. But did it have to be now? Bedraggled, muscles cramped from hours crammed into the pitch-black hold, rattling along with the trunks, half afraid the coach would overturn in the maelstrom, starved, and to make matters worse, in need of the facilities.

She studied his hard expression and knew better than to suggest a delay.

She opened her mouth, but before she could utter the first syllable, Caden bounded across the narrow divide and mashed his large, warm palm over her mouth. He smelled good. Like the soap he favored and warm male skin.

She glared at him and resisted the urge to bite.

Then she heard masculine voices. The scrape of a cabinet opening and closing. Clinking glass.

She nodded her understanding, and Caden withdrew his hand, albeit with evident reluctance.

After a moment the voices receded in time with the thump of heavy footfalls climbing stairs.

To her surprise, rather than renew his demand for answers, Caden gave her a resigned look. "This is not the best venue to hold a private conversation."

"What do you propose?"

He smiled sardonically. "Let us get you a room...sister."

He lowered the carriage step then helped her down, giving her as wide a berth as humanly possible in the cramped stall.

She waited as he disappeared once more into the coach interior. He emerged seconds later hoisting two cases, one black, the other a fine looking, medium-sized pastel trunk embellished with ribbons and tiny flowers.

She peered at the latter. "Is that mine?"

"You don't know?"

She shook her head. "Lady..." she pressed her lips together, uncertain whether she ought mention Lady Wentworth's part in all this.

He sent her a long-suffering look, then jutted his chin for her to precede him from the building.

As soon as the door closed behind them, he turned to her. "What about Lady Wentworth?"

When she hesitated, he sent her an icy smile. "Who else would dare stow you in my—Harrison's—coach? Unless you have another benefactress amongst the guests at Femsworth Manor?"

He made a valid point.

Lightning flashed, followed by a rumble of thunder. She inched closer to him.

"Lady Wentworth both packed and stowed my things before I even knew I was to depart."

He glanced down at the feminine trunk he held. "Very helpful."

She nodded her assent, ignoring his sarcasm. "Do you think we ought to go inside?"

"Come on, then."

They made haste crossing the rain drenched courtyard to the inn.

A few minutes later, a bemused proprietress showed Anna, Caden in tow, to her room, all the while grumbling about why on earth the good sir hadn't thought to mention his sister in the first place.

"Lucky for you, we still have a room to let, what with this night's weather. Guests've poured in all evening, and the storm don't appear to be lettin' up any time soon."

Caden made no comment. He surveyed the chamber appraisingly before depositing her trunk on the bed. His gaze slid to Anna. He eyed her up and down.

Her face throbbed with mortified heat. She could only imagine what a fright she must look. She hugged herself and told herself she could handle whatever insult he doled out.

"Madam, kindly have meals brought up for myself and my sister."

As if seconding his motion, her stomach emitted a low growl.

Her eyes met his. His lips twitched and she sent him a tentative smile, helpless to resist.

"She also requires a bath."

Her smile vanished. She resisted mentioning he looked far from fresh, himself, with stubble darkening his cheeks, not to mention the blue tinge above his brow. Although, come to think of it, the wound didn't look half bad. The work of her salve, no doubt.

He arched a challenging brow at her scrutiny. She arched both her brows in response.

Seemingly oblivious to the silent interchange, the innkeeper balked. "At this hour? It'll cost ya dear, sir."

"Be that as it may, my sister has had a trying evening."

"Aye, sir." She scurried from the chamber, muttering under her breath.

Caden followed, tossing over his shoulder, "Until tomorrow, sister." He closed the door softly behind him.

Anna stood in the room's center and stared at the paneled door, contemplating his parting words. *Until tomorrow.*

Until tomorrow, what? Did he mean to question her then be on his way, leaving her behind? And why wouldn't he? He owed her nothing. Not a paid night at the inn, and certainly not a carriage ride to Derbyshire followed by an extended stay at Chissington Hall.

Why hadn't Lady Wentworth informed her whose carriage she climbed into? Why hadn't Anna thought to ask?

In fairness to herself, her main concern had been escape.

She searched her mind, trying to recall the dowager duchess's exact words as she closed the luggage hold, plunging Anna into darkness. *Stay silent and all will be well. Do check the contents of your trunk when you arrive at your destination...carefully.*

She approached the pretty flowered trunk lying atop the neatly made bed.

She popped the trunk's latches and lifted the lid—then blinked in confusion at the heretofore unseen contents. *Was* this the trunk Lady Wentworth had packed for Anna? Who else's could it be? But on first glance it appeared Lady Wentworth had packed none of Anna's servant's gowns.

She riffled through the layers of clothing, spying several fine day dresses, at least one evening gown similar to those Lady Bernadette had loaned her, fresh undergarments and a white, lawn sleeping gown. And, nestled at the bottom, she was gratified to see, were her new boots.

She nibbled the tip of her pointer finger and stared at the trunk's contents as if doing so might reveal the where, why, and how Lady Wentworth had procured the garments. She drew a solid blank.

Check the contents...carefully.

A satin pocket ran along the inner side of the trunk. Cautiously, Anna slipped one hand inside. Her fingers closed over buttery, smooth leather. A book? Too thin. Some sort of packet?

She withdrew what looked to be a lady's leather billfold and peeked inside. She gasped at the substantial stack of crisp British pound notes. Lady Wentworth had sent her off with a minor fortune. And something else, too.

Anna withdrew a small bit of folded wax paper. She peeled back the corners—and stared. Her mother's ruby? It couldn't be.

Hands trembling, she re-wrapped gemstone, and slid it back into the billfold.

Her thoughts churned. Lady Wentworth somehow knew about Lord Bolton, had aided Anna in her escape, had provided her with clothing and funds—and what appeared to be Anna's mother's ruby, which Anna had pawned two years ago.

How? Why? Nothing about this night made any sense.

A knock sounded at her door, followed by a muffled voice announcing her bath's arrival.

She closed her eyes. A hot bath would feel divine.

Everything else could wait.

Chapter Fifteen

C aden crossed the threshold surveying the neat, traditionally furnished chamber in the *Jolly Pumpkin* feeling anything but jolly. Having Anna mere steps away was akin to having an itch he couldn't reach to scratch. So close yet, for all practical purposes, half a world away.

He stripped off his damp great coat, slung it atop the bed, then dropped into the armchair next to the crackling hearth. He pried off his boots, then sat, fingers steepled, and stared into the flames.

She was here, having stowed herself onto Harrison's traveling coach. Why?

His mouth curved in a grim smile. At least now he knew why he couldn't get that infernal, mind-drugging, luscious scent of hers out of his nostrils.

The moment he'd laid eyes on her climbing out of the luggage hold, everything in him clenched up tight like a tiger crouched to spring. He'd wanted nothing so much as to grab her, pull her close, and beg her to forgive him—*him*—for the things he'd said.

Then he'd remembered her lies. Her marital status. *Her* dismissal of everything he'd offered—save his kisses. She liked those well enough.

Bitterness and longing and wounded male pride clashed inside him, and the best he could was keep his mouth shut and let *her* do the talking.

Then those those damned stablehands started moving about. He hadn't wanted them hearing Anna's voice and coming to investigate. So he'd shut her up the quickest way he knew, with his hand sealed over her lips. Big mistake. Huge. The moment he touched her, his self control hinged on the head of a pin.

He'd still wanted answers, but he *needed* his hands on her, his mouth on hers, her body under his, none of which could happen, ever again.

Right.

Come morning, after a good night's sleep, he'd have himself in hand. But tonight, *Christ,* knowing she was just down the hall might kill him.

Frenetic knocking sounded on his door.

Perspiration blooming over his body, he crossed the cold wooden floor on stockinged feet and swung the door open.

He found the once cheerful inn keeper, now wearing a harried expression.

"Yes?"

"Mr. Thurgood, sir, there's a mite problem."

"What is that?"

She gave him a pained smile. "Y'see, the weather's bad, like I told ya."

Like he could hear with his own ears. Wind rattled the window panes and howled down the chimney chute as if mother nature sought to relocate the entire building. "So you did."

"The thing is, I've a lord, what's arrived. Claims he's a baron."

The hair on Caden's nape prickled. But, really, what were the chances *that* particular baron had arrived to this particular inn, tonight? "And?"

"He's in need of a room and is in a fine fettle at the thought of bedding down in the barn. Sir, what I'm trying to say—ask—is would you mind, overly, sharing with yer sister. I know it's a tad inconvenient—"

"—Fine." A hot rush of anticipation filled him even as he cursed himself for a fool.

She sent him a gap-toothed grin. "I knew you t'be the agreeable sort. If you wouldn't mind gatherin' your things? I'd...er...move yer sister, 'xceptin' she's in the middle of her bath."

"I see." He swallowed. "I won't be a moment."

Caden approached Anna's door at the same instant a serving lad arrived with their meals. He waved the lad off and grasped the rolling cart laden with two covered dishes, a carafe of ruby colored wine, and two crystal goblets. Taking a bracing breath, he rapped his knuckles twice on the door before inserting the key into the lock.

Steam and fragrant oil a-la-Anna greeted him upon opening the door. Next came the sound of contented humming and gentle splashing, as if she hadn't heard the knock. She'd turned down the wall lamps, and most of the illumination came from the glowing hearth.

He drank in the sight of her, unable to move a muscle.

Something—a draft from the open door?—alerted her. Her humming ceased, water sloshed, and she dunked herself to the neck and twisted 'round to gape at him.

"Caden, what are you doing here?" she squeaked.

Sparing a moment to unburden himself of his valise and greatcoat, he pushed the meal cart further into the room and closed the door with a kick of his booted foot. He managed, just, to staunch the grin trying to curve his lips.

She stared at him, cheeks glistening, her dark, wet hair fanning over the water behind her like a sea nymph's.

Everything in him wanted to peel out of his clothes and climb into the fragrant bath with her. His smile faded as he imagined the feel of her. Skin slick and warm, every curve and hollow bared to his touch. His cock went ramrod hard and he thanked the stars she'd turned down the lamps.

"Well?" Water splashed as her hands emerged, spreading wide.

"The arrival of another patron forced the innkeeper to get creative in her chamber designations."

Her fine brows puckered. "Meaning?"

"There's one room to be had. We're sharing."

"That's hardly proper."

"My dear sister, I think we can manage for one night." He sounded as if he meant it. Impressive. "You don't mind if I eat? I'm starved."

She humphed and turned her back on him with dramatic flair.

He rolled the cart toward the chair near the window. It was uncomfortably cool on this side of the room, but it put him as far from Anna as possible. He still had an unobstructed view of her in that damn tub.

She shifted again, keeping her back to him, and sat up taller in the tub. She took a moment to twine her hair on the top of her head, exposing the graceful column of her neck. Her skin glowed in the firelight. Rivulets of water streamed down her nape and the center of her back, and, he could only imagine, over her breasts.

He tore his gaze off her and lifted one dish cover to reveal still-steaming beef stew, crusty bread, and a chunk of hard cheese.

The meal didn't look half bad. He pulled the stopper from the carafe and splashed some wine into one of the goblets.

He sipped. Forked up a bite.

Heard more splashing. Breathed in more of Anna's elegant scent.

He'd thought it fresh by the window? The room was too bloody warm by half. With one crook of his finger he unknotted his cravat and whipped it across the room to land near the door.

"What was that?" she demanded.

"I'm sure I have no idea." He ripped off a piece of bread and swiped up stew. "You might as well tell me your story tonight since we're both here. In this room. Together."

His gaze found its way back to her. He shoved the stew-sopped bread into his mouth.

She glanced over her shoulder at him. "You sound very strange."

"It's been a very strange night."

She was quiet a long minute. "You mentioned a family emergency called you away from the Fenton's party?"

"The earl's taken ill."

"I'm so sorry to hear that. Nothing serious, I hope?"

He growled in frustration. "I don't know. Your story?"

She scrunched low in the water and shimmied 'round to face him. "I'm not sure where to start."

"That's easy. Start at the beginning."

***

Anna frowned and considered where the beginning of her tale might be. The arrival of Angelique into her life seemed as good a place as any.

"After several years as a widower, Father remarried an apothecary whose shop he frequented. Her name is Angelique LeClare. A striking woman, tall, dark haired. He took a fancy to her on sight. I thought it a good thing. He'd mourned mother a long while."

"Fair enough."

"Angelique began to personally deliver the herbs and powders father requested. A particular friendship developed between them. An engagement ensued, and, soon after, a wedding."

"How did you feel about them marrying?"

She gave a one-shoulder shrug and suppressed a shiver. The bath water had gone tepid. Cold seeped into her bones with each passing minute. Eventually she'd have to get out. Having never found herself in such a situation—naked, in a tub, in the company of a man—she wasn't exactly sure how to broach the subject. Best to stay submerged a bit longer.

"He'd been terribly forlorn since mother's death. He was utterly devoted to her. Mother would not have had it any other way." She chuckled, remembering how her father had doted on her mother who always seemed to take his adoration as her due.

"Explains a few things," Caden muttered.

"Beg pardon?"

He raised his brows and sent her a guileless grin. "Nothing important. Go on."

She sniffed, and continued. "Angelique's presence seemed to lighten his spirits. It wasn't as if she tried to parent me. I was twenty when they wed, after all. My life went on as usual, at first.

"Then, for some reason, she let our housekeeper go. She claimed she wanted to see to the cooking and cleaning, only...most of the time, those duties fell to me. Especially when, after nearly a year of marriage, my father took ill."

"How do you mean?"

"He became distracted. Confused. Clumsy. It soon became evident he had developed an ailment, but I'd never seen anything like it. Angelique claimed to have knowledge of it, and, so, assumed his care. Nevertheless, his condition declined rapidly. He went from virile, to bed-ridden in a matter of months. One day, he simply didn't wake up.

"It all happened so fast. I hadn't considered what would befall us after his death. Certainly we'd never been poor, and I assumed he would have seen to me in his will. But..." She shook her head. "After meeting with father's solicitor, Angelique sat me down and informed me we were penniless. She said my mother's jewels had been sold off to pay father's debts. I hadn't known he had any significant debts."

Caden leaned forward in his chair, gaze intent. "I'm confused. You told me your husband left you penniless after stealing your inheritance, or something to that effect. Now you're saying you had no inheritance to speak of."

"If you'll let me finish? You're jumping ahead. And, Caden?"

He studied her, an unreadable expression on his face. "Yes?"

"The water is quite chilly."

Several seconds passed. "Shall I hold the towel for you?"

She blinked, unable to tell if he teased her. "No, of course not. Just...er...close your eyes?"

"Of course," he agreed easily. He leaned back in his chair, legs stretched out before him, arms folded over his chest.

She peered at him. He sat very still, eyelids closed, silent as a church mouse. The bland expression on his face proclaimed him bored beyond measure.

Feeling unaccountably deflated by the notion, she rose, water sluicing down her body. Goosebumps fanned over her skin as the chill night air enveloped her. She climbed over the edge of the tub, grabbed the towel the maid had provided, and scrubbed the rough white cotton over her skin.

Something made her pause. She squinted over her shoulder at Caden.

He had not moved one iota, as far as she could tell. She sniffed and resumed drying herself with the small linen.

Apparently he could care less she stood naked not ten feet away from him. He clearly no longer desired her. She could blame that entirely on his learning she'd married Baron Bolton. Only, hadn't he pushed her away mid-kiss not once but twice, prior to learning about Bolton? Maybe he hadn't liked how she kissed. Maybe her inexperience repelled him.

She wound the towel around the length of her hair, squeezing out the moisture.

Whatever the reason, it was clear his attraction for her had waned. Even so, he remained chivalrous to a fault. Rather than toss her out on her ear when he found her crawling out of the luggage hold, he secured her a chamber, a hot meal, and a steaming bath.

"Finished?" He sounded irritated. Probably he was anxious to get to the end of her tale.

"Nearly." She abandoned her efforts to dry her hair and ran on tiptoes toward the armoire where she'd hung a morning dress meant for tomorrow.

Eschewing a chemise in the interest of time, she yanked the gown off its hanger and tugged it over her head, wrestling it over still-clammy skin. She tightened the ribbon at her bodice with clumsy, half-frozen fingers.

She faced him. "You can open your eyes now."

He stirred, eyelids slowly lifting. He uncrossed, then re-crossed his ankles, cocking his head to study her.

"Go sit near the hearth where it's warm, Gloriana." With that, he unfolded himself from the chair.

She padded to the wingback armchair, the wooden planks warming under her bare feet as she neared the grate. She sank into the chair. The cushions were deliciously toasty and their heat flowed through the folds of her gown, cocooning her with warmth. She groaned.

In the act of dragging the cart, Caden stumbled, cursing under his breath.

"Everything all right?" she asked.

"Fine," he muttered, situating the table in front of her.

He removed the cover from her dish, filled a goblet of wine and handed it to her, then strode back to the window. He grasped the wooden chair he'd vacated with one hand, returned to place it opposite hers with the table between them, and resumed his seat.

He picked up his fork, pausing before continuing his meal. He frowned at her untouched dish. "You need to eat something, Anna."

Her heartbeat thumped painfully in her chest as hope blossomed inside her. "Why are you being so nice to me?"

He scooped up a bite, lips twitching as he chewed. He dabbed his napkin at his lips. "When it's so obviously not in my nature, you mean? You were expecting me to look after my own needs and to hell with yours? Not to worry. You're in fine company with that opinion."

"*Don't.*"

He smiled in sardonic amusement, his eyes glinting glacial blue. "Beg pardon?"

"Please don't turn my words into something ugly. I meant, why are you being so nice to me when I don't deserve it?"

He gazed at her for an interminable minute, an unreadable expression on his beautiful face. "I'm not being overly-kind. I'm doing what any man in my position would do."

She disagreed, but before she could argue the point, he went on.

"You stopped your tale with finding yourself penniless. What happened next?"

She had her answer. The bath, the food, all his small niceties, owed to nothing more than his inherent chivalry. He no longer had any special feeling for her, if he ever had.

Little fool. As her father often said, "If wishes were horses, beggars would ride."

He cocked his head. "I don't follow."

She'd spoken her thoughts aloud again. She must be more exhausted than she realized. "It's just an expression."

Her answer seemed to baffle him.

She went on before he could ask again. "Things went from bad to worse. Not only were we penniless, we were drowning in debt, in imminent jeopardy of losing the house, all our be-longings, and likely bound for the workhouse to pay off father's debts—or worse."

Their eyes met. For a split second, she thought she saw a flick-er of compassion in his eyes, rather than the infernal detached curiosity.

"Angelique came up with a plan—to save us, she said. She said the simplest solution was for me to marry. When I pointed out I hadn't any suitors, she brought the baron to meet me. Before I knew it, a contract was drawn-up and signed, and we both moved into his"—Her face crumpled in distaste—"home in London. She insisted the living situation would enable he and I to become better acquainted."

His jaw tightened in evident disapproval. "I see. And did it?"

Anna stirred her stew, recalling the dark and dingy ramshackle-of-a-mansion that she soon realized was more of a prison than an abode.

She shook her head. "Oddly, the man was not in residence—at first."

"That is odd."

She gazed at him, considering. "Caden, earlier tonight, you indicated you knew Lord Bolton. "

His expression turned grim. "I wouldn't say I know him. I know *of* him. I did have occasion to meet him as a boy, with my father. The two were friends. I did not care for him in the slightest."

He broke off a chunk of bread and handed it to her.

She accepted his offering, nibbled, and waited for him to elaborate.

"My personal opinion aside, it's common knowledge the baron cares nothing for his title, nor the responsibilities that go with it. He's long since lost any non-entailed lands. He's all about the drink, horse racing, and the hells—which is precisely why I can not fathom..." He broke off abruptly, picked up his wine, and took a healthy swallow.

"How did this Angelique expect your *courtship*"—He stressed the word in such a way as to indicate he saw it as nothing of the sort—"to advance in his absence? For that matter, how did this Angelique come to know Baron Bolton?"

She swallowed a morsel of cheese and laughed, self-conscious. "I'm embarrassed to admit, I haven't a clue how she knew him.

As for the two of us getting acquainted, I'm convinced she wanted nothing of the sort."

Caden leaned back and crossed his arms over his chest. "Why-ever not?"

"I believe the man to whom I was introduced, the man with whom I believed myself engaged, was not Lord Bolton."

"What are you saying? That your step-mother introduced you to a decoy? You're certain?"

"Certain? No. Angelique denied it when I asked her about it."

She ate more cheese, questioning her own memory for the thousandth time. "Maybe I had it wrong. Maybe I saw what I wanted to see at first. So much is a blur about those early days after my father's death."

"I see." His tone said he didn't see at all.

She lifted her chin. "I'd like to make one thing clear. Even before I met the true Lord Bolton, I decided I could not possibly go through with the marriage. I planned to find employment—as a tutor, a companion, a nanny. Angelique could go back to working in the apothecary. As for father's debts, I wasn't exactly sure what to do. I assumed Angelique and I would work it out together."

He set his fork down with exquisite care. "You changed your mind about the marriage?"

"I did."

"Why?"

"I didn't see the point. Perhaps, for some, marriage is a business arrangement. That's not a good enough reason for me to wed."

He searched her face. "What would be?"

For some reason, she found it hard to draw a steady breath. "We're straying from the subject."

He inclined his head.

She sipped some wine, then started on the stew. The beef all but melted in her mouth.

She scooped up another bite before continuing. "When I shared my decision with Angelique, I expected some resistance. I never anticipated the rage she flew into. She shook me 'til I thought my teeth would fall out, then ordered her pet footman to lock me in my chamber. Brutus, she called him. He was a beast of a man, more paid muscle than house servant."

"Good Lord, Anna."

She smiled a humorless smile. "My goals changed in a blink. First and foremost, I needed to escape, which meant pretending to come to my senses. Angelique was no fool, however; She kept me under guard. I never said a word in protest. Rather, I became a dutiful daughter, acquiescent and aiming to please."

Caden snorted.

She slid him a quelling look and he sobered, though his eyes twinkled with a mischievous light that eased some of the growing tension inside her and tempted her to smile at the rogue. She bit the inside of her cheek, resisting the impulse.

"When she went out for the day, as she often did, I combed the house, searching for anything I could use for my eventual escape. I knew I would need to find work, so I sequestered myself in the reading room and wrote out several fine letters of recommendation for myself."

"Ah. The infamous forged letters." He lounged back in his chair, wine glass in hand. "And what of Bolton? He didn't...er...trouble you?"

She shrugged and toyed with a damp lock of her hair. "I won't say he didn't occasionally leer at me. But more often than not, he was simply too far into his cups to present much of a threat."

Caden gave an indeterminate grunt.

"One afternoon, after Angelique went out, I waited near her bedchamber for the lone, harried chambermaid to carry out the used bedding. As I hoped, she didn't bother with locking the door behind her when she left. I stole inside." She clenched her jaw. "That's when I discovered my mother's jewelry had not been sold. It sat in a drawer in Angelique's vanity. Angelique had all of it. My mother's pearls, the wedding ring my father had given her, her ruby pendant."

Should she tell him about pawning the ruby, and finding it in her trunk? She supposed she should finish explaining her entanglement with Lord Bolton, first.

"That raises some interesting questions."

"Indeed. She'd lied about my mother's jewels. What else might she have lied about, and why? Regardless of what her possible motives, I was furious enough to take the lot. But...if she noticed, I had no notion how far she'd go to punish me. So I left everything exactly as I found it—save mother's pendant. She'd always worn it; I could never remember seeing her without it, and I...I couldn't help myself. I hid it under my mattress with the letters I'd written and vowed to leave that night, somehow, some way."

He leaned forward, elbows propped on his knees. A muscle in his jaw ticked. "They caught you, trying to escape?"

She shook her head. "They drugged me. Angelique is an accomplished apothecary, but I had never considered she might try something like that. One minute I was eating my evening meal, the next..."

She drew her fist to her mouth. "I have vague memories of being in Bolton's moldering chapel. I recall standing before, I assume, a priest, Lord Bolton beside me, Angelique behind me, whispering if I answered wrong, she'd make me regret it."

She squeezed her eyes shut. "So I thought, just keep quiet. Don't say a word. Maybe the priest would notice something amiss and offer assistance."

Cursing softly, Caden shoved the table from between them. He took both of her hands between his.

Funny. She hadn't realized her fingers had grown so cold until the warmth from his palms seeped into hers.

"Angelique wouldn't have it. She took me aside and slapped my face, hard, 'til I promised I'd answer correctly. God help me, I did.

"Afterward, they sent me to my room. I must have fallen asleep because, when I woke, it was full-on night. I heard voices—probably what awakened me. Angelique screamed at Bolton. She told him she hadn't gone through all the trouble she had for him to blunder everything in the final hour. She said she didn't care what he did with me afterward, but that he needed to..." She swallowed, "...get the deed done before she returned. I gathered she meant..." Her words died in her throat.

"She meant for him to bed you," Caden said, his mouth set in a grim line.

"Had I been thinking, I'd have barred my door. Instead I stumbled out to the landing in time to witness Angelique flying out the front door. He looked up and saw me, frozen at the top of the stairs. He said, '*Come on girl. Let's get this over with.*' I ran back to the bedchamber. He pursued me."

Caden ducked his head, tunneling his fingers through his hair. "Sweetheart."

"I tripped. I was still groggy."

"Sweetheart, it's all right. You don't have to—"

"—He grabbed my ankles and tried to pull me across the floor toward the bed. I resisted with all my might. He must've given up, because I heard him unfasten his trousers. He said we could do it the hard way. When he fell atop me, his legs bracketing mine, I didn't think. I grabbed for whatever I could reach, then swung it 'round with all my might."

Admiration and a glint of moisture shone in his eyes. "Little hellion. Fire poker?"

She'd never said a word of this to anyone. For some odd reason, she felt better, lighter, with the telling.

She sent him a tremulous smile. "Chamber pot. I thought I'd killed him."

He blinked once, then threw his head back and roared with laughter. "Only you. Death by chamber pot. Would've served the bastard right."

Chapter Sixteen

aden's humor faded as quickly as it had come. Anna had survived a harrowing ordeal. More than survived. She'd triumphed against a devil-spawned step-mother, and a vile excuse for a man.

And he'd assumed the worst about her. He hated himself in that moment.

"I'm sorry. For the things I said, back at Femsworth Manor. You didn't deserve any of it."

"Apology accepted," she whispered.

Just like that. Despite his cruelty, how harsh he'd been.

"You're incredible," he breathed.

Cheeks going rosy, she waved his words away. "I'm an idiot, more like."

He glanced at the table he'd shoved away when his need to touch her had overridden all else. "You barely ate a thing."

He rose and pulled it back into position in front of her.

Damn, but she smelled good. Fresh from her bath, her delicate scent wafted off her skin like evening blossoms.

He snapped up the folded serviette beside her plate, then bent to lay it over her lap. His gaze trailed over the loosely tied front of her gown and his breath caught in his throat.

The woman would be the death of him. In her haste to don a gown, she hadn't taken the time for undergarments, as he well knew. The result? The rosy outline of her coin sized nipples were just visible through the bodice—if one happened to be looking.

He straightened and dragged his gaze to the plaster-tiled ceiling. "*Bon appetite.*"

"*Merci, mére,*" she said, a smile evident in her voice as she tucked in to her now, undoubtedly, tepid stew.

"As for your self-proclaimed idiocy..."

She snorted, clearly anticipating a snarky comment.

"Tell me again why you're to blame for any of this?"

She took a moment to swallow her last bite before replying. "Only an idiot would agree to a marriage after one meeting, as I did, even if the man—the decoy, as you dubbed him—was a much younger, pleasant seeming chap."

Caden had begun pacing the room, mostly to put some distance between them. Her words stopped him in his tracks. "Who was the man, I wonder?"

She picked up a piece of cheese, examining it between her fingers. "Bolton's secretary? I'm not at all certain. As I said,

Angelique denied I'd met anyone other than Lord Bolton." She nibbled the cheese.

Caden frowned. "You said she drugged you the night of your so-called ceremony. Maybe she'd started plying your wits with something before that."

Anna gaped briefly. "You know, I never considered that. I should have. It's not as if I've no experience in such matters, having helped mother create her tinctures. Too, I assisted father for years. I should have known."

"Why should you have? At the time you had no reason to question her."

She gave him a grateful smile. "I still have no notion why it behooved her to marry me off to the man. Except that it obviously did."

Unable to peel his eyes off her, Caden sauntered back to the spindly chair. He spun it around and straddled the seat, then rested his folded arms on the seat-back.

"I think we can safely assume she had a financial motive. Bolton hasn't had a pot to..." He cleared his throat. "...hasn't had means for some time, so it's unlikely she expected a payoff from him. That leaves you."

"Me?"

"Yes. Perhaps your father left you as sole heir to his estate?"

She appeared to give his words some thought, then shook her head. "I don't think so. He would have told me, and, besides, I don't think he would have done that to Angelique. He appeared quite fond of her before his illness took him."

"Hm." It was about money. Caden could feel it.

She lay her serviette across her nearly empty dish and sent him a replete smile. Faint, dark circles underscored her eyes. "That was lovely. Thank you."

Their gazes caught and held. Something warm and intoxicating invaded his chest and spread like wildfire to all his extremities. Having learned the truth of her ordeal, her bravery, her utter blamelessness, every defense he'd erected against her siren's call vanished. Mere lust he could handle. What flooded his veins now was...something more.

He was suddenly grateful for the chair and cart and every scrap of distance between them.

Still, the moment stretched, with neither of them looking away. When her eyelids dipped and her lips parted Caden's control stretched to the breaking point.

Enough.

He would not take advantage of her again. For that was exactly what he'd done, misapprehension about her situation or no. He had noted her incongruous innocence, and nearly made love to her regardless. Then he'd learned of her married status and insulted her to boot.

Dear God. Anna was—had to be—a virgin. Bloody hell.

He cleared his throat and shoved up from the chair. He carried it back to its place near the window and sat. Outside, the storm had finally died down. If it cleared up by morning, he'd be heading for Derby. And Anna? Did she plan to continue the journey with him?

As if he would give her a choice. She would accompany him to Chissington Hall, and that was final.

"Let's see if I can work out the rest of your story. You left Bolton's that evening, took those letters of recommendation you'd so presciently forged straight to an agency, and somehow lucked into your position with Lady Wentworth."

"You have the gist." Anna stretched and made a sound that was half sigh, half yawn. "I endured a terrifying, if successful, visit to the pawn brokers and a rescinded offer of employment before Lady Wentworth happened upon me. She hired me on sight, thanks to having no time to verify my references. I don't understand how she came to know the details of my marriage, nor why she went to so much trouble to assure my safety."

"Perhaps she looked into your background after hiring you on, as a precaution. The natural affinity the two of you share probably explains the rest."

"Perhaps..." Bending her knees, she drew her feet up to curl them under her skirts and rested her cheek against the wingback cushion. She stared into the glowing grate as if it held the answers to all life's mysteries.

In the reflected firelight she looked beautiful and fragile, like fine-boned china. But she wasn't weak. Far from it.

He found himself smiling, despite her harrowing tale. There was only one other woman he knew with such a strength. Kitty, his brother's wife. She would like Anna, he decided.

Her face softened and her eyelids drooped as exhaustion overtook her.

"You should go to bed. You're half asleep already."

"I'm fine here. You take the bed."

"I insist. Go lie down." He rose and headed for the door.

"Where are you going?" she asked, sitting up.

He un-shot the lock and wrapped his hand around the cold brass lever.

"You'll want to change into your night dress before getting into bed." He swallowed hard and continued in a voice that sounded almost normal, "I'd rather that happen while I'm gone." Without waiting for her reply, he let himself into the hall.

***

He stalked down the dim, musty-smelling corridor to the wide staircase. He trotted down the stairs, anxious to put distance between himself and Anna.

He was in serious trouble. The ache to make love to her was now compounded by an even greater desire to fold her up in his arms. He wanted to cherish and protect her so no harm befell her, ever again.

Absurd. He was no Prince Charming, and well she knew it. He'd offered her proof positive at the Fenton's when he berated her after nearly bedding her.

Lucky for both of them he had a compelling need to step out. A baron had claimed Caden's chamber tonight. Certainly,

England boasted more than a few. Could be a coincidence. On the other hand, it could *not* be one.

With grim certainty, he knew a fool-safe method to determine whether Bolton was on premises. He need only visit the bar.

He crossed the vacant lobby. Shouldering aside the red velvet-drape divider, he passed through an archway into the inn's pub-style eatery. The smell of moldering bar mats, stale tobacco, and too-oft spilled-upon carpets warred with the kitchen's hardy fare, to permeate the air.

Well past the dinner hour, all of the wooden tables lining one wall of the narrow establishment sat empty, but a fire still burned in the grate and a barman still manned the short bar.

A lone man stood before him, huddling over what appeared to be a snifter of brandy.

A tall man, he wore a coat and trousers fashioned of black superfine. At first glance, the patron's attire reflected wealth and status. But upon closer inspection, the suit of clothes had a shoddy, faded appearance that matched the man himself—a man Caden recognized all too well.

Baron Bolton had lost the air of vitality that had made him seem somehow larger than life the few times Caden had the misfortune to encounter him. He'd lost some height and his broad shoulders had narrowed. His thick cap of hair, once dark brown, had gone dingy gray, and was badly in need of a cut.

Oblivious to Caden's perusal, Bolton carried on a one-sided conversation with the barman. He gestured, snifter in hand, then threw back his head and laughed uproariously.

A chill ran up Caden's spine. That laugh. Like time reversed, he saw himself, nine years old, trailing after his father as he made his social rounds. In his youthful naiveté he'd imagined his presence might sway his father from his usual debauched lifestyle. He'd told Zeke as much, prompting his older brother to predict Caden would only provide an audience for their father as he drank and gambled his way across town.

As usual, Zeke's words proved correct.

When they called on Bolton, it hadn't taken long to recognize the baron and his father as birds of a feather. Caden found himself in the baron's dark-paneled, tobacco smoke-filled game-room. He watched the mantle clock tick in mounting misery as the two men played billiards, waxed laconic over their perceived woes, and drank themselves stupid.

Long buried images flooded his mind. Bolton complaining about tenants, shrewish women, and gambling losses. His father, stumbling around the green-baize table, bemoaning the death of his wife and the lack of sympathy shown him by his father, the earl. And then there was the problem of Zeke.

Caden shook his head to clear the memory. It stuck like a red-wine stain on a white linen shirt.

Jaw clenched, he joined Bolton's party of one. To the barman's look of inquiry, he gave a gruff, "Ale."

A moment later, a frothy-topped stein appeared before him on the polished bar.

As if suddenly cognizant of Caden's presence, the baron leaned onto his elbow, angling his body toward him.

A nearly overwhelming compulsion to smash his fist into the man's face threatened to overwhelm Caden's good sense. Bolton deserved that and worse for what he'd nearly done to Anna.

But he did not have the luxury of indulging his need for vengeance. Not now. Not yet.

The older man's thick brows arched, as if he recognized Caden's malevolent intent and found it vaguely intriguing. "Do I know you?"

Caden couldn't bring himself to speak for fear of what would come out of his mouth.

A slow smile curved Bolton's thin lips. "By God, you're one of Thurgood's boys. I'd recognize you lot anywhere. You have his look—right down to that shiner. He had more than his share of those."

He scrutinized Caden, eyes narrowing in thought. "You're not the heir, though. The younger, I think." He snorted. "Your father didn't have your flat stare down, that's for certain. If he had, he might have occasionally bested me at cards." Bolton chuckled. "Name's Bolton. Believe I met you when you were a lad."

Caden wrestled his anger under control. Barely. "I believe so."

"I tell you, Bolton, when I look in my eldest son's eyes I see my father, the stingy prick who won't give over the title and funds rightfully mine."

"That's a bloody crime, Thurgood."

"Mark me, Ezekiel's just like him. Looks at me like I'm dirt. Then there's this one." He aimed his cue stick and a fond smile at Caden. "Makes me proud. He's got my joie de vivre, *my charm. Already he can talk a penny off a miser, and no female alive can resist him. When he's a man, he'll be just like me."*

With a ruthless effort of will, Caden banished the long-ago memories. The present needed his full attention. So far, he was doing a bang-up job.

Bolton's brows furrowed, as if he didn't know what to make of Caden's attitude. Finally, he shrugged and took a large swallow of brandy.

"What brings you to York?" Caden asked, striving for a conversational tone.

"Heading for a house party. You're not, by any chance, on your way to one?"

His hands clenched into fists. He slid them into his trouser pockets. Soon, he'd deal with Bolton. "Leaving one."

"In this weather? Get caught with the wrong man's wife?"

If he only knew. "Matters at home require my immediate attention."

"Pity." The baron's eyes turned sly. "By any chance, leaving Femsworth Manor?"

Caden issued a nod. "As it happens."

"Rumor has it the Dowager Duchess of Wentworth's a guest."

He pretended to consider the question. "I did make her acquaintance, briefly. The lady keeps to herself."

The baron nodded with greasy satisfaction. "I hear tell she travels with a young companion."

He drew the snifter to his mouth and downed the remaining liquid with one toss of his head.

Caden's blood boiled with renewed rage. Sweat trickled down the center of his back.

"Another," Bolton barked at the barman. "And one for my friend. Tonight is a night for celebrating."

Caden slashed a hand at the barman. He'd accept nothing from the bastard. He grasped his stein of ale so tightly his knuckles turned white. "What are you celebrating?"

Bolton smirked into his full snifter. "A long awaited return on investment."

He referred to Anna, of that Caden had no doubt. *Return on investment.* Damn it, *how* would marriage to her benefit Bolton financially? All he knew for certain was that the baron had attempted to cement the legality of his marital claim by doing the unthinkable with the woman Caden—

His mind went blank, and time seemed to stop.

With the woman he *what?*

Acid burned in his gut. Seeing Bolton had his mind—and body—in a tailspin.

He could sort everything now by simply wrapping his hands around the man's neck and squeezing the life out of him. But if someone stopped him, or if someone didn't and he wound up in irons, who would protect Anna? He'd made so many mistakes with her already. He would not foul this up, too.

He pushed his half-full stein toward the barkeep. He had the answer he sought. He'd get Anna to safety. Then he'd deal with Bolton.

***

The chamber door gave a soft click. Anna came fully awake, though she didn't move so much as a muscle. She lay still, bedsheets pulled to her nose, listening.

She'd nodded off after lying in bed staring at the plaster tiled ceiling, waiting for Caden to return. She had no idea how much time had passed, but based on the notable lack of heat in the room, and the absence of light behind her eyelids, the fire in the hearth had long since died.

Rustling noises sounded near the door. Then one boot heel thumped the wooden floorboards, and he gave a low curse.

After a moment she heard his soft footfalls and the faint brush of his trousers as he padded toward the basin, *sans* boots.

Fabric whispered as he stripped. Her mouth went dry imagining that supple, bronzed skin, bared. Water splashed oh-so-quietly, then she heard a scrubbing sound as he washed. Something warm and decadent pulsed in her belly.

He crossed the room. A scraping noise sounded within the grate, followed by loud pops as embers ignited in the hearth. Soon, light flickered behind her closed eyelids and warmth dispelled the chill.

The armchair creaked in protest as Caden, she presumed, settled in for the night.

She rolled onto her back, sheets rustling, mattress squeaking, her eyes pinched shut.

He had to have heard her. Did he study her even now? Her heart thudded hard in her chest as she waited for him to say something.

He huffed out a muffled, disgruntled sigh, shifted his weight, then nothing.

Seconds ticked by. He either hadn't heard her move, or didn't care that she might be awake.

She opened her eyes, suddenly, unaccountably vexed. Before she could stop herself, she said in a too-loud voice, "You don't—"

Caden gave a yelp of surprise.

"—have to sleep sitting up." She giggled and said more softly, "I didn't mean to startle you."

He grunted, noncommittal. "I didn't mean to wake you."

"You didn't," she lied, then cleared her throat. "There's plenty of room on the bed for both of us. You must lie atop the cover, of course."

He made no comment.

"Caden?"

"Go back to sleep," he growled.

Her heart sank for reasons she chose not to examine. "Are you angry with me?"

"No," he clipped out.

She sat up, and fingered the long braid she'd tied her hair into before slipping into bed.

He'd positioned the armchair to face the hearth, putting his back toward her. His thick hair gleamed in the firelight. Gads, but his shoulders were broad. They barely fit in the chair.

"You can't be comfortable there."

"I'm fine." His subsequent shift belied his words.

"Stubborn to the end."

He heaved a long-suffering sigh. "Leave it, Anna. Trust me. I'm fine here. I don't imagine I'll sleep tonight, regardless." Raw emotion underscored his words.

Her insides twisted. Something was eating at him. Was it what she'd shared earlier? The complications she brought to the table? Or was it the earl? She licked her lips, then flung off the bedcovers and slid her legs over the side of the mattress.

His head jerked in her direction. The silhouette of his profile, limned in the low firelight, revealed a severe frown. "Anna?"

She recognized both wariness and a warning to stay back in his tone.

Undeterred, she crossed the room to face him, her backside absorbing the delicious heat of the fire.

Sprawled atop the armchair, long legs outstretched before him, he glared at her. He wore his thick silk robe. Loosely belted, it exposed a large amount of naked torso. He had refrained from removing his black trousers, but had taken off his boots and stockings, leaving his well-shaped feet bare.

In the stuttering light of the fire, the hard lines of his face combined with the blueish stain above his brow to give him the look of a privateer of old—or the Robin-hood of their childhood, grown to manhood.

His blue eyes glittered like cut glass. "Anna, go back to bed."

"What's happened, Caden? Something has. I feel it."

He laughed without a trace of mirth. "What's wrong? Aside from everything?"

She lifted her chin as guilt assailed her. "I see. You're upset because of me. Because of the position I've put you in. I...never mind." She started back toward the bed.

Quick as a snake, his big hand darted out and grasped her wrist.

"Anna," he whispered harshly. "I'm not upset because of you."

He released her and unfolded himself from the armchair. The silk tie of his robe unknotted and the lapels gaped. He brought himself toe to toe with her and grasped her shoulders.

Her heart raced—from his nearness, his touch, the scent of warm male skin teasing her nostrils. "If not me, then what? I know something's put you in a mood. Something's different since you stepped out of this chamber."

Silence stretched between them, punctuated by the snapping logs in the hearth. She longed to wrap her arms around him, to press her cheek to his bare chest, but she resisted, fearing he'd push her away.

It was all well and good for Caden to rescue her, to take on the role of Prince Charming to her Princess—now as when they were children. But him, admit a weakness or need? Ha. The charming, laughing, oft-times irascible Caden would not give up his cavalier veneer easily.

With shaking fingers, she settled for reaching up to trace the blue tinge above his wound. "As predicted, you look quite ruggedly handsome."

One corner of his mouth kicked upward in a wicked grin that had her stomach doing somersaults.

"Do I?" His tone was easy, but his hands, tightening on her shoulders, told a different story.

Her fingers cruised over his stubble-covered jaw to curve around his warm nape.

Her voice dropped to a whisper. "You owe it all to my tending, of course. The swelling's vastly improved, and hardly more than a tinge of color testifies to your injury."

He closed his eyes and a shudder went through him. "You see? I'm fine. All thanks to you."

He released her shoulders, and grasped her wrist. With gentle pressure, he peeled her hand from him neck.

The rejection stung. "Caden, please."

He searched her eyes as a muscle ticked in his jaw. "What do you want from me, Anna?"

"You've asked me, repeatedly, to trust you, to confide in you. I'm asking the same of you."

His mouth worked, but no words came.

Just as she gave up hope he would confide in her, his rumbling baritone curled into her ear. "Did you ever meet my father, Glory?"

She released the breath she hadn't known she'd been holding and shook her head.

His mouth twisted into a smirk. "Count your blessings. He was a right bastard. In his cups more often than not. Selfish. Weak."

He shifted away from her to face the flames, tunneling his fingers in his hair. "Zeke's nothing like him."

She blinked, trying to follow the thread of his thoughts. *Zeke* wasn't like their father? "Did someone say he was?"

"Oh, he resembles our father. We both do. But inside..." He broke off to thump the center of his chest with his fist. "Inside, he's nothing like the man who sired us. No, Zeke took after the earl. Steadfast. Responsible. Someone you can count on to always know—and do—the right thing."

She arched a brow. She remembered Zeke as an arrogant, bossy boy who carried himself like a king and had no use for girls.

Caden gazed into the flames as if seeing into the past. "I told you just before attending the house party I quarreled with Zeke and the earl. I never said I instigated the entire affair. Suffice it to say I sought Zeke out, ironically intending to offer to my services in the overhaul of the quarry, to ease him of the responsibility. I ended up overhearing the two of them in a heated discussion about me."

He slanted her a look. "Zeke was grousing to the earl about my wastrel ways. Claimed I'd perfected the art of gallivanting about England, jumping from house party to house party, doing nothing productive with my life. The earl defended me, of course."

He switched his attention back to the grate, his jaw hard as granite. "Said I wasn't frequenting hells like our father, as if that was some sort of major accomplishment."

He huffed out a mirthless laugh. "He was wrong, by-the-by. I've spent many a night at the hells. I just happen to be lucky—unlike our father. As I've had no need for their assistance in digging myself out of a catastrophic loss, neither the earl nor Zeke have a clue."

She licked her lips. "I see. You got angry after overhearing your brother saying some not very nice things about you, and your grandfather not doing such a stellar job defending you to him. Understandable, considering what you intended to offer. I presume you lost your temper?"

"In spades, and you know why that is? Because the best defense is a good offense. Zeke's accusations hit a lot too close to home. I said something to the effect of, 'if you think I was a bad bet before, watch out.' Then I left—and ran straight into you." With that, he issued a bitter laugh that had gooseflesh springing up all over her body.

She started to ask what seeing her at the Fenton's house party had to do with this conversation, but some sixth sense had her biting her tongue.

Hands fisting at his sides, Caden paced the darkened chamber, prowling the room like a caged lion. "I mentioned earlier I'd met Bolton. I was a child, nine or ten years of age, hanging onto my father's apron strings like some damned toddler, all the while hoping my presence might somehow convince him to give a damn about Zeke or me or himself for that matter. It was after our mother had died.

"Father had truly sunk into the abyss—not that I understood that. I only saw it clearly in retrospect. To be honest, I now know he wasn't the staunchest of men before her death."

"Oh, Caden," she whispered, heartbroken for the little boy he'd been.

"Zeke told me not to bother. Told me I was wasting my time. But I refused to listen. As usual, Zeke's words proved true."

"What happened?"

"We were in London for the season. Father was making his social calls and I begged to join him. We arrived at Bolton's and there we stayed. They drank—my father, into a stupor—and played an interminably long game of billiards. I distinctly recall my father bemoaning the cruel fate that had prematurely stolen his wife and landed him with Zeke for an heir. I stood up, meaning to defend my brother."

She gave him a tender smile. "Caden. Ever the champion for justice."

"There was nothing noble about my motives, Anna. Father's criticisms were unfair and unfounded. Regardless, before I could say a word—" He broke off and drew a ragged breath.

He held out an arm, acting out his memory. "My father pointed his cue stick at me and said....I was just like him. That I would grow up and be *just like him.*"

Anna could not stay still one moment longer. She flew to him and wrapped her arms around him.

His skin was slightly damp, and feverishly hot. After a moment he returned the embrace. His arms, tight around her, felt so good. So right. She'd thought never to feel their strength surrounding her again.

"Oh, Caden, what a perfectly dreadful memory. Your father was ill. He spoke nonsense. You have to know that."

To her utter disappointment, he released her, untwined her arms from around him, and took a full step back, putting distance between them for the second time in a span of minutes. In the meager light from the grate, his face was harder than she'd ever seen it.

"No, Anna. You don't understand. He was right. And Zeke was right. I think I've always known it. I just didn't allow myself to see it until now. Until you."

Chapter Seventeen

Anna didn't like his brutal assessment of himself, nor how he twisted her into his self recriminations. "All true? Until me? Rubbish."

"I beg your pardon?"

"You heard me, Caden Thurgood. Your summation is utter nonsense. You are nothing like the man you just described. Unless you're always in your altitudes and have somehow managed to hide that truth from me and the rest of the world?"

She began examining his face, jaw and neck.

"Allow me to point out—what in God's name are you doing, Anna?"

She stopped her perusal and arched a brow. "I spent years helping my father treat men such as your father, dissipated from excessive drink. I'm sorry to refute your basis for self-loathing, but I don't see the loose jowls, saggy neck, nor any other of the physical signs of long-practiced debauchery."

He snorted, and Anna was encouraged to see a brief glint of humor in his eyes.

"I'm no drunkard."

"Then you're addicted to cards? Horse racing? To the disgusting practice of rooster fighting?"

"Rooster fighting?" He sounded appalled. "Of course not."

"To laying outlandish wagers on fights or duels or any number of unknown outcomes, then?"

"No." He drew out the word as if speaking to an ignorant child. "I do, however, play for sport, in spite of my family's understandable views."

"Because you can't resist the call of that unattainable, life-altering win. Is that it?"

He rolled his eyes. "I've never heard any particular call."

As she'd surmised. "Then what? Do you at least make a practice of wagering all you own and then some?"

She expected a ready, *No.*

Instead, he paused before replying. "It's not a practice. But, there was a time I did just that."

As if in emphasis, a glowing log in the grate snapped. Embers erupted up the chute.

She wrapped her arms around her midsection. "Go on, then."

"It was during my days at university. My last year. By then, Zeke traveled almost constantly, seeking the elusive pot of gold at the rainbow's end—for the family."

Anna made a scoffing sound. "Another sort of gambling if you ask me."

Caden slanted her a quelling glance. "I wanted to take some of the burden off him. Our father had squandered Claybourne's resources 'til there was virtually nothing left to draw upon. Zeke and the earl had to scrape together every shilling, call in every favor, to keep the estate running and undo the damage caused by father's mismanagement and, as it happened, outright siphoning of resources.

"As if by miracle, Zeke kept food on our tables and all our servants employed. He kept the creditors off our backs and Chissington Hall from crumbling at our feet."

"You admire him greatly, do you not?" she murmured, gently.

Caden laughed softly, as if seeing the truth of her words and somewhat surprised by them.

"I suppose I do." He cleared his throat. "I wanted to help. I had a year left before I graduated Oxford. I told him, thanks to my marks, I'd acquired a benefactor who'd agreed to pay my tuition, housing, expenses, for my last year."

"I take it there was no benefactor?"

He shook his head. "The previous year, I scrimped and saved my quarterly allowance, sometimes going without food. I ventured into the hells, father's stomping grounds. I watched. I learned. I played. I won. I doubled down. Then tripled. I couldn't lose. Neither Zeke nor the earl had a clue."

Anna stayed silent, riveted by Caden's tale.

"I was more than lucky, I had—have—a knack for reading people at the tables. I know when to fold, I know when to ante up. I know when to walk away. I don't *need* the game...I'm good at it, if that makes sense? Even now, especially now—since then—I only dabble for fun."

"Since then. What happened?"

"A school mate of mine came to me, in financial straights. He'd heard of my skills and asked for my help. Said he knew of a tourney. Very secret, very high stakes. He convinced me to combine our funds to raise the sum necessary to enter. Every penny we had went into the pot."

"And you lost."

Caden scrubbed a hand over his jaw. "Not only did I lose, but it turned out my friend's contribution came from borrowed funds. His creditors beat him to within an inch of his life when they learned he couldn't pay. They threatened to kill him if he didn't come up with the scratch. The money he needed was....exorbitant. I could have killed him myself when I realized what he'd done—and that I would have to go to Zeke."

"Your brother bailed you out?"

Caden laughed without mirth. "He did. And discovered in the process the game was rigged. He got most of my money back. But by then, his suspicions were aroused. He set up a meeting with me, the dean, and the minister of finance. Needless to say, everything came out. That there was no benefactor, that I had been gambling to cover my tuition, my expenses, that I was the biggest disappointment of his life since father."

"Caden, that's not fair. However misguided, he had to know you were trying to help—both him and your friend."

"I nearly got my friend killed."

"*Your friend* nearly got *himself* killed. Correct me if my suspicions prove incorrect, but you had paid all your bills. Your share came from what was left."

"That's not the point." He glared at her, clearly irritated over her refusal to see him as a debauched, irresponsible, lout.

She threw her hands in the air. "So what *is* the point? That you made a mistake when you were young enough to not know any better?"

"The point is, Zeke had a strong basis for the recent assumptions he made, and his observations were spot on."

"Oh, now I see. Your perfect, paragon of a brother catalogued your sins and, now you've had a moment to stew on it, you've bought his judgement hook, line, and sinker." She paused. "We are referring to the man who left the country for long stretches, pursuing his own dreams over a period of years, thereby leaving you and the earl to fend for yourselves in his absence?"

Caden's tawny brows furrowed. "Someone's been keeping up with the happenings in my family."

She lifted her chin. "It's common knowledge."

He gazed at her sidelong. "I see. In any case, Zeke traveled because he had a responsibility to replenish the family coffers which our father had depleted."

"Which your father depleted, which your grandfather permitted," she said, not bothering to hide her exasperation. "Lots and lots of mistakes to go around, Caden—as in every family. Maybe your brother did sacrifice himself. So did you—scrimping and saving and doing everything in your power *not* to ask him for anything. Except for when you tried to help a friend."

His scowl deepened. He opened his mouth to reply.

She held up a hand, palm out. "I wonder. Did your brother never consider that something might happen to the earl during his long absences?"

"Of course. He knew I would look after our grandfather should the need arise."

She sniffed meaningfully.

"When I wasn't away at some party or other," he added in a sullen tone.

A fond smile pulled at the corners of her lips. She crept forward and grasped the lapels of his robe, needing to be near him, the stubborn fool.

"Caden, it seems to me you're guilty of nothing more than growing up slowly, perhaps due to a lack of supervision. Your heart has always been in the right place, and immaturity is not a crime. It's a far cry from the sins perpetrated by your poor, weak, father, who, by the way, you are nothing alike."

He stared into her eyes, then covered her hands with his. Heat from his palms seared her skin. "I don't know why you're defending me. Especially after the things I said to you. The assumptions I made. The liberties I took."

She lowered her gaze, her heart thudding painfully in her chest.

"Anna, what happened between us was entirely my fault. I saw the signs, I should have known you were an innocent—"

Her gaze shot to his. "The signs?"

"Yes. Your innocence was right there in front of me." His eyes warmed as he smiled down at her. "Your tell-tale blushes? Needing me to spell-out everything concerning the relaxed societal rules at house parties? Among other things."

She glared at him.

"I took advantage of you. I missed the signs precisely because I wanted to miss them."

She'd had enough. "Caden Thurgood, you did not take advantage of me. I am a woman grown, fully capable of making my own decisions. May I remind you it was *I* who came to your bed chamber earlier tonight, alone, knowing full well what the ramifications of that decision might be? It was *I* who initiated the last kiss we shared."

"Yes, but--"

"Furthermore, I find it insulting that you hide behind platitudes rather than admit the plain truth."

He cocked his head, a frown pulling at his mouth. "Which is?"

She lifted her chin. "You have no taste for greenhorn, inexperienced women and now find me," she swallowed, "repugnant."

An odd expression crossed his too-handsome face.

"You needn't worry. I don't expect a repeat of," she made an inarticulate sound and a vague gesture with her hand and prayed the golden firelight would not reveal the hot flush scalding her cheeks. "In fact, I suggest we go on as if nothing untoward ever occurred. But I will not, *will not,* allow you to treat me like a child who did not act of her own free will."

"Anna—"

"Perhaps I'm being too hard on you. You can't help taking responsibility. Your innate chivalry drives you to take up the cause for everyone and everything that crosses your path—"

"Anna," he said more loudly.

Misery settled over her. She'd said too much, as usual. "Yes?"

A soft laugh of incredulity escaped him. "Did you really conclude that I no longer find you desirable?"

"It's as plain as the bruise on your face, and of no consequence, I assure you."

One corner of his mouth curved up in a laconic smile. "How very clever of you to work that out on your own."

"Thank you." She imagined herself stomping down hard on his bare foot. Not that she wore any shoes. It would probably hurt her more than him.

"Before we conclude this fascinating conversation—"

"As far as I'm concerned we've quite exhausted the topic—"

"—I need to tell you something."

A change in subject suited her just fine. She folded her arms over her chest. "Go on."

"Earlier, I went out intent on uncovering the identity of the guest whose arrival precipitated one of us"—He gestured toward himself—"vacating his room. There's no easy way to say this."

"I always find the direct approach works best."

"So you do." He reached out to squeeze her shoulder, his grip warm and gentle. "Baron Bolton arrived tonight."

She jerked and he grasped her other shoulder, steadying her.

"I planned to wait 'til morning to discuss the matter but one of us insisted on talking tonight." His full mouth quirked upward as he tucked an escaped lock of her hair behind her ear.

She shivered at the tenderness of his touch, and reminded herself not to read anything into it. He'd admitted he no longer desired her. This was Caden being Caden, offering comfort, offering strength.

"We must exercise caution, of course, but in light of his inebriated state when last I saw him, I assume he won't arise with the dawn. An early morning departure will work best."

"You're taking me with you," she said, happiness bubbling up inside her. Because she had known he would, even though he owed her less than nothing. He might not want her any longer, and helping her might yet bring calamity down around him, but he could never abandon her, not and still be Caden Thurgood.

Only the sure knowledge he now found her less than alluring kept her rooted to the spot instead hurling herself against him to rain kisses over his face.

"You are the most confounding woman. After everything, did you really expect me to leave you here? By God, I ought t—"

Her good intentions flew out the window. Hands fisting his lapels, she dragged her face into his warm neck. His rough stubble scraped her cheek but she didn't care. "Don't be daft. I knew you never could."

His arms came around her, hesitantly, as if he didn't know whether to hold her or shake her. "But you just said..." He cursed softly. "Tell me you're not crying."

"I'm not crying." She rubbed the tip of her nose against his collar bone. She never cried. She had no idea why her eyes leaked.

His powerful arms tightened, pulling her into his hard, warm body. One of his hands cruised over her middle back in a slow circle she felt all the way to her toes. She steeled herself against the melting sensation swirling through her. He was merely offering comfort.

"Your non tears are soaking my skin. Anna, look at me," he demanded, voice gruff.

She tilted her head back.

Their gazes met. The tenderness in his eyes stole her breath.

He brought one hand to trace the salty tracks on her cheek. "I'll take care of you, no matter what."

A wobbly smile curved her lips. One of her hands released its death grip on his robe to cup his cheek. "I know," she whispered. "Just like when we were children."

His teeth flashed white as a bark of laughter escaped him. "You've lost me. What are you talking about now?"

"Your favorite childhood game, Robinhood? Outwitting the villains to save the less fortunate?"

The softness in his gaze vanished. A muscle ticked in his jaw and something hot and primal swirled in the blue depths of his eyes. "I'll let you in on a secret. Prince Charming rescues the stolen Princess was my favorite game, with you at least, particularly when we were older."

"But you opposed it so vehemently." Awareness of his body, everywhere it touched hers, tingled through her.

He grunted softly. "Because kissing you felt...good. Too good. Left me restless, edgy, irritable."

"Oh."

"I'll tell you something else. There's nothing, not one damned thing, I don't desire about you, Anna."

"That's not true," she argued. "We just agreed—."

"No. You assumed. You need me to spell it out?" he growled.

She nodded, anticipation igniting all her senses.

"You call me chivalrous. Gallant. There's nothing gallant about how I feel every time I lay eyes on you. Every time I smell your scent. Every time I recall the sweetness of your mouth, the softness of your skin. Christ, if I were *gallant*, I'd be bedding down in the barn with the grooms, not sharing a chamber with you."

Her words came out a breathless whisper. "That's impossible. The innkeeper would wonder why since I'm your sister. I...I thought you'd begun to think of me as such."

His mouth twisted in a sardonic smile. "I assure you, there is nothing fraternal about what I feel for you. Nothing gallant. Nothing chivalrous."

She licked her lips. "You're certain?"

He choked on a laugh, then lowered his lips to her ear. "I watched you climb from your bath and envied every last water droplet that had the good fortune to touch your skin."

She gasped, shocked—but not aghast as she ought to be. Instead delicious heat unfurled in her belly.

"I drank in the sight of you, pink and naked and delectable. From the moment I discovered you in that damned coach the need to ravish every square inch of you has consumed me. I close my eyes to shut out the sight of you, then fantasize about touching you, tasting you, having you. *Christ.* I'm no bloody paragon, Anna. You may as well get that out of your head."

His rasping words set her body aflame.

"Well?"

She cleared her throat. "I never used the word paragon."

He made an inarticulate sound that she interpreted as half frustration, half amusement. "Anna, do you want me to kiss you? Because I swear by everything holy, if you don't you'd better tell me n—"

"Yes. *Please.*"

He cupped her nape with hands she could swear shook. Then he bent and pressed his lips to hers, softly, so softly she thought she might expire from the pleasure of it.

With the gentlest of pressure his tongue played at the seam of her lips, parting them, then easing past. His mouth was hot and tasted of sweet ale and heaven. She never wanted his mind drugging kiss to end.

She clung to him as her bones turned liquid and her knees threatened to give out.

As if aware of the effect his kiss had on her, he scooped her into his arms. He carried her to the bed and sprawled onto his back, cradling her atop him as the mattress jostled and squeaked its protest.

Feeling audacious and bolder than she had a right to, she parted the lapels of his robe, baring his chest, and levered herself onto her forearm to drink in the sight of him, long and lean and stretched out alongside her.

The supple skin of his torso glowed bronze in the stuttering firelight and that intriguing line of glistening tawny golden hair fanned out from below his belly button, then narrowed to disappear beneath the waistband of his trousers.

Her gaze dipped lower, taking in the bulging evidence of his arousal. Her breath caught as joy and delight, anticipation and longing swirled inside her. He did want her.

He swallowed audibly and lifted one hand to trace the curve of her cheek. "What's going through that pretty head of yours, Anna?"

"I…" She licked her lips. "I was so sure you didn't want me…"

"You little fool."

She fell into him, her fingers kneading the rippling muscles of his chest, her lips pressing into the base of his throat. She dipped her tongue into the tender hollow where his heartbeat pulsed.

His skin was warm and firm and tasted of salt and Caden.

He drew in a ragged breath and she felt him loosening her braid. "Yes, darling. Touch me. Everywhere."

Reckless, giddy, unfathomable delight filled her to overflowing.

With a groan, he speared his fingers into her now-loose hair. Gooseflesh rippled over her body and she shivered with pleasure.

Cupping her nape, he drew her face level with his.

She met his gaze and sucked in a breath at the raw desire she saw reflected there.

"To be clear, I want you, more than I've ever wanted anyone or anything in my life."

If she could speak, she'd tell him she felt exactly the same way about him.

He dragged her face toward his and their lips tangled in a voracious kiss. She wound her arms around his neck, pulling her body against the hard plains of his chest. A whimper of need sounded in her throat. She was too lost to care.

Caden's answering half groan, half growl was all the warning she got before, in a lightning swift move, he shifted their positions.

He lay atop her, his forearms bracketing her shoulders, his muscular thighs cocooning hers, his hips nestled into hers.

He cupped her face between hot, slightly damp palms. Slowly, deliberately, he lowered his head, brushing her lips with lingering kisses that turned her insides to melted wax.

When his tongue began slipping in and out of her mouth, her own body's demand for more emboldened her to touch the tip of her tongue to his. A shiver went through him.

A moment later he tore his mouth from hers and pressed his face into her neck. "I need to taste you," he whispered against her skin.

She had no notion of what he meant, but his gruff words curled into her, causing her insides to tremble with violent need.

He nibbled his way to her ear, then nipped at her earlobe.

His soft mouth, his hot breath, his sharp teeth, had her wriggling in unfathomable excitement.

"You squirming is driving me mad," he murmured, not sounding the least bit annoyed.

His fingertips cruised down her neck, over her décolleté, to cup one breast.

The heat from his palm seared her skin through her nightshift. He squeezed lightly then his fingers found her nipple to toy with it through the thin fabric. A delicious shock of pleasure rippled through her with every gentle pull.

His hair tickled her nose as he lowered his head. When his teeth clamped softly over her other nipple, an inarticulate sound of awe escaped her. He suckled her through her gown, gently, reverently.

She closed her eyes and gave herself over to the wondrous, drugging sensations. Each pull of his mouth tightened her insides in a conflagration of heat, and nameless need. For Caden.

Only Caden. It had only ever been Caden. Her nails scored his nape and she arched upward inviting the delicious torture.

"More, minx?" He blew on the damp fabric.

She couldn't speak. Could only nod and gaze at him, hoping he could read the pleading in her eyes.

He seemed to understand. Abruptly, he propped himself onto his knees, tore off his robe, and flung it to the ground. The dying firelight reflected the blue heat swirling in his gaze as he stared down at her like a starving man eyeing a feast.

Wherever his gaze landed, his hands followed.

With maddening gentleness he traced a path down her center, from her breastbone to her belly button, as if she were naked before him rather than clothed in a prim white nightgown.

The area between her legs thrummed as if he'd touched her there. She wanted him to touch her there. She felt brazen and wicked, and didn't care a jot.

"Mm," he murmured, his hand cruising lower to cup her sex, depressing the fabric to burrow his fingers between the hot petals guarding her secrets.

She drew in a sharp breath at the unspeakable pleasure.

He dropped onto one elbow and stared down at her, desperation in his eyes.

Never shifting his gaze, his hand gripped fistfuls of her nightdress, bunching the material upward, ever upward. Cold night air brushed her calfs, then her knees, then her thighs. She shivered as goosebumps sprouted over her flesh, despite the red-hot flames of need licking at her insides.

"What have we here?" His gaze raked over her bared flesh, his fingertips tracing up her naked thigh, over her hip.

Uncontrollable tremors wracked her. She reached for him, cupping his nape to pull him toward her.

He acceded to her wordless demand, his mouth taking hers, his tongue slipping past her parted lips as his fingers explored—her belly, her curls, and finally, *finally* the aching flesh between her legs.

She moaned, enraptured by the molten thrill of his touch.

Swallowing her choked pleas, his fingers found and lingered over one particularly sensitive spot.

She clutched at him, arching into the most intoxicating sensation she'd ever known. *"Caden. Oh, Caden."*

"You like this?" he whispered gruffly, his clever fingers playing over her.

Her insides went taut, like a spring coiled dangerously tight. She crooned, desperate, wordlessly begging for...she didn't know.

But Caden knew. He drove her closer. Closer. So close she could almost taste it—and then she crested a rolling wave, crying out as she rode it higher, higher, finally reaching the pinacle where glorious glittering sensation exploded within her.

He swallowed her cries with his mouth, his fingers coaxing every last bit of pleasure from her body, until she lay limp and utterly replete.

She had no notion of Caden removing his trousers or easing atop her. She only knew the weight of him pressing her into the mattress felt right, his manhood nudging her opening righter still.

He shuddered, his face a rigid mask of, she'd swear, pain. The thick tip of his erection pulsed against her sensitive flesh. "Anna," he choked.

She gazed up at him, understanding his unspoken need. "Make love to me."

"Are...you...sure?" He gritted out the words, his face glistening with a feverish sheen.

"Make love to me," she repeated softly.

A strangled whimper sounded in his throat and, with one slow thrust, he sank himself inexorably inside her.

She flinched as the unexpected pain pierced her core, but did not push him away. She sensed if she did, even a little, he would withdraw from her completely.

She wanted this. Wanted him inside her, wanted to be claimed by him, if only for tonight.

"Anna," he breathed against her lips, her name a plea. He cupped her face and kissed her with a tender desperation that reached inside to capture her very heart.

His hips pumped into hers. Slow. Deep. Stretching and filling her. "You. Feel. So. Good."

Everything in her gloried in his raw delight, which somehow eased the sting within her. Her body softened, welcoming him, stretching to accommodate him. Her hips responded to his rhythm as if with a will of their own, lifting in a tempo matching his.

"Mine," he whispered. *"Mine."*

An exquisite tightness coiled inside her. She clutched at him, lips parting in awe.

He kissed her, whispering praise and nonsensical words against her lips until, with no warning, glorious pleasure unfurled inside her, swift and lush, like an exotic flower, coming to sudden full bloom.

She'd wanted—needed—to hold him close, to feel him inside her, to be claimed by him. But this burst of dazzling sensation filling her felt like their souls joining. Ecstasy overflowed from within her, and she sobbed out his name.

Her cries seemed to unleash something in him. With an exultant roar, he reared up. His hips pistoned into hers, faster, harder, deeper. A hoarse groan sounded in his throat a moment before he tore himself from her body and threw himself face down onto the mattress beside her.

Anna could only lay there, tingling with the aftershocks of their lovemaking, utterly awed. She wanted to giggle. To cry. To plaster herself onto Caden and profess...her love.

She loved him.

His lovemaking had knocked down all her walls. She was that love-addled girl from long ago all over again, vulnerable and bared. For tonight, at least, she couldn't bring herself to care.

"Mmm. You're too far away. Come here, minx."

He wrapped one steely arm around her and dragged her close, his hard body cocooning hers. One-handed, he grasped the bedcovers, somehow crumpled at their feet, and slung the mass atop them. Soon warmth from his body enveloped her, turning her boneless.

Replete, exactly where she ought to be, she closed her eyes, and slept.

***

Caden slept, too—for all of ten minutes. Then his eyes snapped open as the enormity of what he'd done slammed him into full wakefulness. His heart pounded so hard the rush of blood in his ears threatened to deafen him. Sweat dampened his brow and trickled down one temple.

And the soft, sweet smelling woman using his arm as a pillow sighed and snuggled closer, wriggling her soft bottom into his groin—which brought that part of his anatomy instantly awake, as well.

He considered sliding his arm free and vacating the warm bed. But, no. Gritting his teeth, he determined to suffer through his inconvenient arousal rather than wake her. His cock twitched with approval at his decision and he bit back a groan—or laughter—he couldn't say which.

He needed to think. With his head.

One truth resounded inside him with the force of an anvil striking hot steel. He'd certainly proved his point. He was a cad. He'd taken advantage of her, again, gratifying his own selfish need to claim her as his. And, oh, how very satisfying the claiming had been.

He should have resisted his carnal urge. Should have shuffled Anna back to bed and refused to engage in the emotionally charged conversation until he had himself under control. Only, when it came to Anna, he had no self-control, and now the damage was completely, irrevocably done.

Which brought him to a second, unalterable truth. They'd have to marry.

The thought filled him with...*peace* of all things, which made no sense at all. Hadn't he spent much of the night owning up to just how *un*-marriageable he was?

Irrelevant, at this point. Marriage it would be, as soon as he could manage the thing. Not that he had any notion of how to be a decent man, much less husband. But, perhaps he could make himself into the right sort of man. For Anna's sake, he'd try.

He still had the hurdle of her current marital status to clear. He would secure her freedom from Bolton, by God.

After that, he'd convince her to marry him. He hadn't a bloody thing to offer as an enticement. No house of his own. No lands. No rank.

He'd acquired a large nest egg thanks to his investments, which would be even larger once Zeke repaid him for his quarry expenses, but he had no steady source of income, thanks to his recent altercation with Zeke and the earl.

Damn. The earl. As usual, Caden was selfish to the bone. In his preoccupation with the soft, warm, utterly enticing woman curled into him, he'd forgotten about the earl's plight for all intents and purposes.

The bottom line was he needed to hasten them to Chissington Hall, while avoiding at all cost Anna crossing paths with Bolton.

Bolton. How he managed not to smash the man's face into oblivion tonight was beyond him. Even now everything in him tightened with impotent rage. A duel was called for. But not yet. Not till Anna's safety was assured.

She sighed and rolled onto her side to face him. Her fingers curled into his chest and she snugged up against him, just like she belonged there.

Damn, but she felt good, and the intoxicating scent of her skin and hair was wreaking havoc on his already inflamed senses. His cock pulsed against her soft, warm belly as if the fine material of her nightshift didn't exist.

It was going to be a long night.

***

Contrasting sharply with last night's maelstrom, the morning boasted a cloudless sky. The sun's rays beamed through the travel coach's window panes, filling the well-appointed cab with warmth.

With effort, Anna kept a placid smile firmly in place. She perched on the bench, opposite Caden, who lounged in a recumbent sprawl, every inch of him at apparent ease. For the last quarter hour, he'd gazed outside. Evidently the passing landscape held inordinate fascination for him.

She gritted her teeth and resisted the urge to scream.

All morning he had been unerringly polite. He had not uttered an untoward word. He simply acted as if nothing out of the ordinary happened last night, when in fact everything had changed. It was maddening.

She sniffed and plucked at the soft linen skirts of the fine traveling dress Lady Wentworth had procured for her. Ought she broach the subject herself?

"Have you taken ill?" he asked.

Her heart lurched at the unexpected sound of his voice after a good half hour of lapsed conversation, and she answered more sharply than necessary. "No, of course not. Why do you ask?"

"I've heard quite a few sniffles from your side of the coach."

"I'm sure I have no idea what you mean."

He gave a one-shoulder shrug and resumed his study of the passing scenery.

She chewed the inside of her lip. Why bother discussing last night at all? He seemed disinclined, and it wasn't as if she was free to entertain an elicit affair. She was—technically—married, on the run, and heading straight for the bosom of Caden's immediate family, one member of whom was an earl.

She ought to focus her mental energy there, and how Caden intended to explain her presence.

Abruptly, his head angled to face her. His gaze skimmed over her, brows furrowed, mouth curved downward in a matching scowl.

Finally, he meant to raise the subject of last night. "You may as well say what's on your mind, Caden Thurgood."

"I beg your pardon? Why assume I have something on my mind?"

"You're frowning."

He gave her a chagrined smile. "I'm not frowning, I'm confounded. When I'm tired, the two can look the same. *I* didn't get much sleep last night."

She did not miss his subtle stress on the word 'I'. Heat stole up her neck. She'd slept like a baby, ensconced in his lovely, warm embrace. "I see." She hoped he hadn't noticed the breathless quality of her voice. "May I ask what has you confounded?"

He rubbed a hand over his clean-shaven jaw. "If you must know, it's your gown."

She looked down at herself. The traveling dress, fashioned of fine, royal-blue linen, fit her perfectly—and was cut in the first stare of fashion, unless she missed her mark. She might be mistaken. She hadn't had occasion to shop for anything other than footwear in an age.

"You don't like it?"

"It looks…" He broke off, blowing air out his cheeks. Slumping deeper into the corner, he stretched out one long leg and bent the knee of the other. His gaze roamed over her in a leisurely manner "…very nice," he finished softly.

Her stomach did a slow, rolling somersault.

"Oh." She cleared her throat and fought the urge to grin like a dolt. "This bothers you because...?"

Eyes narrowing, he sat upright and crossed his arms over his chest. "Because the gown fits you as if made for you and, based on the size and weight of your trunk, appears to be one of many."

"No mystery there. Lady Wentworth asked Lady Fenton to procure several of her daughter's cast-offs for my use. In truth, I can't imagine why Lady Bernadette wished to part with them, especially as none show the least sign of wear."

She didn't voice her suspicion that Lady Wentworth had not so much requested as demanded the frocks. What had inspired her to do so? Anna had many questions for Lady Wentworth, and the clothing she now possessed did not begin to top the list.

"Lady Bernadette's cast-offs you say? She's heaps taller than you, and a good deal more..."

"More what?" She recounted the lady's ample bosom, especially as compared to her own. "And she's not heaps taller."

His lips twitched and a gleam of wicked amusement sparkled in his blue eyes. Oh, but the man was too clever by half.

"I wasn't complaining. You're perfect as you are."

Pleasure bloomed within her at the softly spoken praise.

Her gaze dropped helplessly to his mouth. He hadn't even kissed her this morning. He'd been up and dressed and ready to depart before she opened her eyes.

"My point is, Lady Wentworth went to a lot of trouble for you. Granted, she displayed an unapologetic fondness for you before all and sundry. Still. Stowing you away in Harrison's vehicle and furnishing you with a posh wardrobe…"

And a tidy sum of pounds. And mother's ruby.

"Seems like a monumental effort for a mere paid companion. And how about the fact she seemingly knew of your disastrous marriage to Bolton?"

"She obviously knew more than she let on. There's something else, too."

His blue gaze sharpened. "Go on."

"She…er…" She hadn't broached either the large sum of money or the ruby she'd found inside her trunk. Not because she wanted to withhold the information from him. She'd simply been preoccupied with other things last night—namely, him.

Telling him now, however, felt awkward, as if she had been once again keeping secrets.

"Hello?"

She owed him the truth.

"She tucked funds and, I believe, though I can't be certain, my mother's ruby into the trunk she packed for me."

Caden launched upright, hoisting himself across the narrow divide to sit beside her. "What on earth? The one you pawned?"

She nodded.

"It can't be. How would she have come to possess it? How would she even know you'd pawned the thing? It must be another stone. But even so, ruby's are more costly than diamonds.

None of this makes sense." He slanted her a glance. "Unless you and she *were* in cahoots."

Her heart sank. He doubted her. She couldn't blame him.

"Caden, I've told you everything. No one could have been more stunned than me when she spoke Bolton's name last night."

He appeared to weigh her words, finally looking more intrigued than accusatory. "What, precisely, did she say?"

"She informed me she'd packed for me and said I must leave straight away lest I find myself departing with

Lord Bolton. I questioned her, of course. How could I not? She'd never once let on she knew anything about my past, when, in actuality, she knew more than I did."

He cocked his head. "How do you mean?"

"You'll recall I thought I'd killed the man. Lady Wentworth seemed to not only know of our...um...connection, she knew he was alive—when I thought him dead. Else why pack a valise for me to escape him before even I knew leaving was a necessity?"

He slung one arm across the upper cushion behind her and his gaze drifted over her. "Why indeed?"

Her skin prickled, her breasts tightened, and everything in her went hot. *Kiss me.* "Do you believe me?"

His eyes met hers. Seconds ticked by. "Yes."

A tentative smile curved her lips. "Thank you."

"Anna, have you given any thought to what you'll do once we reach Chissington Hall?"

The swift change of topic caught her off guard. "What I'll do?"

He inclined his head in a fractional nod.

"I suppose I'll…I was rather hoping I could stay in Derby for a day or two."

Fire flashed in his eyes and his nostrils flared. "Stay in Derby?" he erupted.

Her stomach dropped to her toes. He didn't want her there. Now she understood why he wasn't broaching the subject of last night. It had meant nothing to him.

She forced a smile. "I understand."

His expression turned leery. "Understand what?"

"Rest assured, I'll be off straight away."

"Off? Are you mad?" he erupted. "You'll stay in Derby, by God."

Relief turned her limbs to water. "In that case, I'm not sure what you're asking, Caden."

He shook his head, clearly exasperated. "I'm asking if you've any idea how to end your sham of a marriage. I would assume that's the first order of the day for us."

"For us?" She sounded entirely too hopeful.

His cheeks went ruddy. "For you," he corrected.

She gave up trying to understand his quicksilver mood. "I suppose I must ask for an annulment, not that I know how, nor on what basis one might be attained."

"As to how, I'm sure we can get the earl's man, Hallis to submit the paperwork. Concerning the grounds…" he paused.

"Unfortunately, I know of only one sure-fire way to achieve such an end."

"What is it?"

He lowered his eyes. "If one can show proof she's never lain with her husband, one has grounds to contest the marriage's legitimacy."

Of course. Angelique had wanted to close that particular loophole. Hadn't she commanded Bolton to *get the deed done?* She shivered.

Beside her, Caden leaned forward, propping his elbows on his knees and steepling his fingers. "Thanks to last night, that option's no longer viable."

Last night. All morning she'd wanted him to broach the subject. Now she understood why he had not. *Careful what you wish for, Gloriana*, her father always said.

Words tumbled out of her mouth before she knew what she meant to say. "Do you regret it so much?"

He straightened slowly, his eyes wary. "Regret what?"

In for a penny..."Do you regret making love to me?"

His lids lowered to half mast. "Ah."

Misery settled over her. The man was buying time rather than answer her. Never a good sign.

"Do *you* regret what happened, Anna?"

Answering a question with a question, now? She lifted her chin. "Oh, no, you don't, Caden Thurgood. I asked you first."

Chapter Eighteen

Do you regret making love to me?

The carriage slowed as it rumbled downhill, beneath a canopy of trees. The coach's interior went dark despite the fact it was barely one in the afternoon, and, facing aft, Caden and Anna both lurched back into the cushions.

Anna yelped and reached for Caden. He took her small, gloved hand and tucked it into the crook of his elbow. She turned her head to face him.

His eyes had adjusted enough to make out her anxious expression. "Not to worry. The road will soon level out," he assured her.

Meanwhile, he could only thank the heavens for the seconds the changing terrain bought him to consider how best to answer her question—a loaded one if ever he heard one, and one he had not anticipated.

He'd assumed Anna would stay true to form and avoid any and all topics that might put her on the hot seat. He ought to have known. With Anna, he never could keep his footing.

The coach leveled off, though they remained shrouded in shadow.

"Regret? Not a term I would use, precisely."

Beside him, her body went rigid, and she gave him her most haughty profile.

"What I mean to say—" He broke off. He wanted to reassure her. However, he had no intention of giving away his entire hand. Not yet.

He took a bracing breath. "There are certainly regrettable aspects to what transpired. The fact of your virginity, for one, your current marital status for another."

Her shoulders rose and fell in a heartfelt sigh, and her chin dropped. "I see. I did ask, didn't I?"

The coach shifted again, starting up another slight incline. Caden's grip on her hand tightened, locking her beside him. He didn't want to risk her toppling off the bench, he told himself.

She turned to face the opposite window. "You dislike lying with virgins?" she asked in a small voice. "Or was it how I...what I..."

His resolve to hold his cards close crumbled. He crooked a finger under her chin, urging her to face him.

"I disliked hurting you. That is all. Aside from that, I can say without a moment's hesitation..." His voice lowered seemingly of its own accord. "Making love to you was..."

The forest of trees surrounding the carriage thinned, and diffuse light spilled into the coach to light-up Anna's heart shaped face. Gods she was beautiful.

"Yes?" Her voice held an unmistakable note of hopefulness.

He could withhold nothing from her. "...Everything I could have hoped for and more."

Her rose-colored lips parted briefly in surprise. "I see," she said again. Same words, different meaning entirely.

A smile tugged at the corners of his mouth. How inordinately pleased with herself she sounded.

"What of you? Do you regret what happened between us?"

She didn't hesitate. "No." A tremulous smile curved her lips, despite her obvious attempt to staunch the grin. "Last night was..." she swallowed.

Unable to refrain from touching her face again, he traced his fingertips over her cheek. "Did you enjoy my lovemaking, Anna?"

"Yes, I did. Very much."

He'd battled a simmering arousal all morning—nothing new where Anna was concerned. Everything about the woman seemed to ignite his carnal appetite.

Now, hearing her softly spoken admission, he went instantly hard. The need to feast on her plump, inviting lips, toss her skirts up, and take her, right here, right now seared his senses.

Feigning an interest in the surrounding area, he released her hand and shifted to face away from her. Closing his eyes, he laid his forehead against the sun-baked window panes. *Christ.*

"Not much longer now," he ground out.

"Caden?" A tone of uncertainty laced her voice.

He prayed she didn't require any further proof of her desirability. He could not withstand further temptation.

Bracing himself, he glanced at her over his shoulder. "Yes?"

"I assume you've given some thought as to what you'll tell your family? About me, I mean, and why I'm traveling with you, unchaperoned."

"I plan to tell them the truth."

She lowered her gaze, but not before he saw the flash of alarm. "I see."

Everything in him wanted to take her in his arms. He could not risk it. "Trust me?"

She lifted her eyes to meet his. "I do trust you, Caden."

The constant desire he felt for her was hard enough to manage. But this. This hot sensation flooding his chest at her gentle assurance stole his breath.

It also felt unreasonably, intoxicatingly good. He wondered briefly if this was how Kitty made Zeke feel during their courtship. If so, it explained a lot—and served Zeke right.

***

The coach had been moving at a steady clip for the better part of an hour, during which blue skies gave way to a cloudy dome and the sun eased lower in the western sky.

Now, alerted by the musty scents of damp vegetation and the slight tinge of garlic in the air, Anna pulled aside the velvet curtains to view the Derwent River, its wide expanse of gently rippling water reflecting the late afternoon sun.

The coachman guided the horses onto the old, three-arch stone bridge marking the eastern perimeter of the Claybourne estate.

Soon, the coach crossed through a thicket of forest, then turned onto a cobblestone road. Anna stared, unblinking, at the vista unfolding before her.

Rolling green hills bracketed by miles of forest announced the *pièce de resistance* centered on the hilltop like a crown, the castle known as Chissington Hall.

Bathed in the slanting sun's rays, the imposing limestone fortress radiated a fearsome bronze, as if it shone with a light all its own. The sight of those achingly familiar towers and parapets pinched her insides, making it hard to breathe.

She'd always loved Chissington Hall. It was every bit as beautiful as her memory held. As a girl she fantasized about living in one of the towers with Caden, she a princess and he, her own Prince Charming.

She was no longer a child, and was certainly no princess. Caden, however took on the part of her rescuing prince like he was born to it. Some things never changed.

She shot him a searching look. Over the last hour, he had shown a marked disinclination to converse beyond offering monosyllabic replies to her every attempt to draw him out.

She couldn't know precisely how the sight of his familial home affected him, but the muscle, rapid-fire ticking in his jaw said his thoughts were far from placid.

He'd told her of his bitter argument with Zeke and the earl before he'd departed for Femsworth Manor. Was that where his thoughts had gone? Or was he simply concerned about the earl's unknown illness?

Another possibility existed which Anna could hardly bear to contemplate. He might be worried over his family's reaction to her plight and its potential to bring scandal down upon them.

Caden had asked her to trust him. She did trust him. It was what the rest of his family might do that gave her qualms.

The coach rumbled to a halt in the wide, graveled forecourt. After so long on the road hearing the clatter of the wheels, the relative silence felt like a breath of fresh air.

Caden waggled his brows at her, vaulted out of the vehicle and placed the stoop. He reached for her hand, helping her down.

Her legs trembled like jelly as she descended.

Here she stood outside Chissington Hall, about to enter the forbidding walls for the first time in her life. She wrapped her arms around herself and waited in silence as Caden and the coachman carted their luggage to the wide front steps of the castle's entrance.

He returned to her side, neither speaking as the travel coach set off in the direction of the stables.

Their eyes met.

Suddenly she found it hard to breathe. "Caden, I'm not sure you—we—thought this through properly. What if the earl—"

"—Shh." He shifted to face her, his back to the castle.

Gripping her shoulders with gentle hands, he gave her a reassuring smile. But it was his guileless blue eyes boring into hers that somehow calmed the hysteria trying to well up inside her.

"What's this? My bold girl who single-handedly thwarted a mad woman, fought off a villain, and braved the streets of London now trembles in fear of meeting the gentlest of men?"

"Gentle or not, he is the Earl of Claybourne," she muttered. "What if he sends me back to Bolton?"

"That, my darling, will never happen."

"And what of your sanctimonious brother?"

He looked over his shoulder, squinting as if he could see through the solid stone walls to the man himself. "You need not concern yourself, Anna. My brother may possess an overinflated view of his own judgement in all matters, but his loyalty to family knows no bounds."

"Family being the key word."

He shifted his attention back to her. One corner of his mouth crooked upward. An odd expression lit his sky blue eyes. He seemed on the verge of speaking when one of the massive front doors swung open.

Brows arched, Caden turned. "Ah."

He tucked her fingers into the crook of his arm and, led her, unhurried, toward the broad front steps.

Looming in the open doorway, a tall, powerfully built man with the bearing of a demigod stared down at them—Lord Ezekiel Thurgood in the flesh. The similarities in his appearance to Caden would mark him as none other, even if she had never met him.

A bemused, pleased, and still somehow arrogant expression animated his ruggedly handsome face.

"This is a surprise, brother. I had the impression we'd not see you..." he broke off, arching his brows meaningfully. He cast a quick glance at Anna before finishing with, "anytime soon."

He trotted down the flight of stairs, then reached his arm to squeeze Caden's shoulder. "Welcome home."

Caden frowned in evident confusion. "I'm gratified by your warm reception, but my arrival is hardly unexpected. You did send a messenger to Femsworth Manor, did you not? About the earl?"

"Messenger? What about the earl?"

Caden shot Anna a perplexed look before returning his attention to Zeke. "His recent illness? The messenger claimed I needed to return to Chissington Hall post-haste."

Zeke gave a slow nod of understanding. His eyes lit on Anna, then their combined luggage, before returning to Caden. "It's just the two of you, then?"

Caden frowned. "Yes. But the earl. Is he...?"

Zeke sent his brother a reassuring grin. "Thanks to Kitty, the earl is fitter than you or I. You're under a misapprehension, brother."

Caden opened his mouth to speak, but Zeke forestalled him with a hand raised, palm out. "Let us continue our discussion indoors. Kitty won't thank me for leaving her out of an exchange which promises to be, at the very least, interesting, not to mention she'll be delighted to see you."

Zeke's gaze traveled once more to Anna. "You can introduce your friend to both of us at once, as well."

His casual suggestion seemed to Anna more of a command.

Lifting her chin, she determined not to budge an inch until Caden gave his assent. She slid her gaze toward him.

His warm eyes twinkled at her as if he read her intent. He proffered his arm.

The three proceeded indoors.

Inside the thick walls of the manse, the house was almost chilly, despite the warmth of the day. The combined scents of lemon oil, fresh flowers and long-standing wealth filled the air.

She'd entered into the Claybourne dynasty lair. Lord only knew what fate would befall her now.

"Kitty will be reading, unless I miss my guess. She's headed up a ladies' book club dedicated to the advancement of women's legal rights, if you can believe that."

Caden snorted, and a look of private understanding passed between he and Zeke. "Oh, I can believe it."

They moved unhurriedly through a winding maze of corridors to a destination seemingly known by both.

Moments later, they entered a small drawing room. One glance told Anna the family used this space for intimate gatherings. Still elegant like the rest of the manse, the chamber had a comfortable, lived-in feel.

A small fire burned in the grate. Silk-paper covered the walls, the green and cream painted scrollwork barely visible behind floor-to-ceiling shelving, filled with objects d'art and books. Plush carpets lay over gleaming hardwood floors, and the furnishings—velvet covered wingback chairs and a sturdy looking sofa—nestled around a large walnut table on which a leather-bound tome lay open.

"I see the book, but not my wife. Can't have gone far."

Anna skimmed the book's title. Mary Wollstonecraft's *A Vindication of the Rights of Women.*

Zeke approached the east-facing wall, where two exterior doors opened to a cozy terrace. The sun's glowing rays poured through the open doorway like an offering from heaven. He peered outside.

In an instant, his cool countenance metamorphosed to one of utter besottedness. "Kitty, darling."

Anna heard a woman's small start of surprise. Second's later, Zeke's wife appeared in the doorway. Gem-covered combs held her long, ebony hair back from her face, while the length of it spilled down her back. She was, to Anna's mind, stunningly beautiful.

In her apron were several long-stemmed roses which she'd obviously just clipped. She aimed a warm, affectionate smile at Zeke. Then, something must have alerted her to the presence of others. She turned and spotted Caden. Her face lit with unabashed delight.

"Caden, when did you arrive? Zeke, did you know? Why-ever did you not inform me? And who is this with you?" All of this came out in an exhilarated rush as she flew across the room toward Caden.

Slowing just enough to remove her apron and set it aside, she launched herself at Caden, who caught her up in his arms with a hardy chuckle.

"For your information, Caden's arrival is as much a surprise for me as it is for you." Zeke came up behind his wife and rested his hands on her shoulders. "Through some odd miscommunication, he got word the earl had taken ill."

Lady Thurgood looked nonplussed. "The earl, ill? Nothing could be further from the truth. Wherever did you hear that, Caden?"

Caden arched a brow. "A very good question. Where is the old man now?"

"Resting after our afternoon walk," she answered.

"Kitty's a hard task-master. She insists Claybourne get his regular exercise," Zeke said.

Caden sent her a fond grin.

Anna was beginning to feel like an unwelcome voyeur when the future countess turned her pale green gaze on her. "Now then, who is this you've brought home with you?"

Was it Anna's imagination, or had a strange look passed over the woman's face before her mouth curved in the placid smile she now wore?

Zeke's attention shifted to Anna, his expression sober.

"Yes, well," Caden cleared his throat and moved to stand beside her.

Her palms went sweaty in her kid-skin gloves. She braced herself for his explanation, and their reaction to learning they housed a member of the peerage's run-away bride.

"Mrs. Jones..."

Her gaze snapped in his direction. He was introducing her as Jones?

"...may I Introduce my brother and his future countess, Lord Ezekiel Thurgood of Claybourne and his wife Lady Christine Thurgood."

She somehow managed a polite greeting and curtsy.

"Zeke, my lady, I am very pleased to introduce you to Mrs. Anna Jones." He paused a beat. "My fiancé."

A stunned silence greeted Caden's pronouncement.

Anna belatedly realized her mouth hung agape, and she closed it with a snap. *Fiancé?*

The room grew increasingly dim until it dawned on her she held her breath. She gasped in a greedy lungful of air, simultaneously noting Caden's brother and his wife exchanging matching, unreadable looks. Surprise? Horror? Disbelief? She couldn't say.

"Mrs. Anna Jones, you say?" Zeke asked, with a slight stress on the word Mrs.

"Yes. My fiancé is a widow."

Zeke and Lady Thurgood stared at Caden with expectant expressions.

A moment later, Caden's sister-in-law fixed him with a glower, hands fisted on her hips. "Surely you don't expect to get away with this, Caden."

Anna's skin went clammy.

Then, Lady Thurgood burst out laughing. "How did you come to be engaged? What plans have you made? You can't just announce your engagement and leave out all the juicy details."

"Details. Of course," Caden replied, not quite masking his relief, at least to Anna's ears. "But perhaps we could save the explanations for later, when the earl is about. This way we can share our good fortune once. Much more efficient that way."

Brows beetled, Lady Thurgood opened her mouth, as if to argue.

Zeke's words stayed her. "An excellent notion."

She scowled up at him.

Seemingly unaware of her displeasure, he continued. "Speaking of the earl, the two of us should pay him a visit now, eh, Caden? He would hardly appreciate us leaving him in the dark about your homecoming."

"Nothing I'd like more. Regardless of the happy report regarding his good health, I travelled all this way, anxious over his welfare, and I'd rather like to see him with my own eyes."

Zeke inclined his head in a regal fashion. "We'll go directly. Kitty?"

All signs of her irritation vanishing like it never existed, the ebony-haired beauty crossed the invisible divide between the two couples and linked arms with Anna.

"Never fear, I shall see Mrs. Jones settled." Her inscrutable, pale-green gaze captured Anna's. "However far you've come, traveling is always exhausting. I'm sure you'd like to freshen up."

Dismay filled her. More than anything she wanted to get Caden alone to demand an explanation. Instead, she pasted what she hoped passed for a polite smile on her face and lied through her teeth.

"Thank you, Lady Thurgood. Your hospitality is most welcome." She turned to Caden. "I'll see you soon?"

He sent her a crooked grin. "Count on it."

***

In unspoken agreement, Caden and Zeke waited, still and silent, for the ladies to depart.

The door closed. The ladies' footsteps receded in the hall.

"Right." Zeke moved to the credenza housing the brandy.

He poured two healthy snifters, then made his way back to Caden. He handed Caden one of the snifters and indicated the armchairs near the grate. Without waiting for Caden to follow, Zeke took a seat.

So much for visiting the earl.

Caden sat. Waited.

Zeke raised his glass in a toast.

Caden returned the gesture.

Zeke downed the contents of his glass, then set the crystal on the polished wooden side table between them with a decisive click. "Surprised to see you, after everything you said when you left."

Caden felt his face go hot. "I may have overreacted slightly. Not that I was wrong, you understand."

"Of course not," Zeke said in his standard condescending manner that, for some reason, wasn't getting Caden's goat like it usually did.

"The thing is, when I heard about the earl's illness—"

"The earl's supposed illness which turned out to be false information?"

Caden nodded once. "The very same. When I *thought* the earl ill, my reasons for leaving in the state I did seemed..." Damn. He was not going to call himself childish—even though he had been—and substantiate everything Zeke had said about him.

He started again. "That is, I realized worrying about your low opinion of me might be a waste of my time and not worth drawing a line in the sand over."

Zeke raised his brows. "I see."

Caden took a healthy swallow of brandy. The rich amber liquid slid down his throat, warm, smooth, and neat. "Should we go see the earl now?"

Zeke drummed his fingers briefly on his knee. "Actually, if you don't mind, before we share the news of your engagement with the earl..." He sent Caden a pleasant smile. "I'd like to know what in hell you're up to."

Typical Zeke. Caden snorted and tossed back the remaining brandy in his glass. "The normal manner of things, I expect. One gets engaged, posts the banns, sets a date—"

"Yes, but *normally* one does not get himself engaged to someone who's already married."

Caden froze a beat. "You saw the ad the bastard posted? Color me surprised you paid it any mind."

"I remarked on it precisely because I recognized the chit. She's the one you pined over for months after her family—Masters, was the name, if I remember correctly?—departed for London never to return."

Caden scowled at his brother. "Pined? I did no such thing."

Zeke smirked. "Please. I pointed the ad out to Kitty and said, 'That's the girl whose family summered in Derby when Cade and I were boys. Caden had a mad *tendre* for her.' I assumed the poor girl ran away from Bolton once she figured out what sort of scum she'd married?"

"Something like that," Caden grumbled. He scrubbed a hand over his stubble-roughened jaw. "Hell and damnation. Do you think Kitty recognized Anna as the woman in the ad?"

"Anna, eh? That's what she goes by now?"

Caden grunted his assent.

"As to whether or not Kitty recognized the woman—"

"My fiancé," Caden corrected, striving for patience.

Zeke's brows shot up. "Fiancé? I assumed…Wait. Don't tell me you got the girl with child?"

His patience reached its end. He fixed his brother with an icy stare. Then a thought hit him like a solid punch, square between the eyes and his vision blurred.

Anna very well *may* be carrying his babe. He'd attempted to avoid such an outcome. Still. Nothing was fool proof. He could well imagine Anna's belly, round and full. A hot rush of wonder stole his breath.

"I'll be damned," Zeke murmured.

Caden blinked. "Eh?" He shook his head and dragged himself back to the present. "I seem to have lost the thread of conversation."

One corner of Zeke's mouth hitched upward. "You asked me whether or not Kitty recognized your *fiancé*." He stressed the word, almost as if poking fun at Caden. "Hard to say."

"Supposing Kitty did. What are the odds she'll question Anna directly?"

Zeke grinned. "Is that a rhetorical question?"

"Hell and damnation," Caden groused again, then sighed. "Thankfully Anna is, by no means, a shrinking violet. Too, the facts were all meant to come out eventually."

"I'm relieved to hear you meant to fill us in before bringing scandal crashing down upon our family."

Caden arched a brow, amused in spite of himself. "Is scandal something you're worried over, these days?" He refrained from iterating the obvious—to his mind, at any rate—that they'd all braved scandal quite recently—for Kitty's sake.

"Worried is too strong a word. I'll admit I would prefer to avoid one if possible."

Caden examined his nails. "And if it isn't?"

He looked up in surprise when Zeke reached over to squeeze his shoulder.

"In that case, forewarned is forearmed. I'm with you, brother, no matter what, always. Now, kindly bring me up to speed on where things stand before we present your situation to the earl."

The door to the family parlor swung open. The earl, looking hale and fit and every bit the patriarch of the family, burst into the room. "So it's true. My youngest grandson has returned to the fray—with a fiancé, no less."

Chapter Nineteen

"**G**randfather." Caden rose, crossing to the old man to wrap him in an embrace. "It's good to see you looking so well, my lord."

"And why wouldn't I? Have you met my young tiger?"

He referred to Kitty, his one-time servant-slash-companion who, at that time, went by the name of *Kit*.

Caden and Zeke exchanged amused glances.

"For some odd reason, I received word at the Fenton's party that you'd taken seriously ill."

The earl's bushy gray brows furrowed.

Caden shrugged. "I'll take it up with Harrison when next I see him—right after I thank him. As it happened, my fiancé and I needed to make ourselves scarce."

Claybourne looked from Caden to Zeke, then fixed his gaze on the empty brandy snifters. "Do I need a drink to hear the rest of this tale?"

Slapping his hands on his knees, Zeke unfolded himself from his armchair. "Sit. I'll pour, while Caden fills both of us in."

The earl grinned. "And here I feared things might get boring around here."

"Boring?" Zeke groused, half way to the credenza.

The earl waved his hand in a vague gesture as he settled onto the sofa. "No more damsels in distress—"

"—disguised as boy servants. I see your point," Zeke agreed.

He splashed brandy into a snifter for the earl, then refilled his and Caden's empty glasses.

Caden dropped into his vacated armchair and steepled his fingers. "Do you remember the doctor and his wife who leased the old cottage near the river on the other side of the bridge? Years ago, when Zeke and I were boys."

His grandfather accepted his brandy with a nod of thanks for Zeke. "The couple who summered here and had the pretty little girl to whom you were devoted?"

Caden slid Zeke an accusatory look.

Zeke barked out a laugh.

"I was nice to her. That is all," Caden said.

The earl's blue eyes twinkled. Abruptly the twinkle faded. "Are you saying she's the one you plan to marry?"

"She is."

"I see."

The room went silent save for the *tick-tick-tick* of the clock on the mantle.

Caden cleared his throat. "I take it you saw the ad?"

"If you refer to the one placed by Lord Bolton in search of any information leading to the return of his missing bride, then, yes, I saw it."

"Excellent. That saves a bit of time catching you up to Zeke."

"Before you entered the room, Caden was about to explain how he and Mrs. Jones became engaged."

Claybourne gave Zeke a perplexed look. "Who in blazes is Mrs. Jones?"

Caden glared at his brother. "That's the name Anna—formerly Miss Gloriana Masters—was going by when our paths crossed several days ago. She's been using the alias since escaping Bolton and her wicked stepmother—"

"Her stepmother?" Zeke interjected, looking well and truly appalled.

Caden nodded once, anger over what Mrs. Angelique LeClerque Masters had tried to do to Anna in boiling up inside him.

"Her late father's second wife orchestrated the entire affair. She convinced Anna she needed to marry Bolton in order to save both of them from a life on the streets, after claiming Masters died penniless."

"I recall the physician being well-off, if not outright wealthy," Claybourne said. "Granted, we knew the family years ago. Circumstances change."

"As we experienced first-hand," Zeke muttered under his breath.

Caden shrugged. "I can tell you Anna did not anticipate finding herself destitute at her father's death. Thanks in no small part to the shock of it, she initially agreed to her step-mother's suggestion to marry Bolton. Soon after, however, she decided against the marriage. When she informed her loving stepmother, she found herself imprisoned, drugged, and ulti-mately a coerced participant in a sham ceremony."

The earl sipped from his snifter. "Poor girl."

Zeke drummed his fingers on the arm of his chair. "I wish I could say I'm surprised Bolton would stoop to such a level. The perplexing thing is why he'd bother if she brings no money to the table."

"Oh, there's money involved," Caden said. "I just don't know how, where, or why. Yet."

"How did she manage to escape after the ceremony? Where did she go?" Zeke asked.

Pride welled up in Caden's chest. "During her captivity, she forged several letters of recommendation for herself. Suffice it to say she fled the night of the wedding with the letters and a piece of her mother's jewelry, which she hocked for cash. From there she landed herself in the role of companion to the Dowager Duchess of Wentworth. "

Claybourne's eyes sharpened. "Wentworth, you say? Of Northumberland? A guest at the Fenton's party, I take it?"

"Yes," Caden replied.

"I've seen neither hide nor hair of the lady in an age. She used to pay us a visit on occasion, en route to London. Always during the summer, never the spring. She didn't move much in society, even when the duke lived. As I recall there was some sort of tragedy in the family. Can't remember exactly what," the earl mused.

"The Dowager is a distant relation to the Fenton's. To Randall, as well, through the Marquis. I assume that's why she attended the festivities, which resulted in my path crossing with Anna's after all this time."

Zeke and the earl fixed Caden with matching, expectant looks.

"Yes?"

His grandfather gave an exasperated sigh. "You saw each other and, what? Professed your undying love for each other from childhood?"

Caden barked out a laugh. "Hardly. I recognized her, but couldn't place her. She, on the other hand, denied having ever laid eyes on me and let me know in no uncertain terms she wanted nothing to do with me."

Zeke grinned. "You mean to say a woman exists immune to Caden Thurgood's infamous charm?"

Caden smirked. "I did mention she's now my fiancé?"

Zeke hooted with laughter. "So you did. But how did you go from stranger to fiancé?"

Caden propped his chin in his hand and considered which details to share. "Suffice it to say I did, eventually, recognize her."

He rose from the chair and paced to the open terrace doors, where he stood, looking out. "I told her the ruse was up, we became reacquainted, and I...er...proposed. The thing is..."

Seconds ticked by with neither Zeke nor the earl uttering a word, but Caden felt their eyes boring into him.

He pivoted to face them. "The problem we have is how to get her out of the damned marriage. While she managed to escape hours after the so-called vows were spoken, Bolton's been searching for her. He means to have her back, and we know he traced her to the Fenton's party."

"Know, how?" Zeke asked.

"I saw him at the inn where we rode out the storm."

"I see," the earl said.

"It won't take much digging on his part to discover she and I spent a great deal of time together prior to my departure and her disappearance. We can assume he'll wind up here sooner than later."

The earl crossed his arms over his chest, looking resolute. "We'll have to get the marriage annulled quickly, then."

Zeke eyed Caden. "There's only one sure way to achieve that. As you stated, Cade, she ran away after the ceremony. It'll be uncomfortable for her, but a quick examination by a physician and—"

"—No, no, no," Caden interrupted, knowing all too well where Zeke was going. "She won't want to submit to anything like that. Too...er...undignified. Too...public."

Hell's teeth. His cheeks throbbed with scalding heat. It wouldn't take a genius to glean why Caden wouldn't want Anna examined for proof of virginity.

The earl glanced up to the ceiling as if seeking divine guidance.

Zeke coughed into his fist. "Of course. Do you have any other ideas for a more *dignified* basis of annulment?" He pressed his lips together.

The bastard was laughing. Caden feigned ignorance. "We investigate the cur, then use something we find to scare him off."

The earl nodded. "Good thinking. We can leverage the information to get him to agree to the annulment, and then," the earl met Caden's eyes, "get the two of you to the alter. *Quickly*."

Caden inclined his head, taking his medicine in stride. At least he'd beaten them to the punch announcing his engagement. Now all he had to do was convince Anna to accept his proposal.

***

"Here we are." Lady Thurgood pushed open the heavy paneled door and crossed the threshold into the large, sunlit chamber.

Anna followed, gazing about the high-ceilinged antechamber. "How lovely."

"I'm so glad you like it. It's one of my favorite suites. I do hope you'll find the rooms comfortable for the length of your stay."

She felt like a princess out of a fairytale. Silver and blue painted silk papered the walls. Two large oriel windows afforded a clear view of the Derwent. Their shutters had been left open, allowing for a soft, fragrant breeze which riffled the sheer drapes and caught at Anna's hair.

Through an open double doorway, she spied a large canopied bed with a beautiful blue brocade coverlet, along with the usual accompaniments—a dresser, side tables. And there, on a chest beside the wardrobe, her unopened luggage.

The future countess moved through the chamber, examining surfaces, the vase of fresh cut flowers beside the bed, the wicks in the oil lamps. She was beauty and vitality incarnate, and she made Anna feel positively dowdy.

"A tray of tea and biscuits is coming directly. I'll just wait on that if you don't mind?"

"Of course, though you need not trouble yourself if you've other things to do?" She finished on a hopeful note.

"Nonsense. What could be more important than getting to know my future sister-in-law?" Lady Thurgood faced Anna, hands clasped loosely behind her back. "I do wish we'd had some notice of your arrival, but then Caden assumed we did know, as he believed himself summoned by Zeke. How very odd."

"It is odd." She ducked her head. "I'm sorry for any inconvenience my presence has caused, my lady."

She had no notion of the true inconvenience Anna would cause them. Not yet.

The future countess waved her apology aside, smiling warmly. "Caden and Zeke will sort out the conundrum of the messenger. The important thing is you're here—and you've brought our Caden home. Would you like to sit? Let's sit."

With that, Lady Thurgood took one of two plush looking velvet armchairs situated near the hearth. She arranged her skirts with efficient flicks of her fingers then fixed Anna with an expectant eye.

Feeling a bit like a cornered fox under that frosty green stare, Anna had no choice but to follow suit.

"I have so many questions. You don't mind if I ask just a few? While we wait?"

Anna swallowed. "Er...I believe Caden wanted to—"

"Where did the two of you meet? Of course, I myself have known Caden only a little while in the grand scheme of things. Have you known each other many years, or are you more recently acquainted?"

After a moment's consideration, one of her father's adages came to her. *Whenever possible, stick to the truth.*

"As it happens, Caden and I were acquainted as children. We met again, quite by accident, at a house party hosted by Lord and Lady Fenton."

Lady Thurgood nodded, a satisfied expression on her face. "We knew, of course, that Caden accompanied Lord Randall's younger brother to the party. A happy coincidence, then, that you both wound up attending. You say you knew each other as children?"

"Yes."

A pregnant silence ensued.

Anna held herself very still though inwardly she squirmed under the lady's watchful gaze.

"It's the most extraordinary thing, perhaps unrelated, but only recently Zeke told me of a family who spent many a summer nearby, in a quaint little cottage on the river, not a five minute carriage ride from Chissington Hall. He mentioned a young girl who was a particular friend of Caden's. That young girl wouldn't happen to be you?"

Anna shrugged clumsily as her pulse raced. "It seems likely, my lady. My family did summer not far from here, and Caden and I were friends, as I mentioned."

Lady Kitty's green eyes softened. A small smile played at her lips. "Zeke said Caden had a terrible crush on you."

Anna barked out a laugh, then immediately clapped a hand over her mouth as the mortifying sound reached her own ears.

She cleared her throat. "I beg your pardon, my lady. I can assure you, Caden did *not* have a crush on me."

Amusement glinted in the future countess's feline eyes.

Yes, that was what her eyes brought to Anna's mind. A graceful, watchful cat.

"You sound very sure of that, Mrs. Jones. I shall have to put the question to Caden, to see if he gives a similar response."

Anna's cheeks went hot. She peered over her shoulder at the door. Would the tea tray never arrive?

"Widowed, and at such a young age. Do you mind if I ask for how long?"

She plucked at her skirts. The surprising change of subject caught her off guard, not to mention she did not want to lie to this woman. She'd never been particularly good at it, and she had the distinct impression the lady would see right through her.

A soft knock sounded just before the antechamber door opened. A fresh-faced, white-capped maid pushed a rolling cart laden with a gold tea service and a two-tier plate piled with fruit, scones and finger sandwiches.

Making no move to rise, Lady Thurgood smiled her thanks as the young woman parked the cart and departed. The door closed behind her with a soft click.

She picked up the ceramic teapot, filling two delicate looking tea cups. "Sugar? Milk? You were saying?"

"One sugar, please." Anna hated the tremor in her voice. When next she saw Caden, she intended to brain him for the third time this week.

"It's a rather difficult conversation," she finally said in all honesty.

"I see." Eying Anna, she held her cup to her lips to sip.

Anna felt the lady's unwavering stare as she stirred the sugar cube into the steaming jasmine scented tea, watching it dissolve. She picked up her delicate cup and took a tentative sip of the smooth, hot liquid.

Across from her, Lady Thurgood set her cup into its saucer soundlessly. "I see I shall have to come straight out with it. I fail to ascertain how you can be a widow and engaged to Caden while married to Lord Bolton."

Anna met the woman's eyes and said the first thing that came to her. "The thing is, I thought I had killed him. I only just learned he survived."

After a beat of silence, she said, "I think you'd better start at the beginning."

***

"And that, my lady, is how I ended up here."

Anna sat back in her chair, oddly relieved. It had taken over an hour, but she'd told the future Countess of Claybourne everything. She'd glossed over certain details, such as those concerning Lord Bolton's attack on her person which precipitated her hitting him in the head.

As far as the intimacy shared by she and Caden, she'd left that out entirely.

Lady Thurgood had listened, quiet and attentive, throughout the long discourse, save for occasional murmurs of commiseration and concern. Now, she regarded Anna with compassion-filled eyes.

"You poor dear. You lost your father, and never had a moment to grieve." Brows beetled, she rose and moved to the open window.

She gazed toward the waning sun on the horizon. "I can't help but feel a certain affinity with you. I'm not sure what, if anything, Caden shared with you of my experience prior to marrying Zeke."

Anna joined her. It felt good to stretch her legs and breathe in the balmy air. "He did not disclose any details. He mentioned a difficult time you'd been forced to navigate, which you managed with evident grace and courage. He can't sing your praises enough."

She chuckled. "I'm not so sure about the grace part. But yes, I underwent a difficult ordeal. Suffice it to say, with the earl's help, and of course that of Zeke and Caden, I escaped marriage to my guardian, who we believe planned to marry me, then murder me."

"Oh, my," Anna murmured, pressing her hand to her heart. They did share a similar story.

"I ran for my life, on the cusp of the death of my beloved grandfather. I'd lost both my parents several years before that, and at the time, believed my brother dead, as well. So I know a bit about what you must have suffered—what you undoubtedly suffer, still."

"I miss my father terribly. Both of my parents, really, though my mother has been gone for some time and the sting of loss is less acute."

"I understand. No other family to speak of?"

Anna shook her head. "My father's family relocated to New York. After losing both his parents to illness, he set sail, returning to England where he attended university, became a physician, and sometime thereafter, met my mother.

"Mother rarely spoke of her past. She told me enough for me to know she was an orphan, with no family to speak of. There was only ever the three of us."

"I'm sure the two of them loved you very much. Your father probably remarried hoping his new wife would be a second mother to you. How *could* she contrive to sell you off to Lord Bolton?"

Anna screwed up her face. "I still can't figure out what was in it for either of them. Caden believes there was some sort of financial motive, but I can't figure how. Angelique swore father left us destitute. Even if she lied about that, whatever fortune he had would have gone to her.

"As for Lord Bolton, the shape of his home alone tells me he hasn't the funds to pay Angelique a dowry for me. Whatever they stood to gain by having Lord Bolton marry me is a complete mystery. Frankly, I don't care why. I just want to be free of both of them."

Lady Thurgood nibbled the inside of her cheek. "I can understand your position. I, however, do care to know the why's and wherefores." She grinned at Anna. "I'm inquisitive by nature."

Anna grinned back.

She cocked her head and tapped her chin with one graceful finger. "My guardian wanted to marry me to inherit my family's title. Did your father hold any sort of honorific?"

"Oh, my, no."

She arched a single, ebony brow. "It's maddening, missing the puzzle pieces. There are, however, two things we know for certain. One, Bolton is still searching for you."

"Yes." Anna agreed. "And the other?"

"That you ended up in the right place at the right time. Crossing paths with Caden was the best thing that could have happened for both of you."

"Both of us?"

"It's obvious he cares for you very much."

Anna's cheeks went instantly hot. "I'm not sure where you got that idea."

She gave Anna a bemused look. "He asked you to marry him—"

"—Oh, but"

"—He secreted you out of harm's way in the dead of night—very romantic, by the by."

"Yes, but—"

"Finally, he brought you here, to the breast of his family. That alone tells me everything I need to know."

Despite her need to set the lady straight on nearly every point she made, her curiosity got the better of her. "Why do you say that?"

She rested one elbow on the window sill. "Has Caden mentioned anything to you about his...er...relationship with his brother, Zeke?"

"You refer to their recent argument?"

Her green eyes gleamed with satisfaction, as if Anna had just proven her point. "Precisely. When Caden left, I feared we would not set eyes on him for a long, long while. Yet, here he is."

"He came home because he understood the earl to be ill."

"And to get you to safety—and introduce you to us."

"I believe I explained I stowed away in his vehicle."

"He discovered you"—she cleared her throat discreetly—"*after* stopping for the night at a roadside inn?"

Blood flooded her cheeks. She must be glowing a bright shade of red. "Yes, and there procured two rooms for us." He had. At first.

"Of course. Caden is nothing if not a gentleman. My point is, he could easily have left you behind, rather than bring you with him and place himself on the mercy of his brother, for that is exactly what he has done."

Horror filled Anna. "But I have no wish to cause him distress. I've told him so repeatedly."

Lady Thurgood took both of Anna's hands in hers. She squeezed gently. "Please, do not trouble yourself. Distressing or no, mending the rift between the two of them is the best possible outcome for both of them regardless of who blinked first. I'll add Caden used a large measure of wisdom in turning to his family for assistance. Zeke did the same when faced with our particular crisis.

"The point I'm trying to make is, I believe Caden chose to swallow his pride and make amends..." she paused, "...for you."

Anna batted back a rush of tenderness and a sense of belonging she had no business feeling. "My lady, forgive me, but you're overlooking Caden's nature. He could never leave me behind once he understood my predicament. Defending those in need is a part of who he is."

The lady's knowing laugh conveyed an obvious fondness for Caden. "He is a good man, I'll grant you. But he could have helped you without bringing you here, Mrs. Jones. Miss Masters. Bah, either sound so horribly formal. May I call you Anna?"

"Of course, my lady."

She smiled warmly. "And you must call me Kitty—especially as we're to be sisters."

Anna sucked in a breath and her cheeks pulsed with heat. "Oh, dear. I thought I made it clear. Caden made-up the part about us being engaged in order to explain my presence."

Lady Kitty laughed with delight. "You hadn't a notion of him saying so? More of his gallantry at work, then, do you suppose?"

"Well, yes. I mean, no. I mean, I wondered how he planned to explain my presence. When I asked him, he told me he meant to tell you all the truth."

Lady Kitty gave Anna a delighted smile. "Are you so sure that is not precisely what he did?"

Anna blinked.

"Never you mind, darling Anna. I insist you put all of this from your mind for the next little while and take a well-earned rest. We will sort this mess out, together, as a family. Matter of fact, I wouldn't be surprised if Zeke, Caden and the earl have already concocted a plan."

Without further ado, she hastened toward the chamber door, throwing over her shoulder, "I confess I can not wait to discuss all of this with Zeke and compare my new knowledge with his."

Her green eyes twinkled with mischief. "Later, I shall send a maid to help you with your toilette, then collect you myself to escort you to the dining hall. This old castle has so many twists and turns, you'd never find your way on your own."

Before Anna could tell her not to go to the trouble of sending a maid, she was gone, door closed behind her, leaving Anna to wonder just where she'd gone wrong in her story-telling. She'd been forthright—mostly.

Yet, Lady Kitty believed Caden intended to marry her. If she only knew what had transpired between them at the inn, she could have no doubt whatsoever.

Anna's breath caught in her throat. How could she have been so stupid? How had she missed the obvious? Lady Kitty was right. Wrong about Caden's feelings, but right about his intention.

He did plan to marry her.

He'd said nothing of the sort on the drive to Chissington Hall, then proceeded to shock her with his blithe announcement of their supposed engagement. She'd assumed he'd made the claim out of expedience.

She paced the elegant chamber, wringing her hands. The idiotic, wonderful, too-noble-for-his-own-good man intended to marry her. But not because he had affection for her as his sister-in-law supposed.

Anna knew he didn't love her. He'd said nothing of tender emotions. He'd spoken only of wanting her, craving her. But that was a far cry from love.

He'd marry her out of duty, honor, responsibility.

She could not allow it—even if the thought of *not* marrying him now left her feeling as if someone had carved her very heart out of her chest.

Chapter Twenty

Anna came awake slowly. She lay atop the comfortable, down-covered bed in her fairytale bedroom suite.

She'd left the drapes open to allow the breeze off the river to sweeten the air, then lain awake, heart heavy, mind spinning, certain she would never sleep. But she had slept. She wondered for how long. The slant of light across the room told her dusk was nearly upon them.

A bone deep longing for Caden, for his presence, his smile, welled up inside her. But he wasn't hers, no matter that he'd willingly sacrifice himself for her for the sake of his honor.

Not hers. She needed to get that through her head.

A soft scratch sounded on the ante-chamber door. The promised maid, come to help her dress for the evening meal?

"Come," she called loud enough to be heard in the hall, and dragged herself into a sitting position.

A moment later. Caden's dark blond head appeared in the doorway, and her heart lurched.

He stepped inside the bedchamber, closed the adjoining door behind him, and leaned against it, arms folded over his chest. "You have no idea how hard it was to get here undetected."

She swung her legs over the side of the mattress, her heart in her throat. He shouldn't be here. She ought to insist he depart this instant.

Instead, the sight of him, freshly shaven, dressed in formal dinner attire, turned her bones to jelly and her brain to mush.

"I see you had a nice cat-nap." His eyes did a thorough sweep, starting at the top of her head, moving down to her stocking-covered toes, then eased back up to her face. An appreciative smile curved his lips.

Gooseflesh sprouted over her body as if he'd run a fingertip down her spine.

With effort, she found her voice. "Should you be here?"

He cocked his head and, in no hurry at all, closed the distance between them. "You don't wish to see me? I find that rather surprising."

The mattress dipped as he lowered himself to sit beside her, close enough that their hips brushed, and her stomach did a neat somersault.

"Your hair looks lovely, all sleep-tousled and mussed."

Her hand moved automatically to her crown. She'd forgotten she'd unpinned it.

Caden scooped the mass off of her nape and let it sift through his fingers.

She tried and failed to suppress a shiver. "You shouldn't be here. It isn't proper. Someone will see you."

"Who?"

"The maid arriving shortly to help me dress, for one."

"I see." He wound a thick lock of her hair around one finger, then let it fall. "I'd have sworn on a stack of bibles you'd be climbing the walls waiting to talk with me. But if you're certain..." He half rose.

"Wait."

With no hesitation, he dropped back onto the bed.

She nibbled her fingertip, eyes darting to the closed door. "Are you aware your brother and his wife know precisely who I am?"

His face said he was. "Evidently Zeke saw the ad Bolton placed and pointed out same to Kitty. I hadn't considered that. It rather sped up the process of explaining things, so no real harm done."

"No harm done?" she squeaked. "You told them we were engaged. They clearly understand that to be an impossibility as I'm already married."

A muscle ticked in Caden's jaw. "An impossibility, you say?"

"Of course."

"Why? Are you planning on returning to the man?"

"No, as you very well know."

"You do mean to dissolve the marriage as planned, then?"

"Again, you're aware that is precisely what I mean to do."

"Why, then, call marriage between us an impossibility?"

She drew in a lungful of air. "Caden, before we bother continuing this inane argument…"

He arched his brows in silent query.

"Are you, by any chance, proposing actual marriage to me?"

He crossed his arms over his chest. "I believe I am."

Anna searched his eyes.

He returned her gaze with an unblinking stare.

"I assumed you made the claim in order to explain my presence, *sans* chaperone. I did wonder how you intended to rescind your bald declaration."

"Well, now you know." His jaw hardened. "I intend nothing of the sort."

Lady Kitty had been right. He wished to marry her. To make her his wife.

An image of the two of them walking hand in hand down the graveled lane leading to—of all places—the cottage where her family had summered filled her mind. Her gut twisted with a sharp, painful yearning for what could never be. Not like this.

Still, a tiny piece of her heart ignited with hope. "Why?" she couldn't stop herself asking.

"Why?"

"It's a simple question."

He unfolded his long legs from the bed, jammed his hands into his pockets and began to pace. "I should think it obvious."

"To you, perhaps."

Brows furrowed, he moved back toward her, not stopping 'til he loomed over her. "Anna, you were a virgin—"

"—I knew it." She sprang to her feet, hands fisting at her sides. "You intend to entrap yourself. I won't have it."

He pinched the bridge of his nose. "I don't consider it thus."

She threw up her hands. "Every girl's dream. To receive an offer of marriage based on a man's misplaced sense of obligation and duty."

The casual smile he sent her did nothing to disguise the sudden bleakness in his expression. "There's nothing misplaced about it, darling. The fact is…" His eyes softened, crinkling at the corners. "…we made love."

Her insides trembled at the softly spoken words.

"…and now we shall marry."

She held fast to her resolve as her heart broke in a million pieces. "It's not that simple."

He nodded. "I'm aware you didn't choose this—to find yourself altar bound, and with me in particular. But it's where we are, darling." His voice lowered to a whisper. "I vow I *will* try to make you a good husband."

Anna blinked rapidly. He had everything all wrong. He was exactly the man she'd choose to marry, was she free to do so, and were his reasons for proposing based on love and affection.

Me in particular, he'd said. And what was that nonsense about him *trying* to make her a good husband? Of course he'd be a good husband. He'd be a marvelous husband.

Abruptly she understood. Caden didn't see himself as she saw him—as he truly was. He thought he wasn't good enough. They'd discussed his skewed opinion of himself at the inn. She'd thought she'd disabused him of the notion. She ought to have known better. Caden, the man, was nothing if not stubborn.

Thus, he'd handed her a way out. All she had to do was agree with his summation of himself as a profligate philanderer ne'er do well.

She wouldn't do it.

"You must admit I have the right of it."

"I admit nothing. I do not wish to marry you for the reasons you cite."

"I see." He studied her, his expression inscrutable. "What reason, do you suppose, would justify you wanting to marry?—me, specifically, by the by."

Heat bloomed over her, pulsing off her cheeks. The word *love* hovered on the tip of her tongue, but, of course, would remain unspoken.

He traced his fingertips along her jawline. "You were saying?"

Heaven above, that felt good. Her eyes drifted closed and, helpless to resist, she pressed into his touch. "I think...I think..."

"Yes?"

"I would very much prefer to be *un*-married before discussing any future engagement."

"Ah. An excellent point." He spoke the words in a gruff whisper.

His hand curved around her nape, while his free arm encircled her waist, pulling her ever-so-slightly closer.

She tried to recapture her resolve. It slipped out of reach like a fish in water.

He was too close. His allure, too powerful. Her defenses were no proof against his hands on her body, or the clean, masculine scent of him teasing her nostrils.

"There's one glaring problem, Mrs. Jones." He lowered his lips to her ear. The velvet rumble of his voice curled through her, turning her bones to jelly.

"What's that?" came her breathless reply.

"We want to do all sorts of naughty things together. Or don't you want me to kiss you, and touch you and fill you until you come apart in my arms?"

Just like that, her insides simmered with delicious molten heat.

"That's quite…" she drew in a shuddering breath and, knees gone wobbly, promptly plopped onto her rear on the mattress. "…a bold assertion."

He sent her a cocksure grin. "You haven't denied it, however. I'd call you a liar if you did. It's written all over your beautiful face."

She glared. She couldn't decide which of them at this moment annoyed her more. Him for his utter arrogance, or her, because he was right.

He lowered himself to sit beside her, his thigh brushing hers. He leaned back propping himself on his elbows. "No need to get your feathers ruffled. I did say *we.*"

So he had. Her gaze strayed to his mouth. She did so want him to kiss her.

"At any rate, consider it fodder for thought." Abruptly he rose from the bed.

He strolled across the room, and leaned against the windowsill. "Hadn't we better compare stories before supper?"

She blinked at him, disappointment washing through her. "Beg pardon?"

He arched a brow. "I tell you what Zeke, the earl and I discussed, and you fill me in on yours and Kitty's conversation."

Of course. Why hadn't she thought of it? Probably something to do with being distracted by Caden's mouth, and hands, and...Closing her eyes briefly, she shook her head to clear it.

"Quite right. Tell me how you left things with your brother and the earl." She applauded herself on sounding almost normal.

"As I mentioned, Zeke remembered you as a girl."

Lady Kitty had said as much, as well. She'd also shared Zeke's theory Caden had harbored a childhood crush on her. She considered asking Caden if that was true. Then dismissed the idea. He'd only deny it.

But was it true?

"He saw Bolton's ad in *The Times*, mentioned same to Kitty. I hadn't considered he'd have recognized you from so many years ago. After all, I didn't recognize you straight away when you hovered not two feet above me. In fairness to myself, Zeke had the benefit of reading your name in print alongside your likeness.

"And so, forewarned, he questioned me the moment you quit the room. Then the earl joined us. You'll be gratified to know we reached a decision about what's to be done to sort your situation."

"Oh? You've decided? Do tell."

If he heard the sarcasm in her tone, he gave no indication. "Assuming Bolton has been apprised of your presence at the house party and subsequent disappearance in conjunction with my departure, we expect to find him on our doorstep sooner than later. We devised a plan to enlist the earl's man-of-affairs to uncover everything he can on Bolton—concerning his finances, business ventures, personal circumstances, etcetera, etcetera. In short, we're searching for leverage, something we can use to free you from the sham of a marriage which Bolton and your step-mother wrangled you into."

"You make it sound so simple."

Caden shrugged. "No reason it shouldn't be."

"What about the rest?"

He arched his brows. "The rest?"

She cleared her throat. "What did you tell them about our so-called engagement?"

He tugged at his waistcoat, not meeting her eyes. "A consensus was reached. As soon as the annulment is procured, we'll proceed with the wedding post haste."

"Post haste?"

He winced apologetically. "Let's just say it escaped neither Zeke's nor the earl's attention that the one sure-fire way to get you out of your marriage we rejected out-of-hand."

"Proof of my virginity. So you, what? Admitted we..." She couldn't finish her statement. Could barely breathe. She waved her hand in a vague, all encompassing gesture.

"Don't be daft."

She glared at him.

"Nothing specific was said."

"But they know," she hissed, humiliated beyond measure.

He turned to look out the window toward the river. "They're two intelligent men. Of course they know, just as they know precisely where to lay the blame for the situation."

Blame. Did he even know what that one word revealed about his true feelings? *Blame* implied someone was at fault. Implied someone made an error in judgement. The fact he viewed himself as that person didn't lessen the sting.

"A good plan is in place. The first step ought to meet with your approval, at least."

"Dealing with Bolton," she murmured.

"Precisely."

Without making the conscious decision to do so, she rose and joined him at the window. She simply wanted—needed to be near him.

"What did you and Kitty discuss?"

She gave a one-shouldered shrug. "I told her nearly everything."

Caden eyed her with mock shock. "Was she scandalized?"

She gave his shoulder a half-hearted swat. "I said *nearly* everything, including the fact that we are not actually engaged."

Caden grunted. "What did she say to that?"

"She insisted I was mistaken. *Me*. About whether I'm engaged. I don't know whether to thank you or scold you for this latest entanglement, Caden Thurgood."

"You'll let me know when you've decided, I'm sure."

She gazed up at him.

Though the sun had not completely sunk, the moon had risen and its reflection off the river gleamed in his eyes, currently fixed on her lips. A muscle in his jaw ticked.

Her insides shimmered. A mind numbing, all-consuming need filled her, blotting out every other consideration. She wanted Caden to kiss her, now. To make love to her again, right here in his grandfather's manse.

She opened her mouth intent on telling him everything he'd said about her wanting him to kiss her and touch her was true.

Abruptly, he tugged on his cuffs and sauntered for the door. "I'd best make myself scarce before the maid arrives and my presence scandalizes the household."

She frowned, barely resisting the urge to chase after him. "You're going? Now?"

"Hadn't I better?" he asked, turning to gaze over his shoulder at her, all innocence.

"Of course," she snapped out.

With a crooked grin of farewell, he exited the chamber. A moment later, she heard the antechamber door open and close.

She stared at the empty doorway, a cacophony of emotions roiling inside her. Restlessness and yearning, safety and warmth, happiness and belonging. Because she was here, with Caden, and he wanted to marry her.

Where was her affront at a marriage proposal born of duty rather than affection? She had until her marriage with Bolton was dissolved to figure out how to let Caden go. That was what she ought to do, wasn't it?

Kitty seemed to think he cared for her. He must, beyond the call of mere duty, mustn't he? Would that be so wrong a basis for marriage?

Probably. But, God help her, she wanted it to be enough.

***

Caden met Zeke and the earl in the family parlor. The three had agreed to convene slightly ahead of the appointed hour when the ladies were due to arrive.

A fire crackled merrily in the hearth. The earl lounged in his usual armchair, while Zeke, decanter in hand, splashed ruby-red liquid into three of the six glasses set out on the credenza.

"Ah, Caden, just in time." Zeke held out a glass to Caden before delivering the earl's wine and taking the seat beside his.

Caden joined them, lowering himself onto the adjacent sofa.

"It's good to have both my boys home," the earl said, raising his glass in a toast.

Caden lifted his glass to the earl then sipped. How things had changed from the last time he was home. Instead of chomping at the bit to be away from his older brother, he felt settled. Instead of alienation, he felt camaraderie. A clear sense of purpose and resolve replaced the usual restless, aimless energy that plagued him in recent years.

Thanks to Anna. She'd changed everything. She'd changed him. He liked the changes if he was being honest.

"You'll both be pleased to know Carson Hallis responded to the telegram we sent out today," the earl said.

Far from seeming annoyed by the potential difficulty posed by the *Bolton complication*, as the earl deemed it, Caden's grandfather appeared energized. His and Anna's future wedding plans likely played a part in the old man's attitude.

Unfortunately, Anna had denied their engagement during her *tète-á-tète* with Kitty. Who knew what she'd say to the earl when they met. By the end of the evening, would they or would they not be engaged in the eyes of his family? More importantly, would Anna ever agree to the engagement?

"What did Hallis have to say?" Zeke asked.

Caden eyed the earl expectantly. Inside he brooded. It must have occurred to Anna she might be carrying his babe. Even so, she seemed markedly resistant to the idea of marriage to him.

He couldn't blame her. What did he have to offer? He was not of the same ilk as Zeke and the earl. He was, by all accounts, his father's son.

Even so, he had no intention of letting her go. And so, faced with her evident opposition, he had no choice but to play the ace he'd been born with and hope the gamble worked. His entire future rested on it.

The earl rolled his wine stem between his fingers. "Hallis plans to employ his minions to dig into Bolton's court filings, banking records, as well as search out any and all rumors amongst the *ton* and and *demi-monde* concerning his personal affairs. With luck, he'll have something for us by the end of the week."

"I assume you apprised him of the need for discretion." Caden said.

"Never fear, the message covered all that and more," the earl replied.

"Excellent." Caden swirled the ruby liquid in his glass and breathed in the rich aroma of berry and spice. "What if he finds nothing more than a marriage certificate?"

The earl rose from his armchair with the ease of a man twenty years his junior. Zeke was right. He looked more hale and hardy than he had in years.

He stood at the mantle, wine glass in hand, a gleam in his faded blue eyes, every bit the family patriarch. "We'll get the thing annulled. Call in some favors, or, barring that, buy all his gaming debts and pronounce them due."

Zeke, as usual, took a more careful approach. "We should wait and see what Hallis finds. There doesn't appear to be any immediate danger or point in rushing the process." He lowered his voice and muttered, "Let us hope."

Caden bit back a smile. It was the second time Zeke had broached the possibility Caden had gotten Anna with Child. He couldn't find it in him to get too terribly annoyed. He'd been pondering the same thing to the point of obsession, mainly because he was of two minds.

While the thought of her carrying his child filled him with wonder and stole his ability to think straight, the truth was, he didn't want Anna to marry him out of necessity. What kind of fool did that make him?

"There are some family matters we need to see to, sooner than later, however," Zeke said.

Caden eyed his brother. "Such as?"

Zeke returned his stare. "As you're to be wed and will have a wife to provide for, your current financial situation will have to change."

Caden straightened and set his glass on a side table with a decisive click. This was the opening he'd hoped for.

Zeke continued. "You'll, of course, resume living in the Hall. Once married, you and your lady wife will move into a wing more suited to housing a family, rather than make-do with the chamber in the bachelor suites where you habitually reside. Your quarterly allowance shall be reinstated, and…" he flashed a magnanimous grin, "…we shall forget all about the unfortunate incident that precipitated your recent…er…"

"Fall from grace?" Caden put in dryly. "How about, no?"

Zeke's grin vanished and a flash of annoyance sparked in his blue eyes. "No? I had hoped you'd matured enough to move past this stubborn streak."

Caden pinched the bridge of his nose, striving for patience. He no longer had the luxury to tell his brother to stuff it, nor, oddly, the inclination. Anna's influence, no doubt.

"I appreciate the offer, Zeke. However, I have an alternate proposition to make—one that I believe will clear up the recent misapprehension on your part regarding the funds I requested."

Zeke's look of annoyance faded, replaced by one of grudging intrigue. "Do you mean to say you actually intend to explain yourself, rather than leave the earl and I to our suppositions and conjectures?"

Caden met his brother's eyes with an unblinking stare. "I fully intended to explain myself, and would have, had I not heard insulting suppositions and conjectures spoken behind my back."

"I'd hardly call a private conversation between the earl and myself speaking behind your back. One could argue you had no business listening-in to our private discussion. As for the rest, you never gave us a chance to—"

"Boys, enough." The earl's gruff tone brooked no argument. He held one hand outstretched like a maestro holding a section of the symphony in check. "This is not the time for another of your squabbles. The ladies are coming."

Only then did Caden note the muted, distinctly feminine voices echoing down the hall, announcing the ladies' impending arrival.

"Might I suggest we continue this"—Caden cleared his throat—"*discussion* after supper?"

Zeke snorted. "I can hardly wait."

The ladies' chatter grew louder. Anticipation tightened Caden's gut.

In moments he would introduce, Anna, his future wife, to the earl, and he had no earthly idea what she might say. For that matter, he had no notion of what the earl might say.

The black sheep of the family, he had announced his engagement to a married woman on the run from her psychopath husband—a woman apparently not overjoyed by the prospect of marriage to him. It was anyone's guess how the next hour might unfold.

He closed his eyes briefly and inhaled through his nose, slow and deep. He'd faced worse odds. He thought.

A sudden image of her, strolling one-slippered down the stone corridor, formed unbidden in his mind and he choked back a laugh. He'd carted Anna's lone satin slipper with him all the way from Yorkshire. Most likely she hadn't bothered keeping its match. He still didn't know why he hadn't surrendered the thing to her the night she'd lost it. No doubt the set had cost her a pretty penny.

He'd make it up to her with a dozen such pairs. Fine slippers or boots or whatever she preferred. Of course, cementing his financial resources meant repairing the damage he'd done with his knee jerk reaction in rejecting Zeke's authority and all things to do with his familial estate. One thing at a time.

He opened his eyes.

Aunt Lillian entered the chamber, her evening attire impeccable, her white hair piled high in typical fashion. Next came a smiling Kitty, whose pale green eyes shot immediately to him, expectant, and, as always, warm.

Then came Anna.

She had indeed dressed for dinner. She wore one of her new-to-her, oddly well-fitting gowns. This one was fashioned of a pale gold-ish amber that seemed particularly suited to her coloring and which hugged her curves to perfection. Her chestnut hair was styled in a classic chignon, allowing for soft tendrils to frame her crowd-stopping face.

She paused just past the threshold, eyes searching the room, and, spotting him, sent him a tentative smile that hit him like a punch to the gut and drew him to her like a magnet to steel.

In seconds, he held her silk gloved hand to his lips. "Good evening. I trust you had a pleasant rest?"

She nodded once. Her almond-shaped eyes held his, uncharacteristic uncertainty swirling in their depths.

An overwhelming urge to shield her from any discomfort or harm filled him. He'd never in his life felt such an affinity for someone *not* his family, and certainly had never felt the need to side-up against his family. But this was Anna. *His* Anna. With her, all bets were off.

He tucked her fingers into the crook of his arm and shifted to face the room with her locked at his side. "Come. It's past time you meet my grandfather, the Earl of Claybourne."

Chapter Twenty-One

Anna hesitated only a fraction of a moment before allowing Caden to lead her into the small, luxuriously appointed parlor.

She held her chin high, silently commending herself for maintaining a calm veneer in the face of her audience—an earl, his heir, a future countess, and an earl's sister, blue bloods all, through and through.

She studied the earl as they made their approach. As a young girl, she had, on occasion, seen him, say when he frequented the village market, or rode one of his many horses, or took the road past their cottage sitting atop his dashing barouche. Yet she'd never met the man, despite the fact his grandson had befriended her, and her family resided not a five minute carriage ride away.

Thanks to that, or perhaps due to her mother who always cautioned her against trusting the nobility, she'd imagined him as aloof and disdainful of those whose social status placed them beneath him—which encompassed almost everyone.

Now she weighed her childhood image against the man himself.

Broad shouldered and tall, he stood—presided?—at the marble mantle, the unapologetic master of his domain. Marked with age by his lined skin and white hair—albeit, a full head of it—he nonetheless emanated a keen, nearly palpable sense of authority. But she detected none of the haughty and forbidding characteristics she'd anticipated. Instead, he emanated strength tempered with a kindness and warmth that set her immediately at ease.

Zeke, sitting in an armchair near the earl, was another story entirely. The carefully neutral expression on his handsome face did not disguise his distrust for her. Something icy in that royal blue stare said if she intended to lure his baby brother into harm's way, she had another think coming.

She could tell him she held little sway over Caden and his too-noble ideals, but she sensed the attempt would be akin to arguing with a brick wall. At least, to some degree, she understood the issue Caden had with his older brother.

Caden. His arm felt so very solid under her hand, promising safety, the heat from his body, offering comfort.

But he was no pussycat to be toyed with. The sleek, powerful energy he emitted with his every move spoke of the essence of the man at her side—one hundred percent alpha male—which explained the trouble his elder brother had with *him*.

He halted in front of the earl. "Miss Anna Masters, may I introduce the infamous Earl of Claybourne, otherwise known as my grandfather. My lord, Miss Masters." He paused. "My betrothed."

A split second after he spoke, Lady Kitty's joyous, "*Yes,*" pierced the air.

Zeke, the earl, and, a quick glance told her, Caden, all fought grins over the lady's cheeky exclamation.

Though inwardly gratified by the lady's show of approval, Anna's cheeks burned. How could he put her on the spot like this?

On the other hand, hadn't he told her, as far as he and the family were concerned, they were well and truly engaged?

The earl took her hand. Blue eyes, a shade darker than Caden's but not so deep as Zeke's, twinkled at her. There was no other word for it.

He pressed a kiss to her fingers and expressed his pleasure at meeting her, charming her and setting her instantly at ease.

Caden thought he took after his father? Bah. He was every inch his grandfather's grandson.

The earl extricated her hand from Caden's arm and led her toward a tall, ornate crystal floor lamp.

"Let me have a look at the beauty you've brought home to us, Caden." He studied her face, and a bit of her discomfort returned. "You are quite correct, Kitty, love, she does have the most extraordinary eyes."

Kitty appeared at Anna's side as if by magic. "Exotic, don't you agree?"

Anna sputtered, flustered beyond measure. "Oh, I don't think—"

"Exotic, and...oddly familiar." He cocked his head, still contemplating her face.

Curiosity overtook her embarrassment. "Oh? Did you know my mother, perhaps? My family did reside nearby many a summer."

"Yes, I'm aware," the earl replied. "Your parents let the old game-master's cottage for a time."

Zeke unfolded from his chair, moving to stand beside Caden. "You mentioned you'd met them on several occasions, but that was years ago. You recall her mother's face so clearly? I hope I'm half as sharp when I reach your age, old man. While I remember a pretty, dark-haired woman toiling in the garden and the occasional sighting of a lanky, studious looking man, I'd be hard pressed to give any better description than that."

The earl's focus shifted to his older grandson. "I never said I recalled them, per se. I said she looks familiar." He grinned at Anna. "Perhaps I am thinking of your mother, or perhaps a painting hanging in a gallery. Who knows? You'll have to forgive the mental cogitations of an..." he cleared his throat and eyed Zeke meaningfully, "...*old* man when confronted with a young beautiful woman."

She smiled. "You did meet my parents, my lord? I never knew."

"I invited your family to visit on several occasions. Most times I received word your father was away on business."

"He did attend frequent lectures and the sort." She nibbled her lower lip, then froze, hoping Caden had missed the so-called tell. She hadn't exactly lied; her father had attended many lectures. Just not during their time in Derby.

If she wagered a guess, her mother had manufactured the excuses to beg off attending. She had never been overly social, especially when it came to the nobility, for whom she had a distinct distrust. She frequently warned Anna off of them. Off Caden. *Guard yourself with the likes of him, Gloriana. With the nobility, the title always comes first, even before family. When you're grown, you'll understand. Best to find a good man. A loyal man. Steer clear of the likes of them...*

She gave herself a mental shake, dragging her thoughts from the too-vivid memory.

"Staying up on all the latest scientific discoveries is an admirable trait in one's physician. Your parents did come to tea once—one afternoon while you and Caden explored the countryside, no doubt."

"Oh?" They'd never mentioned.

The earl's gaze found Caden, bespeaking a deep fondness that endeared him to her all the more. "As I recall, on those months your family resided in the cottage, that's all the boy ever did. Especially the later years."

Following the earl's pronouncement, a simultaneous snort came from Zeke, and a groan from Caden.

Anna flicked a glance toward Lady Kitty who gazed back at her wearing a beaming I-told-you-so smile. Before she could staunch the reaction, something warm and wonderful flooded her chest and spread to all her extremities.

Her mother's words came to her again. *Don't be charmed by the likes of that Claybourne boy. With the nobility it's the title above all—even each other. Even over family.*

She shivered.

"Have you caught a chill, my dear?" the earl asked, concern evident in his eyes.

Now she knew where Caden got his too-keen powers of observation, too.

"Not at all."

"Nevertheless." He led her back toward the intimate seating area before the hearth, helping her onto the sofa. "Caden, be a good lad and call the footman to serve the champagne."

"Certainly," Caden murmured. He sent Anna a brief wink.

Anna arranged her skirts, discomfited by her ill-timed memories. Her mother's dire predictions had never amounted to anything. Quite the opposite, in fact. Caden had proposed to her, for goodness sake, and hadn't he risked his family's censure bringing her here? Hardly an example of putting the title first. So why did she suddenly fear the other shoe dangled, ready to drop?

She was safe, welcomed by Caden's family with open arms, with the possible exception of Zeke. As for Caden, he would never knowingly hurt her.

He settled beside her, holding two flutes of champagne, tiny bubbles still rising to the rim, and handed her one.

Accepting the chilled crystal, she banished her mother's words to the recesses of her memories.

A footman distributed the remaining champagne flutes 'til everyone in the room held one. The earl took one armchair, Lady Lillian the other, and Kitty and Zeke moved to stand before the hearth.

Zeke wrapped an arm lightly around his future countess's waist, then held his glass aloft. He met Anna's, then Caden's eyes.

"To the two of you. May you live a long and healthy life together, and," he broke off and shifted his focus to his wife. Affection softened his expression.

Kitty's answering gaze, equally lovelorn, had Anna stifling an urge to sigh aloud.

Zeke's focus shifted back to Caden. Was Anna seeing things, or did his lashes glisten with a sheen of moisture?

He continued, voice gruff. "May marriage bring you the happiness and joy it has me. That is my wish for you."

A lump tightened her throat as everyone in the room heralded Zeke's toast with *Here, here.* The backs of her eyes stinging, she sipped her champagne. Its sweet effervescence softened the hard constriction.

Caden's warm palm gripped her free hand and squeezed.

Her eyes met his. "Here, here," he whispered, his blue eyes filled with tender promise.

Hope and belonging and so much love rose up in her that it was all she could do to not confess her heart to him right then and there. Heaven help her. What was she to do?

***

With the plates cleared, the ladies adjourned the dining hall for the music room, leaving Caden, Zeke, and the earl to enjoy an after dinner brandy.

Dinner tonight, *sans* guests, was an informal enough event that no one would have objected if Caden, or any of the three men, had opted to escort the ladies into the parlor or out on the terrace.

Though tempted, Caden hadn't. While he suffered with an unreasonable desire to not allow Anna out of his sight, his pride didn't relish the idea of anyone else knowing.

Besides, he and Zeke had unfinished business concerning Caden's—and thus Anna's—future.

Hand resting atop the white table linen, Zeke lifted one finger in a silent command. In an instant, waiting footmen set about clearing dishes and cutlery and serving the brandy goblets, before departing and closing the doors behind them.

Zeke drew his glass toward him, eyes on the shimmering aromatic liquid. "I gathered from our earlier conversation, you have some things to say concerning your allowance, brother?"

"I say, m'boy, Caden only arrived home today. Surely such matters as quarterly allowances can wait?" The earl smiled an apology at Caden.

Caden held up a hand. "Please don't worry on my account, my lord. Zeke has the right of it; I have some things I need to say—to both of you."

The earl's bushy grey brows shot up. He leaned back in his chair and lifted his snifter to his lips. "Go on, then."

"The thing is—" Caden cleared his throat. This was harder than he'd anticipated. Best to get the worst part out. "The thing is, Zeke, a large part of what you observed about me was true."

He had the momentary pleasure of seeing Zeke's dumbfounded expression. That was something.

Bolstered, he continued. "I have spent these past several years following my education in negligence and disrepute. Rather than pursue any proper vocation or calling, I squandered my time, fraternizing with a certain class of women, frequenting house parties and the like." He paused. "Gambling for the fun, I'll admit, despite the incident you bailed me out of.

"I want you to know, however, It's the former I regret. I don't have a gambling addiction, Zeke. I have, however, lived a meaningless existence. Recently I tried to change that."

Zeke nodded once. "By change, do you mean you needed one last large withdrawal from the family account to cover a gambling debt? Because, I have to tell you, that screams of a gambling problem."

"The money wasn't for a gambling debt."

Zeke closed his eyes briefly in a silent show of relief. "You needed to pay off, or house a woman, then?" The implied *whom you impregnated,* remained unspoken. "Best we know now to minimize any damage going forward. Your wife will certainly not thank you for your bastard child showing up on her doorstep."

Caden told himself he deserved this. The good news was, for once, Zeke had the key points all wrong. "No—on both counts. Though I can see why you'd assume as much."

"But—"

Caden held his palm out for silence. His grandfather, he noted, gratified, had not uttered the first word. "Let me finish, please. I am coming to my point."

"Very well." Zeke drummed his fingers on the white table-cloth.

He couldn't help himself, Caden supposed.

"Go on, son," the earl said, with a tap on Zeke's forearm, bless his grizzled heart.

The drumming ceased.

"I think I'd come to the same conclusion as you. No, I *had.* I took stock of my life and realized it was past time for me to change, thanks, in large part, to your influence, Zeke."

"Mine?" Zeke sounded dumfounded.

"Witnessing your metamorphosis after Kitty came into your life, seeing you"—Caden searched his mind for the right words—"allow yourself to be vulnerable, showed me a strength in you I'd never realized until then was missing."

Zeke shifted in his seat, his cheeks turning a dull shade of red. He made no denial. To do so would be to lie. His brother was no liar.

"It caused me to contemplate my own future. Well, that, and Kitty's relentless humanitarianism."

Both Zeke and the earl chuckled knowingly.

"When I looked in the mirror, I saw a shallow, self-absorbed man. One I'd thought was so different from our father, but who was really the same—minus his unluckiness."

The earl looked sad at the mention of his son, but Zeke looked downright thunderous. "You are nothing like our father. He was a weak, selfish man."

Caden's brows shot up, as if to point out Zeke had made his point for him.

"Zeke's right, Caden. I loved your father. But you are not like him. Granted, you are blessed with some of his better traits, his charm, a jovial attitude that draws the fairer sex, and more than his share of luck, but the rest," His grandfather broke off, shaking his head in vehement denial.

Caden fought down a rush of emotion he hadn't expected. He grasped his forgotten snifter and took a large swallow. The heady liquid burned its way down to his belly. It helped.

Zeke spoke again. "So, you lost a bundle of money, perhaps in an investment gone awry. It's just money, Cade. There are worse things. Thankfully you don't make a practice of racking up debts. I can only hope, now that you are engaged—"

"Zeke, for God's sake, will you let me finish?" Caden's words sounded gruff, but his heart did not carry the heat of anger it once had—except for a small portion aimed at himself.

Why had they not talked like men about this before Caden left, half-cocked? Oh. Because Caden had erupted like a child instead of broaching his grievances like a man.

Zeke clenched his jaw, and gestured for Caden to get on with it. He picked up his glass and drank.

"The money—which I was forced to raise on my own, pilfering my own investments, and yes, I'd like to be reimbursed, did not cover a debt, gaming or otherwise. Neither do I have a woman clamoring for my support."

Zeke and the earl exchanged brief, relieved looks.

"Then...?" his brother's one-word query dangled, open-ended in the air between them. "Why the secrecy?"

"I wanted to surprise you, as a sort of wedding present. I needed the money for equipment, ordered, and due to arrive any day, for the quarry."

Zeke frowned. "By God, I got word from the foreman of some unknown shipments which started showing up late last week."

"You refer to the limestone quarry?" The earl asked.

"Exactly. Excellent. I hadn't realized the machinery would arrive so quickly," Caden mused.

Zeke propped his elbow on the table, closed his eyes, and rested his chin on his fist. A small smile played at his mouth.

"This wouldn't have anything to do with my wife, now, would it?"

Caden arched a brow. "I take it you've heard her grumbles over the estate's longstanding contract with the military? A contract she sees as inhumane—nay—barbaric?"

"What's this?" The earl demanded. "The Claybourne estate has a long history of supporting the Royal Navy."

Zeke sat upright and drummed his fingers on his knee under the table. He simply couldn't help himself, Caden mused.

"Something Kitty detests, old man," Zeke said. "She claims the military uses the limestone to, and I quote, poison, blind and maim."

The earl's expression turned considering. After a moment he nodded with reluctant agreement. "I see."

Caden went on. "She painted an all too vivid picture for me. It got to where I couldn't sleep at night imagining the horrors propagated by our unwitting association."

One corner of Zeke's mouth kicked up. "My wife. She does has a way about her."

Caden spread his hands wide. "She does, indeed. During your honeymoon, I did ample research. Turns out the estate itself, and the villages under the Claybourne mantle, can benefit from the limestone in a multitude of ways, benefits which would not only offset any loss of funds caused by terminating the contract with the crown, but should out-pace the lost income."

"How so?" The earl asked.

"Besides the usual shoring up of roads and buildings, Limestone uses include purifying drinking water, re-mineralizing farm soil, and enhanced metallurgy."

Zeke's eyes sharpened on Caden. "Mayhap this is true. But such an over-haul can't happen on its own, equipment or no. Someone with the wherewithal to manage what promises to be a massive undertaking would have to take charge. Production, transport, implementation, oversight. In short, every aspect."

Finally. He spread his arms wide. "That's where I come in, brother. Meet your new overseer of operations." Caden sent the earl and his brother his most magnanimous smile. "All I require—"

Zeke barked out a good-natured laugh. "This ought to be good—"

"Is the deed to the cottage where Anna's family once lived, signed to me, a hefty salary, free rein to run the quarry as I see fit, and..." He met first his grandfather's, then Zeke's, eyes. His smile vanished. "...your trust."

A pregnant pause ensued.

Then his grandfather stretched out his hand to Caden. "You have mine."

They shook, then both turned expectant gazes on Zeke.

He pushed away from the table and stood, then rounded the corner approaching Caden.

Caden rose, uncertain what to make of his brother's odd silence.

Zeke dragged him in for a rare, warm embrace. "You have my trust, along with my thanks, and, my apologies. You were right. I should not have given up on you and I should have asked why you needed the funds. It goes without saying you'll be reimbursed."

He pulled back and met Caden's eyes. "You grew up while I was away, chasing my mines and running from my life. I should have noticed. Kitty did."

"Did she?"

"She told me I'd underestimated you. Said I shouldn't make assumptions about why you needed the money and"—He shook his head ruefully—"said I should ask you about your future plans. One thing's certain."

"What's that?"

"Her *I told you so* is going to be of epic proportions."

Caden, the earl, and Zeke all burst out laughing. They roared until tears leaked out of their eyes, because they knew what he'd said was nothing short of the truth.

***

Anna awoke early for her walk as planned. She doubted she could have slept late even had she wanted to. She laced up her boots and silently admitted the truth: She didn't want to miss a single moment of what currently comprised her life, here and now, in Chissington Hall. She felt just like the princess in the fantasies she'd created in her head as a child.

She even had her Prince Charming.

She paused, and gave her waist a little pinch. Sure enough, it hurt.

A helpless smile splitting her face, she reached for the bell pull above her bed. She hated to pester one of the servants who surely had tasks aplenty, but she dare not try to find her way out of the sprawling manse on her own.

Less than a minute later, a soft knock sounded on her antechamber door. Awed by the household's efficiency, she hurried forward swung the door open wide, and found herself face to face with Caden.

Freshly shaven, hair damp and combed back, dressed in tweed and smelling divine, he stole her breath.

He flashed her a brilliant smile. "Good morning."

"What are you doing here?" she hissed in answer, and grabbed his sleeve to pull him inside. An image of him kissing her breathless filled her with giddy anticipation despite her chastising tone.

He didn't budge from his wide-legged stance in the hallway. He waggled one finger at her. "Best if we maintain a modicum of decorum, darling."

She scowled at him. He had nerve, showing up on her doorstep uninvited, and then rebuking her.

It was like he'd read her mind.

She crossed her arms over her chest. "Perhaps you'll answer my question, then?"

He gave a mock, long-suffering sigh. "I came to escort you on your walk. I thought you might enjoy a guided tour."

Her heart swelled at his thoughtfulness. "I would like that very much."

To her utter delight, his tour started inside the castle. He revealed hidden treasures she never would have noticed on her own, and shared snippets from his childhood that warmed her heart.

Here, the schoolroom where he and Zeke and countless Claybourne children before them practiced their letters and, according to Caden, drove their nan's, governesses, and tutors to distraction. There, the music room, the billiard room, the men's wing.

And now, the formal ballroom.

"I've never seen a real ballroom, Caden."

"No? Can't say you're missing much."

She disagreed. She clasped her arms behind her, tilted back her head and executed a slow pivot. A real, glittering ballroom, with high-high ceilings and massive crystal chandeliers.

She gazed across the expanse of polished marble-tiled floors spying artful alcoves, strategically staggered, where, she imagined, couples sought out privacy for quiet *tète-a-tètes* between dances, out of listening range of young ladies' ever present chaperones.

She glanced up at the balcony which would house the musical quartet. She could practically hear the strains of a waltz now, could see a crush of dancers sweeping over the floors.

Anna had never attended a real ball. Still, the scene unfolded before her, clear as day. A shiver of longing coursed through her and whispered if she stayed, if she and Caden wed, she might experience such an evening first-hand.

In the arms of the man I love. Caden, whom I've always loved.

She turned to stare, wide-eyed, at Caden, her heart lodged in her throat. Should she tell him? But what would that accomplish? It was clear he felt something for her, but *something* hardly equated with undying devotion.

He must be the one to broach the subject of affection, even if it wasn't love precisely. She stared at him, willing him with all her might to do so, now—or at least kiss her.

Caden gestured toward the doorway. "Ready to venture outdoors?"

Not waiting for an answer, he took her arm and led her out of the ballroom and down another corridor. "We'll exit through the portico."

"Delightful," she said, annoyance pricking her.

They were alone. Not a soul in sight. They hadn't crossed paths with a single servant. No one would witness Caden sweeping her into his arms to kiss her as she ached for him to do.

As she'd ached for him to do since yesterday afternoon, in her bedchamber.

But no. Caden's chivalrous streak had evidently asserted itself the moment he blithely announced their engagement.

What happened to the passionate man who betrayed his own sense of honor to make love with her? Had their lovemaking left him unmoved? He'd implied otherwise when they spoke of it in the carriage.

What if he lied to spare her feelings? What if he no longer desired her? What if he wanted to marry her out of duty alone?

That, she could not bear.

She nodded woodenly as Caden pointed out pristine potted plants and overflowing flower baskets adorning the portico.

She had to know the extent of his feelings for her. At least, if they shared passion, they had a chance for love to grow—or so she believed. But what if the passion was all one-sided?

In the coach, he had told her he found their lovemaking *everything he had hoped and more.* At the time, she'd taken his words as high praise. In retrospect, he could just as well have been hedging.

She clenched her jaw. She loved the man and was *this close* to accepting his proposal. How could she not? Despite his words to the contrary, he was everything she could want in a man and more. What kind of fool would she be to reject him?

A fool in love, evidently, because without some sign he cared for her, at least a little, she could not marry him. It would kill her.

"Are you listening to a word I'm saying?" He demanded, stopping in his tracks.

Anna stumbled to a halt beside him. "Um…Yes?"

He scowled down at her. "You've hardly said a word about the grounds. Not the winding path, nor the fountain, nor the pond." As he spoke he gestured hither and yon, as if pointing out same.

She glanced around her, surprised to find they had walked quite a distance from the castle and now stood beside a small pond with a delightful fountain depicting a mermaid riding a large fish.

Caden continued in an peeved tone. "I thought you'd enjoy the estate's famous secret garden. But if you'd rather turn back—"

"Secret garden? As in hidden?"

"Oh, you are awake." He inclined his chin toward the dense forest on the eastern side of the path into which the gravel walk seemed to vanish. "Hidden, invisible to the naked eye, and so on. What do you think? Should we go back?" One corner of his mouth quirked upward.

"I wouldn't miss it for the world." A garden, safely tucked away from any possible onlookers? Once there, she *would* coax a kiss out of the man, if she had to plant one on him herself.

Chapter Twenty-Two

Leaves and bramble crunched underfoot as Caden led Anna off the graveled path onto a worn foot path leading into the forest. As always, the proximity to the river left the morning air thick with moisture.

Above, the sun had burned off much of the overcast sky, but the prevailing cool temperature hinted at fall's arrival. Upon entering the dense thicket of trees, the air grew downright frigid.

Whether from the sudden absence of light or the knotted roots beneath their feet, Anna stumbled.

Caden caught her easily, one arm about her waist. He shifted to face her. He told himself she needed a moment for her eyes to adjust to the green tinged other-worldly darkness enfolding them.

Their eyes locked for a timeless moment.

Then her gaze dropped to his mouth and her lips parted.

Now, he thought, *finally.* She would come to him, ready and willing and, *Christ,* he was as hard as an untried youth.

Lifting her chin, she fisted her skirts in her hands and marched past him toward the clearing on the opposite side. "This way?"

Frustrated desire ate at his resolve to stick to his plan. "Right-o."

They emerged into a clearing of sweet smelling grass liberally dotted with yellow and white wildflowers. A limestone wall standing two stories high ran the length of the property as far as the eye could see. Rich green vines covered it.

She spread her arms wide. "This is lovely, but I'd hardly call it a secret garden. More like a remote picnic spot."

"This is not the garden." He nodded his head toward the massive wall. "One would think the wall marks a perimeter. Which it does. It also encloses the estate's hidden-by-design garden."

"Why did you never show me this when we were young?" she asked, her tone half accusatory, half dubious, as if she doubted the garden's existence.

"It would hardly have been proper to bring you here, where we'd have been completely unsupervised."

She arched a brow. "You expect me to believe you kept this place a secret due to your moral ethics?"

He kept a straight face for a full second, then barked out a laugh. "Hardly. I myself learned of its existence after you'd been gone a long while. For some reason my parents, or, more likely, the earl, thought it best not to reveal such a rife location for mayhem to two rambunctious boys."

She laughed. "Fair enough. But now..." she pressed her palms together, steepling her fingers under her chin. Her eyes sparkled with unabashed excitement. "Show me."

Everything in Caden wanted to drag her close and plaster her with kisses until he had his fill. Instead he sent her a jaunty smile, as if his insides weren't tangled in knots by unfulfilled desire. "As you command, my lady."

He reached unerringly for the hidden lever, gratified when he heard a soft click. He tugged, overcoming a modicum of resistance thanks to the overlapping vines, and out swung the low-hung arched iron-and-stone gate. "After you."

Anna ducked inside, and he followed.

The delight in her expression as she took in seemingly every nuance made the torture he'd endured in bringing her here without breaking down and kissing her worth it.

"It's beautiful, Caden. Like a dream."

Peeling off his leather gloves—because it was warmer in the garden than on the open path, and not because he meant to expose and touch every inch of her flesh she'd allow—he made his way to the lone slatted bench where he sprawled, legs outstretched, arms spread along the back, and tried to see the space as she might.

Sunlight entered through the domed, trellis-styled roof, across which grape vines grew in abundance. Velvety green vines and brilliant climbing florals covering the walls, swallowing, reflecting and softening the light so it appeared ever dusk or dawn.

Birds chirped merrily atop the trellis. A few had found their way inside to bathe in the trickling, large marble fountain where ecstatic angels frolicked.

Riotous English rose blossoms in pink, white, and red abounded. He didn't know all the other flowers by name, but he thought he spied clematis in blues, purples and pale lilac, and in the raised beds, peonies, pansies, and herbs—sage, lavender, mint, certainly. The combined scents of flora and fauna sweetening the air almost rivaled Anna's own intoxicating scent.

The place *was* bloody magnificent.

"Caden, I hope you know how grateful I am you brought me here," she said in a feather soft voice. She moved toward him.

"I thought you'd like it."

"No. I mean, thank you for bringing me *here*." Gloved hands twined before her, she lowered onto the bench beside him. "I've been thinking."

Sitting this close, her rosy cheeks and creamy complexion called to him. He could no longer resist touching her. His fingertips grazed her cheek. Soft and dewy as a newborn babe's.

"About me kissing you breathless?"

So much for his plan. Now she would know beyond a shadow of doubt how badly he wanted to—

"Yes."

Everything in him stilled. "Yes, you've been thinking about me kissing you?"

Her unblinking eyes met his. "Yes."

In an instant, he had her face cupped in his hands and his mouth on hers. He'd imagined devouring her. Instead, he found himself savoring her sweetness.

Tremors vibrated his hands. Was he shaking or was she? Maybe both of them were.

Her lips parted, welcoming his tongue into her warmth, and she loosed a tiny mew of need.

Longing, fierce and intense and so hot it threatened to incinerate him from the inside out swept through him. How did she *do* this to him?

Her arms twined around his neck and she pulled herself into him, or was that him pressing her close to touch every part of her he could? He didn't care so long as nothing separated them.

"Anna, *Anna,*" he murmured against her lips. "I've been so desperate for you. I can't...I need..." He couldn't finish his thought.

His mind whirled and his insides seemed to liquify into the richest, hottest wax. He pulled his mouth from hers and pressed his forehead against hers. "I want you," he said in a gravelly tone he barely recognized as coming from him.

"You do? Truly? I thought..." Her magnificent eyes lowered and her cheeks, already flushed, bloomed scarlet. Her words came out in a tumult. "I thought you'd had your fill of me and proposed only to do right by me, and I swear, Caden, if that's the only reason—"

His choked laugh cut her off mid-sentence. "Sweetheart," he smiled into her now glaring eyes. "I restrained myself for both our benefits."

"I don't follow."

He inclined his head. The last thing he wanted now was a long, drawn out discussion. But he could spare a moment to clarify matters.

"I wanted you to feel what burns between us for yourself, to wipe any and all doubt from your mind as to our suitability. I think I accomplished my aim."

She stiffened. "Well, that seems..." She sniffed. "...calculated and a tad arrogant."

He pressed a soft kiss to her lips and her body went satisfyingly pliant in his arms.

"It's not arrogant if it's true." He kissed her temple, nuzzled the tender spot beneath her ear. "Do you want me to kiss you, Anna?"

He brushed his lips over hers, feather soft, teasing her, and torturing himself.

"You know I do, Caden," she said, her voice breathless. "*Please* kiss me."

His words came out a hoarse whisper. "Glad to know I'm not alone in this madness. I haven't for one moment stopped wanting you, Anna. God knows I tried."

"*Caden.*" Fisting his lapels in her hands she arched up to kiss him with a desperate, sweet ardor that stole his breath.

He pulled just out of her reach, and she huffed out her displeasure.

This was it. Time to play his ace.

"Then it's agreed? When this is done, when we have your...*situation* sorted, you'll marry me?"

Her brows furrowed. "It's what you really want, Caden? It's not just gallantry?"

"This again?" He took her hand and pressed it to his cock, straining against the fly of his trousers. "Does this feel like a man focused on gallantry?"

She drew in a shocked gasp. But rather than tug her hand away the moment he released her, her fingers traced the ridge of his erection, tentative and exploratory.

A helpless shudder rolled though him.

Far too soon, she withdrew her hand and brought it to her mouth to remove her glove with her white teeth.

Then she lowered it to cup him and all rational thought fled.

He reached for her, dragging her into his chest. His lips found hers, hungry, desperate, as if he could swallow her whole. Everything in him went hot like a volcano ready to erupt. At this rate, he'd lose control and unman himself.

"You make me crazy, Anna, make me burn. You make me want things I shouldn't." His words came out choked, as if ripped from his lungs.

Her hands smoothed over his shoulders and crept up his neck to twine into his hair. She'd rid herself of her second glove and her cool fingers against his fevered skin made him gasp.

She leaned back to gaze into his eyes. "What *do* you want, Caden?"

I want you. Your body, your heart, your promise to be mine. But he couldn't speak the words. He closed his eyes and trembled with the force of his desire for her.

As if gentling him, her lips found his cheek, his jaw, his neck. Her tenderness threatened to derail him from the inside out.

"I need to taste you." He lowered his head, nuzzling her collar bone while his clumsy hands fumbled with her bodice.

After a moment, he had her ribbons untied. He tugged at the gown, lowering it to expose an expanse of creamy curves and the tantalizing edges of small, rosy, puckering nipples.

When his lips sealed over one of the cresting buds, her head lolled back, and a tiny whimper of need escaped her.

He wanted to roar his triumph. His lips suckled, his tongue laved, and his groin tightened like an over-wound spring.

As if it had a will of its own, one of his hands wrestled with her skirts, fisting them upward to dive underneath.

He slid his palm between her legs, over her inner thigh. "Unconscionably soft," he murmured, dizzy with the dewey feel of her satiny skin. He cruised higher, reaching her cruchless undergarments and pressing the sheer fabric aside.

He groaned. Warm, wet, plump flesh.

He took his time exploring her exquisite petals. Beneath his touch her sweet flesh quivered. Little by little, her legs parted for him, inviting his intimate touch.

"*Caden.*"

"Darling." He pulled her, pliant, onto his lap, her back to his chest, her legs straddling his.

Her head fell back on his shoulder as his fingers danced over her, drawing forth shiver after shiver of pleasure, and her nectar of feminine dew. She was so ready. So open. Completely his.

She came apart under his touch, sobbing his name.

Her release and the delicious friction of her hips, pressing and sliding over his erection flared his own passions to the point of agony.

Grasping her by the waist, he lifted her and turned her to face him, settling her with her skirts bunched around her hips and her legs astride his.

She looked like a goddess, eyes dazed, cheeks flushed, lips parted, her chemise hanging low, exposing the creamy swell of her breasts.

With one arm around her waist, he held her close. He feasted on her lips and used his free hand to rip open the fly of his trousers. Unerringly, his raging cock found her opening, and in one thrust, he filled her hot, silken channel.

She closed around him like a glove. Sweet heaven on earth.

She cupped his cheeks with damp palms and kissed him, her lips clinging to his as he plunged into her, again and again.

He heard a moan, or a growl, or a groan and realized the sound came from him.

"Caden, darling, *yes*," she murmured against his lips.

It undid him. He erupted, his hot seed spilling into her. He couldn't stop himself if he wanted to. Like jumping off a cliff into endless ecstasy.

When he was utterly spent, he flopped onto his back dragging Anna with him. His legs hung over one side, Anna still straddling his hips, their bodies joined in the most intimate way possible. Their hearts pounded into each other's so he couldn't tell whose was whose. It felt right. *She* felt right.

She was his. His.

She had agreed to marry him. Their lovemaking, as far as he was concerned, sealed the promise. God help anyone who tried to take her from him now.

He could lay like this, listening to the fountain softly gurgling, the birds cooing, the wind whispering through the trees beyond the garden walls forever, so long as Anna lay with him, her cheek nestled into the curve of his neck.

Her fingers toyed with his hair brushing his collar. She sighed and nestled closer. Yes, he could stay like this forever, Anna in his arms.

***

After all the worry and indecision, being made love to by Caden, knowing they would spend forever together, left Anna more contented than she could remember being, ever. He had not told her he loved her in so many words, but he had shown her with his touch that he cared.

"Do you remember the two of us, whiling away those long summer days along the river bank? You dictating the rules of the game and never relenting? When I rescued my stolen princess, I had to bestow a kiss on her. Always."

His question came out of nowhere. Spoken in a soft voice that felt like a caress, it nevertheless dragged her from the near idyllic state she'd been in.

She stirred in his arms, lifting her head to look at him.

A small smile played at his lips and his eyelids were open a mere crack.

She traced her fingers over his jaw, her heart overflowing with love. "So I did, as you've already established *many* times. You recently admitted you liked kissing me. Too much, you said. Or will you deny that now?"

"I will not. Do you recall the last time we saw each other? In Derby, I mean."

She folded her hands on his chest and rested her chin on them. "I do."

"What do you recall, Anna?"

She licked her lips, suspecting he meant to garner her admission she'd wanted his kisses more than he'd wanted hers, yet unable to work up any heat at the moment.

"I was moping about, our day of departure looming ever closer. You said you felt sorry for me, and offered to play Prince Charming rescues the stolen princess as a way to cheer me. I agreed."

"Agreed? You leapt at the chance," he teased and tugged a lock of her hair. "What else do you remember?"

She closed her eyes, feigning concentration. In reality, she remembered every detail. Lying at the base of that large yew tree, ignoring the knotted roots poking into her back, pretending to be in a dead faint.

Caden swooped her up in his arms and carried her to a shaded, grassy knoll overlooking the river bank. She could still feel the warmth of his firm, lithe body as he held her. Could hear the gentle cascade of water flowing, smell the foliage, and damp earth as he laid her on his coat.

She could see the blue of his eyes as, slowly, he lowered his mouth to hers.

He'd kissed her before. Hard, quick presses of his lips that left her giddy and giggling for days. This time was different. He kissed her so gently, so tenderly, her heart threatened to burst from her ribs. Rather like it had a few minutes ago.

Unlike today, he ended the kiss with an abruptness akin to a bucket of ice-cold river water dumped over her head.

Before she could open her eyes, he was on his feet, grabbing her hand, all but dragging her to the path leading to her family's cottage, where he left her to take off in the opposite direction.

His apparent anger baffled her—and grew into a hurt more painful than she could have imagined. Especially as she never saw him again.

She had no intention of telling him any of those things.

Instead, she opened her eyes and sent him a studious look. "We were in the forest clearing, equidistant between our homes. You rescued me, delivered me to safety, and then...kissed me."

He nodded. "I see. Not such a momentous occasion for you, then. For me it was," he paused, blew air out his cheeks, "...beyond anything."

Her pretense of indifference vanished. She stared at him, heart in her throat.

"Before that summer, you were a playmate, a younger one at that whom I needed to protect. That summer, the moment I saw you, I knew things had changed. You seemed different. Not only the bullying termagant from the years before, but..."

She could not speak, much less work up any heat at his less than flattering description. Butterflies swarmed her belly, squeezing in around her heart.

He huffed out a self-conscious laugh. "You were all girl, with eyes that seemed to see through me, and a mouth that...I thought about way too often. That day, that *kiss*. It left me—" He raked a hand through his hair. "I didn't know whether I wanted to throttle you or kiss you again."

He slid her a wry glance. "That's not true. I *wanted* to kiss you again, and touch you, and touch *myself*, for God's sake."

He snorted and looked up at the dome. "Meanwhile I didn't understand any of my feelings, other than to know being with you left me restless and murderously desirous of something I was sure I should not want.

"One minute you were the demanding little girl down the lane, and the next you were…" He shook his head. "… always on my mind. The first person I thought of when I woke, and the last before I slept. Practically my obsession, I'm embarrassed to admit." His expression turned somber. "And then you were gone."

Her heart lodged so tightly in her throat it threatened to choke her. When she found her voice, it echoed all the emotions swirling within her.

"Maybe you didn't understand your feelings for me, Caden Thurgood, but I knew mine. I was mad for you. From the moment you told your brother and his mate to fob off, I was putty in your hands."

His face went ruddy but he barked out a laugh. "Putty? More like porcupine."

They grinned at each other, until, gradually the humor of the moment faded, becoming at once achingly poignant.

She felt herself ridiculously on the verge of tears. *She*—who never cried.

"I never thought I'd see you again, Caden. Imagine my shock when I discovered you face down at the one and only social event Lady Wentworth deigned to attend since employing me."

He tucked a lock of hair behind her ear, his finger tips lingering over her cheek. "Shocked and appalled and clearly not overjoyed at the reunion."

Her mouth curved upward. "Not precisely true."

A voice sounded in the not too far distance, crashing into Anna's dreamlike state with the force of an anvil. With a yelp, she sprang off of Caden, yanking down her skirts, and attempting to right her bodice.

"Caden? Who *is* that?"

He grinned at her. *Grinned*, despite the very real danger someone would discover them here—like this.

In seemingly no hurry, he unfolded himself from the bench, tucked in his shirt and refastened his trousers.

Turning to face her, he shifted his stance, positioning his body to conceal her from anyone who might happen through the gate. "Probably just a groundskeeper."

"Groundskeeper?" she squeaked. "Don't I look as if..." As if she'd been recently tumbled, she left unsaid. She stared at him, horrified.

His gaze assessed her and his expression of amusement vanished. He swallowed audibly. "You look like a goddess," he breathed. "Come here."

Delight over the emotion he did not bother to hide overrode her anxiety. She hurled herself into his arms.

Her face pressing into his chest, she heard him mutter under his breath. She could not quite make out the words. It sounded as if he'd said, *Will I ever* not *react to you this way?*

"Caden? Are you here? Is Anna with you?" came the deep, rich voice of Zeke.

She groaned in dismay.

"We're here, Zeke," he called in a loud voice. "What in God's name are *you* doing here?"

The hidden door swung open.

Anna sprang away from Caden, putting a good two feet between them just as Zeke's head bobbed inside.

His eyes went from Caden, to Anna, then back to Caden. He almost managed to hide his smile.

"Sorry to interrupt your...er...tour of the grounds. Miss Masters has a visitor."

"A visitor? At this hour?" Caden sent Anna a bemused look. She shook her head.

"My sentiments exactly." Zeke remarked. "If not for the identity of her visitor, I might've refused her."

"Who is it?" Caden asked, sounding more curious than annoyed.

"The Dowager Duchess of Wentworth, and to say she's impatient for Miss Masters to return from her walk would be putting it mildly."

***

Zeke departed, allowing them a few minutes to, as he put it, finish their tour of the garden.

Wearing an indulgent grin, Caden smoothed and tucked her mussed hair 'til she was forced to swat his hands away. She did allow him to amend her efforts at tying the bow at her bodice so that it resembled an actual bow rather than the knot she'd accomplished in her haste to cover herself.

She would never recover from her embarrassment over Zeke discovering her and Caden in such *flagrante dishabille*.

Not that she had time to worry over his opinion of her. She had bigger problems to sort.

"Are you looking forward to reuniting with your ex-employer? You appear to be in quite a hurry." Caden spoke in a neutral tone.

His long legged stride kept pace with Anna's trot with seeming no difficulty at all.

"I am. Although…" She paused, unable to put into words the renewed anxiety building within her. "I'm unsure what to expect from her."

"What do you mean?"

"I mean, has she come to collect me to resume my duties?"

Caden slammed to a halt, his hands grasping Anna's shoulders, turning her to face him.

"You're not going anywhere." His voice brooked no dissension. Still, faint worry lines etched his forehead.

Did he fear she might choose Lady Wentworth over him? She did care for the woman, a great deal. But her heart belonged to Caden. Had it escaped his notice she'd agreed to marry him before their magical lovemaking in the garden?

"I'm not, no," she agreed softly.

His expression relaxed, but he lifted one hand to rub the pad of his thumb between her brows.

"What on earth? Do I have a smudge of dirt between my eyes?"

"You're scowling so hard you're in danger of giving yourself a permanent crinkle. What are you afraid of, if not that?"

"I'm not afraid." She bit her lower lip, then stopped when his gaze tracked to her mouth.

"The truth is, I don't know why she's come. *Now,* I mean. And why so anxious to lay eyes on me? I can't help feeling..." she shrugged, helpless to explain. "As if everything in my life is about to change."

He wrapped her in his arms. He was warm and solid and, despite what he thought of himself, everything good in a man.

"The *grande dame* probably wants to see for herself you made it, safe and sound. Or mayhap she has news of Bolton. Either way, we'll hear her out together."

Together. The word sent a little thrill of happiness through her, dispelling her sense of doom. "I *am* glad she's here. I owe her so much and have so many questions."

He sent her his most devastating smile. "Let us go get your questions answered."

Chapter Twenty-Three

A footman stood at attention on the portico near the back door. He informed Caden and Anna the household awaited them in the grand parlor.

Hand on the small of her back, Caden led her through a maze of corridors.

Soon they neared a massive doorway opening into a chamber Anna had yet to visit. A muted din of somber voices greeted them as they crossed the threshold.

They entered a large parlor, lushly appointed with gilt filagree trimmings, marble statuary and hearth, velvet drapery and cushions. It was large and, most definitely, formal, unlike the one where they usually convened. It occurred to her the family had treated her as one of their own since her arrival.

As their presence became known by one and all, all conversation ceased. Five sets of eyes turned in their direction.

The earl and Zeke stood before the massive, marble mantle. A low burning fire glowed in the grate. Lady Lillian and Lady Kitty shared a sofa situated near an oriel window overlooking a formal garden. Lady Wentworth held herself ramrod straight before said window, her back to the view. Sunlight streamed in behind her.

A knife could cut the tension in the room.

"Good morning," Anna said, a tentative smile on her face. "Lady Wentworth, it is so very good to see you."

She spoke the truth. Her odd feeling of dis-ease not withstanding, she had missed the older woman, with her sharp tongue and dry wit. She hastened toward the dowager, whose entire frame seemed to sag with unabashed relief at the sight of her.

"There, you see? Hale and hardy as promised," Lady Kitty said in her melodic, soothing voice.

"I'll be the judge of that," Lady Wentworth replied, though her tone held no real heat.

She reached for Anna's hands with both of hers as if they were dear old friends, reuniting after a long time apart, rather than an employer and employee. It probably seemed strange to Caden's family. To Anna, the greeting felt somehow right.

"Let me have a look at you." Lady Wentworth eyed her head to toe. "How do you fare, my dear?"

Anna's eyes burned for no good reason. "Very well, thanks to you." She smiled at Caden. "And Mr. Thurgood, of course. I didn't expect to see you quite so soon. It seems a lot of trouble for you to go to—again."

Lady Wentworth's expression sobered. "I had to come immediately. I bring news that you will want to hear."

A fresh wave of dread rolled through her. "You saw him. Lord Bolton." It was a statement more than a question.

"I more than saw him, I dealt with the blackguard. That's what I need to tell you. I've handled everything. You're free of the man."

Anna blinked. "You handled everything?"

Caden appeared at her side. "How so?"

Across the room, she heard the earl's low voice. "By George, I knew she looked familiar. Lill?"

"You know, I think you're right, Horace," Lady Lillian murmured in response.

"What is this about Bolton no longer being a problem?" Zeke demanded, crossing the room toward them.

Lady Wentworth drew herself up like a general facing down troops. "As you all apparently know the relevance of the name, I'll cut to the chase. He has agreed to have the marriage annulled. All it took was some persuasion of the fiscal variety."

"Well, that's bloody fabulous," Caden burst out. "The man kidnaps Anna, forces her to wed him, stalks her, then makes out like a road bandit."

"You'd rather a drawn-out legal battle, Thurgood? Be glad I've taken care of the problem." Her eyes narrowed on him. "Just in time to deal with the next."

"The next? And what might that be?" Caden sounded more curios than indignant.

"Yes, do tell," Zeke said, folding his arms over his broad chest.

"As if you don't know, Caden Thurgood," Lady Wentworth admonished.

"Oh, dear." Zeke sounded resigned, and very much as if he knew the so-called problem to which Lady Wentworth alluded—which was more than Anna could say for herself.

Her gaze shifted between Lady Wentworth, Caden, and his brother. "Excuse me, gentlemen, Lady Wentworth. Before we move on to the next subject, I have a question." She met Lady Wentworth's eyes. "Why?"

"Why?" she aped.

"Why have you done," she opened her arms in an all en-compassing gesture, "any of this? Helping to secret me away, rectifying my appalling marital status...For that matter, how did you know of my situation? At Femsworth Manor, you knew I needed to depart before I did. You worked out my escape to the letter. Clothing, funds, transportation. My God," she exclaimed with sudden insight. "You made up the earl's supposed illness, did you not? To make certain Caden would leave, straight away, thereby securing my escape?"

"Clever girl," Lady Wentworth said, a fond light in her dark eyes.

Anna scoffed at that. "Not clever enough by half. I don't understand any of this. I'll ask you again: Why have you gone to so much trouble on my behalf? Surely not out of loyalty for my service?"

"The girl doesn't know?" came the earl's hushed query.

"Horace, I think it's safe to say she does not," Lady Lillian answered in a low, censorious voice.

"Know what?" she demanded of the room, scanning each of their faces in turn.

Everyone—save Lady Wentworth—wore some degree of the same piteous expression. A sense of inescapable doom filled her. Like watching a carriage accident unfold but being unable to look away or stop it. She'd known something terrible was coming.

"We've strayed from the point," Lady Wentworth said in her most imperious tone.

"Which is?" Zeke demanded.

Anna wanted to scream. She wanted answers, not this deflection.

"Why, that on the road to Derbyshire, Anna and Caden spent the night in an inn. Together. In the same chamber."

A deafening silence followed her pronouncement, broken after a beat by the tap-tap-tap of Zeke's finger on his bicep. "Lady Wentworth, are you, by any chance, implying that my brother and the lady should marry?"

"I'm more than implying. I'm insisting. His honor demands it."

Anna should've wanted to crawl under the carpets and disappear. Instead, morbid curiosity outweighed even her mortification. She would not leave until she grasped Lady Wentworth's stake in all this.

Zeke eyed the ceiling. "Here we go again."

"I beg your pardon?" The older woman sputtered.

Zeke started to reply, but Caden stayed him, holding up one long finger.

"Lady Wentworth," he drawled. "You are, unfortunately—or fortunately depending on one's take—a hair slow on the draw." He bestowed on her his most devastating smile. "Anna and I are already betrothed."

The corners of her lips curved up slightly, and some of the rigidity went out of her posture. "I see. That's fine, then."

"So glad you approve," he said, dryly.

"Enough of this." Anna exclaimed. "I ask again. Know what? What does every other person in this room seem to understand that I do not?"

Caden grasped her shoulders in a gentle grip and shifted her to face him. Compassion filled his eyes. "Lady Wentworth is—I believe—your grandmother."

"My grandmother? What? No." She choked out a half laugh, which died on her lips when Lady Wentworth averted her gaze.

"Should we...perhaps..." Lady Kitty's words grew hushed as she neared the doorway, through which she ushered the others—save Caden who remained, rooted beside her.

He laid a hand on Anna's shoulder. "Do you wish for me to stay?"

She considered his offer for a long moment, replaying his words from earlier. *We'll hear her out, together.* Finally, she shook her head.

With obvious reluctance, his withdrew his hand. "Call out if you need me."

Seconds later she heard the soft click of the door as it closed, leaving she and Lady Wentworth—her grandmother?—in a lock-eyed stare.

Anna felt like a fool. Now that she knew, she could not help but label herself a blind, idiot. How had she missed the obvious signs? Their similar frames, height, expressions, down to the stubborn sets of their jaws. She recalled noting their feet had a particular likeness. High arches, skinny ankles, and crooked pinkie toes—much like Anna's mother's feet.

Her feet? She was thinking of feet in light of the momentous revelation leveling her?

"May we sit?" Lady Wentworth sounded, for once, uncertain.

Wordlessly, Anna indicated the nearby sofa.

They each took a corner, angling their bodies to face each other. Two cups of now-cold tea sat on the polished table before them, and Anna caught the sweet scent of bergamot in the air. What she wouldn't give for a bracing cup of steaming hot tea about now.

"I would dearly love a cup of tea," Lady Wentworth said, echoing her thoughts. "Or perhaps something stronger."

"I can call for—"

"—No. First I'll answer the questions you no doubt have for me. Afterward, if you do not wish for me to leave, tea would be most welcome."

It was on the tip of her tongue to tell her of *course* she would not wish her to leave. Then it dawned on her. Depending on what the lady shared, that may well not be the case.

"Are you really my grandmother?"

"Yes. Emmaline, your mother, was my daughter."

As she'd surmised. Now that she knew, it explained another coincidence. The myriad books in Lady Wentworth's library on horticulture, healing herbs, and the like. The books must have belonged to her mother, once upon a time.

"My parents never told me of you. Why is that?"

A far away look came into the older woman's dark eyes. Dark eyes, like her mother's. "That would be because your mother wanted nothing to do with her father and me, with good reason."

"Such as?"

"The late Wentworth, your grandfather, my husband, came from an old, distinguished family. The bluest of blood ran through his veins. To say he had conservative ideas about how society should function would be to put it mildly."

Her mother's words echoed in her mind. *With nobility, the title always comes first. Even before family.* She twined her fingers in her lap.

"Meaning for him, the title came before all else?"

Lady Wentworth looked taken aback. "You sound exactly like your mother—before she left."

"She may have said something to the effect a time or two." Or fifty.

"She spoke of him?"

Anna smiled sadly. "No. She merely proffered her opinion regarding nobility as a whole. Mother had strong opinions about many things."

"She could be a force." A faint, fond smile accompanied the statement. "In this instance, she had good reason for her staunch belief. Her father, the duke, arranged what he believed was a good marriage for Emmaline. A nobleman from an old established family. She did not outright agree to the match, but she did concede to consider allowing the man to court her. To that end, he visited our estate in Northumberland where he stayed one month's time.

"After several weeks, Emmaline was less than keen on the idea of marriage to him."

She drew in a deep breath and continued with her tale. "The morning of his departure, Emmaline came to us distraught. Apparently in a private conversation with the man, she expressed her intention not to wed him. She claimed this nobleman, a man highly esteemed for his rank and wealth, became enraged and attacked her."

"And? What did the duke do? Did he call the man out?"

She pressed her lips together briefly. "No. He told her to grow up. Said it made no difference in the scheme of things. I'm not sure he even believed her. He said she did not have to like him in order to wed him."

A sick feeling rolled through Anna. "And you? What did you say?"

She fisted her gloved hands on her lap. "The man was handsome, charming, rich. I couldn't imagine him doing anything so barbaric as attacking our daughter in our own home. I decided she must have embellished the truth. When I said as much, she did not argue. She informed us of her intent never to see the man again and clammed up tight. Wentworth was furious. A silent war ensued. And then...she turned out to be with child."

Anna's hand went to her throat. She couldn't breath.

"Pragmatic as always, Wentworth determined that the two of them should marry as soon as the license could be obtained. Emmaline took his decision surprisingly well. Indeed, she made not a peep of protest."

"What happened?"

"The morning her wedding was to take place, we woke to find her gone. I thought Wentworth would have an apoplexy. Even so, I argued—too little, too late—that we hadn't done right by her. Not only should we not force her to marry the blackguard, but we should beg for her forgiveness and..." Her cheeks flushed an angry red. "...*murder* the bastard who'd hurt our daughter."

Anna nodded her agreement in vigorous accord.

Lady Wentworth's eyes grew haunted. "Wentworth said any daughter who would disrespect him like that was no daughter of his. He said I must choose where my loyalties lie—with her or him. And I…" One tear coursed down her lined cheek.

"You chose him."

"I did. But…I couldn't live with my decision. I grew to despise him—and myself. Nothing was worth the loss of my one and only daughter." She shifted in her seat and gazed out the window. "Unbeknownst to him, I hired a runner. It took some time. Years, in fact. But eventually the runner found her. Found you all, here, in Derbyshire.

"So to Derbyshire I traveled. I told Wentworth I wished to visit London for a shopping expedition, which brought me through Derbyshire. Nothing out of the ordinary for Claybourne, a peer of my husband's, to put me up for a few days respite from the road."

"So that's how he recognized you—and somehow noted a resemblance when no one else did."

Lady Wentworth arched a brow. "I wouldn't say no one else. But, in Claybourne's case, he did meet me when I was much younger. Perhaps I looked more like you, then." She smiled faintly.

Anna could not help the slight, answering smile. She had a grandmother.

"I arrived in Derby full of hope—to visit with Emmaline, to make amends." She sent Anna a watery smile. "That was the first time I laid eyes on you. You were such a beautiful child."

Anna frowned. "I don't recall meeting you."

"Because you never did. Emmaline refused to see me. Nor would she permit me anywhere near you. That didn't stop me from spying on you every chance I got. As for your mother, I gathered from your father, who I did meet with, briefly, that she was content with her life."

Anna wrapped her arms around herself. "You say she was pregnant when she left home."

Lady Wentworth nodded.

"With me?" Her voice was a mere whisper.

She nodded again.

"So, the man who raised me? The one I called father?"

"Was your father in all the ways that mattered. I met him only the once, but I could tell he would protect both of you with his life. Unlike Emmaline's own parents."

"How did they meet? Do you know?"

"She sought him out, initially, to oversee her pregnancy and to deliver her baby when the time came—you. She offered to be his housekeeper in exchange for his services." Lady Wentworth gave a sad chuckle. "He must've loved her at first sight. Emmaline didn't know the first thing about housekeeping when she left home."

"He did love her, very much." Tears she could not hold back blurred her vision. "She told me many times the trick in life was to find a good man who loved you. She warned me to stay away from the nobility because with them, the title always came first. Now I understand."

Lady Wentworth made no reply.

A large part of Anna wanted to reach out, to wrap the woman in her arms and offer comfort. With an effort of will, she pushed the feeling aside. Now was the time for answers. As her father always said—*her father*—when in doubt, focus on the facts.

"How did I wind up in your employ? I assume you arranged that?"

She inclined her head. "I kept watch over you for years, my only recourse since Emmaline never acceded to any of my pleas—to meet you, to finance your education, or clothing, or sponsor a come-out. I needed to do *something*. To enrich your life in any way.

"I hoped, after her death...but your father refused to dishonor her wishes. I did the only thing left me. I set an investigator on you, in case you should ever need me. I'd long ago set up a trust in your name, one which you would inherit at the age of twenty-four, or when you married, whichever came first.

"I never told your mother of the trust. I couldn't risk her undoing the thing. My solicitor informed your father's solicitor only after both your parents passed. I suppose that's how word of it got to Bolton, for he indeed knew of it."

"Angelique must have learned of my inheritance first. My father's second wife," she offered by way of explanation. "She has some tie to Bolton, the basis of which I haven't a clue. The two of them colluded to force me to marry him. At least their plotting makes sense now in light of the trust. But none of that explains how I ended up working in your household."

Lady Wentworth gave a one shoulder shrug. "It's a rather simple tale. The investigator had eyes on Lord Bolton's home, watching for any sign of you. His employees followed you when you left in the dark of night, overheard you hailing a hackney to convey you to a pawn shop, subsequently followed you there and sent word to my solicitor who soon-after arrived..."

Anna's lips twitched and a welcome flash of amusement flitted through her. Simple, eh?

"...and saw that you received a large overpayment for your items, which he then purchased on your behalf—"

She closed her eyes briefly. "It *is* my mother's ruby you sent with me."

"*Your* ruby."

Anna swallowed over the hard lump lodged in her throat. "I thought I'd never see it again. I assumed it could not possibly be one and the same. I also couldn't comprehend why you would give me such a precious stone, period."

"Well, now you know. It was your mother's, and was always meant to be yours. Regardless of how we leave things today, the ruby belongs to you. May I continue?"

Anna nodded.

"I was not at all certain what to do next. My man-of-affairs notified me you'd registered with that perfectly dreadful agency in a seedy part of town."

Anna opened her arms wide. "I chose it as the look of the agency told me the agents might not go to the trouble of verifying my falsified references."

Lady Wentworth smiled her cunning smile. "You are nothing if not resourceful." She spread her hands wide. "You know the rest. I conspired to hire you."

"After you got me un-hired from another household." Anna held up her hand when the older woman opened her mouth, presumably to defend her actions. "I understand. Clearly I inherited my resourcefulness from you."

A brief, comfortable silence passed, until the momentousness of their conversation seemingly overtook both of them again.

Anna met the older lady's eyes. "Why not simply tell me the truth? Why, after my father passed, did you not seek me out and introduce yourself? Surely that would have been easier than relying on investigators, solicitors, and agencies."

Her shoulders rose and fell in a deep sigh. "I feared, once you knew what I'd done, you would turn me away as your mother had. I decided to settle for some relationship rather than risk your hatred and banishment."

Frowning, Anna rose and paced to the window. "I confess, what you've shared is almost more than I can take in."

"I understand." She rose. "I'll take my leave now, if that is what you wish, and stay out of your life."

She turned to face her. "You think I mean to cut you from my life, *now*? After all you've done for me and all you've gone through yourself? You suffered for the choice you made so many years ago, and, though your apologies fell on deaf ears, watched over me still."

She gave a self-derisive snort. "I did a bang-up job, did I not? Allowing that horrid man to get his hooks in you."

"I got myself into that mess, but you managed to rescue me nonetheless. First getting me out of London safely, later secreting me out of Femsworth Manor, and now, garnering Bolton's promise to release me from my marriage."

Hope lit her eyes. "What are you saying, Anna?"

"You're my grandmother, my only living relative, and perhaps the only person in the world who cares if I live or die." She paused. "Aside from Caden."

The sparkle of unshed tears shone in Lady Wentworth's eyes. "The gift of of claiming you as my granddaughter is more than I ever thought possible. What now?"

Anna crossed back to the sofa. "I don't know, exactly." She took the older woman's hands in hers and sent her a cautious smile. "But I want to find out."

"I want nothing more in the world." She looked down at their clasped hands. "Anna, I said some rash things concerning the status of yours and Caden's relationship."

Anna released her hands and arched a brow. "That's putting it mildly."

"I thought, if I could arrange a meet between you and Caden—"

"—You *arranged* that?"

"Well, why else would I subject myself to a house party?" She shuddered with dramatic zeal. "He was the only male from your past you'd ever taken an interest in as far as I and my sources could tell. Too, I knew he and his family had the wherewithal to protect you from Bolton should anything happen to me. But now…"

A sudden feeling of falling off a cliff upended her stomach. She did not want to hear what the woman would say next.

"…I could retract my previous statement. You could come home with me. If you want me to, that is. Anna, what do you want me to do?"

***

Caden paced the edge of the portico and glared up at the stalled morning sun, refusing to budge an inch in the cloud-dappled blue sky. Rain would be preferable to this infernal good weather.

His stomach growled, mocking his decision to eschew the breakfast hall while Anna and Lady W—her *grandmother*—talked. His need to be alone, to calm his growing disquiet, had won out over hunger.

He gripped the stone balustrade 'til his fingers turned white, and stared out at the thick glade of forest before him.

He ought to be content as the cat who stole the cream. Less than two hours ago, he'd escorted Anna through those woods, into the secret garden beyond. They'd made love. She'd all but agreed to marry him.

The arrival of Lady Wentworth, together with her blithe announcement that he had debauched Anna at a roadside inn, had only cemented his claim on her hand.

What's more, Lady Wentworth had, purportedly, cleared the one tangible obstacle to their marriage, namely Anna's previous marriage to Bolton.

His family approved the chit. Everything was set for a post-haste wedding. Everything was fine. Better than fine.

So why did he feel all he'd ever wanted—and when exactly had Anna become that to him?—slipping through his fingers?

Damn it all to hell. His mind was playing tricks, plain and simple. Anna was, for all practical purposes, his.

His life finally made sense. He'd mended fences with his family, brought home a bride, and, for the first time in his life, he saw a clear path ahead of him. One he'd chosen, rather than stumbled onto—unless he counted finding Anna again.

Calmer now, he shoved his hands into his trouser pockets and wandered toward the corner of the portico.

He took in the evergreens separating Chissington Hall from the rest of the world, and blocking his view of the hallowed ground of the riverbank where he'd escaped his reality as a child more times than he could count.

In his mind's eye, he saw the root-knotted grassy knolls where he and Anna had so often frolicked as children. Where he'd kissed her that day before she left, never to be seen by him again—until Harrison knocked him face down in the muck.

Little did he know, his would-be rescuer, a woman with exotic, enthralling, and somehow familiar amber eyes would reshape his entire future.

He closed his eyes, and recalled to mind their recent interlude. He could feel her pliant body, hear her excited breathing, even smell her tantalizing scent.

And he was getting hard again. God's teeth, the woman had him well and truly ensnared in a fog of perfect lust. Once he had her in their marital bed, he intended to keep her there a solid week.

He laughed under his breath, opening his eyes and inhaling deeply of the fragrant air, oddly Anna-esque.

He stilled. The last time he'd *imagined* smelling her perfume...Anticipation flooding his senses, he pivoted on his heel--and found her standing not five feet away.

She stared at him, an inscrutable expression on her face. A gentle breeze riffled her skirts, stirring the soft chestnut tendrils of hair she hadn't yet combed into submission following their lovemaking, and imbuing the air with a fresh wave of her intoxicating scent.

He could pick her out of a crowd, blind-folded. A helpless smile tugged at his lips and he started toward her, needing to close the distance. "How did you leave things? Did you invite Lady Wentworth to stay with us a while, or...?"

"How did you know? About her being my...being related to me?"

He stopped an arm span from her. She had hedged. Rather than answering his question, she'd asked one of her own. Maybe it meant nothing. Maybe.

"I'd love to tell you I worked it out before today. Alas, I merely put together a story Harrison told me in passing with all the other oddities--her obvious affection for you, secreting you away, the clothing she acquired for you, the ruby, and finally, showing up here and going on the offensive like someone's angry, well, grandmother."

He studied her. She had a distracted look, as if she only half-listened.

"You'd have come to the same conclusion eventually," he said.

She nodded, brows furrowed.

"Are you well? Following the unveiling, so-to-speak? Did she give you any explanation for why she hadn't come forward in the last twenty plus years?"

"She did. It was...is...a lot to take in."

He waited for her to elaborate.

She didn't. Instead, her expression grew resolute, as if she braced for opposition.

The feeling of dread he'd talked himself out of moments ago returned with a vengeance. A trickle of sweat coursed down the center of his back, though the temperate breeze on the shady portico belied the summer season.

"You never said how—"

"Lady Wentworth has—"

They stopped speaking in unison. Smiled at each other in awkward apology.

Caden gestured for her to continue. "Please."

She cleared her throat. "I simply wished to share with you that, following our discussion, Lady Wentworth deemed it proper to recant her previous accusation."

"That was kind of her--but completely unnecessary, in light of the obvious."

Her questioning look annoyed him.

"The fact we were—are—already betrothed?"

"Ah." She ducked her head "You heard her say she took care of the Bolton problem?"

"I did. Your point?" he asked through set teeth.

"As I'm no longer in danger, we no longer have to keep up the pretense of a...fake engagement."

Fake engagement? "Anna, there is nothing fake about it, and well you know it."

Pressing her lips together, she pushed past him to stand at the stone railing, facing out. She heaved a visible sigh. "I'm not doing a good job of this, am I?"

He moved to stand beside her. He glared at her profile. "Depends. What exactly are you trying to do?"

She shifted to face him, her expression devoid of any discernible emotion. She, who had no poker face. The lack thereof said it all.

Meanwhile he employed every ounce of will he possessed to hide the feelings running roughshod through him. Fear. Anger.

A gut-wrenching need for her to give him one shred of evidence she had ever actually cared for him. And disgust—at his own weakness. When had he become this pathetic excuse for a man? If he wasn't so bloody miserable, he'd laugh at the caricature he'd made of himself.

"Your reason for offering for me, if you can call it that, no longer exists. You wanted to keep me safe. Well, now I'm safe."

"There is also the small matter of our having lain together--on multiple occasions. There could be consequences."

She lowered her lashes, and a muscle ticked in her jaw. So she did feel *something*.

"You refer to the possibility I am with child?"

"Obviously."

"In light of..." She hesitated, her cheeks turning a furious shade of pink, "...your actions at the time of our...your, er..."

Her show of vulnerability, however minute, cut through his veneer of icy calm. He couldn't stop his impulse to trace his fingertips over her jawline.

"That's not a fool-proof method, darling. And that was only the once. This morning, I spilled my seed inside of you. Or don't you recall?"

She closed her eyes briefly, then took an unsteady step backward, as if recoiling from his touch. "In any case, I can deal with such an eventuality, I'm sure, should the need arise."

His stomach pitched. "Like hell. As if I would ever shirk responsibility for my own child."

Her scoffing laugh turned his blood to pure ice. "Your responsibility. Yes, of course. God forbid Caden Thurgood not step in as honor would demand."

He jammed a hand through his hair. "You act as if honor is a bad thing."

"It's a fine thing. One of the traits about you I ado—" She broke off. "—admire most."

"Why do I hear a but at the end of your statement?" Coldness filled him, spreading to all his extremities.

She met his eyes with an unblinking stare. "A child may be reason enough for you to wed, but, for me, there needs to be... there ought to be, something more." Her eyes pleaded with him to understand.

At once, her meaning hit home—and gutted him.

Her dismissal of his reason for marrying was mere camouflage. The truth was as evident as the lack of emotion on her face. She did not want him. It was all well and good to wed him when he offered safe harbor, when he was the lesser of two evils and came with the force of the Claybourne title behind him.

But now, with Bolton no longer a threat thanks to Lady Wentworth's machinations and her newly established financial means—she was the granddaughter of a dowager duchess after all—her reasons for marrying Caden had evaporated like mist. Unless she proved pregnant. Even then, she seemed less than thrilled at the prospect of marriage to him.

She did not want him as her husband. He couldn't blame her.

He straightened, linking his hands behind his back and looked anywhere but at her. "I see."

"You...do?"

He forced a bland smile. "I apologize for my previous inability to grasp the obvious."

"Which is?" she drew out, sounding suddenly wary.

You do not want me as your husband. Though the words burned through him, he could not bring himself to say them aloud.

"Your situation has changed," he said instead. "You no longer need rescuing. No reason to saddle yourself with a less than sterling husband when the wolves no longer breathe down your door, eh?"

"Less than—*No.* Caden, you've twisted my words."

He nodded, still wearing his forced grin. "The point is, I take your meaning. I shall, of course, accede to your wishes to end our arrangement. However"—He met her eyes, trying to impress the import of his words—"I must insist, should our indiscretions bear fruit, you contact me immediately. I will not abandon my child. No matter what."

He'd cross that bridge if it came to that. Whereas he'd previously imagined such an eventuality with an odd combination of awe and desire, he now didn't know how he felt. Imagining Anna carrying his babe while not belonging to him, body and soul, bloody hurt, like he imagined being trampled by a horse might feel.

And whereas before he'd been disinclined to exact her promise to marry him based solely upon a happenstance pregnancy, he'd been more than willing to do so should the need occur. Now, the thought of forcing her into marriage under any circumstance was more than he could stomach.

When at last she spoke, her words came out a mere whisper he had to strain to hear. "I will."

He arched his brows, his expression deliberately nonchalant. "What now? I assume you have a plan? I didn't think to ask. Have you informed my family of your decision?"

She had the audacity to look affronted. "Informed your family? *My* decision?" she all but hissed. "I have not. If we are in agreement, we should tell them together...unless you'd rather have a private discussion with them?"

In *agreement*. Caden could only shake his head no.

She lifted her chin. "Very well. As to the rest, I expect Lady Wentworth and I will start for Northumberland this evening. Tomorrow morning at the latest."

He wanted to hurl something. One of the man-sized potted plants preferably. "In that case, we should make haste informing everyone. I wouldn't want to delay your departure. As you say, we'll tell them together. You can say your goodbyes at the same time. Two birds with one stone and all that."

All color drained from her face. Likely fearing the reaction of the earl and Zeke. As if he'd let anyone rebuke her.

He wanted to shake her. To kiss her. Hell, he wanted to drop to his knees and beg her not to leave him. What kind of a fool did that make him?

He had never experienced this conflagration of need and ire and tenderness and lust. Except...maybe he'd had some of these feelings before, for her, all those years ago. Hell, maybe Zeke had the right of it and he had fallen for the chit way back when. And as she had then, she would walk out of his life without a second look.

At least his pride remained intact. He would never, ever, beg for the affections of a woman, especially one who so obviously wanted nothing to do with him. No one, least of all her, need never know how deeply her rejection cut him.

Chapter Twenty-Four

Caden issued a summons, gathering everyone in the formal parlor, his face dishearteningly emotionless. He could, at least, feign a modicum of disappointment for appearance sake.

All parties filed in, positioning themselves within earshot and viewing distance of the sofa where he and Anna sat.

Lady Kitty took the armchair opposite them, while the heir apparent stood sentinel behind her. Lady Wentworth, shooting a sidelong glance at Caden's brother, chose an adjacent settee. Lady Lillian perched on an armchair beside Lady Kitty's, and the earl presided over all from his vantage before the mantle.

Anna glanced around the room, taking in anew the plush carpets, the gilt adornments, the velvet and satin covered cushions, and gleaming, polished surfaces. This beautiful parlor had seen all her dreams crumble at her feet. If she never again stepped foot in this luxuriously appointed chamber, it would be too soon.

Misery settled into her very bones, making her ache. Her plan had seemed so simple. Tell Caden he no longer had to marry her, and wait for him to confess his true reason for asking had less to do with obligation and everything to do with his desire to spend his life with her. She wasn't greedy. She could wait for him to fall in love with her, but she needed some indication he had tender feelings for her.

Instead, in less time than it took to make his breakfast selection from the sideboard, he opted to let her go. She was leaving. Today. Just like that.

Acid burned in her stomach and she swallowed convulsively. Lucky for her she'd eaten nothing today. Any food would surely have come back up.

"Well," Lady Kitty began, anticipation lighting her eyes, "What is it you wanted to share?"

Caden sent Anna a bland smile. "Would you like to do the honors, or shall I?"

Anna attempted a smile in return, but her cheeks trembled with the effort. "Y-you."

She cursed the stammer in her voice and lifted her gaze to the one person who, she assumed, guessed what was coming. Her grandmother.

Lady Wentworth's eyes held hers, compassion, encouragement, and love in their depths. Anna grasped the connection like a life line.

"You all understood, I'm certain, the grounds of Miss Masters' and my recent betrothal." He paused. "As she is no longer in danger of being absconded with by her previously held husband, the need for her to...to..." His words died a painfully slow death.

Anna could bear the concerned stares—or glare in Lord Thurgood's case, aimed directly at her—no longer.

"We've decided to call of the fake engagement," she blurted.

A deafening silence greeted her pronouncement. For a full two seconds.

"What of Lady Wentworth's claim that my brother stole your virtue?" Zeke demanded, his glare bordering on menacing. The knuckles of his hands, gripping his wife's seat back, had gone white.

To Anna's great relief, Lady Wentworth answered on her own behalf.

"I spoke out of turn, out of concern for my granddaughter. I apologize. I withdraw my statement."

"Withdraw?" Lady Kitty burst out. "You can't simply withdraw your statement. Not if it's true."

The older lady sniffed and lied through her teeth—for Anna. "That's just it. I made it up."

"I see," the earl said. He and Lady Lillian exchanged matching, disgruntled looks.

Lady Kitty's eyes turned pleading. "But...Caden? Anna? Is this truly what the two of you wish?"

Unwilling to outright lie, Anna turned to Caden, brows lifted. In truth, she wondered how he might answer.

He tunneled a hand through his hair, still, evidently, at a loss for words.

Please, she thought. *If you care for me, say so.*

Abruptly, he slapped his hands on his thighs and rose. "It is what's best for all involved. We discussed matters, and came to a mutually agreed upon decision that Anna is best off with her grandmother, the Dowager Duchess of Wentworth. They plan to depart immediately."

Best for all involved? Bah. He wanted to rid himself of her, and his last statement made that glaringly obvious. Her cheeks throbbed with heat. She lowered her gaze to her hands, fisted in her lap

He made his way around to the back of the sofa, planting himself directly behind her. "Isn't that right, Miss Masters?"

She itched to shift around, to search his eyes for any sign he wanted her to stay. Absurd. He'd had ample opportunity to tell her he cared.

She stared straight ahead. "Of course."

An odd crunching sound came from behind her, and she lost the battle with herself. She turned to look over her shoulder, and saw Caden crossing away from her, making for the door. What on earth?

"As for me," he began, "I have much work ahead of me at the quarry. Now that all is resolved as concerns Miss Masters' safety, I..." He broke off when he reached the threshold. Without turning around he said, "Lady Wentworth, Miss Masters, I wish you a safe journey and godspeed."

With that, he left. He *left*.

***

It was well on night by the time Caden returned to Chissington Hall—by design. He could not chance witnessing Anna and Lady Wentworth's egress. A quick check at the stables verified they had departed this afternoon.

He had visited the quarry, where he made a cursory study of the newly arrived machinery. Afterward he rode an aimless path through the nearby village with a loose plan of searching out roads, rooftops, and buildings in need of repair. He barely took in what he saw.

In truth, he hadn't left to satisfy any burning desire to begin repurposing the quarry. He left because he feared what foolish thing he might do if he stayed—such as staring after Anna's carriage like a lovelorn fool, or worse, chasing after it, or *much* worse, begging her not to leave him, period.

He trudged up the broad front steps, more weary than he could remember feeling in a long, long time. God willing, the rest of the household had all retired.

On the cusp of framing that fruitless wish, the front door swung open. He looked up, hoping to see George, the earl's longstanding butler.

Instead, Kitty pounced the moment he cleared the top step.

"I was beginning to wonder if you'd ever return. What are you going to do, Caden?"

"Do?" He knew, of course, she referred to Anna and their broken engagement. Not that they'd ever been engaged, according to Anna.

"You can't simply let her leave."

"And yet, that is precisely what I did."

She threw up her hands. "So you did, like a man who could not care less. Are you saying you don't love her?"

It was like taking a punch to the gut. He pushed past her, hastening to the grand staircase, which he climbed two steps at a time. "I'm not discussing this."

She didn't say another word, and he didn't look back. He knew what he'd see if he did. Disappointment, and worst of all, pity.

***

Caden awoke early. Too early. He couldn't not. He was exhausted, having had not nearly enough sleep, but, like yesterday, the morning sun shone into the bedroom like a beacon.

He muttered under his breath, and rolled onto his side, away from the offending glare.

Home, sweet, home.

Two days ago, one day following Anna's defection from his life--he rather liked that word to describe her rejection of all he had to offer—he moved into the cottage where Anna and her parents had once lived, the cottage he'd demanded Zeke sign over to him when negotiating his and Anna's future.

He'd intended to give it to her as a wedding present, after renovating. It hadn't been lived in for years and thus lacked updated bedding, curtains, furnishings—basically all the things that made a place comfortably habitable.

After her defection, he decided to take up residence immediately. He considered his dismal living conditions as a sort of penance. Believing for one second his so-called inherent charm coupled with her evident attraction for him might entice Anna to marry him after her safety was no longer threatened had been pure foolishness on his part.

Worse, his family knew he'd been a fool, and, he suspected, also knew he'd fallen for the chit. That realization above all else drove him from Chissington Hall as fast as his legs could carry him. He couldn't bear the piteous glances his family cast his way when they thought he wasn't looking.

If they knew what he meant to do today—what he *had* to do, because he couldn't not—they'd really think him a candidate for bedlam. Perhaps he was.

He'd meant to sleep a bit longer, hoping a full night's rest might enable him to put his best foot forward on his fool's errand. Alas, further sleep eluded him.

He swung his legs over the edge of the lumpy mattress and noted the faint scent of freshly brewed coffee in the air, coming from downstairs. God bless Kitty who had insisted he accept the loan of a housekeeper and cook until he got his household up and running.

He splashed water on his face from the basin and reflected, not for the first time, on how dear was his brother's bride. The best thing that ever happened to Zeke, to their entire family, was Zeke finding and marrying Kitty.

Still, her too-keen insight, combined with her forthright tendency, sometimes made her insufferable. Like the day Anna left.

"Are you saying you don't love her?" He could still hear her asking.

No, his insides screamed in reply, *I love her more than life. I need her more than the air I breathe.*

And it hurt like hell.

He dressed in plain white sleeves and clean trousers and trotted barefoot down the stairs. Hot black coffee and something to stave off hunger, then he'd do what he had to do.

At the base of the stairs, he caught the sound of distinctly feminine humming. His heart slammed into his ribs before he could school himself.

Not Anna. Anna had left him.

Still, that angel's voice didn't belong to Cook. He made his way toward the kitchen, fairly certain of who he would find.

The mouthwatering scent of fresh baked bread wafted over him as he stepped foot in the warm, sunlit room. A gleaming silver pot of coffee sat atop the counter beside a mound of thick sliced bread, butter and confiture, and assorted fruits. His stomach loosed a low rumble, reminding him he'd neglected dinner last night. When had he eaten last?

He was still pondering the question when his raven-haired sister-in-law burst into the kitchen through the back door opening to the gardens. A plethora of fragrant blossoms and greenery spilled from the apron she held out in front of her like a basket.

She offered Caden a warm smile of welcome as if she, and not he, lived here. "Good morning. I hope we didn't wake you."

"We?"

As if in answer, a sober-faced Zeke trailed in after her.

"Ah. May I?" He gestured toward the spread they'd prepared.

"Please." She rummaged in a drawer, finally locating a small utility towel.

"Your hospitality knows no bounds," he said dryly.

Ignoring his sarcasm, she lay the small towel atop a clear section of counter and began sorting her clippings.

"When Zeke told me he planned to pay you a visit this morning, I asked to tag along to get a look at your gardens. Though sadly overgrown, they boast numerous herbs and other leafy greens, in addition to the myriad flowers."

"Fascinating." He poured himself a cup of coffee then plucked up a slice of still warm bread. "Would either of you care to join me?"

Zeke grinned. "Don't mind if I do."

Soon, he and Zeke sat across from one another at the scarred wooden butcher block style table in the kitchen's center.

Caden took a bracing sip of steaming black coffee and felt some of the night's cobwebs fall away.

"You have something you wish to discuss, Zeke? If it's a report on the status of the quarry you're after, I'm afraid I won't have much to share for several weeks. I've increased production and brought on more workers to see to some much needed road repairs, but the other projects will require those road repairs completed to make transport to specific locations feasible."

Zeke eyed him over the rim of his cup, a considering expression on his face. After a moment, he set the cup down with a decisive click.

Out of the corner of his eye, Caden saw Kitty turn her back on her work to face them, arms clasped behind her.

Caden glanced between the two of them. "Is everything all right with the earl?"

"The earl is fine," Zeke replied.

Caden nodded in relief. So he was to be the recipient of a stern talking-to for some unknown reason, likely the fact he'd moved into the decrepit cottage, something each member of his family had tried to dissuade.

"You may as well get on with the lecture. I've a busy day ahead."

Zeke opened his mouth to speak, but Kitty beat him to whatever he intended to say.

"Zeke simply wanted to check-in on you. Make certain you're sleeping and eating, that sort of thing."

"Zeke, eh?" He leaned back in his chair and sipped more coffee. "Right as rain, as you can see."

Kitty's dubious expression said she disagreed. "Cook says you've barely eaten any of the evening meals she's prepared."

"It's been two days. I've been working late. I'm sure when I'm not exhausted, my appetite will rebound to surpass your wildest expectations."

In true Kitty fashion, she continued unabated. "You're more than a bit rumpled, as well. We'll send over a valet."

"If you like." He ripped a piece of bread and slathered it with butter and jam.

She glanced pointedly at Zeke who appeared not to notice her scrutiny.

As if losing her patience, she threw her arms open wide. "Zeke? You wished to discuss some things with your brother, I believe?"

He gave a resigned sigh and set the slice of apple he'd cut on his plate.

"Quite right my dear." He gave Caden a frank look. "The thing is, Kitty and I both think..." He eyed the ceiling. "How can I put this?"

Caden had never seen his brother tongue-tied. If it was any-one else, he might guess the subject involved Anna's defection, but, Zeke? Impossible. His brother would never interfere in

Caden's personal affairs, not those involving the opposite sex, at any rate.

Kitty once again spoke up. "We both think you're being an idiot. Meant in the kindest possible way, of course."

"Of course," he said. "You think I ought to move back into the Hall until the renovations are complete."

Zeke gave him a pained smile. "Not quite."

"If this is about the quarry, I already told you—"

"The quarry!" Kitty exclaimed, clearly vexed.

Zeke spared her a brief, quelling glance. "Cade, forget the quarry, and your ridiculous insistence in living in a half-dilapidated cottage. Can you think of any other area of your life where you may have, of late, mismanaged things dismally?"

Yes. Caden glared at his brother. "No."

Kitty snorted.

Zeke gave his wife another speaking look. "I'll spell it out. You clearly love the woman. She clearly loves you. What Kitty and I want to know is, why aren't you fighting for her?"

Caden was struck momentarily speechless. Then he propped both elbows onto the hard wood table top. He scrubbed his hands over his stubble covered cheeks.

"Could you elaborate? The part about..." Heat rising up his neck, he cleared his throat. "About Anna clearly loving me?"

"I knew it," Kitty exclaimed, triumphant. "Zeke Thurgood, if only you'd talked this over with Caden like I suggested before she left. The poor, dear girl—"

Caden's head snapped in Kitty's direction so fast, her words died in her throat. "She. left." He articulated each word.

Her expression softened. "Darling, did you never ask yourself why?"

He erupted from his chair, nearly upending it, and stalked to the counter to stare out the window into the riotous garden beyond. Anna's garden, it was meant to have been.

"I didn't need to ask myself," he said in a low voice. "She asked herself what I had to offer as a husband and found me wanting."

"Caden," Kitty sputtered, "what utter nonsense. Why would you think—"

"Kitty." Though Zeke spoke in a low voice, his tone carried unmistakable command. "If you don't mind, I'd like to speak with my brother alone."

After a brief hesitation, she stalked out to the garden. She did not close the door behind her.

Caden turned, leaning into the counter, arms crossed over his chest.

Zeke rose and moved to stand beside him. "What do you have to offer?" he asked softly, as if considering the question.

He crossed one arm over his chest, propped his elbow on his forearm and his chin in his hand. "Let's see. To date, you've offered to rescue Miss Masters from a well-connected, if disliked member of the nobility, you mended the schism in your family, from whom you had broken ties thanks to me and my pig-head-edness—No, let me finish," he said when Caden opened his mouth to argue that the fault for the rift lie with *his* pig-head-edness.

"You played your part, I played mine. Bottom line, I should have recognized you'd turned into a man and asked questions rather than making presumptions. We've established that much."

"Yes, but I gave you good reason. My whole life I've tended toward our father's bents, whereas you emulated the earl. We both know which of the two is the better man."

Zeke's eyes flashed with ire. "You have some of our father's traits, Cade. That is not a crime. Don't you know men would kill to possess one ounce of your natural charm? Your magnetism, with both women and men alike? Your bloody luck, for that matter, which, I'll add, our father never possessed?"

"These are my so-called good traits? I sound like a shallow, rudderless cove." He snorted. "Thank you for making my point."

"You're actually missing *my* point, Caden. They're not bad traits and they're not your only traits. You're also noble and trustworthy. How, otherwise, could I have left the country for months on end during my own imbecilic phase? I could because I knew I could trust you not to leave England and to see to the earl in my stead—which you did, by the by."

Anna had said the very same thing—not that the fact added up to a hill of beans. "Care to elaborate on what about your actions were imbecilic?"

"I was running—from everything our father taught us to fear, same as you've been running. We just did it in our own ways. I'd probably still be running if not for Kitty. And I believe your Anna is the same sort of…" he broke off as if searching his mind for the right word.

"Anchor," Caden suggested, his voice barely a whisper. "I thought, with her, I could be the man I've wanted to be. I never really tried for fear of failing. No gain ever made the risk worth taking, at least not since my formidable disasters."

"Your…what?"

Caden felt his cheeks heating. He may as well get it all out. "I couldn't help father, and I couldn't help you, despite my best efforts. It seemed nothing I ever did made much of a difference. Then there was University, when my mate nearly died, and then the quarry business happened—"

"—By God, I'm a right bastard, you know that? Caden, you have grown up and you have always made a difference for the better in everything you do, even when things didn't work as intended. I should have told you. I was so worried that if I wasn't tough enough on you…" He shook his head. "I'm sorry."

"This isn't on you."

Zeke shook his head. "It is. I knew something in you had changed when you swallowed your pride for her in coming back here. Even if it wasn't for her, alone, doing so took an inner strength I doubt our father ever possessed, or if he did, he neglected it so long it shriveled and died.

"You've always had a noble streak, Cade. When you tried to save our father, when you stood up for the lonely little girl down the lane who needed a friend, when you tried to take on responsibilities rightfully mine, and your friend's, and God knows whose which should never have been your burdens to begin with. When you went in Sterling's stead to the Fenton's house party—"

Caden held up a hand, palm out. "Stop. That last bit, especially, is a stretch, and we both know it. I've been running wild, and I went to the party with the intent to debauch myself with women, wine, and what-have-you, only Anna's presence curtailed my baser instincts."

Zeke's mouth twitched. "Fair enough. My point with all this is, what you have to offer her is a good man who loves her, who would sacrifice anything for her safety and happiness." He broke off and a look of dawning understanding lit his face. "Which is, apparently, why you let her leave. You made up your mind she didn't want you, in the end. I'm right, aren't I?"

"She agreed to marry me under one set of circumstances. Then her long lost grandmother arrives like a bloody fairy-god-mother and she chose greener pastures."

Zeke fixed him with a frank stare. "Did you give her all the facts?"

"Such as?"

"Did you tell her you love her?"

Caden's jaw hardened. "Ah. You mean, did I beg?"

He laughed. He *laughed.*

"I'm glad you find this funny."

Abruptly, Kitty flew into the house, her skirts billowing behind her. "Caden, only recall how close Zeke came to losing me."

His brother eyed the ceiling, as if seeking divine help. "Eavesdropping again, darling?"

She pressed her lips together. "Yes, well, listening-in, and we can discuss that later. The point is, Zeke, you resisted admitting you loved me, and that was the one thing I needed to hear. Tell him, before he makes the biggest mistake of his life."

Zeke gave Caden a considering look. "She's right. I risked my pride, and Kitty's rejection, by telling her how I felt. In the end, it was the only viable choice. The thought of living my life without her held..." He shook his head. "...no appeal."

Kitty launched herself at Zeke, who caught her up in his arms.

A momentary stab of pure jealousy pierced Caden's guts. He wanted what they had—with Anna, the one woman who'd ever inspired such insipid longing in him.

"If losing her is an acceptable option—"

"Enough," Caden cut in, his voice hoarse with the effort of holding back his emotions. "Enough," he said again, resigned.

"But Caden," Kitty began, only to be silenced by a touch from Zeke.

"She deserves better than me, Lord knows she does," Caden began, "and, despite your claims to the contrary, she made her choice."

Kitty opened her mouth to protest further, but Caden held up his hand.

"Even so, selfish bastard that I am, I made up my mind last night to do anything and everything in my power to convince her to spend the rest of her life with me."

Kitty bounced on her toes, all but vibrating with excitement. "Does that mean what I think it means?"

One corner of his mouth quirked upward. "It means I'm going after her. It does not mean I shall be successful. I had intended to get an early start, and the sun is creeping higher as we speak, so if you don't mind..."

"We'll get out of your hair," Zeke said. "But first, allow us to give you this." He pulled a folded piece of parchment from his inner vest pocket.

Caden took the paper, frowning. "What's this."

Grinning ear-to-ear, Kitty answered. "It arrived last night. It's from Lady Wentworth, addressed to me. In it she states only that she and Anna are guests at the Black Swan Inn, and that they intend to depart later today for Northumberland."

Caden blinked. "But why would she...?"

Kitty lifted her chin, her expression one of feline satisfaction. "Isn't it obvious? She loves her granddaughter, and she believes her granddaughter loves you."

"Huh," was all Caden could think to say. Hope blossomed within him, as intoxicating as it was terror inducing. He raked a hand through his hair.

Kitty sent him an impish grin. "Did we mention we brought one of the earl's best horses for you?"

Chapter Twenty-Five

Anna made a thorough search of the guest chamber. Satisfied she'd packed all of her belongings, she moved to the bed and snapped her luggage chest closed. That was that. They were leaving. Time to crawl out of the pit of despair where she'd allowed herself to wallow since riding away from Chissington Hall—and Caden.

If only it were that easy.

A knock sounded at her door. Her grandmother, coming to collect her for breakfast, no doubt.

She crossed the room on stockinged feet, fixing her sunniest smile on her face.

As predicted, her grandmother stood in the hallway, dressed in a spiffy traveling gown of silvery-grey silk.

"Good morning. How was your morning walk?" She bustled into the chamber.

"Invigorating. The sunrise this morning was spectacular."

Lady Wentworth regarded her a long minute. "Oh, my dearest. As bad as all that, is it?"

Her forced smile faltered. "I'm not sure what you mean?"

The older woman made a tut-tut sound and ambled toward the small sitting area. She sank into one of two armchairs.

"I'm old. I'm not blind. You've been heartsick from the outset of our journey. It's one of the reasons I decided we should stop."

She'd thought she'd kept her dismal feelings under wraps. Caden's many admonitions that she refrain from playing poker rang in her head.

"I don't understand. I thought we stopped here for you to rest prior to continuing our journey home."

Joining her grandmother, she took the adjacent wingback chair, curled her legs under her skirts, then propped her chin on her knees.

"I wanted to give you some time to be certain of your decision."

She heaved a sigh in chagrin. "You must think me a total ninny, pining after a man who doesn't love me."

"I think nothing of the sort. If anything, I feel responsible for your current state. If you recall, I hand-picked your young man for you. We attended the Fenton's party precisely to bring the two of you together."

"You certainly had me pegged. I fell hook, line, and sinker, whereas he..." Anna shook her head. The truth spoke for itself. "...did not."

"Are you so sure?"

"He let me go," she whispered. "When I told him we no longer had to go through with the fake engagement, he…" Her brows puckered, remembering.

He had gotten quite obviously annoyed. For a split second she'd thought he meant to fight for her. She'd all but forgotten that.

"What precisely did he say?"

Anna's cheeks flamed with heat. She would *not* mention the possibility of a child. Not unless circumstances dictated she must.

Ducking her head, she plucked at her skirts. "He said there was nothing fake about it. Then I said I didn't want marriage based solely on his need to always do the right thing."

Her grandmother gaped. "You mean to tell me, he wanted to go through with the thing, and because he showed integrity, you rejected him?"

"That's very close to how *he* reacted. He sputtered something to the tune of *you make honor sound like a bad thing.*"

Lady Wentworth's peeved expression said she agreed with Caden.

Anna bounded from the chair to pace. "It's not that I don't want a man like Caden, who does right, who protects those he cares for at the expense of himself."

Her grandmother's brows shot up. "Well, then? Why did you call things off?"

"Because I want him to love me, grandmother. I couldn't bare the thought of him marrying me only for honor's sake."

Understanding flickered in her eyes. "Because you love him."

"I do." She covered her face with her hands. "And now I wish I never laid eyes on him."

She heard the creek of wood and the rustle of skirts as her grandmother rose from her chair. A moment later, her arms went around Anna.

"Darling, did it never occur to you he took your rejection as a sign you didn't really want to marry him? After all, you never said a word about your feelings for him, did you?"

She peeked at her grandmother through her fingers. "No. I didn't want him to feel obligated."

"It seems to me you have a choice. We can return to Chissington Hall, today, now, and you can tell him how you feel. Or..."

Anna met her grandmother's eyes. "Or?"

"Or we can wait him out a day or two longer. I believe, if he truly loves you, he'll come to his senses before too long and come after you."

Anna's heart filled with equal parts agonizing hope and desperate fear. Her chin trembled. "And if he doesn't? We can assume he doesn't love me?"

Her grandmother pursed her lips. "He may or may not in that case. If he doesn't love you, good riddance. If he does, but doesn't have the spine to speak up, then I suppose you still have the first option."

She frowned. "What should I do? What would you do?"

Lady Wentworth tapped her forefinger on her chin. "I'd say, any man who couldn't bring himself to risk his pride to have you isn't one worth having. But that's just me."

Anna pressed her lips together. "Say he does come for me. What about you?"

"What about me?"

"I only just found you. I don't want to be apart from you again."

Her grandmother's eyes welled with tears in an instant. "I suppose I could be convinced to stick around Derby for a while."

A knock sounded on the door, and they stared at each other for a timeless moment.

Finally her grandmother waved her toward the closed door. "Only one way to find out, girl."

Her heart in her throat, she approached the door. Bracing herself, she opened it, and found not Cade, but a stooped chambermaid whom she'd seen crossing the corridor earlier that morning.

The woman shot a furtive glance inside the room, head downcast as she hunched over a rolling cart, carrying a tea service and two covered dishes. "Breakfast, m'ladies."

Tamping down an unreasonable flood of disappointment that Caden had not magically appeared, she turned to her grandmother. "You ordered breakfast?"

Her grandmother spread her delicate hands. "I didn't. Perhaps the innkeeper took it upon himself as we had yet to come down to eat."

The white-capped chambermaid pressed the cart inside.

Anna studied her. Poor thing. Despite the maid's thick mop of curly red hair, something about the way she moved told Anna she was not a young woman, as were most of the inn's chambermaids.

Having parked the cart between the arm chairs, the maid turned and hurried from the room, with a muttered, "Pull the call bell when ye've finished, if ye please." The door closed behind her with a bang.

"Good help is hard to find, even in the nicest of establishments," her grandmother said with a sniff.

Anna eyed the cart. "Nevertheless, I could eat."

"Solving the world's problems does work up one's appetite. Shall I pour?"

Anna resumed her seat and unfolded her serviette.

"What have you decided? Shall we away to Chissington Hall after we eat?"

She lifted her chin. "If it's all the same to you, I'd like a day to consider my best course of action."

They tucked into dishes consisting of boiled eggs, ham, and toast, and sipped lukewarm tea in companionable silence.

Anna felt better than she had in days. Despite the ever-present heart ache, having shared her inmost feelings with her grandmother had eased some of her pain.

She smiled at her grandmother, who blinked back at her and issued a giant yawn.

The act proved contagious, and Anna yawned, as well.

They both chuckled—and yawned again.

"Perhaps some more tea to wake us up?" Anna asked, already pouring.

"It's not the best tea I've had. Their standards are slipping."

Anna nodded, sloshing a bit of the tepid liquid over her grandmother's cup into the saucer. "Oh, dear." She giggled.

Her grandmother squinted at her. "I feel...not quite whight." She shook her head. "...*whight,*" she repeated, once more mispronouncing the word.

Anna chuckled. "I'm not sure why everything seems funny." She picked up her teacup and sipped, watching as her grandmother reached for hers.

It slipped from her fingers, crashing into the saucer. Tea splashed over the surface of the cart.

Anna flopped back in her chair, dismayed by the task of cleaning the spill. "I'll wipe that...moment...need to...rest..."

She awoke from a bizarre dream involving Caden and her late father's wife. In it, Angelique had hidden her away in an attic while Caden wandered the town in possession of one of her slippers—half the set she'd worn at the Fenton's house party. She never had found that missing slipper.

She tried to open her eyes and found her lids resistant as if held down by glue. She moaned softly. Her head hurt, she was very thirsty, cold to the point of shivering, and her shoulders ached of all things, probably because she had fallen asleep in the carriage, slumped sideways, with her arms behind her.

The carriage. They'd departed? Hadn't they discussed waiting? She tried and found it impossible to pull her arms from behind her. With effort, she peeled open her gritty eyes.

She noted several things at once. Though she indeed traveled by coach, she was not riding in her grandmother's pristine vehicle. Her nose, and the light from at least one low burning lamp illuminating the cabin interior, told her that much. The cushions, the fabrics, the musty pervasive scent, in short, everything about her surroundings screamed dingy.

She slid her gaze to the window nearest her. Someone had drawn the short curtains, but slits of light coming from beneath and between the folds said the sun shone outside, albeit weakly. How long had she been out?

She took a bracing breath and straightened in her seat, fighting off an ensuing nausea. When it passed, she peered around her, freezing in place as a shock of recognition jolted through her.

Angelique sat across from her, eyes glittering with malice. Her dark hair was sleeked back into a ruthlessly tight bun, pinned at her nape. She wore a chambermaid's uniform, down to the white apron. Only the cap was missing. *And the mussy, red hair.*

Angelique and the stooped, wild-haired maid were one and the same.

"Ah. She's awake," came the woman's caustic voice.

Gooseflesh spread over her limbs. She closed her eyes briefly and repressed a shudder. Angelique had found her, drugged her and somehow taken her from the inn. But why?

A more urgent question surged to the forefront of her mind, bursting from her lips with a croak. "Where is my grandmother?"

A malevolent grin spread over the woman's face, chilling Anna to the bone.

"Where is my grandmother?" She mimicked in a nasty tone. "Look at you, in your fine clothes, your wealthy grandmother in tow, staying at the best inn money can buy. You must think yourself very clever, indeed." Rage infused every word.

Anna's pulse raced at the venom directed at her. She concentrated on schooling her breathing and remaining calm. She needed answers and to get those, she sensed she must do nothing to inflame Angelique further.

"Not particularly, no. I have no idea what you want with me. I never did."

Her meek tone appeared to mollify Angelique, slightly.

She leaned back as if preparing to share a long tale. "No, you wouldn't, would you? Stupid child. I had it all planned, every detail worked out to the letter. All I had to do was get you married off to Bolton—which I did," she hissed and one of her hands fisted before her.

"I was so close. Then he let you slip away, the fool. After all I did, all I sacrificed, putting up with your father, pawing at me, putting up with you underfoot, nearly two years of playing the perfect little wife. I didn't even realize how much money was on the table 'til he died and I uncovered a virtual treasure."

As she and Caden had surmised, Angelique had, indeed, discovered Anna's inheritance after her father's death.

"Then Bolton, in his altitudes as usual, let you slip away. We looked for you. Two more years passed! Finally we find you and your dear sweet Grandmother thinks to make a deal with Bolton and take everything I worked for from me. Well, she can think again. Bolton does what I say. We'll take her money and yours."

Anna swallowed and risked posing the question burning through her again. "She's...she's all right, isn't she?"

Angelique gave Anna a sly look. "She's fine. For now. I left her sleeping like a baby, watched over by my very good friend. You remember Brutus?"

Anna did. He'd been one of Bolton's so-called footmen. Not only had the man looked ridiculous in livery, with his massive chest and boxers' hands, Anna had never seen him accomplish any task save for keeping a watch over her. She'd known even then he was hired muscle.

"What do you mean, 'for now'?"

Angelique smiled, seeming pleased by Anna's grasp of the pertinent facts. "Since Bolton can't be trusted to manage this thing, I decided to take charge. We're going to meet up with him shortly, and the two of you *will* consummate your marriage. You'll do it, or the old lady falls asleep and never wakes up. *Just like your father,*" she finished, her tone low and menacing.

Just like her father? Dear God, had the woman murdered her father? Her sweet, gentle father? For what? For money? And now she threatened to do the same to her grandmother.

Fear unlike anything she'd ever known washed through her—and beneath that, a deep, simmering anger ignited.

"Do we have an agreement?"

Anna stared.

"Do we?" Angelique screeched.

"Assuming I do what you say, how do I know you'll keep your word?"

She pursed her lips. "You'll have to trust me. And, if you can't do that, there's also this." She slipped her hand into the pocket of her apron, and pulled out a small pistol, which she aimed directly at Anna.

***

Caden had anticipated many scenarios. In one, Anna welcomed him with open arms. In another, she slapped his face and told him she never wanted to see him again. Another still, she listened to him with cool disdain and sent him packing.

In none of his visions did she outright ignore him. And yet, he'd been standing outside her guest chamber knocking for several minutes. She refused to utter a simple "Go away," much less open the door. He had attracted many a stare. Soon, management would probably demand he leave.

He contemplated that—for about five seconds.

She wanted to make a point? Fine, he'd leave her in peace if that was what she truly wished. But she could bloody well tell him to his face.

The Black Swan's proprietor had barely been persuaded to reveal Anna's and Lady Wentworth's chambers, even after Caden presented the latter's hand written note. He suspected the man would outright refuse to unlock Anna's door for him and risk the wrath of the dowager duchess.

However, convincing a chambermaid was right up his alley.

He strolled casually toward the chamber into which he'd witnessed a maid entering minutes ago. He pasted on his most debonair smile and rapped twice on the door jamb.

Minutes later he and the blushing maid approached Anna's door, only to have it crash open.

Instead of Anna, he found an ashen-faced Lady Wentworth. She clung to the door like a lifeline and gazed up at Caden with terror-filled eyes.

A terrible sense of foreboding hit him like a punch to the gut. "Where is Anna?" he demanded, not bothering with the niceties.

"Caden, thank God you're here. They took her. You've got to get to them—before it's too late."

With a hell of a lot more calm than he felt, Caden extracted what information he could from Lady Wentworth and a handful of the hotel staff.

Evidently, a chambermaid had delivered a breakfast cart, stolen from another maid whom she had incapacitated and left bound. The food or tea must have been laced with a sleeping agent because Lady Wentworth recalled feeling unaccountably woozy, then nothing more until she woke to find Anna gone.

Other servants witnessed an unknown chambermaid and a brawny looking man exiting the building, lugging a very heavy looking laundry cart onto a carriage. The servants claimed they believed the cart was filled with toxic items needing to be disposed of through burning, something which apparently happened on occasion.

Personally, Caden assumed the large man's so-called menacing air lent itself to the pair departing unquestioned.

By Caden's best guess, they left just prior to his arrival on scene.

"By God," he muttered to himself. "I saw them. I saw them leaving."

He'd ridden right past them when he turned onto the hotel's access road. He'd been too caught up in his own worries to give more than a passing notice, but upon reflection, hadn't he witnessed the oddity of an ancient carriage, its insignia covered by a black tarp, driven by, not a groom, but a beast of man dressed in servant's garb?

"Which way did they go?" Lady Wentworth demanded, her frail hand grasping at his sleeve.

He had not seen the direction they turned. But he knew—just as he knew who must be behind the entire sordid scheme. Anna's stepmother, Angelique, and Lord Bolton, the double crossing schemer. They would be heading to Lord Bolton's residence. It was the only place that made sense.

Why hadn't he foreseen this as a possibility? He knew Bolton had no moral compass. If he and Angelique hurt Anna, it would be all his fault. Him and his stupid, worthless pride. If only he'd told her how he felt. If only he begged her to stay and not to leave him. If he'd found a way to convince her, she would be safely ensconced in Chissington Hall at this very moment.

He met Lady Wentworth's eyes, his insides hard as forged steel.

"They're en route to London. Send word to Chissington Hall. Tell my brother to meet me at Lord Bolton's London address."

"Lord Bolton?" the older woman sputtered. "But—"

"He's behind this. He and that wicked Angelique." And that was all the explanation he had time for. His princess needed rescuing.

Chapter Twenty-Six

The poorly sprung carriage seemed to find every rut in the cobbled road. Whomever had bound her following her drug-induced slumber had strung her arms tightly behind her, and her shoulders screamed in protest as her body, perched atop the threadbare bench, jostled and lurched. She willed herself to ignore the pain, as well as the gun Angelique held.

She had to think. Her grandmother's life depended on her keeping her wits.

Angelique had told her she'd left Lady Wentworth with Brutus. Anna was fairly certain the lady lied.

Doubtless, she did not have an unlimited number of male servants at her disposal whom she could drag with her across the countryside. Therefore, assuming she had only Brutus, he would have to be the man driving the team, wouldn't he?

If so, she could cease worrying over her grandmother for now.

That left her tasked with disarming Angelique, removing herself from the moving carriage, and evading Brutus. She scoffed inwardly. Was that all? No matter. She had to try.

"Where are we going? Can I assume you're taking me back to Lord Bolton's London mansion?"

"Keep your mouth shut. I'm tired of answering your questions."

"I understand," Anna replied, her tone deliberately meek. "Only, you don't suppose Lord Bolton might...Never mind."

Angelique's gaze sharpened. "Might, what?"

"I only wondered if Lord Bolton might not fear incurring Lady Wentworth's wrath. Perhaps he's not even waiting for us."

The woman snorted. "I told you. He does what I tell him."

"Really? Because, I think he's more likely to cross you than Lady Wentworth, don't you? Perhaps you should reconsider your course of action while you still can."

"Stop. Talking. You have no idea about anything, you silly twit. Bolton is my..." She broke off and sent Anna a canny smile. "He'll be there."

Anna tried another tack. "But what if you're wrong? I could save you both time and trouble. I could pay you whatever amount you name, if you let me go free."

Angelique snorted in dismissal, but Anna thought she caught a gleam of interest in the woman's eyes.

"I could give you my mother's ruby. It's worth a fortune."

She saw immediately she had struck a nerve.

Angelique's face lit with greed and renewed malice. "*My* ruby. The one you stole. I assumed you'd pawned it. You kept it?"

"Of course. It was my mother's."

Angelique scoffed. "Stupid little fool."

Still, she appeared to give Anna's claim some thought. "Perhaps we could work something out. Where is it?"

She swallowed. It was now or never. "I'm wearing it."

Angelique's eyes flicked over her. Her gaze settled on the ribbon tied around Anna's neck, disappearing into her bodice.

"It's on a ribbon, tied around my wrist." She bit her lower lip and scooted on the bench, angling her body ever-so-slightly, purportedly to show Angelique her wrists, bound behind her. "See for yourself."

Angelique leaned forward and peered over Anna's shoulder, eyes narrowed.

Anna prayed she could see nothing. Her entire plan depended upon it.

"Lean forward, you stupid cow," Angelique barked.

Anna made another infinitesimal shift, forcing the older woman to bend precariously over the aisle. Evidently, she finally had Anna's wrists in sight, because she let out an angry shriek. "*Liar*. You're not wearing any rib—"

Anna shoved off the bench with all her might, jamming her knee into the woman's midsection, and the two toppled to the floorboards.

She heard Angelique's muffled "Oomf," and, at the same moment, a masculine shout sounded from outside. Then came a loud *Bang!* as a gun exploded.

The carriage braked, hard, slamming to a jerking halt.

"Get. Off. Me." Angelique shouted, their combined skirts muffling the woman's voice.

Gritting her teeth, Anna fought with every fiber of her being to keep the woman beneath her as she strained toward the door. If she could just nudge the handle with her—

Abruptly, sunlight streamed into the can as the carriage door swung open wide.

Anna blinked at the sudden brightness, and then Brutus's broad chest filled the open space, blocking out most of the light.

She sagged in defeat. Her last ditch effort had failed. She cringed as the man reached in, one handed, and with a surprisingly gentle grip, pulled her from the coach.

"Anna, tell me you're all right?" Caden demanded.

Caden demanded?

She wobbled on violently shaking legs and gaped at the most beautiful sight she'd ever seen.

Caden, here. He'd come. Her very own Prince Charming had come.

And he was in danger.

She glanced around, frantic. In a blink, she took in Angelique, trying to right herself, and the driver's box, empty. "Where is Brutus?"

"Hold still," he ordered, and began patting her down, one-handed.

"By Brutus, do you mean the man whose head I fired over? He's charging down the street on foot, directly toward the magistrate."

"You *are* wearing my ruby! It's there around your neck. Give it to me." Angelique sprang from the coach cabin, launching herself toward them.

"She's got a pistol," Anna shouted, turning her body to shield Caden's.

"Woman," he growled. He wrapped one arm around her waist and moved her aside. She heard the cock of his pistol. "So do I."

"No," Angelique screamed and reeled back. "You can't do this."

Never taking his aim off Angelique, he turned to Anna, his free hand untying her wrists.

She'd never seen his face look so hard. Yet, when he spoke, one corner of his mouth cocked up. "Evidently she never heard the tale of Prince Charming rescues his princess."

Anna gazed at him, certain he could see her love for him written all over her face and not caring a jot. "Evidently not."

"Although, I'll say it looked as if this princess was doing a fair job of rescuing herself."

***

Several hours later, having returned to the Black Swann Inn to first assure herself of her grandmother's safety, and then to answer questions of the magistrate, Anna found herself alone in her chamber.

She had bathed, dressed, and now awaited Caden—with increasing impatience.

She had yet to speak with him privately.

In stoic silence, he stayed by her side as she submitted to detailed questioning by the magistrate, who, by then, and with Caden's assistance, had apprehended Angelique and her fearsome associate.

Caden was seeing the man off when Zeke arrived.

Zeke, it turned out, had not come because he'd been summoned. He had already departed Chissington Hall to deliver salient news.

According to the earl's man-of-affairs, Anna and Lord Bolton had never actually been married—not legally. Neither had Angelique and her father been properly wed.

Because, as it happened, Lord Bolton and Angelique had been married to each other for many years. For reasons unknown, they'd kept their nuptials secret. Nonetheless, the truth was recorded in black and white. Neither Bolton nor Angelique had been free to marry another.

It was certainly good news. She was neither related to Angelique by marriage, nor did she face the necessity of acquiring an annulment. Meanwhile bigamy would be added to the list of crimes for which the two would certainly answer.

Under normal circumstances, Anna would have been over-joyed by the discovery. Due to the tumultuous events of the day, however, all she really cared about was getting Caden alone.

She finally thought the moment had come when the magistrate made to leave. Instead, grim faced, Caden told her he needed to fill his brother in on all that occurred, and suggested she and her grandmother take some time to rest after their ordeal.

She didn't want to rest. She wanted to hear from Caden, in his own words, why he had come. She wanted to throw her arms around him. To tell him she loved him and wanted to marry him whether or not he loved her.

She wanted him here. *Now.*

What was keeping him? Had he left with Zeke?

Unwilling to wait another second, she marched toward the door and reached for the lever just as a soft knock sounded.

"Anna? It's Caden. May I come in?"

Her heart in her throat, she smoothed suddenly damp palms over her skirts and opened the door. Finding it hard to breathe, much less speak, she gestured for him to enter.

No sooner had he closed the door, than he pulled her close and covered her mouth with his.

With a cry of unabashed delight, she twined her arms around his neck. He was warm and strong and she never wanted to let him go. Dizzying joy bubbled up inside her.

Never taking his lips from hers, he slid one arm around her shoulders, one under her knees, and strode to the bed. He lowered to sit, Anna cradled against his chest. Only then did he break off the kiss. He sent her his slow, pirate's smile, one that, oddly, didn't reach his eyes.

"That was past due," he said.

"Past due?"

"The Prince always claims a kiss from his princess upon rescuing her."

She reached up to cup his cheek—a smooth, freshly shaven cheek. "Oh, Caden. You came," she half choked.

Misery filled his eyes. He ducked his head, grasping her hand to press a kiss into her palm. "I'm sorry. So sorry it took so long."

"What do you mean? Your timing couldn't have been more perfect. Even the magistrate said so."

"Wrong. That mad woman should have never had the chance to grab you. I should never have let you go, at least not without a fight. I should have told you how I felt. How I *feel*."

Her heart beat so hard against her ribs, she wondered he didn't comment. "How do you feel, Caden?"

He wrapped one warm and slightly damp hand around her nape. His eyes blazed with ice-blue fire. "Like you're the most beautiful, most brave, most delectable creature on this earth. Like I don't deserve you—"

"Oh, Caden—"

"—and don't care a fig that I don't. I don't care because I love you more than life. More than breath. I told you I never bet it all on anything, and I meant that. I don't. People call me lucky, but the truth is nothing has even been worth gambling everything on. I've never wanted anyone or anything the way I want—no, the way I *need* you. You make me believe I can be a better man.

"So this is me, begging you to be my wife. To spend your life with me. Not because you may be with child—though I vow, nothing could make me happier—and not because you need rescuing, but because I love you—so bloody much it hurts."

"No," she said, shaking her head.

His expression turned bleak. "I'm too late?"

"Never."

He frowned in confusion, even as hope lit his eyes.

"I meant, no, you can't be a better man, because you're already the best man I know." Her vision blurred as tears filled her eyes. "It's me who doesn't deserve you, my very own Prince Charming. But I'm so glad you love me because I was giving you one more day to come to your senses before I stormed the castle of Chissington Hall to demand you marry me."

His own eyes went suspiciously damp, and one corner of his mouth curved upward. "Is that so?"

"Yes."

He crooked a finger under her chin. "Does that mean you love me, Anna?"

She laughed softly, one fat tear coursing down her cheek. "Didn't I say so?"

He shook his head.

She sent him her most brilliant smile. "I do love you, Caden Thurgood. So much. I think I always have."

"In that case," he said. "I suppose I can give you this back." He reached into his inner waistcoat pocket and withdrew a small item fashioned of gold satin.

"My...slipper?"

He arched a brow. "Not sure. Let's see if it fits. *After.*"

With that, he rolled with her onto the bed, and showed her exactly how much he loved her, in a language older than time.

Epilogue

Derbyshire, England, April 1880

It was a fine spring day, cool and crisp. Puffy white clouds dappled a pale blue sky. A soft breeze played over the river Derwent, casting ripples over the water and whispering through the trees.

As they did on most Sunday afternoons, Caden and Anna enjoyed a picnic atop a blanket they'd laid out on a grassy knoll overlooking the river.

They ate their lunch beneath the shade of an old yew tree, the very tree where Caden, not quite a man, but no longer a child, bestowed the fateful kiss on his stolen Princess Anna, marking him as forever hers.

He lounged with his back against the tree trunk, long legs stretched out. Anna nestled between his legs, leaning into his chest, half dozing as he caressed her growing belly with leisurely strokes.

"I rather enjoyed today's fare better than last week's, madam wife," he mused. "Fried potato slices dipped in melted chocolate. Who'd have thought the two foods would make such a flavorful combination."

Anna chuckled. "Your babe, evidently. I never imagined eating anything of the sort before this pregnancy."

"It certainly went down better than the orange slices and malt you concocted last week."

"Yet you still managed not to leave so much as a spoonful," she said, a smile evident in her voice.

He arched a brow. "True. At this rate, I stand to gain all of your baby weight. That's hardly fair."

"According to the doctor Kitty recommended, I am eating for two. But one of us is only the size of a thimble." She chuckled briefly. "But you and I both know I'm as big as a house already. Kitty's bump is barely visible even though she's two months further along than I."

"I know nothing of the sort. You're perfect as you are."

She pulled his hand briefly from her belly to press a kiss to his palm. "Are you very upset over Kitty and Zeke claiming first rights to the earl's name for their babe should he be a boy?"

Caden considered that. "No. They can have *Horace*. I have a few other names in mind." He paused. "The truth is, I'm rather hoping for a girl with her mother's eyes."

"Are you?"

"Mm hm."

"Do you have a name in mind for her, as well?"

"I do."

When he didn't immediately offer it, she turned in his arms to swat his chest before twining her arms around his neck. "Tell me this instant."

He traced a finger over her cheek. "I was thinking we'd call her Evelyn," he said softly.

Wonder filled her eyes. "You want to name her after my grandmother?"

He nodded.

"Caden Thurgood, you are the sweetest, most thoughtful husband—"

He laughed, cutting her off. "Stop right there. There's nothing thoughtful about my choice. I credit her with bringing you back to me. Without her machinations—meant to entrap me, I might add—I never would have found you again. The mere thought of not having you as my wife is enough to give me nightmares." He shivered for dramatic effect, then sobered. "I owe her more than I can say. I love you, Anna."

"I love you more," she choked and sank against him, nuzzling her face into the crook of his shoulder.

"You're crying?" he asked after a moment.

She sniffled. "I never cry."

If the Slipper Fits, Mrs. Jones, he thought, but only said, "Of course not," and hugged her close, allowing her happy tears to soak the front of his shirt—again.

The End

I hope you enjoyed reading If the Slipper Fits! If so, please consider leaving a review for others, and don't forget to read books 1 and 3 in my "Hidden Hearts" series, The Trouble with Tigers and Beautiful Viscount, Beastly Bride.

Also available now: my steamy Regency series, "First Comes Marriage" set in Dragonblade Publishing's Lyon's Den Connected World. book 1 The Lyon Whisperer, book 2, The Lyon Returns, and book 3 A Lyon's Tangled Tale

About the Author

A word about the author...Kimberly Keyes knew before she was old enough to drive writing was her passion. She writes steamy historical and contemporary romance, laced with a bit of mystery and suspense. She loves crafting un-put-downable romances that take her readers away and leave them hungry for her next book!

Her favorite tropes are marriage-of-convenience, fake relationships, grumpy/sunshine and close/forced proximity. You can count on "steamy" yumminess intertwined with that delicious falling-in-love feeling romance readers crave.

The bulk of her time she spends writing and rewriting, plotting, and dreaming up ways to perplex the characters living inside her head. You can also find her toiling in her garden, walking her dogs and trying to keep up with her social media posts!

There's lots of ways to connect with Kimberly and she loves to hear from her readers. If you love one of her books, PLEASE let her know. It keeps her writing!

Want to learn more and stay in touch? Visit her website at kimberlykeyes.net where you can learn about her books, upcoming releases, watch book trailers and sign up for her newsletter. Every newsletter offers at least one awesome giveaway.

More ways to connect—my moniker is always "Kimberly Keyes Romance":

Facebook

Instagram

TikTok

Pinterest

Bookbub

Goodreads

Thank you for reading The Trouble with Tigers. If you enjoyed the story, Kimberly would appreciate you letting others know by leaving a review! Reviews are an author's life blood, and it really means the world to her to receive them!

THE TROUBLE WITH TIGERS , a steamy, grumpy/sunshine, hidden identity, fake engagement, forced proximity Victorian romance and book 1 in Kimberly's "Hidden Hearts" series.

As a favor to his grandfather, the earl, Lord Zeke Thurgood reluctantly agrees to act as Lady Kitty's fake fiancé. But the more time they spend together, the deeper their feelings grow. When an unforeseen threat brings their an arrangement to a sudden end that promises to take her from him forever, Zeke will risk everything to convince her to marry him.

"...An exciting and steamy love story with enough twists to keep you flipping those pages furiously. I couldn't stop reading this book, even when I got a headache from staring at my Kindle for too long! The ending was perfect, with suspense and surprises around every corner..." Amazon reviewer

BEAUTIFUL VISCOUNT, BEASTLY BRIDE, a steamy, enemies-to-lovers, grumpy/sunshine, forced proximity, marriage-of-convenience Victorian romance, and book 3 in Kimberly's "Hidden Hearts" series.

Lady Annabelle tracks Viscount Randall to the frigid north to demand a confession from him regarding her brother's death, and finds herself caught in a snow storm and forced to seek shelter in his remote castle instead.

THE LYON WHISPERER, book 1 in Kimberly's "First Comes Marriage" steamy Regency series set in Dragonblade's Lyon's Den Connected World. A Marriage-of-Convenience, Forced Proximity, Grumpy Sunshine, steamy Regency Romance. Available in Kindle, Kindle Unlimited, and Paperback.

When a fortune-wrecking wager at the notorious Lyon's Den tasks the "Iron Lion of Barrosa" with marrying an earl's reckless daughter, he'll tame her by any means—unless she shows him the true meaning of surrender first.

"...absolutely impossible to put down. It held the reader so very captivated that, once started, it was very hard to get any sleep. Two nights in a row this reader was up till 3:30am trying to find a good stopping point...A huge bravo to Kimberly Keyes." Dorothy C, Amazon reviewer

"This was my first foray into The Lyon's Den Connected World and now I can say I'm going to need a lot more reading time to explore all of the books! Kimberly Keyes has written a smoking hot romance novel that was so impossible to put down, that I had to stay up very late to finish it the same day I received it. I don't want to spoil it for anyone, but Amelia is a wonderfully strong protagonist and an animal advocate, so what's not to love? I'm going to lend the book to a friend, but not before I read it again." Sonya R., Amazon reviewer

THE LYON RETURNS, book 2 in Kimberly's "First Comes Marriage" steamy Regency series set in Dragonblade's Lyon's Den Connected World.

A fake marriage, forced proximity, bluestocking bride, widow/widower Regency romance.

Gwen, a wealthy widow with no desire to wed again must find herself a husband. After paying an exorbitant fee to the notorious Black Widow of Whitehall for a husband who, she's assured, is "almost certainly dead," her husband, the alluring Gideon Devereux returns from the grave.

"Fabulous historical romance. Great addition to Lyon's Den, and Keyes has a new fan. Rings every bell. Had a very hard time putting it down." Texas Librarian, Amazon reviewer

"...absolutely loved Gwen and Gideon's love story!! It was awesome!! The book was a lot of fun and very entertaining to read. It had just the right amount of romance and mystery within it that the story kept flowing and the pages turning....I highly recommend this book!!" GH, Amazon reviewer

A LYON'S TANGLED TALE, book 3 in Kimberly's "First Comes Marriage" steamy Regency series set in Dragonblade Publishing's Lyon's Den Connected World. A fake marriage, amnesia trope, rake and wallflower, Brother's Best Friend, forced proximity romance.

When unassuming wallflower Lady Georgina learns the dashing rake she's loved from afar, her brother's best friend, has returned home from the war an amnesiac, bound for a madhouse, a daring rescue mission ensues in which Georgina pretends to be Teddy's wife.

"Seriously one of the best in the Lyon's Den series. An emotional, exciting story from beginning to end. The Dove-Lyon dynamic is perfect. Georgina is a treasure. Teddy was...well...a serious hunk of treasure himself. Kept me reading almost straight through." Amazon reviewer

"Loved it!! Brother's best friend + successful novelist FMC + amnesia + rescue from the madhouse = histrom PERFECTION..." Hannah, Amazon reviewer

. ♥ . ♥ . ♥ . ♥ . ♥ .

LOVER'S LEAP, a steamy, friends-to-lovers, mistaken identity, forced proximity contemporary romance.

Recovering from a break-up, Candace escapes to a friend's luxury vacation home and meets the lethally hot Logan Shaw, her temporary roommate who she wrongly assumes is gay, and her best friends lover.

"This book pulled me in from the first moment. I bought it for a plane ride and had finished it by the time the plane landed!" Amazon reviewer

"Take a smoking. hot photographer with striking blue eyes and a curvy blonde fireball on the run from a thunderstorm, put them together in a mutual friend's upscale Lake Tahoe retreat and you have the makings of a steamy, made-for-each-other romance." Kat Drennan, Award winning author

PLAYING HER SONG, a steamy, small-town, second-chance, contemporary romantic suspense.

Jackson doesn't do relationships, especially not with women like Julia, his one-time tutor, back after 13 years. But does that rule out a no-strings fling?

"Let me start by saying what we're all thinking, Jackson is seriously hot. And not just his looks. He's everything a rockstar hero should be and Julia is the perfect heroine for him..." Anij, Goodreads reviewer

"News flash: PLAYING HER SONG is SPEC-TACULAR! I'm OBSESSED with this book!" ~Betty Bookstagrammer @_Book__Cafe_